never-contented things

also by sarah porter

Vassa in the Night
When I Cast Your Shadow
Tentacle & Wing

The Lost Voices Trilogy
Lost Voices
Waking Storms
The Twice Lost

never-contented things

sarah porter

TOR TEEN

A Tom Doherty Associates Book
New York

NEVER-CONTENTED THINGS

Copyright © 2019 by Sarah Porter

A Tor Teen Book
Published by Tom Doherty Associates
175 Fifth Avenue
New York, NY 10010

www.tor-forge.com

Tor® is a registered trademark of Macmillan Publishing Group, LLC.

Library of Congress Cataloging-in-Publication Data

Names: Porter, Sarah, 1969– author.
Title: Never-contented things / Sarah Porter.
Description: First edition. | New York : Tor Teen, 2019. | "A Tom Doherty
    Associates Book."
Identifiers: LCCN 2018046897 | ISBN 9780765396730 (hardcover) |
    ISBN 9780765396754 (ebook)
Subjects: | CYAC: Fairies—Fiction. | Foster children—Fiction. | Brother
    and sister—Fiction. | Sexual orientation—Fiction. | Love—Fiction. |
    Magic—Fiction. | Supernatural—Fiction.
Classification: LCC PZ7.P8303 Ne 2019 | DDC [Fic]—dc23
LC record available at https://lccn.loc.gov/2018046897

Our books may be purchased in bulk for promotional, educational, or business use.
Please contact your local bookseller or the Macmillan Corporate and Premium
Sales Department at 1-800-221-7945, extension 5442, or by email at
MacmillanSpecialMarkets@macmillan.com.

First Edition: March 2019

Printed in the United States of America

0 9 8 7 6 5 4 3 2 1

For Tera

contents

Part Three
joshua korensky

Part Four
lexi holden

Part Five
unselle

Part Six
ksenia adderley

Part One

ksenia adderley

Do you not remember Jeanie,
How she met them in the moonlight,
Took their gifts both choice and many,
Ate their fruits and wore their flowers
Pluck'd from bowers
Where summer ripens at all hours? . . .
While to this day no grass will grow
Where she lies low:
I planted daisies there a year ago
That never blow.
You should not loiter so.

Christina Rossetti, *Goblin Market*

how could i leave josh behind?

I think about it a lot, how it all happened, how we came to be here. It's not like I have anything else to do in the dull ebb of this place. Even the days here feel like a technicality, as if they don't actually mark time. As if they have no function, except to help keep up the illusion that this is a real town, and that we still count as real people now that we live inside it.

I don't know why I'm so preoccupied with going over my memories, getting them exactly right. My story won't save anyone else. No one else will ever know it. Or if they do, that will mean it's too late for them too.

Because I have to assume that this is it for me, for life. More of the same nowhere, with everything that makes it seem like *somewhere* just an empty gesture. A fraud. Because even if I could find a way out, how could I leave Josh behind? He'd never agree to escape with me.

After all, he's the one who chose this world for us.

we'd never seen them before

It was blue, the night, though dusk should have been over and done with, and we were already at least half-drunk. I should have pried the flask away from Josh half an hour before. He was barely sixteen and not much for pacing himself, at anything. But we'd been talking—about the future, which usually seemed too sickening to contemplate, since I was eight days from the age where foster care implodes with a pop—and though Mitch and Emma were actually kinder than otherwise, and wouldn't want to spew me out on the street, they were reminding me on a frequent basis that I should *explore my options, make arrangements, think about my next steps.* The whole thought of where and what next felt like a giant blowing-apart, unthinkably steep and wide and high all at the same time. I was suffering from a kind of omnidirectional vertigo that must be what the helium feels inside a balloon as somebody leans in with a lit cigarette.

So we kept wandering, and the night colored blue all over us like it wanted to steal our shapes and paint us into being part of it forever. It was almost comforting, and better than being at home, where no one was waiting for us. Mitch and Emma were on vacation and they'd told me to take good care of my foster brother—which I thought I was, in my way—and to not trash the house, which they said half-kidding, almost trusting me. And even almost-trust shows how lucky we were to have them, and for six unbroken years at that, after the various dicey pseudo-homes Josh and I'd both cycled through before we found each other. I'd make sure that Mitch and Emma found their house pristine, cleaner than they'd ever seen it before. If we drank or smoked, we'd keep it outside in the dark, and there would be no spilled scotch on the sofa or burns scored into the carpet.

I couldn't imagine what next, though I knew what Mitch and Emma had in mind: a group home for ex–foster kids, clear across the state. A lousy job and community college classes at night. They wanted me to have a decent life, as long as it was far away from Josh. There were programs for kids like me; the state would help with my tuition.

And I said *yes, yes,* but privately I kept hoping I could come up with something else. A different what-next, one good enough that I could bring Josh with me without destroying him. That was the goal: to hold on to my unexpected brother, the one who'd lurched into my heart out of nowhere when I was already twelve, without that being a cruel and stupid and careless thing to do.

But I couldn't see how to pull that off on minimum wage, and I didn't have a realistic prospect of earning more than that. Should I run off to the city and try desperately to make it as something-or-other? I wasn't deluded enough to think that would work. So Josh and I didn't like to say it, not directly, but we both knew we'd have to separate.

Mitch and Emma had said, to our faces, that our relationship had an *unhealthy intensity.* That it was *compensatory,* a punch in the teeth to all we'd lost. And they loved Josh, had even started the process of adopting him. Legally, he was too young to leave the system. If they knew we were hoping to live together as soon as we could figure out some way to do it, they'd do anything to stop us. Maybe even forbid me from visiting. Josh wouldn't turn eighteen for two whole years. Neither of us was willing to face that long without the other.

That's why, even drunk, Josh was getting restless. Twitchy with a conversation that kept reminding us of all the ways we could blast apart. If you let yourself feel how empty the sky is, you know you're always falling into an enormous hole. An oubliette, I think is the right word: a place for things meant to be forgotten. Even starlight forgets the brutal fusion it came from by the time it reaches the Earth, because the sky is just that fathomless.

"Kezzer," Josh said, with an odd waver in his step, "let's go see if there's anybody at the gorge."

It was edging toward midnight and our flask was almost empty. I said okay.

We swung by Carly's Pizza first—it was the worst pizza in town, with strange gummy cheese, but it was also close by and open— and bought slices.

"You and your sister partying hard tonight?" the college boy at the counter asked me. Sandy-haired and smug and too dumb to deserve the education he was getting, or at least that's what I assumed—though at the same time I knew it was my own vile mood talking, and he might not deserve my contempt at all. Even so, I wasn't about to reply with more than a snort.

But Josh grinned, even though the joke was getting old—that strangers can never look at us without saying *you and your sister* to me, or *you and your brother* to Josh. Josh's glitter eyeliner and long hair layered in three colors are enough to make him a girl to them, or my bowler hat and straight body are enough to make me a boy. Either way, it seems people take us for necessarily two of the same, and most often we play along.

At least they always understand at a glance that we're family and not just friends, even though we don't look alike so much. That, I appreciate.

"Raging," Josh said, and draped his torso sideways over a stool with such a blast of sex appeal that the boy gawked. He looked to me like the type who'd be horrified if he realized he was ogling another guy. "What time are you off, anyway?"

Not that we'd ever show, but the counter boy started scribbling down an address on the edge of a paper plate, trying to sell us on meeting him at a party in an hour. We got free sodas out of it and Josh doubled up laughing as soon as we were through the door.

It was Friday night, it was lush buzzing June, and only a week into summer break. I'd just graduated, along with the rest of the senior class. The gorge's rim should have been thick with kids we knew. I'd been expecting that our friends Lexi and Xand would be there, at least, though maybe Lexi was out of town and I'd forgotten, and Xand wouldn't come looking for us without her.

But there was no candlelight staggered by the tree trunks, no visible slices of sequins or denim. It was silent apart from the rattle of the bugs, and it was blue and banded violet where the gorge opened into midnight, and our faces went a blending-in blue again as we walked along chewing our pizza. Josh stopped and nuzzled his cheek, kittenish, into my shoulder, which is a thing he does and the way he is, especially with me.

"Doesn't anybody want to see us, Kezzer? Doesn't anybody care?" His voice was teasing, but also not. And of course I thought it too: that there must be something else going on, something better than the usual beers and mason jars radiant with sweating candles, and we'd been left out. Which might be understandable if it was just me, but who doesn't want Josh at a party, to sass and dance and smile, never showing off or getting in the center of things but just softly glimmering in the corners? Who doesn't want the chance to maybe make out with him, right before dawn, behind their parents' hydrangeas? He's a shade chubby, in a sinuous way—it's part of what makes people take him for a girl—and he makes chubby look prettier and sultrier than anyone else can.

That was when we heard sounds coming from a clearing farther along than the one we typically used. Laughing voices and a song that was new to me, dark but piercing, with languid harmonies and scattered bells. That was when our eyes opened wide to take in their lights, still mostly blocked by trees, but with a crystalline sharpness that wasn't like candle flames. Maybe they were rich college kids with some kind of new LED setup. It didn't make a lot of sense that we were only noticing them now, and so out of the blue, but there they were, and we crept closer. I wouldn't have bothered with people I didn't know, but Josh was already smiling. I knew he could follow that smile straight into their circle; even if he was young, he was so unmistakably deft, so ready to be one of them.

And I felt guilty, for no reason at all. I might have been edging toward weariness, I might have preferred to go home and watch a video together, but I knew Josh was eager to play. I felt like I had something to make up to him, though there was nothing I'd actually done. So it seemed like he should go have his fun, and I'd look after him, and get him safely home no matter how late it got or who tried out the softness of his skin.

That was what I thought, but that wasn't what happened.

"Ooh, Kezzer," Josh crooned. "Just look at them!"

Because they were beautiful. Maybe nineteen or twenty kids who looked like high school juniors or seniors, college freshmen at most. Josh and I should have known them at least by sight, but we'd never seen them before. For half a moment I thought they must be models, dancers, on break between takes of a music video, because they had the glitz and seduction of pure images. Most of them were spinning, undulating their arms, but a few perched in intimate pairs on boulders around the edge of the clearing.

There was a girl with blue-black skin and pink dreads past her hips and patterns like neon butterfly wings painted up to her eyebrows, a pale boy in shiny black leather tights and a white billowy jacket like a ship under sail, a milky blonde dressed in surreal Victoriana with a mink head sewn, openmouthed and snarling, right over her heart. Dripping red poetry was written on her skirt, and I thought she might have used blood. I looked, and looked again, and then gave up trying to take in all the details. It was too much, it scattered and refracted when I looked too hard. All that I could truly see of them was their glamour.

Josh stepped out of the tree shadows before I could catch his arm, and they pivoted toward him.

They smiled knowing, comfortable smiles. I wasn't sure I liked them, but I couldn't leave Josh there alone, so I followed, into the ice-blue twinkling of their lights.

"How can I not *know* you?" Josh asked, with a full-on blast of wonder. His tone was beguiling, disarming; I could feel the strangers warming to him. "Unless you're just visiting here?"

"We've met before," the pale boy said. His white jacket caught too much of the light. There was a burning cast to its pallor that made me look off, but I could feel how his stare lanced at us. "I can't believe you've forgotten that . . . Josh."

There was a lilt to the way he said Josh's name, and I was nearly certain of what I'd heard: it was the *ping* of a lucky guess. A long shot, maybe, but I knew that no one who'd met them would forget them. It wasn't possible.

But Josh's eyes widened, then spun searching through the leaves. "That's right! It was here. Was that sometime last spring?"

"Something like that," the pale boy agreed. "We had a thoroughly wonderful time." The pink-dreaded girl shimmied up to Josh and wrapped her arms around him, giggling confidentially, and the pale boy's attention beamed toward me. "You and your brother here stayed up till dawn with us." When I looked at the boy, his smile leaped all over me. Prodded like a dog's claws.

He was waiting for me to introduce myself, but I didn't. We'd never seen them before, I was sure—and *Josh* is common enough that him saying it didn't prove anything. But if he could hit on the name *Ksenia,* I might start to question my own memory.

That, or question if they'd spied on us somehow. Either way, it set me on edge. If part of me thought I should be more open to new people—especially to gorgeous, wild new people—the offness of how they were acting completely killed the impulse.

"I'm sorry, I can't recall your name," the boy said. Too formally, I thought, for a teenager. "It begins with a K, I think? Kelvin?"

"Close," I said. Josh was absorbed in the dark girl's banter but now he glanced at me, and I shot him a look to say *Keep your mouth shut.* "It's Keyshaun, actually."

"Keyshaun," the stranger repeated. I felt the tiny slap of his doubt. "I remembered the K, and that it was something a bit unusual."

Josh had been gawking, on the edge of outing me, though it wasn't anything new for us to invent names to match what people thought we were. He didn't like me lying to these brand-new, very old friends of his, but at that he subsided.

"Keyshaun," Josh said, and smiled blissfully. "You remember now, don't you? How much fun we had? You were dancing for hours with . . ." And he scanned the crowd like he was trying to find his own memory out in the night, pick it up, and slot it into his brain. "With that guy in the blue."

A boy in blue holographic leather came up to me then. Amber-skinned, deep-eyed. The look of him, the look of all of them, was too perfect, too cutting, but for Josh's sake I didn't shy away when he slipped an arm around me and pulled me into the center of the glade.

The gorge yawned ten yards distant. We were dancing and the music chimed and chattered in a way that made my tongue prickle. Bells seemed to be ringing in my head. The night took on an unctuous gloss that sent me gliding too fast through time.

I watched Josh from the corner of my eye. Pink Dreads and White Jacket had him in a triangular hug, three faces leaning in together, cheeks touching, and that was how they were dancing. No one had told us their names, I realized, but my thoughts felt slippery and it seemed too late to ask.

I watched them press a drink into Josh's hand; not the usual beer, some kind of moody, earth-smelling wine. He gulped it down. I had a full glass too, and I couldn't remember taking it from anyone. Something in the scent of it bothered me. When I got a chance I set it down on a tree stump, and if anyone noticed they didn't say anything. A girl wearing—what? Silver snail shells?—smiled at me sidelong and reached to run a nail along my cheek.

The night started to feel like the continuation of a story I'd be-

gun and then lost track of somehow. I could see how Josh had believed them, but why had they lied? He swooned backward,
supported by their crossed arms, his head upside down and his
red bangs trailing over the stones. They spun him like that and he
laughed.

The boy in blue tugged me back against a tree and kissed me,
hard, and the prickling in my mouth got louder, like something was
singing in there. It should have been thrilling, but I wasn't sure how
I felt about it. I thought dawn must be coming soon; I thought that
then I would have an excuse to drag Josh away, though it was
clear he'd never choose to leave on his own.

I'd closed my eyes, but I opened them in time to see the pale
boy in white and the dark girl streaming pink as they led Josh away
into the shadows. He fired me a last round-mouthed *Oh my God*
face over his shoulder, like he couldn't believe his luck. My muscles flinched with the urge to go after him, pull him back, though
it wasn't our way to interfere.

The boy in blue pressed in harder and slid his hands up my shirt,
at which point he should have realized that my name probably
wasn't Keyshaun. He didn't seem to care.

Because they'd given up on me for the moment, though I didn't
understand that then. They'd picked their first target and I just
needed to be kept out of the way. The kiss slid down my throat like
biting insects, like a prancing thing with too many needle-fine feet.

I was getting dizzy, and I tried to push him off. And then my
mind was one big black buzz and I was down on the grass and
stones. I could feel the cold lumps digging into my shoulder blades.
The ground seemed too chilly, and too unsteady, for June.

There was a fading-away, where I had just enough of my mind
to catch the trail of disappearances: voices dialing out in mid-
sentence, the music shedding its notes. I remember trying to stand
up, even thinking I *was* up, only to feel my body still sucking the
cold from the sod. I remember trying to call out for him. It was up

to me to keep Josh safe, so I couldn't just pass out. That thought kept blaring at me in anxious bursts. I held on to it—*Get up, get up*—and clawed at the ground.

When I woke up, everyone was gone. My bowler hat had rolled away and come to rest in a patch of moss.

what was i supposed to do?

There was a blue sky slamming through the trees and I tried to stay calm; he'd gone off with his new friends, he didn't see me and assumed I'd headed home. I called and got his voicemail—*Who do you think you are, calling me? Just kidding, you know I love you!*—three times in a row. Panic started blasting at me with the blue. My phone seemed to jump in my hand.

Worried, I texted. *Call right now!* He'd think I was being too smothery, probably, but it wasn't like him to leave without me, and without a word. It was already after eleven; I'd been out a long time. Maybe he'd gone under too, somewhere out of sight, curled beneath a pine's feathery arms. I walked back and forth for a while in the direction where I'd seen him weaving away into thickening shadows, calling his name and poking at the undergrowth. It was useless. Birds nattered in their nerve-shaking soprano and there was no sign that anyone but me had been here last night.

Then I thought that he might be back at the house—Mitch and Emma's demure, butter-yellow split-level ranch—where we'd lived for the last six years. His head burrowed under pillows, his eyeliner smudged halfway down his cheeks, sleeping it off. So I ran, even though every footstep drummed it into me: that it wasn't true, that he wasn't there, that I'd find his bed empty. Then I told myself that was just paranoia ragging at me. He'd be there. He had to be.

I had three long miles to get through, under foliage and past peonies and enough vinyl siding to encase an iceberg, and the whole way my thoughts rolled back and forth like dice: from *Josh is gone* to *Josh wouldn't do that to me.*

It hadn't yet quite occurred to me, or I wouldn't let it, that they might have stolen him. Kids don't kidnap each other, do they? Maybe his friends at the gorge were older than they looked, but they couldn't be more than twenty-one or -two.

I'm a good runner, but pelting at this speed I was still out of breath and streaky with sweat. Sunspots bounced off parked cars like a shining pulse. By the time the yellow house hove into view I was getting dizzy and I almost had trouble picking it out, as if I'd been away for years and my memories were confused.

My hand shook and at first I couldn't fit the key into the lock, but then I was inside: rooms that seemed too gray-dark after the sunlight, silence that sounded brick-hard.

Down the half flight of stairs and then the hallway, my footsteps mute in the heavy mustard-gold shag. I flung open Josh's door like I still thought I'd find him there, but the truth is that I knew. The emptiness was already inside me before I found it in his room. Messy bed and wadded black jeans and the plastic horses he'd slathered in glitter and rhinestones, but no sleeping boy and no breath but my own, heaving out of me.

I stood there, sick with my own abrupt stillness, stunned by the next impossibility: deciding what to do.

Who knew what drugs they'd fed him? He could be with them, having the time of his life, so high that he hadn't remembered to text me. That wasn't like him, though; for all his ingenuous manner Josh was keenly aware of his impact on people. So maybe he was trying out a new degree of thoughtlessness. Maybe with Mitch and Emma gone he felt like I was being too clingy or too protective, and this was his way of rebelling against me. Maybe he just wanted me to miss him. If that was it, then calling our foster parents, or the police, would be the worst thing I could do. I'd get him in trouble for nothing but a little attitude.

But it was my job to look after him, to replace the family he'd lost when he was small. That was what I was good for. And if the strangers at the gorge had taken him—it was the first time I let that thought sit in my head, let it leer at me—then the sooner the search began, the better our odds would be of finding him unharmed.

It was precisely noon. I decided to give it an hour or two. Give him a chance to sober up and say, *Oh hell, Ksenia must be flipping out by now.*

I made myself coffee, slugged it down, and ten minutes later puked brown bitter acid into the toilet.

It seemed like the strangers must have slipped me something, but how could they? I hadn't touched their wine. So why had I passed out like that on the stones?

I made myself take a shower, wash the leaves and clumped soil out of my jagged hair. I turned the jet as hot as it would go but my skin stayed clammy. When I was dried and in clean clothes just forty minutes had gone by, and I wasn't sure I could stand to keep waiting. I sat at the kitchen table for ten more minutes, staring at my phone, in case I'd missed something.

When I called him again I didn't hear his usual message. Instead there was a new recording: a peal of shrill bells. The sound of them brought some of last night's needling static back into my mouth.

If he'd changed his outgoing then he must be awake, ignoring me, and that made no sense at all. We hadn't fought. I hadn't stopped him from doing whatever he wanted to do. A smolder took over my heart and entrails, like the stink of a chemical fire buried somewhere too deep to put out.

What's wrong with you? I texted. *This is bullshit. Tell me where you are!*

Nothing, and nothing, and nothing. It rang in my ears, it bit at my tongue, its teeth sent a sympathetic resonance singing through my skull. I paced around the kitchen, stopped at the sink to rinse my mouth. I couldn't wash out the prickling, or the acid tang of bile.

Maybe someone else had gotten into his phone somehow, slipped in those chimes. That didn't seem good either.

I'm giving you ten minutes, I wrote. *Then I'm calling the cops.*

Because what was I supposed to do?

There were two things that came next: one that I did, and one that I didn't do.

I didn't contact Mitch and Emma. They hadn't had a vacation alone together in ten years; why not let them enjoy their cruise, since obviously Josh would turn up soon? That spared me the boiling shame of telling them I'd lost him somehow, that I'd let him get drunk to where his judgment was impaired. That on my watch he'd fallen into the arms of strangers who'd do who-knows-what to him. As if I didn't know what who-knows-what is like.

What I did do, when I was seated on Emma's couch with its Tuscan Wheat Ultrasuede, the two officers across the coffee table so that their stares held me braced: I said I'd tried their wine. Only a few swallows, because it tasted wrong. I said I'd gotten dizzy soon afterward, lost consciousness, and come to on the ground. Everything I told them was true, except the dark wine going down my throat.

I wished horribly that I had drunk that wine. It would have made Josh's disappearance a little less my fault. Even claiming it had happened was enough to ease the pain, very slightly. I almost started to remember the wine's sullen zing.

I didn't say that I thought the beautiful strangers might have drugged me, because I could let the cops tell themselves that. I saw it in the looks they passed: the woman with pinkish-tan puffed hair, exactly the color of her dust-dull skin, and thick slashes of terra-cotta blush; the bulky, sad-mouthed black man with cheeks as loose as pudding. I didn't need to say I was afraid they'd drugged Josh too. The officers did the work for me; their eyes spun around to that exact conclusion. I could watch the movie playing on their faces: a naïve sixteen-year-old boy at the mercy of this band of freaks. Maybe the strangers were addicts, or pimps, or some kind of sick cult.

They were very interested in his new outgoing message, those brightly tolling bells, and listened to it again and again.

I waited for them to call Mitch and Emma with the news that their foster son had vanished, but oddly they didn't seem to think of it. Maybe they assumed that I already had, but they never asked.

These were the kind of cops who work hard to prove that they're human, compassionate. At all costs, that they're *not bad people,* no matter what anyone thinks. They leapt at the crisis, the missing child, the missing orphan, and I encouraged them.

"Josh is so sensitive," I said. "So vulnerable. One problem with losing his parents so young is that now he gets impressed way too easily by people like that, who are older and cooler and confident."

They took notes.

By nightfall half our town was on the move in shuffling bands, flashlights sweeping. Josh was a known entity around here: a weirdo, but such an innocent one, who carried in groceries for old ladies; a pansexual libertine, but so adorable about it that half his old hook-ups were vaguely in love with him. ("It's not that I like *both boys and girls,*" Josh had vented once at Mitch in exasperation. "I like *people!*")

So nearly all the high schoolers who weren't on summer trips had joined in. Lexi was there, of course, though she seemed like she was avoiding me, even having trouble meeting my eyes. Did she blame me for what had happened? Despise me for losing her best friend? If she did feel that way, I guessed she had a good enough reason for it.

At first it seemed like no one else had seen the strangers—*They weren't from around here,* everyone said. *Those weren't kids from State U.*—but as the darkness wore on, people began to sidle up to me, to tell me they'd sighted them earlier yesterday evening, buying gas or drinking milkshakes at Denny's.

I didn't believe any of them. They'd been thinking too hard about the story I'd told, that was all. Their minds were infected by the dream and they were starting to see what I'd seen: the billowing white jacket, the mink frozen in mid-snarl, the rainbow bends on peacock leather. They watched visions seeded by my words, then said, *I remember now!*

It made me feel a little better, though, that I wasn't the only one rocked by waves of panic. That I wasn't alone with the lash of pink dreadlocks and Josh's look of round-mouthed delight as they led him who-knows-where. It soothed my fear enough that I could almost ignore the unending fact that we still hadn't found him.

A group combed the bottom of the gorge, edging down the treacherous path along the cliff's face to the dried-up creek and patchy willows at the bottom. I hadn't let myself think about that, either, and I stared after them for a while, too afraid they might be right to follow. But they didn't find a broken body on the stones, or dangling in the branches.

One funny thing: it wasn't just the cops who didn't mention Mitch and Emma, the importance of keeping them informed. No one did. As if the two of them leaving town amounted to a wisping away into oblivion, and a ten-day trip equaled utterly gone.

I couldn't stand the way Lexi wouldn't look at me, though. Even if I had it coming, couldn't she at least pretend to act supportive? I finally worked up the nerve to walk up to her. "Lexi. Hey." It wasn't enough. "I really did pass out. I know how you must feel, but I seriously would have done anything—if I'd just thought in time—"

That got me a sidelong glance out of her black almond eyes. "Oh. Ksenia, it's not that."

Her voice was low, broken. She was trying not to cry—obviously to protect me from seeing just how much harm I'd done, to her, to everyone who cared about Josh. I watched her for a minute, not saying anything, because how useless would it be to prattle *I'm sorry, I'm so sorry?* She was looking down again. Intermittent sweeps from a flashlight limned her dark-brown profile in golden strokes, caught in the twists of her hair. Out of everybody, I realized, she was the one I needed to forgive me. I just didn't know how to make that happen.

"I know I screwed up," I tried at last. Stupid or not, it was all I had. "Lexi, I'm so sorry."

She was dying to get away from me. I could tell by the lift of her shoulders, the twist of her head. "It's not that," she repeated; Lexi's voice is always soft, but now I could barely make it out. "I'm the one who's sorry."

Xand waved to her from another group, just turning right along the edge of the gorge, and Lexi shot me an apologetic smile and practically ran after him. I knew then that, if I wanted her to forgive me, words weren't going to cut it. Nothing counted except for finding Josh, bringing him back again. Memories kept projecting on the darkness: how hard Lexi had laughed after Josh hid out in the school all night, to write *creep pervert scumbag* in neon pink all over Sean Miller's locker. Sean had pawed Lexi in the hallway, and the writing was Josh's idea of revenge. He'd even added a few smiley faces with fangs, just to bring home the point. *It's totally not water-soluble, Lexi. He'll have to scrape at it for hours! He'll have to use his teeth!*

Once we had Josh back, I knew how it would go. The rescued orphan boy would eat homemade vegan brownies and sop up hugs and then we'd all say to ourselves, *You see? I'm not a bad person. After all. After everything.*

we need to be happy while
we can

By two in the morning everyone was peeling off, giving up for the night. There was a feverish tinge to the air, stars suppurating in the dark, and one person after another offered me a ride home or a place to stay, so I wouldn't be alone. And I fended them off, one at a time, standing on the roadside near the gorge. Of course we'd searched the site of that party time and again, we'd paced between the trees in widening rings, kicked up the dirt outside the clearing. No one liked to say it, but after a while I realized they were testing for churned soil. For a shallow and hasty grave.

You know I won't live that long, Kezzer, Josh had said. *We need to be happy while we can.* His voice kept incanting those words in my head while we searched, until I thought my flashlight beam could claw up the ground.

We'd found nothing: not a dropped cup, not a scarf, not even the scuffs of dancing feet. I was half aware, or more than half, that the lack of any sign of those strangers made me look bad, like I'd invented the whole thing. I could hear people murmuring doubtfully just out of view, behind the trunks or hidden by boulders, and I almost wished I'd faked some kind of evidence. I knew it had happened, I knew it was true, and I wanted them to feel it with me—quickly, before they stopped imagining that they'd seen pink dreadlocks hanging out of a van's window—at a traffic light, that was it, down on Fulton Street.

But that wasn't why I felt the need to search one more time, alone.

What was it in the night—something like a quality of reserve or shyness, something like a voice not quite ready to speak—that gave me the sense that the time wasn't right for Josh to turn up, but that he might soon? That, even if he was injured or unconscious, the swarm of people stomping around and yelling for him might have scared him off?

No matter how irrationally, I thought I might have better luck alone. I sat down, cross-legged, just where I'd seen him squeezed by the two strangers, swaying with them. Muggy blue air; dripping stars snagged in the branches. Shrill intermittent wind.

"Josh?" I said. "It's me. You can come out now. Even if you're . . ."

But I didn't know how to finish the sentence—what did I think he would be, if not a warmly smiling, chubby boy with dyed-red bangs and long wavy hair layered blond over chocolate? I felt like there was something I needed to say, but I couldn't guess what. I gave up and waited. I felt the ground until its coolness smacked my own pulse back at my palms.

Some time went by, I couldn't tell how much. My thoughts began to list in my head like foundering ships. My bowler hat tipped over my face.

Then I heard a voice crying out. I sprang to my feet still in a state of flawed, sleep-smudged consciousness, shoving my hat back, and spun in the direction it had come from: a mess of moonish trunks and slotted darkness, just like every other direction.

I knew the voice didn't sound like Josh's, not really. It was more like a little girl's, distraught and weeping. But it didn't feel like a meaningful distinction. In that darkness, anyone in trouble seemed like Josh to me. I went in pursuit.

I went in desperately, thrashing at the undergrowth and shouting. At first I completely forgot there was a flashlight in my pocket, and stumbled on in the moon-specked dark. The voice wailed again and I shoved forward, crying to her that I was coming, I was coming, and I wouldn't let anyone hurt her.

That was when I caught the side of my foot against a stone. My ankle twisted under me with a brisk twinge and I went down, onto my hip and then my ass. The back of my neck took a scraping thwack from a branch, and then I was sprawled against the sticky roots, gasping and laughing.

Because as I'd fallen the voice had come into focus in my head and I'd recognized that it wasn't a sobbing child at all. Some kind of night bird, its call filtered through my longing for someone I could help. The bird cackled again and I wondered how I'd made it into something human, something that was almost my missing brother.

I turned on my flashlight, scooped up my fallen hat, dragged myself upright. The ankle wasn't so bad, just tweaked enough to give little chirps of pain when I circled my foot. That was good, since I had to walk the three miles home.

Once I was alone in the lighted kitchen I tried calling Josh one more time, and heard the bells pealing. They made me sick. I needed sleep. I stretched out on the sofa near the front door instead of going to my room, just in case he came back.

In the morning the cops came rapping on the glass beside my head. Would I answer some questions.

Sure I would, Officer.

It felt like I'd heard them in my sleep: the things they were thinking. I felt like I'd been eavesdropping on their mental process in my dreams, so I wasn't surprised. I didn't ask what the problem was. I didn't ask for anything, not even time to get changed. I'd gone to sleep in my clothes—a ruffled vintage tuxedo shirt, gray skinny jeans—and that was what I wore to the station. I probably stank.

When they stopped for coffee and doughnuts, they got some for me too. From that I knew they hadn't entirely made up their minds.

They sat me at their table, in their little bright box of a room. They told me I wasn't in trouble, but some things had come up. Some questions needed straightening out.

The dark cop with the pudding cheeks asked, "So, you'd gone to sleep by the door? Why weren't you in bed, Ksenia?" His voice wobbled, gargling and liquid. The woman had left and we were on our own. For the first time, then, I took in the name on his chest. Rodriguez.

"I was waiting for my brother. I thought he might come back."

People complain about me, that I'm distant, or cold. I don't intend to come across that way. But to most people, honesty seems like coldness. That's what I think. Warmth is usually a performance, a way of covering up for something deeper. Something frozen. Inside us it's like the ocean: the temperature drops as you go down. And if that wasn't how it was with Josh, if he was warm all the way through? Well, he wasn't normal.

"But Joshua Korensky isn't actually your brother."

I bristled. "Of course he is."

The cop waved a file full of papers. I knew enough to guess that those pages were blank, that he'd just yanked a stack from the copier. "Some of the kids from your school seem to think that he's a whole lot more than that to you. *Good* friends of Joshua's. They would know."

I didn't take off my hat. I didn't run fingers through my hair. I sat with my hands folded politely on the tabletop, very calm, and stared at him. It was deliberate: physical repose, full eye contact, those are supposedly signs that you're telling the truth.

"What do you mean?"

"So that's why I bring it up, that he isn't your brother. Just in foster care with you. You never laid eyes on him before you were twelve, isn't that right? And young kids, thrown together . . . hormones raging . . . it's understandable, am I right, Ksenia? Outsiders might not be so sympathetic, but it's not actually incest at all."

I knew what he was doing. You don't spend your early years with a mother like mine, and not know. She'd taught me. *See, Sennie, they'll make your excuses for you, so you think it's safe to come out and admit it. Like, see, if they think a guy raped somebody, the* cop *will be the one to say, "Hot little number walking around in a skirt like that, of course you thought she wanted it!"* And then she'd cackled. Just like that bird.

"You think I had sex with my brother?" I asked, indignant. "Officer, that's a disgusting thing to say. And it would totally be incest, anyway. Family isn't just who you're blood-related to."

He looked perplexed. Waved his folder. "That's not what his friends told me. They say he said that you two were in love. Going to be together forever."

Maybe he did. And it wasn't Lexi who'd repeated it, I knew that much; somebody else had blabbed.

"Then his friends are liars," I said.

Because I knew where this would go. *Josh was always sleeping around, and that hurt you, didn't it, Ksenia? You couldn't take it anymore, could you? So you did what you had to do, to make the pain go away.*

He left the room, probably to discuss what next to try on me. And the truth wasn't what he thought, but it also wasn't what I'd said.

The truth was deep nights, a lot more than one, when Mitch and Emma were fast asleep and Josh came crawling into my bed and nuzzled close and tried to get started with me. And I'd say, *No, baby, it would be wrong. You're younger. I'd feel like I was taking advantage of you.*

But you literally can't *take advantage of me, Kezzer! Because it's my choice if I love you, and I do. Oh, why do you have to be the only one who worries about that?*

Besides, I'd say, *we're basically brother and sister. Incest is frowned upon.*

What about when I'm eighteen? he'd ask. *When we're together for real and it's just you and me? Then there won't be anybody to be all frowning-upon anything we do. They won't even know how we grew up together.*

Maybe when you're twenty-one, I'd finally told him. Just a week ago, and it was the first time I'd given in. *If you still feel this way, then.*

And that was a tactical error, because he'd bounced like a maniac all over my bed and then thrown himself across me, wrapping my face in his arms and peering down. *Oho! So you're saying it won't be incest anymore, once I'm twenty-one?*

It won't be incest anymore, once you don't need me to take care of you.

Maybe you should let me be the one to take care of you, Kezz. I just want to be with you till I die. His voice had broken, but at the same time he'd reached to pull up my tank top. And I'd stopped him, grabbed his hand, but I didn't kick him out. He'd slept in my arms. Beautiful and soft, my shoulder damp under his mouth.

But the cop didn't need to know any of that.

What they were looking for were reasons why I might have murdered my brother, and since I hadn't murdered anyone I didn't think the rest of it mattered.

I'd never been that jealous of the people Josh messed with, anyway. Not even when he made a display of it, tried hard to get a reaction from me. The thing is, Josh had lost so much that he could be a little compulsive about pulling people in. He'd use whatever worked. It would have been stupid, even heartless, to hold that against him.

Why should I care? I was the one he loved. He loved me more than anything.

He'd always said so.

When the cop came back in he seemed a little confused. Disoriented. It was like he'd lost his train of thought while he was in the hallway. Couldn't remember what we'd been talking about, or what I was supposed to be guilty of having done.

He tried to cover it up, but I could tell. He thanked me too heartily for coming in, for my help with the investigation.

"Sure," I said. "Just so you find my brother. Bring him home."

For an uncomfortable moment I could have sworn he didn't know what I was talking about, or whom. Maybe there was something wrong with him, like early Alzheimer's. "Your brother."

"Joshua Korensky," I reminded him. "We spent all day yesterday going around with search parties? Looking for him?"

"Young Joshua!" he said, with blank enthusiasm. "When we find him I'll be sure to tell him how lucky he is, to have a terrific big sister like you. One who cares so danged much about him."

He showed me out. They had no evidence against me, anyway. Even if I'd done it, I would have had to be an idiot to confess.

They had no evidence of anything at all. Just a lacuna, an emptiness big enough to fit one plump sixteen-year-old and the makeup always running down his cheeks. Would it really have been so hard for him to take off his mascara before bed? He'd left flakes all over my pillows, whenever he snuck in.

Don't make me wait until I'm twenty-one! Five whole years? You know I won't live that long, Kezzer. We need to be happy while we can.

Sure you'll live, I'd said. *Of course you will. Why wouldn't you?*

I'm just not that kind of boy, Josh had told me. And then I'd realized he was crying.

i'm a stranger here myself

For all that day, and the next, the search parties went out, and I went with them. But I could feel what everyone was thinking, their rising futility, and I had to clench my hands. After the first day, they'd all stopped believing we would find him. He'd run away, maybe, or else his body was moldering in a ditch somewhere far outside our town.

Somebody muttered, "She's the one who chucked the body, so why doesn't she just show us where it is? Save us all some time." People hushed him, watched me sidelong. "Well, have you seen her crying? You ask me, girl seems way too calm."

Sun throbbed in the leaves. We went over the same ground. The clearing was well trampled now, but only by our feet.

Sometime on the third afternoon, Josh's friend Derrick cornered me outside a gas station bathroom. A lanky redhead with the all-American face you'd expect above an assault rifle: a perfect face for shooting up malls. He'd been growing out the hair to look cooler, started a lousy band, but I didn't think it was helping much.

"It's your fault Josh went off with those people," Derrick hissed. "*If* he did, *if* that's what happened. You know he only did that stuff because he couldn't stand waiting for you."

There was the tingling stink of gas and stale urine. A filthy sparrow bashing its beak on a peanut M&M, blue. Why did they choose such an ugly, snappy blue?

"It's my fault, that Josh did exactly what he wanted to do?" I said. Except that Derrick was partly right: right that I never should have let it happen.

"He loved you," Derrick said.

"He still does," I corrected. "He loves me now." *Start talking like he's dead, and I'll find a way to make you suffer for it.* I didn't say the words, but I signaled them with my eyes. And Derrick backed off, slinking around the brick wall.

Ooh, Kezzer's getting scary! Josh laughed in my mind. And Mitch: *When you get in these moods, Kezz, you look just like a young David Bowie.*

Shut up, both of you, I thought back. *Josh, just come home, and then you can be as ridiculous as you want. I'll listen to anything you tell me. Hours of it.*

Reports had gone out on the news: the missing boy, the frantic search. And still Mitch and Emma didn't call. It seemed increasingly awkward for me to call them. They were busy with their vacation, obviously not bothering to think about us, and Josh was my concern.

And so we came to the third night, and everyone but me went home. It was sixty-eight hours since Josh had vanished, then sixty-nine, seventy, seventy-one. I went back to the glade. Clouds were rolling in and it was cold for June. I could smell the air starting to think about rain.

I didn't care.

If I wept, it might mean I truly had something to grieve for. Since Josh must be fine, wherever he was, I couldn't risk crying. But it was getting harder not to.

Drops started pocking down. I sat with my knees bent up, back to a trunk. Blunt, dumb rain tapping at my upturned face. It came in waves, thicker and harder.

"Josh," I said. "Enough already. If you're punishing me. If this is some kind of game. Enough. Just come back to me."

And then I heard a moan.

I didn't jump up this time. Instead I stilled, every muscle drawn tight as a chain. I remembered that psych-out with the sobbing bird, how I'd sprung after it. It seemed like something awful would happen, if I let myself be fooled that way again.

A surge of rain came, shaking all the leaves. There was a popping and rebounding everywhere, a stir of mud on the ground.

And then someone who was clearly human moaned, just out of sight to my left, and I felt Josh's dusky tenor taking the shape of each of my organs, liver and heart and guts. I was up, and the dimness became his foot sticking out. Then it became his whole body. He was huddled on his side, drenched and trembling.

I dropped down and uncurled him, opened his arms, and now I was free to cry. His skin was slick with rain and fever, his face was bloated. They'd done something terrible to him.

"Josh," I said. "Baby, it's me. You're safe now, I've got you. I've got you."

He snaked his arms around my neck. His eyes were void and rolling and for a moment I thought he would strangle me.

"Keyshaun," he said, woozily. "Welcome back."

It was a horrible time to be making such a stupid joke, but I couldn't get angry. Or maybe he wasn't joking. Maybe it was delirium.

"It's me," I said again. "Ksenia. Kezzer." He still looked blank. "Ksenia Adderley? Your foster sister?"

"Ksenia!" Josh exclaimed. It seemed like my name brought him more into focus, stopped his eyes from tilting around in their sockets. He wrapped himself around me, pressed his mouth against my neck, so I couldn't see his face. His shivers clattered through us both, his teeth clicked; it was a brisk night, but not *that* cold. I had to get him home. Or, no—to the hospital.

"Yes," I said. I wanted to ask what had happened, but I knew it wasn't the time for that yet. "Oh, baby, I'm so glad I found you. I was so afraid."

"Ksenia, derived from *xenos*. The Greek word for stranger."

"Okay," I said. Though if that was true, how would he know? And why would he bring it up now?

"I'm a stranger here myself!" Josh squealed, and laughed uproariously.

Rain spattered hard on both of us, trickles tangled us up like spider webs. I was trying to lift him to his feet, but he hung limp from my neck, dragging me down. He wasn't in his right mind. I dug out my phone, called 911. Josh sagged passively against me, one hand pawing at my face, while I explained the situation. They told me not to move him. They said they'd come find us. We weren't so far from the road.

"Where did everybody go?" Josh asked when I'd hung up the phone. He seemed a little less insane, now. His tone wasn't as sharp; more the purr I was used to. "Kezzer, I thought they really liked us! Why did they leave? Weren't we all having fun?"

"What do you mean?" I asked. "You've been gone for three days. Those creeps vanished, and they took you. They must have dropped you back here." *Dumped you like garbage. Once they were finished with you.*

He tipped back to look at me, and I used my phone to light his face. It was flaccid, bruised along one side, streaked with dirt. His lips looked like a crushed plum. Brown eyes moon-round and searching inside me.

"But we were just dancing, Kezzer," he argued. "Just now. It was all so beautiful."

He didn't remember anything. Three whole days wiped out.

I was already wondering how I could hurt them, those glamorous scumbags who'd done this to sweet Josh. How I could track them down, and what would be the worst thing I could do. Though technically, I should do it to myself too. I hadn't protected him.

I had precisely one function, one excuse to be alive, and I had failed at it.

"Kezzer?" he said. All at once he was getting hysterical, maybe slipping out of his trance. "You have to hold on to me. Tighter. Hold me as tight as you can!"

I didn't know what kind of injuries he had, was the problem.

But he clung and begged and whimpered until I gave in and squeezed. And when the EMTs came stomping through the woods he flailed at them.

"You can't take me away from her! We can't be separated, not ever again! I made sure of that. I made sure!"

"Relax," they said. "Don't worry. Your . . . sister? She'll be right there with you. She'll be with you the whole time."

I held his hand in the ambulance. When we got to the hospital, though, they had to sedate him to make him let go of me. I sat in the glare of the waiting room. The fluorescence skidded over me: a quality of light that feels wet, impenetrable, enameled. My nails dug into my palms. I pictured the boy from the glade, the one with the whitely shining jacket who'd guessed Josh's name, stalking into the room and blanching in fear when he saw me. I pictured my hand raw-knuckled, gripping the key to our front door, and the fleshy blurt as the key punctured his throat. I could smell his blood. It gargled up, gluey and frothing like a chemical reaction. And it wasn't red, but violet.

As Mitch would say, the vision was *compensatory*. As if I could pay back the world for what I hadn't done. But it kept me occupied while the TV blared vacantly and the three Hispanic kids wept silently across the room. I gathered that their father had been in a car crash; they were waiting to hear if he'd live. Their tears held the light in pale ribbons.

I deflected their grief, familiar as it was. Didn't let it touch me. I had enough of my own. Josh, of course, would have gone to them. Maybe read to them from one of the children's books that were scattered around. I even considered it: trying to be him, do what he would do, in case it helped anything. But I couldn't, and even if I'd tried I wouldn't have done it right, wouldn't have managed to comfort them.

After a while words came to me, carried by white coats from the room where they'd taken him. *Concussion, contusions; fever, irregular heartbeat, severe dehydration.* Concern about the possibility of internal bleeding, but nothing broken. As to why he'd lost his memory, they had nothing. He couldn't tell them anything, but none of the obvious markers had turned up in his blood. Not even alcohol. He was asleep now. I should go home and get some rest.

I slept in my chair instead. When he woke up, when he asked for me, I would be at his side immediately.

Once I looked up, and the kids were gone. I never learned if their dad survived. Apart from me, the waiting room had emptied out.

Even with my eyes shut, that awful light skated relentlessly over my lids. It burst like flares, signaling for help, and I was still searching for Josh. He was in a room just down the hall, even in my doze I knew that, but now it was the whole room that had gone missing, folded over or under some complication of the greasy blue-tiled floors, or tucked into an extradimensional pleat in the brightness. Not one of the nurses could remember where they'd put his room, and I screamed at them that they had to remember, that Josh was still inside it.

The next time I looked up, the light was blocked by the same cop, Rodriguez. The pudding face who thought I was an incestuous killer, but only because that was the quickest explanation to hand. He saw me pulling out of sleep. Jumped a little at the sight of my opening eyes.

"Just when we'd gone to the trouble of getting a search warrant," he said, and brayed with laughter. "Now what are we supposed to do with it?"

It struck me as an unprofessional thing to say.

"Are you sorry that Josh turned up alive? It was more entertaining to suspect me of his murder?" It's a bad idea to talk to cops that way, but I was feeling unhinged from the stress of the past few days. Now that Josh was found, I couldn't keep myself locked down anymore.

He jerked his head in the direction of Josh's room. His cheeks shook like there was some kind of small flying animal, a bat or a giant moth, crashing around inside them. "If that's what you call alive!" He was still chortling. "Well—the doctor said—anyway, young Joshua is back, and aren't we all so relieved? I'll be around again later, to talk to him."

Whatever was wrong with this man, I thought then, it must be getting worse. Officer Rodriguez clearly had some degenerative brain disease, and he was trying to hide it so he wouldn't lose his job. There was no point in getting angry. I made myself go cold again, stared flatly. He patted me on the shoulder.

Then he left, and as soon as I was alone, or anyway surrounded by unconscious strangers who'd staggered in during the night, his words started circling back around. Zipping past and flicking at me. *If that's what you call alive!*

What was that supposed to mean? Josh couldn't have lapsed into a coma, could he, while I was slumped in that chair? The thought nagged at me; it threatened to locate some sick premonition in my dream. I was up, aware that I should wait for a nurse to call me, and aware that I wasn't going to wait another moment.

No one stopped me in the hall. No one jerked me back at the door to his room.

The bruises on his face found my gaze first, like a garland of fat purple chrysanthemums. As far as I could tell, he was sleeping peacefully, his lank, unwashed hair spread out in rays of mixed color. He looked so sweet, and so terrible. An IV snaked into his arm.

I bent over him. Watched him breathe. His lashes were fluttering; they seemed too light and frail without his usual mascara.

"Kezzer!" he said. His free arm whipped around my neck. I was shocked by how strong it seemed. He yanked me down to him so sharply my feet nearly skidded out behind me, showered wet kisses all over my cheeks. "Kezzer, they said I was lost for three days? They said you went crazy searching for me?"

I'd told him that last night, too, but it was to be expected that his thoughts were a mess. "That's all true."

"Did you miss me unbearably? Did you realize how totally you love me, once you thought I was gone?"

"I didn't need to realize it, silly," I said. "I've always loved you."

If he wasn't so obviously traumatized, his talking this way would have made me suspicious. I might have wondered if his whole disappearance was a stunt, meant to torment me into doing whatever he wanted. I wouldn't necessarily put it past him; he could act out sometimes, even in extreme ways; he was perfectly capable of starting drama. But, no: it was just typical Josh, fervent and unguarded.

"I strongly believe that you should love me even more. Starting now. Kezzer, say it? So I know I'm back from—wherever I was?"

He unlocked his arm and let me go; I pulled up a chair. "Where *were* you? Do you remember anything else now?"

Josh grimaced. "Flashes, maybe? I don't know what's real. Kezzer, don't ask me about that! It makes me so confused, like I might throw up—I can't stand to think about it."

Hysteria tightened his voice. That was what I'd thought. I'd kill them.

"I won't ask anymore. You know I'll be here if you ever want to tell me." I stroked his hair, carefully. It was so rank with sweat and oil that it stuck to my hand. "The cops are going to come around with questions, though. I can't help that."

His lips twitched; they still looked too thick, engorged. "You haven't said it yet. You *have* to, Kezz. So I won't feel so lost."

"That I love you even more now?" I smiled at him. "*More* would be excessive."

"Oh, like that should stop you!" At least he was grinning back at me, and he seemed like himself again, if only for a moment. Sparkling and impish.

"Oh, fine." He ruffled with expectation. "Joshua Korensky, I love you even more than I used to. Even though I've always loved you a stupid amount. Are we good now?"

There was a purplish throb to the light, as if the current had winced in its wires. A subtle plucking or puckering sensation that might have come from the floor, or might have been just in me. He seized my right hand, kissed the back of it.

"And you—like, you'd do anything to keep me with you? You'd go anywhere? Officially?"

It was getting to be an unnerving ritual. But this was a time for Josh to hear whatever he needed, not for me to stay in my comfort zone. "I'd go anywhere to reclaim you from those freaks, that's for sure. Not that you ever belonged to them!"

The lights cringed again, the ventilation rasped—isn't unreliable power dangerous in a hospital?—and Josh's eyes rolled back. I'd thought he was mostly better, at least physically, but maybe I was wrong. He gave a hacking little laugh and both his hands clutched at me convulsively, fingers digging into my arms. The air transmitted a shudder; it hit me in the guts.

Then it passed. We were just as we'd been, except that Josh's lids were drooping sleepily. A nurse came and shooed me from the room.

They told me they were holding him one more day, for observation. If he kept improving, he could go home.

I wondered if Lexi would come visit; if she'd get over despising me, now that I'd found him, at least enough to look me in the face again. The thing was, Lexi had never screwed up anything in her life, not the way I could. She was always on top of whatever anyone threw at her. It was amazing she'd gone this long without deciding I was worthless.

In our house, the wall between my bedroom and Josh's was thin. Voices sifted through the plaster. I'd had to hear Josh talking, even when I didn't want to. I'd had to overhear him confiding in Lexi, along with her bitching about me. *You can't blame Kezzer,* Josh had said; he'd said words to that effect repeatedly. *It's seriously harder for her than anybody knows but me. She* totally *likes you, Lexi.*

And Lexi: *I get that she's protecting herself, Josh. It's just insulting that she sees me like that, like I'm one more person she has to watch out for? I don't think I deserve the way she's always on her guard with me.*

Of course you don't deserve *it, Lexi! But I don't think you see—I bet Kezz would run into a burning building for you. And that would be way, way easier for her than opening up the way you want her to. The scariest thing in the whole world for Kezzer is letting anyone know her for real. She's afraid of what they'll see.*

But if Ksenia understood me, *then she wouldn't need to be afraid of what I'd think of her!*

I'd sat with my arms clutching my knees, listening to them discuss how *scared* I was. It hadn't been easy. None of it: not when I heard Josh making excuses for me, not when I heard him tell her about my parents. About Owen. Not when he talked to her so seriously about things that he would have joked about with me. But I never said anything about it, to either of them. We'd hang out and wisecrack at the gorge, and I'd pretend I hadn't heard a thing.

If Lexi wanted to know that stuff so badly, it was better if Josh just got it over with.

they might not find their way home again

I finally went back to the house, to pick up clean clothes for Josh and to shower and change myself. Word had gotten out that he'd been found and he had a parade of visitors to keep him busy, bringing him flowers and chocolate and his favorite foods: rubbery vegan brownies, fried tofu wontons. Xand's mom gave me a ride back, dropped me off at 32 Whistler Drive: the same split-level with its butter-yellow siding, its sofa covered in Tuscan Wheat Ultrasuede.

So why did it feel so wrong? The moment I walked in the door I was struck by the conviction that I'd entered the wrong house by mistake: a house that coincidentally happened to look exactly the same as ours. Mitch's red corduroy jacket draped from its hook by the door, but maybe it was just a very similar jacket. Emma's sunflower teapot sat on the kitchen table, but it wasn't as if there was anything distinctive about her taste.

I stepped outside, checked the number on the house. I even walked back to the corner to read the street sign. I had to admit that everything seemed to be in order, but the sense of wrongness, of something altered, kept its grip on me.

So I leafed through the stack of mail that waited on the kitchen table for the day when our foster parents returned. I picked up every envelope in turn and read the names: Mitch R. Delbo, Emma Kossuth Delbo. No amount of staring made the names change.

After twenty minutes or so I had to swallow the truth of it: I was where I should be. If something had switched around, it wasn't intrinsic to the house. It must be me; I must be looking at my old surroundings differently. I decided that my perceptions were slanted by everything I'd been through—it had been a rough night, with brutal days beforehand—and went off to shower. The close, chemical air of the hospital still clung to my skin like a film.

Even though I'd talked myself out of my delusion, I still didn't much like getting undressed in that house. I felt too exposed at the touch of its drafts, too vulnerable. For a while I stood in the bathroom, just watching everything, every toothbrush and towel, as if they would move. One of Josh's multicolored hairs hung over the sink. A stray hair from before; from when he was still—well, relatively—innocent, undamaged. At last I turned on the water, stripped, and stepped in.

In spite of myself, I rushed through washing, then toweled off fast and yanked fresh clothes on. I went to grab his things and get out of there.

Probably that was all that was wrong with the house: that Josh wasn't in it. He'd been gone for too long. The sense of his presence was eroding.

Once he came back, it would all be fine.

I found a shopping bag and headed to his room. As I flipped on the light and started digging through his clothes—I wanted to bring an outfit he especially liked—his voice kept on in my mind: *I'm just not that kind of boy.*

Josh, be real. You'll live because nothing's going to kill you. Would I let you get hurt? I'd wanted to comfort him, and at the same time I was annoyed. I'd suspected he was acting. Being outrageously manipulative.

You can't watch me all the time, Kezzer. In a few weeks you're probably going off to that stupid group home for ex-foster kids, because you won't have any choice. We both know it. And even if we make it through that—it'll happen sometime when your back is turned, that's all.

What will happen? It's not like there's anything wrong with you. You don't even catch colds.

Oh, Josh had said. *I feel like somebody will kill me. Just, you know, sometime when I'm happy, doing whatever I want to do. I'll be so incredibly happy, glowing with it so much, that it will piss somebody off. It'll be obvious that I don't belong on this planet at all!*

I hate to call you a moron when you're already crying, I'd said, and he'd cracked up laughing in mid-sob. *But that has got to be the most ludicrous shit I've ever heard in my life.*

Well, I hate to think of how guilty you're going to feel! His tone was a blend of petulance and teasing. *When you're, like, showering my cold, gorgeous body in white rose petals, and you have to remember how you wouldn't take me seriously!* He'd rubbed his face on my tank top, wiping his tears on me, and I gave in and pulled him up and kissed the salt off his cheeks. Maybe it wasn't fair of me. Maybe I'd acted too much like I was already his girlfriend.

I couldn't be the strong one all the time, constantly enforcing the boundaries. It got exhausting. And maybe he'd really believed what he was saying, anyway.

In an overflowing drawer I found his favorite shirt, with a photo of a kitten dressed as an astronaut. Clean black jeans, his newish ones, socks and underwear, and a hoodie with black glitter stars. Stashed everything in the bag, hung it on my wrist, and turned to go.

In the corner of my eye, something moved. It was near the back of the dresser.

I decided that I'd had enough of it all, thanks. Enough of psych-outs and delusions and the mentally deranged comments made by local law enforcement. I didn't turn my head, but my attention stayed fixed on my periphery, even as I told myself to ignore it. Whatever it was.

Except that Mitch and Emma would have a fit if they came home to mice. If that was what was back there, I should step up and deal with it.

So I looked. It isn't easy to describe what I saw.

It was a fragment of Josh, as if a mirror had recorded his reflection at the moment it shattered. It had one brown eye with heavy glitter liner, a sharp angle of incomplete nose, half of his voluptuous mouth. It was unmistakably Josh, but also not: Josh shrunken and reduced and ugly, a shard of imp. Two feet tall at most.

It glided along the wall's base, mostly flat but sometimes popping into three dimensions. There would be a thrust of cheekbone or a jutting elbow, just for an instant.

I could hear its pained breathing. Its single nostril was broken off, after all.

It saw me watching and flashed me a look: furtive and shamefaced, but also just a bit amused. The corner of its mouth hiked, but not enough to count as a grin.

It hit the edge of the wall and vanished, as if it had ducked under the paint.

The whole thing was unacceptable. It was not in any way okay for my mind to generate sights like that. I'd barely slept, and that might be affecting me in upsetting ways—but sleep deprivation was no excuse for imagining something so grotesque.

Especially since the hallucination had picked on *him*. I would have preferred to see myself deformed that way, or Emma; anyone but Josh, who was sweet and hurt and needed me.

I edged out of the room with quick scissor steps. My breath had stopped completely but my pulse filled my head with a maddening tick, like a metronome set much too fast. For a moment I stood in Josh's doorway, staring back at the corner where the thing had disappeared. Too stunned to slam the door behind me.

Then I did. It banged shut and I started gasping.

It didn't matter if that thing had been a hallucination. There was no way in hell I'd let Josh sleep in the same room with it. When he came home, he'd just have to sleep next to me.

And when Mitch and Emma got back here, only four days from now? What did I think I could do, call an exterminator?

The bag of Josh's clothes had gotten twisted, tight as a tourniquet around my wrist.

The hospital was weirdly empty that night. The only nurse I could find—a twitchy blonde who jerked along like a puppet, like she might have some kind of muscular disorder—was nice enough to let me sleep in Josh's room, in a pile of mangy blankets on the floor. They'd moved him to a double, and now an old man snorted, in seemingly permanent sleep, on another bed across the room. There was the soft beep and wheeze of machinery, the chirr of current in the wires. I didn't tell Josh anything about what I'd seen. He was still fragile. I didn't want him to get weirded out or feel nervous about returning home.

I stretched out below him. Josh hung his arm over the side of his bed, and I propped my elbow on my bag so that I could hold his hand. The nighttime lighting gave the room a silver-black cast. The grit of an old photograph.

"Kezzer? Isn't this awesome?" I laughed; leave it to Josh to think that being stuck in a hospital was something to celebrate. "I don't mean that! I mean, it's like we're already together. We don't have to sleep in different rooms, or worry about Emma or Mitch walking in on us."

It's not that I like both *boys and girls,* Josh had said. *I like people! That's one reason Kezzer is so perfect. She's a million times more of a person than she is a girl.*

But you don't like Kezz like that, Mitch had answered. Quickly. *You don't like Kezz in* that *way, of course, Josh. You love her as a big sister.* And Josh hadn't answered.

Mitch had in fact walked in once when Josh was sleeping in my bed, and he'd completely bought Josh's line that he'd had a nightmare and needed me to comfort him. Then he'd told us that we were too old for that and shouldn't do it again. It didn't look right.

"They'll be back soon," I said. "We need to be prepared for that, emotionally I mean. They'll want to know when I'm leaving."

"Maybe they won't come back," Josh said sleepily. "Then we'll just live together in the house."

Every time I started thinking he was back to normal, he'd say something like this. Something that proved me wrong. "That seems unlikely. Seriously, Josh, you can't be hoping that they'll die in a plane crash?"

"No—oo. I'm not hoping they'll *die*, Kezz. That would be way too mean. I just think they might not ever find their way back here. That's all."

This sounded less like insanity, and more like Josh's way of playing. He'd go off on flights of wish fulfillment sometimes. Giddy and whimsical. If he was just having fun, then I shouldn't shoot him down.

"Right," I said. "That's totally a thing that happens." I was trying to play along, but my voice was taut.

"It is!" Josh said. "This is why people should be very, very careful about going on vacation. They might not find their way home again."

"What about us, then? Will we find our way home from the hospital?"

"Of course we will! We're still right here in town." He squeezed my hand. "Don't you worry, Kezzer. We could be in a labyrinth with walls made out of living snakes, and I'd make sure we got where we were going."

The day when we'd be forced apart was much too soon, and it was coming just when he'd been through hell. That was all this was. Josh was defending himself against the crush of reality by saying crazy things. I could understand the impulse.

"Then next time we're lost, I'll leave it all up to you." My mind was sliding. I could feel my eyes wanting to go out, my vision guttering like candle flames. "Baby? I think it's time to sleep."

"We're lost right now," Josh murmured. "But in a good way."

"In the best way," I told him. My voice sounded slurred. "Because I got you back."

"I love you so *much*, Kezzer," Josh said. "Anything I ever do, that you maybe wonder about? That's why I did it. Like, I can guarantee that in advance." Even through the blankets the tiles felt cold beneath me. My shoulder blades seemed too sharp. The hospital beyond our room was oddly quiet, as if it had been evacuated when we weren't looking.

Josh would be free to leave in the morning. He was safe. That was all that mattered.

you could put it like that

The house packed the same depth charge of quiet and discomfort it had held the day before. With my hand on the knob, I knew I hadn't stayed on Josh's hospital room floor only because he needed me. I was afraid to sleep here alone. To share the walls with some broken-mirror imp that couldn't possibly be real.

But Josh bounced in the instant the door was unlocked. The black glitter stars on his hoodie caught the light and sent it flying, and he yanked the hoodie off and threw it on the sofa. "Oh, it's so great to be home! I feel like it's been forever. Kezzer, let's not go out for the next week? We should make a fort out of the dining table and refuse to leave at all. Like, I'm through with partying, and now I just wanna eat crackers with you in the dark."

I'd followed him in. He plainly didn't sense anything wrong, so how could I justify my fear? I was momentarily distracted, wondering if that disturbed cop had ever been back to question him; if so, Josh hadn't mentioned it.

"We can do whatever you want. Just so we have the house absolutely perfect before Mitch and Emma get back." It should have been a simple matter, our foster parents returning, but now when I tried to think about it, my brain seemed to glitch out. I knew they were due back soon, that was all. "Wait—*when* did they say they'd be home? Thursday, or—? I can't remember the date."

Josh came up to me, smiling. I'd forgotten to bring his makeup to the hospital and his face looked blurred and babyish without it. He locked his hands behind my neck and tipped back, swaying gently. My hat toppled onto the floor and rolled. "Oh, *Kezzer*. Don't worry about that. Seriously, don't."

"I don't want to give them any excuse to say that I'm a bad influence, or too irresponsible to be around you." But now I realized that *someone* would tell them about Josh's three-day disappearance, the search parties that had gone out; it was inevitable.

All at once it hit me: by bundling that secret in myself, by keeping silence, I'd guaranteed that Mitch and Emma would be beside themselves with rage. They'd never let me visit now, much less allow Josh to travel to see me. Looking back, I couldn't understand how hiding the truth from them had seemed like the right move. It wouldn't help to tell them that I had been too ashamed of having lost him. I'd doomed us.

I yanked Josh's arms off my neck, more roughly than I'd meant to. Turned my back on him so he wouldn't see my face. My breath snagged in my throat like burning rope, my eyes blazed. I'd let the strangers steal him, and then I'd compounded that by failing him *again*, slicing myself into failures, crimping and bending the slices into walls, until there was no way out.

"Kezzer? What's wrong?"

I couldn't speak, couldn't glance around. I was afraid I might hit him.

Even though none of this was his fault. Unless I blamed him for being too trusting, which he was—but that was why it was my job to watch over him. Every bend, kink, elbow of the awfulness: they all kept coming back to me.

"Never mind," Josh said. He rested his hands lightly on my shoulders. "I know. You're mad because you're scared. About what Mitch and Emma will do. I wish you'd *listen* to me, Kezzer, because I keep telling you that's not a problem anymore."

I shoved my hands into my armpits, clamped down. My muscles were jumping with the urge to strike out.

"I can't take this right now, Josh. Your bullshitting. Just stop."

My voice came out in a croak. It was hideous. "It's a problem, and it's gotten *worse*, and none of your cute little fantasies are going to help us. All that crap about them never coming back? Let go of me!"

Because now his arms were reaching, rippling to pull me tight against him, and his lips were on the back of my neck.

"It's a nice house, Kezzer. Isn't it?"

Of course he hadn't let go.

"Nice? If you like this kind of crap. If you want to pretend life is a bunch of stupid glass flowers from craft fairs, and banana bread, and emotionally disturbed, white-trash kids who should be eternally grateful that you've given them a decent home!" I was hyperventilating, sobbing. I never, ever let myself crack up like this, except around him.

It wasn't the first time he'd had to talk me down.

"So we'll redecorate," Josh said, and applied a long, slurping kiss to my nape. "You're right that those flowers are crazy ugly. Let's throw them out right now! We can smash them on the patio and say, *You're not your mom, Ksenia Adderley, oh, no, you're not your mom.*"

It was almost against my will, but I laughed at that. Sob-laughed, anyway.

The flowers were in a glass-fronted section of the home entertainment center, a giant slab of bland, pale wood blocking out one wall. They consisted of scribbly twists of lurid red and blue and yellow, vaguely resembling clustered petals, jiggling at the ends of wire stems. A big bouquet of the things in a blue vase. Mitch and Emma were going to hate me anyway. We might as well. They'd blame me and Josh would barely get in trouble at all.

He'd be okay, or as okay as he could be without anyone who understood him. Me? I'd just be gone.

My knees were wobbling. I let them go, let myself sink onto the carpet. He came after me, sort of flopped across my back in a heap. And he was so warm, so velvety, his hands reaching around now to stroke my face and drag through my damp hair. He smudged my skin like finger paint, or dough. How did he always understand so exactly what I needed?

"Mitch and Emma don't *know,* Josh. About what happened. That you disappeared. I thought somehow—if I could just find you it would all be okay, and I'd never have to admit how stupid I'd been. But that was the biggest lie I've ever told myself."

"Oh Kezzer, it *is* okay. You'll see. Let's just forget about that night. Please? I didn't disappear. I've been right here with you all along. We decided to play Parcheesi, and we just lost track of time, and three days later we realized the game was over. And you'd been totally whupped, naturally."

I laughed again, even though I knew it was wrong. "I can't forget about it. Those assholes—they took you, they *hurt* you. Now it's up to me to—"

I didn't finish. Josh knew me to the quick. He'd know what I meant.

"You don't have to do anything, Kezzer. Except stay with me, and love me. And let me make you dinner tonight." He said it fast, like he could crack my thoughts in half. Throw the dangerous part away.

He uncurled me, just the way I'd uncurled him, out in the rain. Nestled himself around me so that he was half-draped across my lap.

"I'm going to find them, Josh. I'm going to make sure they suffer for what they did to you."

"No, you're *not.*"

"How am I supposed to let that go?"

"Kezzer. This isn't about you and Owen, okay? It's not the same thing at all. I'm not like some replica of you, when you were eleven. And you can't undo what happened then by perfectly protecting me."

"Josh!" I couldn't believe he'd brought that up.

"If you want to take care of me, Kezzer—and take care of yourself too—then I really, *really* need you to forget about what happened. Like, if we run into them sometime—the people we met that night?—then I need you to be incredibly polite. Like you're at a job interview."

I stared down at him. His face was pressed against my chest, but the bruised cheek still showed: a trail of swollen blobs shifting into shades of mauve and rotten green. And he was telling me to be *polite* to the creeps who were responsible? But his tone wasn't anything like it was normally; he sounded sharp, decisive. Even bossy.

"That's insane," I said. And then I saw it.

The imp-thing, the Joshling: the slippery, pleated horror that had stolen his image, snapped off a piece of him. It had been hiding in the home entertainment center, in that vase of gross glass flowers. The thing had crumpled itself down until it was camouflaged by the oil-bright petals, but now it was blossoming. A shoulder unfolded, a glitter-crusted eyelid, a stretch of wet teeth too long for the diminished head. It popped out, expanded to its full height, and slithered down the back of the glass like a spill of viscous sludge. And this time I could *hear* it: a piping chitter that might have contained butchered words.

Josh saw my face and rolled his head, still in the crook of my arm, to watch it go. He didn't look surprised, or frightened. He tracked the thing impassively as it scrabbled at an angle across the TV, gripping the screen as if there were handholds in the flatness, then dropped to the floor with a whisking little thud.

Where every piece of it seemed to divide along a mirrored fold, like a butterfly opening its wings. There were two symmetric eyes, sliding out from each other until they were linked by tips of overlapping white; two jouncing, agitated knees, two half-mouths slipping further apart. Until it broke into two separate Josh-imps that dashed in opposite directions. To the edge of the cabinet doors, where they vanished. Just the way it had done before.

Except now Josh had seen it too. And he didn't seem to mind. At the very most, his expression showed a lazy curiosity.

I let out a choked noise that was nowhere near a scream.

Josh sat up and hugged me. Kissed me on the lips, which he

knew I didn't allow, but I was in no state to resist. Was there some of the same prickling, sparking sensation that had flooded my mouth when the boy in peacock leather had kissed me, that night by the gorge? "Kezzer, I need you to listen to me. I need to know you get it. Can you do that for me?"

I couldn't speak. I nodded, with my face pressed between his hands.

"What I've been telling you, that Mitch and Emma aren't coming back? I'm not kidding about that. This is our house from now on, and you don't have to leave. You won't age out of anything when you turn eighteen, okay? Neither of us is going anywhere. Do you trust me now?"

It should have been good news. The best news possible. The weird thing, then, was that I didn't want to believe him. I was sick with the knowledge that the Josh-imp was still nearby somewhere, listening in.

But since I didn't know what else to do, I nodded again. I'd seen what I'd seen, it was no hallucination, so clearly I was no expert on what could be real. Maybe Josh really knew something I didn't, even if that made no sense to me.

"Great. Okay, then. That's a big improvement, Kezzer. But then the thing is—I guess you could call it the catch?—it's that we're kind of guests here."

He really didn't seem like he was joking, or even crazy. "Guests. You mean in the house?"

"Not exactly," Josh said. His hand gave a circular flick. It suggested something more encompassing.

"On the planet?" I asked. It came out with a bitter snap. If that was what he meant, I guessed that it was nothing new, really. Not for me. If I hadn't been a guest, all my life, then I must have been an invader.

Josh kissed me again, very softly, and tousled my ragged hair. "You could put it like that."

what a little savage you once were!

I didn't know what was wrong with me. I sat for a while on the sofa, trying to cry out the feeling of being throttled and compressed by impossibility, until Josh brought me a mug of some kind of herb tea that put me to sleep. When I woke it was late afternoon. He'd spread a blanket over me. And the instant my surroundings entered my mind I jolted, staring around to see what the imp-thing had been doing while I slept. There was no sign of it. Just the usual pale wood and tan drapes, the musty gold carpet, those garish flowers. *We'll redecorate*, Josh had said. Was he planning to attack the place with spray paint?

To my taste, there was nothing he could do that wouldn't count as home improvement. I could hear him scuffling around somewhere; maybe he had started with his room.

Now that I was rested, more mentally together, I felt sure that everything he'd said was madness. Not that I thought Josh was crazy, exactly; just constructing a very complicated system of denial. I'd been wrong to get mad; no one plays games with their own mind that way unless they've been driven to it. But of course Mitch and Emma would come home, and learn the truth, and kick me to the curb. Sputtering with indignation. They would welcome an excuse to keep us apart, free Josh from my unwholesome influence. I knew that. As for what we'd seen? I couldn't guess what that thing was, not now. I'd figure it out later.

"Ke-ezzz-zer!" Josh trilled. He dashed up the half-flight of stairs leading down to the bedrooms, practically skipped across to me. He had his makeup on thicker than ever, concealer slapped over those bruises, and he'd been messing with his hair, puffing and feathering it. "Are you feeling better now?"

"You're the one who just got out of the hospital," I pointed out.

"Well, sure. But I think it's easier for me anyway." He crouched down by the sofa and got in my face. Blasted me with his grin at close range. "Kezzer, if you're okay now? Then I need you to do something for me. Go out to a café or something? I need the house to myself. Just for a few hours."

That was when I noticed that the scuffling noise down the hallway hadn't stopped. My heart tripped. I did my best to ignore the sounds, but they kept on, dry and whispery and insistent.

"I'm not totally sure you should be alone," I said. *With whatever that is.*

"Oh Kezzer, of course I should! And how am I supposed to make a fabulous surprise dinner to welcome myself home if you're sitting there watching me? Spoiler alert!"

"You're making your own welcome-home dinner?" I asked— though in fact he'd said something about this earlier, wanting to cook tonight. And my cooking is abysmal, while his is at least okay. "We still have enough money left that we could go out, as long as we don't go crazy." Mitch had left me cash for groceries, and so far I'd been careful with it.

"I don't want to go anywhere! Kezzer, I won't feel like I'm a hundred percent home until we have a real celebration, right here, together. Right now I only feel like I'm, oh, eighty-five percent home. I wish we had champagne!"

I didn't much like the idea of Josh drinking, not after last time. But if we were staying in it might be okay. I wanted to make him happy, if I could.

The noise down the hall went on, like a crumpled paper stuck to the bottom of my thoughts, dragging and muttering. A singsong rasp, crisp and hypnotic. I knew Josh was hearing it too, but somehow we'd entered into a silent agreement that everything was fine, that that sneaking horror was an acceptable presence.

"If Hadley is around, she'll probably buy a bottle for us." Hadley was a friend, or friend-ish, who worked at the bookstore, and she was twenty-one; she thought Josh was so amusing that she would indulge him. The truth was, I didn't entirely mind having an excuse to get out of here. "I'll see what I can do. And you need money to go shopping, right? It's all on my dresser. Under the shepherdess."

The shepherdess was one of Josh's altered objects: a porcelain figurine of a damsel clutching a lamb he'd bought at Goodwill, then half-encased in a chrysalis of resin-dipped cocktail umbrellas, webs made of discarded jewelry, rhinestones, blobs of paint. He'd given it to me for my last birthday and it was both horrible and awesome.

Josh pulled and prodded and badgered me to my feet, then paused to squeeze me again. "I already found it." He dug in his pocket and handed me a twenty, then put on an exaggerated pout. "For the champagne? Don't you dare come back here without it!"

He was kidding, but he'd also feel hurt if I didn't.

I got my shoes and my bowler hat and left, even though I had a feeling in my stomach as if it had been lined with tinfoil, crinkling and sour and sharp. A feeling too much like I'd had when I'd watched him dancing with those people I was supposed to be so polite to. If I ran into them, that is. So did that mean they were still in town somewhere? What did Josh know?

The suburban streets spread out in front of me, soft with gusting branches, with wisteria cascading off trellises. The lawns were clipped and neon green, the shadows a blue encroachment on the ground. Peace and prosperity, even if a few of those houses had been seized by banks and were sitting empty, their yards starting to fray. Textbook American Dream, give or take.

But the feeling of wrongness, of difference, that had overcome our house yesterday—it was out here now too. There was nothing I could put my finger on, but the wrongness was spreading. Maybe the shadows seemed a bit too active. Maybe there was a vital quality to the air, like something fermenting. And even though it was a beautiful day, no one seemed to be around.

I'd been expecting some relief, getting outside for a while, but that clearly wasn't happening. I got out my phone to text Hadley; if she was working today, she wouldn't care about running into the liquor store when she was on break. It was just three doors down from the bookshop.

I turned the phone on. And it screamed.

Not like a person, exactly; more like a teakettle squalling and babbling through its steam. A piercing hiss that hinted at garbled words, at radios lost in rubble. I flung it away, and it landed on that luminous grass, still piping away at a frantic pitch. It sounded like the voice of something small and not quite human, in terrible pain.

For a while I stood in a world that had ground to a halt, watching my phone where it lay on the grass: its ordinary black plastic shell, its blue screen, but transmitting that hellish little voice. I was sure now that there were words somewhere in the stream of sound, but I couldn't understand them. I could guess, though: the voice was begging me to do *something*.

I dared myself to pick the phone back up: reached down for it, but yanked my hand away before it made contact. Then I tried to tell myself that it was Josh, pranking me somehow. I was still in view of our front windows. I looked to see if he was there, smiling slyly.

All I saw was the yellow siding, the tan drapes. A twitch at the fabric's hem.

It wasn't Josh watching me, but something was. Panic hit me with a metallic snap and I bolted, my feet pounding for three blocks before I thought that if I had a reason to be afraid, then it wasn't safe for Josh either. I wheeled to a stop and stood there gasping, my hand clutching a lamppost.

Unless it *was* safe for him. He'd seemed perfectly secure and confident. When the imp-thing had fanned up out of the glass flowers, he hadn't flinched. Still, I thought of going back for him. I thought of telling him we had to run away. Even if that meant we wound up sleeping in a cardboard box under a freeway off-ramp.

I imagined myself saying all that to him, and also *being* him as he listened to me. I could hear how ridiculous I sounded in his ears, how he felt somewhere between bemused and impatient. *Kezzer, I thought I'd explained things to you? There's nothing to worry about. Now, go buy my damned champagne.*

It felt like a mistake—and everything, everything I did felt like an even bigger mistake than whatever I'd done just before, my failures endlessly inflating and swallowing one another—but I went on. Walking toward downtown. The streets were still unnervingly empty, no cars went by, but at last I saw a few people—children playing in a yard, a man weeding—though always in the distance. I couldn't hear my phone anymore, that part was good.

Downtown consisted of two blandly cute streets at right angles to each other, over by the college. Full of bars and cafés for the students, mostly, though townies like us went to them too. An art-house theater, a ratty gallery full of smeary, huge-titted nudes hanging over a window display of bongs, a Thai restaurant. The usual, for a town with a big state university like this. And the bookstore, right on Grand Street.

Which was dark, its front door locked. I couldn't remember what day of the week it was, but since the bookstore had a sign saying it was open seven days, that shouldn't matter anyway. I stood with my back to its window for a moment, wondering what to do next. A small group of college kids sauntered past, oversized backpacks sagging from their shoulders. They struck me as exceptionally ugly people, their faces weirdly elongated, or much too big, or flat in unexpected places. One of them fixed me with a sidelong look, his eyes skidding deeper into their corners to stay on my face. He grinned.

Something in his backpack was squirming. The canvas bulged and jumped.

I told myself that he was smuggling a puppy into his dorm room. Doing something fairly innocuous. Though he should at least leave the bag unzipped. Let it breathe.

Once they were gone—which took much too long—I walked

over to the liquor store. I had a fake ID, but it was too crappy to work if anyone looked closely. And besides, the owner knew me by sight; his son had been in my year at school.

So I'd try to brazen it out. The worst he'd do was laugh at me.

The lights were on, the door chimed as I stepped through. But there was no one behind the counter. I waited—maybe the owner was in back?—until time seemed to sway in my head. The bottles gleamed in their long rows, the overhead lamps reflecting again and again, and I began to imagine that those rebounding lights were tiny, shining people swarming over everything.

Then I snapped out of it, and the lights were just lights again. I didn't know how long I'd been standing there, but it felt like a while, and still no one had appeared.

When I was younger—thirteen, fourteen—I'd shoplifted routinely. I was good at it and never got caught, but it upset Josh so much—*What if someone sees you, Kezzer, what if the clerk has to pay for whatever you've stolen, what if Mitch and Emma find out and send you away?*—that I'd stopped completely. Now, though, lifting a bottle of champagne seemed like the obvious thing to do. If I left the twenty to pay for it, it wouldn't be so bad.

The bottle I chose was marked $17.99. I was even allowing for sales tax, so Josh couldn't possibly get angry. I tucked the money under the register and helped myself to a shopping bag. Turned to go.

The boy in the white jacket was watching me through the window. The one from the grove, the same one who'd led Josh away. The one I'd mentally rehearsed murdering, in lavish detail. He didn't have his entourage with him this time, and he looked much less handsome by daylight: sickly pale, even faintly gray. There was something off about the angles of his face, as if the bones were slightly out of joint. He still had great hair, I'd give him that, mahogany brown and as thick as plumage. He was stylish enough too, with the big jacket and the same black leather leggings he'd been wearing that night.

Josh had been clear in his instructions: I was supposed to be very,

very polite to this scumbag. I thought of smashing the end off my bottle of champagne and seeing how polite I could be with the part that was left. My legs trembled with the kick of adrenaline. The boy in the white jacket smiled at me: a patient curling of his lips, as if he could see his blood frothing in my thoughts. As if the image was thoroughly charming.

I went to meet him, bells jangling at my back.

"The lovely Ksenia Adderley!" he said. "Now that I see you again, it's clear how absurd it was to take you for a young man. It's a fetching hat, that one, but it threw me. I hope you're settling in all right?"

I grimaced at hearing my name; he wasn't supposed to know it. But then it came to me that Josh must have told him at some point during his three days of captivity. Must have let it slip in a drugged stupor. It wasn't his fault.

"Josh has a bad habit of standing up for shitheads like you," I said. "Who've hurt him, or molested him, or whatever the hell you did. He won't take it the right way, if I get arrested for your murder."

The champagne was still in the bag, but I realized I was holding the bottle by its neck, so tightly I was surprised it didn't shatter. One vicious swing, down on the top of his head: that might do it, with any luck. It would be twenty bucks well spent.

"It's the thought that counts, Ksenia," he said. In that repulsively courtly tone I'd noticed when we first met. His voice was high for a man, reedy; a syrupy whine. "So we can both take my murder as already accomplished, the blood long since swallowed by the earth, roses bursting on the spot. And we can say you've served out your long years in prison, and at last been freed, and now we've met again."

I'd thought at first that he might be in high school or college. A freshman at most. Then I'd thought, no, older than that. But now I got the sense that both those guesses were way off. In the light his skin had an ashy, faceted look, not youthful at all. One of those forty-five-year-olds who can sometimes pass? Up close I could see that his eyes were an unnaturally bright, pale green, as sour as stomach acid.

"Who are you, anyway?"

"That's all behind us, now. We can meet as old friends, and recall the time I stole your brother from you, albeit temporarily, and how you gouged out my eyes with a broken bottle to avenge him. We can laugh about it together, remembering how your hands were gloved in gore up to the elbows. Wax nostalgic as the hours wear on; oh, Ksenia, what a little savage you once were! And now that that's established, may I accompany you on your walk?"

The awful thing was that I almost said yes. It was like his words had seeped inside me, coated my thoughts in grease. "Like hell. Who are you?"

He shrugged, his white jacket lifting in a cloudlike puff with the gesture. The question didn't *interest* him. His nose was long and bony, his cheekbones too prominent.

"Another time, then. I'll show you the sights."

He bent in and kissed me on the cheek, and somehow I lacked the presence of mind to break his jaw. I just stood there and took it, from this kidnapper, this filth, this almost-certainly rapist. Exactly like when I'd been eleven, I was paralyzed and stupid, speechless as a rock. The boy-slim man in the white jacket turned to walk off.

The feeling of his lips stayed with me. A cool, dry *hush, hush* on skin that shrieked and burned.

because we weren't really
home before

I wasn't supposed to go back yet. As far as I could tell without my phone, it hadn't been the few hours that Josh said he needed. My cheeks still raged with heat, my limbs jerked when I moved. There was no chance that I could sit calmly in a café somewhere. He'd seemed so self-satisfied, that creep in the jacket. Like he'd put one over on me, duped me somehow, and he was stopping by to gloat. My heart was still hammering, minutes after he'd disappeared from view.

I stormed back the way I'd come, through the residential streets, with no idea of what I would do. Anything at all except behave myself. Anything but follow instructions, even if they came from Josh. I wished I'd swung that bottle; the longing to have done just what I didn't do jumped inside me like a giant pulse. I even wished I was handcuffed, my black penny loafers tracking stinking blood all over the patrol car. That kiss lingered, branding me with my failure to act while I'd had the perfect chance. Now that I thought about it, there hadn't even been witnesses.

I wasn't looking where I was going. A pair of little girls, crouched low, loomed almost under my shoes. My knee knocked one of them in the head as I swerved, stumbling onto the grass. The bag with the champagne whacked my thigh, hard enough to bruise. What were they doing, blocking the sidewalk like that?

Okay. They had their chalks out and they were drawing on the pavement. Bloated psychedelic flowers, a lumpy, leering mermaid. They turned to gawk at me with wide, vacant eyes. There was some-

thing idiotic about them. Empty as corpses. Or maybe it was just
my foul mood telling me that.

"Sorry," I made myself say. "I didn't see you."

"Olivia, let's draw a dragon next!" It was the blond girl who'd
spoken, to her darker friend. But she was still staring at me, just as
expressionlessly as before. "Olivia, you like dragons, don't you? Let's
make it purple."

"I said I was sorry," I snapped. "Even though I didn't feel like it.
Now it's your turn to say, *That's okay.*"

"I think it should be red," Olivia said. Her two fat braids fidgeted
in midair as if they were sending out signals. Then, tentatively: "I
don't feel so good."

"Not yet," her friend admonished. "That's for later."

I started to step around them. I might give their drawing a few
hard scuffs on my way. Olivia reached out and grabbed my hand,
her expression suddenly moon-eyed and piteous. "I don't want to
die," she said. Clearly to me, this time.

Her hand looked as tender and doughy as any five-year-old's
would. Silky, pale brown skin, tiny dimples, chubby fingers. So the
sensation of her fingers pressing mine came as a shock: her skin felt
like crumbling bark. Her flesh gave the airy, hollow impression of
dry-rotted wood. I yanked my hand back.

"You look fine," I babbled. "Don't be silly."

I'd lunged out of range, but Olivia was still reaching for me. "I
know I'm not whole-me," she said. "But I'm enough-me. Enough
that I don't want to die! Don't let them take me."

I looked at the blond girl, even though all I wanted was to get
the hell away from them. "Are you two in some kind of trouble?"

"She's just playing," the blonde said hastily. "It's part of our game."

"If somebody's threatening to hurt you," I said, "I can call the
police. And I'll wait with you until they get here, and make sure
you're safe." Though I couldn't, I realized. I'd flung my phone on
the lawn, to punish it for screaming at me.

"No, no," the blonde said. Olivia's plump little hand still waved vaguely in my direction, her fingers grasping and releasing nothing. "We are having lots of fun, playing our game. About the dragon. And how it's going to eat her. Olivia, say how much fun it is! If you say it, we can make the dragon red. Like you want."

Olivia looked at her, and then back at me. "It's so much fun!" she said hesitantly. "It's all about a dragon."

"Well, the princess is going to come and save you, right?" I said. "And slay the dragon, in the nick of time? Spill its guts. Then the two of you can dance on its inert body." Josh should be proud of me. I was making such a stupendous effort to be kind, when that was the last thing I wanted to be. My heart still hadn't settled down and there was a jarring, kinetic urgency running through my limbs.

"I'm not sure," Olivia said. She looked concerned.

"It's going to eat her," the blonde pronounced with finality. "Goodbye! Have a nice evening!"

"Goodbye," I said. Though I was aware that the wrongness that had begun by infesting our house had moved on, spreading first through the whole town, and now it had reached these two kids. They weren't quite how children are supposed to be. Healthy, well-adjusted kids don't feel like dead logs, for one thing. But I wasn't sure what I could do about it. They'd said they were fine.

I wasn't feeling all that together either. On consideration. I might be as off and as wrong as everything else.

When I got back to our house my phone was still where I'd thrown it, nestled in the glaring grass. The phone was silent now, its screen gone dark. I sat down beside it and stroked the plastic, wondering who it was that had been shrieking out of it—begging me, I was almost sure, for help. If I hit the Power button, would it start screaming all over again? I wasn't sure I could face it. In my memory its timbre was girlish and thin and frantic. And possibly familiar.

Another voice mingled with it. Josh had flung open the windows and he was singing—such a fantastic voice, all dusk and velvet. I wasn't the only one who thought he could go pro. Knocking pots around. I could hear what was probably the electric eggbeater.

It made me sick with longing for when we'd both been kids, somehow. We'd gotten into the habit of hiding together, clutching each other, in closets or behind furniture. I'd tell Josh stories about my life and he'd make them into rambling, improvised songs, just for me—except that in the songs everything was different, I was always victorious in the end, and it was easy for people to love me. Like, if I told him that my mom had left me alone in the car for hours, he'd have the car start flying, and I'd rescue a boy who'd fallen off a cliff or something.

I knew we were just daydreaming, but it made life feel a tiny bit more possible than it had before.

Once the sun was streaking sidelong, and the air had gone golden, I walked up to the door. Josh must have heard me coming because he was instantly there, pouncing on me with a puff of the flour that covered his shirt. He squeezed me and rubbed his cheek on me and said, "Oh, Kezzer, you're home! I was just getting worried, you've been gone so long, and you didn't answer my texts or anything! Your dinner is so totally ready!"

"I didn't have my phone with me," I said. "But I did get the champagne."

Even though what I'd meant to say was, *Josh, what have you done?*

"Well, that's *something*." Josh pouted. And in fact the world didn't feel nearly so unbalanced now that he was with me, and my long afternoon didn't seem as crazy anymore. Maybe I was overreacting. I do have a problem with doing that. "I'll pop it in the freezer for a little bit. Oh, Kezzer, you're a mess. There's flour all *over* you! You get changed and I'll start serving."

Somehow I did what he said. In my own room, I stared at my shepherdess for a moment, her baby-blue lips smiling through a tangled rain of costume jewelry. She was exactly the same as ever, with shiny black hair and a lace dress painted with pink and blue blotches. The clothes spilled out of my drawers the same way. Lexi's framed photo of Josh and me laughing by the gorge, our faces topaz with candlelight, still hung on the wall, with the same inscription in gold ink: *To the coolest friends in the world. Heart U both! Lexi.*

Another photo, of my dad—except that he'd turned out not to be—in uniform. Josh hated it, that I wouldn't throw out that picture. He once drew an X across it, from corner to corner, in scarlet lipstick on the glass. I could still see the red smudge left under the frame's edge after I'd cleaned it. That hadn't changed, either.

And what had happened today, really? So my phone was broken. So the bookstore had been closed. So I hadn't actually killed anyone, just wanted to—like *that* was new. Some kids had acted screwy. Children's brain chemistry is weird. They're all basically on drugs all the time anyway.

I shucked my T-shirt—oversized, gray—knocking my hat onto the bed in the process. Slipped on a man's tuxedo vest as a shirt, which was a look I knew Josh liked, and put on fresh jeans. Took a quick look in the mirror, to make sure *I* was the same as usual. Tall, bony, blond, with hair like poisonous spines. Fine. Except that I needed my bowler hat.

Sennie, sweetheart, don't cry. Who cares what the darn test says? You'll always be my little duckling. Now, say quack, quack, quack. That's how ducklings say "Goodbye, Daddy."

The one time Lexi had called me by that name, I'd been ready to give her a black eye. Not that she'd had any idea why it got to me.

I walked over to the bed, keeping my eyes averted from the photos, and leaned in for the hat. It had fallen brim up, and it looked like something wet and glossy had gotten stuck in the bottom of it. A black plastic bag, wadded up? How had that happened, when I'd kept my hat on all day? I bent closer.

The object was black and bright acid green. Softly domed, glassy, and circular, big enough that it perfectly fitted the hole where my head should be. Tiny pleats of variegated color, olive and ochre, running through the wide green rim that surrounded a core of midnight.

Iris and pupil. A giant eye was nesting in the bottom of my fucking hat, and it was watching me. I screamed. The pupil dilated, like it could hear me.

My room was the nearest one to the kitchen. Josh came running, leaped down the stairs, slammed back my door. And it was there, in that triangle of space pinned between us, me and Josh and my spying hat, that the force of what had happened came to me. Billowing up and down, huffing alien air in my face. The truth, or what I could sense of it, was a charged zone beating in our midst and holding us apart.

Though only for a moment. Josh broke free first, stomped over to the hat, and stared into it critically.

"Oh, for God's sake. Can't you give us some privacy?" He snatched the hat by its brim and flipped it over, smacking it down on the mattress. I could *feel* the eye going out, fizzling to nothing like a flame. "Oh, Kezzer, I'm so sorry that happened! I don't ever want you to be scared. You, um, you probably should be careful not to leave your hat turned up that way. All right? The thing is—I know that's your special hat and everything—but you were wearing it that night. It might decide to cause trouble."

"Josh," I said. I only realized how hard I was breathing by the distortion it forced into his name. "Josh, where *are* we?"

He hesitated. "We're home, Kezzer. You know that." He reached for me, but I held myself back. So rigid that he gave up, for the moment.

"Home," I said. "It seems different."

"That's because we weren't really home before, and now we are. We finally, finally are. We've both been so lost, for years now, Kezzer, don't you see? But now for the first time in our lives we have a real home, and it's all ours, and no one can ever make us leave, or force us apart." He was getting louder. "Please, please just let us be happy!"

"You did this," I said. *How,* though? "Did you do this?"

Another pause. He seemed flustered. "Kind of? All I want is for you to appreciate it. Kezzer, Mitch and Emma were *scared* of you! They just tried hard not to show it. The way people do with dogs, like fear would make you attack, or something. And they couldn't stand how much we love each other, because neither of them has ever felt anything even close to what we have! They were dying, really dying, for you to leave. I heard them talking about how I would get over it before too long! Like I ever, *ever* would!"

He'd started crying. I couldn't stand it. I went to him and wrapped him in my arms. "Baby," I said, "it's fine. It's going to be fine. I'm just—processing."

Josh snuffled. "So you'll come eat dinner? I've been cooking all day!"

"Let's go eat. I'll open the champagne. We'll celebrate"—I couldn't say *you coming home*, somehow—"that we're back together. Okay? And then I need to get my revenge, for how you slaughtered me at Parcheesi."

Josh laughed at that, hard and sputtering. I stroked his hair.

He slid his hands under my vest and up my bare back. I don't do bras. Very softly, because I didn't want to upset him again, I pulled away. "So, what did you make for us?"

A flicker of worried sadness passed over his face, then shifted into a grin. "I told you it was a surprise, Kezzer! A fabulous surprise. I made us absolutely everything you can imagine."

tiny, sparkly hands

The smell hit me when I walked back to the kitchen. Warm and rich and salty. And there on the table were two plates heaped with mashed potatoes and gravy and what I thought must be lamb shanks. I'd been expecting, oh, tofu fritters or something.

"But you're vegan!"

Josh considered that. "Not tonight. This is the most special occasion possible. As special as if we'd found a rocket ship and we were cruising through space. There are a million stars, and they're all reaching out, just for us! Tiny, sparkly hands." I kissed his cheek and headed for the freezer, got out the champagne. "You don't mind, do you? I thought lamb was your favorite!"

"It is. I'm just surprised. You usually get pissy if I smack a mosquito."

Josh grinned. "You were *supposed* to be surprised. As I informed you earlier."

The champagne popped and fizzed, I poured it, Josh put on music. We toasted each other. And as it turned out, dinner was incredible. Impossibly savory and full of subtle herbal flavors I couldn't identify. The carrots were the most carroty I'd ever tasted—exuberantly so. Every bite made me sad that I'd never get to taste that exact same bite again. This was food that left a trail of longing behind it.

"Where did you learn to *cook* like this?"

"Kezzer, hello? I can read? There are cookbooks? So what do you know, I looked up some recipes. It's good, right?"

Cookbooks. Not the internet. I wondered if we could still access the web.

"It's the best food I've ever eaten," I told him truthfully. "I bet the restaurants millionaires go to aren't this good." There was a tiny edge in my voice; it was *too* good, *too* delicious. I would have had to be an idiot not to notice that.

Josh beamed. "I baked us a cake too! With plums!"

Something flashed into my mind: an image, a nagging dream with insomniac eyes. It was me, or another me: a Ksenia flat on a twilit sidewalk, convulsing in some kind of violent fit. Lexi kneeled beside me, crying my name again and again, her brown arms cradling my head so I wouldn't bash it on the pavement. In that azure light Lexi was able to hold on to herself, to preserve her darkness. But my blond hair and pale skin were painted blue by the glow until I was almost erased. I was only there through the medium of my spasms, my drumming heels.

And then I stilled, and Lexi started screaming. Begging for help. There seemed to be a lot of people crowded around us, actually. More than I'd seen all day.

"Kezzer?" Josh said. He was studying my face with a look of slight anxiety. "What are you thinking?"

"Oh," I said. Snapping back to the kitchen, to my fork in midair with its nugget of lamb. "Just that when I was out today, there weren't a whole lot of people."

I half expected him to argue. To say that everyone must be on vacation or something. So his reaction startled me. He tipped his head and looked mournful.

"Yeah," he agreed. "We couldn't really get people. You know, right off the bat. But it's something where—I mean, I know there's room for improvement."

"Improvement?" I said.

Josh refilled our glasses. Carefully, not looking at me. "Are you done with your lamb, Kezzer? Because personally I am desperate for cake."

My plate was clean, in fact. I was stuffed, but I knew if there was more I would have gone on eating. And at the mention of cake, my mouth flooded with spit and sweet, sharp anticipation. I got up to clear the table. "Sure, baby."

I saw it again. My body on the sidewalk, my face nearly dissolved in blue. A big man I didn't know, hands thrusting at my chest, and Lexi weeping violently. "Do you think she poisoned herself?" someone asked.

Josh was up beside me, dessert plates clattering as he plopped them down. He fetched the cake from the oven, where it had been keeping warm. A plum upside-down cake, dripping with terracotta syrup, dense with fruit as slick and bright as rubies. And the smell: it was unspeakable. A distillation of butter and caramel and flowers that throbbed like hearts.

Josh levered two fat slices onto the plates and spun around, a brash, abrupt grin flaring on his face. "Kezzer? You know, if you want more people here, there's something we can do about that."

"What do you mean?" I said. I must have blipped out somehow, because I didn't remember coming back to the table, didn't remember my slice set in front of me. I'm not usually that into food, but now my fork trembled in my hand. Josh watched while I took my first bite, and I had to close my eyes just to cope with it: the effervescent tang, the tidal sweetness.

"We could have a baby! Hell, Kezz, let's have two. Or three! Raise them so that they never even have to *think* about—the kinds of crap that happened to us. Keep them safe, and warm, and so super loved!"

No one to say to them, *You'll always be my little duckling.* And then never call again. Josh might have his issues, but I knew absolutely that he would never treat a child the way my dad, or actually-not-dad, had treated me. I could almost see the appeal of the idea, except for everything.

"Now you're just being crazy," I said. "You're sixteen? Did that slip your mind somehow?"

"I really don't see why that matters," Josh insisted. "It's not like we'll ever have to worry about money."

That was a new thought. There'd been too much to absorb. "We won't?"

"Nope. We'll have everything we need. Kezzer, to tell you the truth? I knew you wouldn't need money to buy our champagne today either. I just gave it to you to, like, help you adjust."

Ah. "There was no one there. I left the money under the register. I didn't want you to think I'd been stealing."

Big smile. "See? Other people get these whacked-out ideas that you're so edgy and intimidating and everything. But I know how thoughtful you actually are."

I'd finished my cake. When did that happen? I braced myself against the urge to go get more, and then more. I wasn't my mom, Josh had said, and that cake wasn't a bottle of painkillers swiped from a clinic. So not acting like her, that was the important thing.

"It does seem like Mitch and Emma might have made a mistake, being scared of me," I said. "The one they really should've been scared of is you."

I didn't mean it as a compliment, but Josh took it as one. He started bouncing in his chair from pure glee. "Oh, *absolutely*! That is so utterly right. Oh my God, I can't believe sometimes how well you understand me! Even though I should know by now. Yeah, you come across as all remote and threatening, but when—when someone really gets inside you, you're not. And I seem like some adorable puppy that anybody would want to bring home."

And she was still there, that girl in the blue, that Ksenia who wasn't anything anymore. I knew they hadn't managed to restart her heart. The tips of her spiny hair leaked blue poison, her skin was barely a blue ruffling in bluer air. Hope and rage were the same in her, as indistinct as the atmosphere. Her corpse weighed almost nothing. It floated on my thoughts like a slab of ice.

"You're the only one who really gets me, Kezzer," Josh said. His hands were drifting down my neck. It hit me that I would have a decision to make. Not five years from now, but immediately. "I've been hopelessly in love with you since I was ten years old. When you walked in here fuming, acting like you couldn't see any of us. Remember? And you were *all* I could see; you seemed like a completely new kind of human being to me. A new invention. Like, just by existing, you were gonna obliterate everything that came before you."

"I remember." I'd been blind with fury; I'd come so close to having a real home, a real family, and then it had been stolen from me. Yeah, I'd actually been dumb enough to believe Owen's parents might become mine too. Mitch and Emma happened to be next in line. I couldn't feel anything for them, though objectively I knew they were good people: generous, tolerant, and determined. I knew they tried hard to feel something for me, even if they couldn't really manage it.

But Josh never thought he was doing me a favor, by loving me.

He reached to undo the top button on my vest. I stiffened, and he paused, his brown eyes searching. "You do love me back, right, Kezz? You love me for real?"

"I do," I said. "I love you incredibly much. It's just hard for me to show it the way you do." And that was all true. But the question of whether I was *in* love with Josh—that seemed more complicated. And I knew it shouldn't seem like that. It should have been the simplest question in the world. "You're the only person I've ever loved who hasn't betrayed me."

"And I never will, Kezzer. I promise." He got out of his chair and tugged me from mine. "You get that everything is different now, don't you? I think—probably it was just too hard for you, when we thought we were going to have to be apart for so long? Like, it was too dangerous for us to love each other even more, then. But now you can let go, and it'll be totally safe."

Would I even know, if I was in love? I couldn't detect my own heart, sometimes. It could have been doing almost anything, and I wasn't sure I'd notice. Besides, this was what Josh needed from me.

I said, "You know what Owen did to me." I hadn't even meant to. It came out.

Josh wrapped himself around me, kissed my neck. "Oh I know, Kezzer. It's horrible that happened to you. But seriously, seriously, this isn't the same thing at all. Like, you didn't love Owen, and I utterly and forever love you! You really, truly *can't* take advantage of me, because I'm already yours, and I have been all along. Okay? That's what I keep trying to explain. Why won't you believe me?"

That wasn't actually what I'd meant. Maybe I'd thought that was the problem before, but it wasn't.

"I haven't, though. With anyone. Not since then." Though that wasn't really it either.

Josh tipped back, wide-eyed. "Really? But you make out with people!"

"Yeah," I said. "That's all I do. I make out to kill time, until you're done screwing." Did I sound jealous, or bitter? Maybe I did. Probably.

"Why didn't you tell me that before?" Josh demanded. I stared back, couldn't answer. "I only really want you. *I* was killing time screwing random people, until we could be together." He was studying my face, the glitter on his eyelids winking with light. "Kezzer? Are you scared? Of being with me, I mean."

"Yes," I said. It was true, in more ways than I could identify.

"Then what can I do?"

Maybe the wrongness had been in Josh too. But I only really noticed now that he seemed right again. Because that was Josh like he's supposed to be, sweet and openhearted. He was genuinely worried about how I felt. He was trying to help me.

"Sing to me?" I said. What really scared me was hearing my own voice. How it broke, just from saying that.

So Josh switched off the music and sang me love songs in his beautiful tenor, all dusk and velvet, with shivers on the high notes and tiny earthquakes on the low ones. And while he sang he pulled me to the living room and got me in a tangle on the sofa. Between verses he would pause, to dust the smallest possible kisses on my face and throat. I closed my eyes, bit my lip. We both knew I wouldn't try to stop him, wouldn't tell him no. I was done with that. I was in some unfathomable space, where there was nothing to do but go on. Where every step I took burst out into countless unknown directions, skewering the darkness like rays.

This was what Josh called *home*.

Every brush of his fingers felt amazing—too amazing for comfort, actually. I felt like a lab rat, wired into a machine that jolted me with unrelenting pleasure. I was on the edge of plummeting, falling completely out of control.

He slid down my body to tug my skinny jeans off my ankles. And that was when I realized I couldn't breathe. Every inch of me was shaking like a sail in a storm, and a choked, whining noise came out of my chest. I threw myself on the floor, stark naked, and rolled into a ball, rocking and fighting for air. My head knocked against the edge of the coffee table, over and over, and I couldn't seem to stop it. My lungs burned.

And Josh was all over me, stroking my hair and arms, and I knew he was going to hate me for rejecting him again. For going back on our unspoken deal. I tried to say that I didn't mean it. That I wanted to be his. I just couldn't get enough wind to do it.

"Kezzer!" Josh said, "Kezzer! You have to breathe. It's okay, it's okay, just calm down. Breathe for me. You can do it! Nice and slow, okay? Okay?"

I managed to suck in one long stretch of air, just enough to speak; my voice came out in a whistling shriek. I kept picturing Lexi's beautiful face, streaked by tears as she kneeled over my body. Just the idea that she would sob like that because of *me*—it rolled through me like a planet slammed out of orbit. "Josh, I'm sorry, I'm so sorry. I can't. I want to, but I really—I can't! I try and I try and I *try* and I can't do anything I'm supposed to!"

"Shh, Kezzer. Shh. It's okay. It's not your fault. I guess I should have known you weren't ready."

Every breath seemed to get snarled inside me, to fight and jump on its way back out. "I'm sorry. I know you're going to hate me. I *can't.*"

"I will *never* do anything but love you, Kezzer. No matter what." Josh was mostly naked too; only his underwear was still between us. He coiled around me and there was a shifting moiré of sweat and sensation where our skins overlapped. He let out a kind of half laugh, close to crying. "It *does* make me want to kill Owen even more than I used to, though!"

Right. "I guess that's why. It was like a flashback."

"Shh. I know. I want to help fix what Owen did to you, Kezzer, not make it worse! Like once you see what it's like to be with someone who really loves you . . . It's okay. We'll wait till you're ready."

I turned and buried my face against his chest. Squeezed tight. "I thought I was. I'm sorry."

"Come on the sofa, okay? I'll just hold you, Kezz. I promise."

I was getting better. Still shaking, my breath still catching with every gasp, but better. I climbed back onto the sofa and we stretched out in each other's arms, and Josh stroked my face, and everything seemed almost okay. Tears were slowly seeping from Josh's closed eyes and slipping down my throat. Even now that there was no one trying to rip us apart, we still clung to each other, for warmth and hope and some slight sense of reality. I kept my eyelids shut tight. I didn't want to see anything, or know anything.

At some point I gaped around, and found myself staring straight into the single eye of the imp-thing, the shattered, shrunken Joshling. It was perched on the coffee table less than two feet away from my face. Watching us, and leering.

And all I could do was close my eyes again while it leaned close and its gritty finger wandered around my cheek.

it was what we had to give

It was late, as late as the end of the world, when Josh squirmed out of my arms and flopped across my back instead, then started kneading my shoulders.

"Are you okay now, Kezzer? You know, I think this is what we have to do; like, just hold each other a lot, and let you get used to being touched really gradually. It was stupid of me to think you could get there all at once."

I felt a small blurt of fresh panic at the thought of *getting there,* ever, but I didn't want to say that. Maybe Josh was right, for all I knew. Maybe it would get easier. And I was relieved that he was taking it so well, the way I'd flipped out, but I couldn't be sure he wasn't secretly resenting me.

"I'll try," I said. Maybe my voice sounded strained, because Josh's hands stopped dead for a moment.

"If we both know we want to make a life together, Kezz," Josh argued softly, "then it's not about *trying.* It's just, like, about being patient, until what we have is bigger than everything that happened to us in the past. We have to create a whole new world, just for the two of us!"

My face was squashed into Tuscan Wheat Ultrasuede and I couldn't see much of the room, but I had a feeling that, even if I looked around and didn't spot the Josh-imp, it would still be watching somehow. We were already in a new world, I thought then, but *creating* it—that wasn't something I'd had any say in. I was hit by a wave of dizziness, even lying facedown.

"We never smashed those sick flowers," I said. That would eliminate one of the imp's hiding places, anyway.

Josh used my shoulders to lever himself up and sat on my bare ass, jiggling. "Yup. Clearly we need to go do that right now! We need a blast of destruction to start our new life right." He surveyed the room, and I was glad he'd taken so readily to the change of subject. "Practically everything in here could use some destroying, actually, though I guess it's too much to do it all tonight. Maybe we could set fire to that recliner, though? And, Kezz? I've decided we should paint this room purple. With lots of gold and silver stars everywhere? All this beige and tan is just *barbaric*. And then a big silver rocket ship, with you and me sailing up, up, and away!"

"Sure," I said, and rolled sideways so that Josh lost his perch and stood up. My head still swam with undulating shadows, stray lights. I managed to sit but at first I couldn't really see the room. My clothes formed a dim blob on the coffee table. I reached out and felt the satin of my vest.

Josh swatted me. He was being playful, but his lightness struck me as forced. Like he wanted us both to start pretending our night had gone differently. "Oh, Kezzer, you don't need those! Remember, there's hardly anybody here yet. We can run through the streets totally naked and not even think about it."

"I saw a few people," I said—but then I realized it would be better if he didn't ask who they'd been. I didn't want to describe my meeting with White Jacket, and not just because Josh might not approve of what I'd said to him. "There were a couple of kids drawing on the sidewalk."

"Well, kids should be in bed by now," Josh said primly. "If they aren't, then it's not our fault if they get a surprise. And anyway, we're both so pretty that anybody who sees us like this should be extremely appreciative! Maybe just put on shoes, to make sure our feet don't get cut? And I'll get you your hat."

My hat. The vitreous green eye in it, staring at me through a pupil the size of a fist. "You really think it's okay to wear that hat again?"

"It's fine now! And anyway you can't give up that hat, Kezz. It's the you-est thing in the world! I mean, the you-est except for me." He smiled. His makeup had smeared into gooey glitter puddles with his eyes awash in their centers, and he was jamming his feet into laceless high-tops. "Just be careful to keep it upside-up. Okay? So if there *is* anything in there, it can't get out."

Did he think I'd find that reassuring? I got up to fetch my black penny loafers—Josh had chucked them across the room earlier. The sparkle and confusion were clearing from my eyes now. Josh bounced out of the room and down the stairs, thumping for a few moments too long.

It was a short flight down, just seven steps. But now Josh's descent was echoing in my mind, and I felt certain I'd heard him thud down—too many times. Ten?

I went to see. The wood banister attached to the wall was just the same, the bland botanical prints hanging there were the same. The worn cornsilk-colored carpet looked exactly the way it always had, but it folded over too many stairs now. I stood and counted. Eleven.

Compared to everything else that had happened it was a trivial piece of weirdness, but I still didn't like it. "Josh?"

No answer. I went down the first step, then another. The air grazed my body too intimately, and I wished I'd put on my clothes. "Josh? Are you there?" I could see the open door of my room, lamplight spilling out like a welter of bright eyes. If he was in there he should absolutely hear me.

My foot hovered in midair, toes skimming the next step down.

And it giggled.

The stair-step itself, that is. It giggled in a stifled way, like a fifth grader trying not to give away a prank call. I could see the carpet quivering with the effort to hold in laughter. I jumped back and up, catching my heel on the top step behind me so that I landed on my ass, just in time to watch four of those stairs pull themselves free. They bent and petaled into four identical Josh-imps, all shrieking with hilarity, and scattered down the hallway.

The space they'd evacuated closed up behind them, either the top floor dropping or the bottom rising or both rearranged by some subtler tucking-in of the distance. Almost instantly there were only seven steps again. And then Josh came out of my room, naked except for black briefs and his high-tops and a silver sequined scarf he'd wound around his neck. I'd never seen it before. "I found it in Emma's dresser. Do you like it, Kezz? And doesn't it just blow your mind, to think that she was ever interesting enough to *wear* something like this?"

"I was calling you," I said. "You didn't answer." He didn't seem to think it was strange that I was sprawled there hyperventilating. I pulled myself up and he tipped his head, perplexed.

"Really? I didn't hear anything." He had my bowler hat in his hand and he made a show of shaking it out, then climbed the stairs to me, dropped the hat on my head, and slid his hands around my hips. "Are you ready to go on our destructive rampage? Oh my God, Kezz, we're at the start of something so beautiful! I still can't believe it's happening."

I held him. Aggressively tight. His concealer had worn away enough that I could see his puffed mold-green bruises again. In all the vastness of the night he was the only warmth or reassurance I had left. He nuzzled in, squeezing me back, and I knew I couldn't mention what I'd seen.

"Josh? Are any of our friends here? Lexi, or anyone?"

Lexi. I'd seen her cradling me in that vision, seen her *crying* over me, and it had left me with a deeper ache than I knew what to do with. I usually didn't let myself miss people.

Josh kissed my cheek, slow and soft. "Can't I be enough for you? For a while, anyway? I already told you, it's something I have to work on, and I don't know how long it's going to take. I'll really try my hardest ever, though!"

I thought about that. "So we can't get to—wherever they are?"

"Oh, Kezzer, you're usually such an introvert! I knew you might get lonely but I thought it would take a lot longer than this. Like, this is our honeymoon, and it's *supposed* to be just the two of us!"

"Then—say, a month from now. We can't get to them?"

Josh hesitated. "You can't. Not until they trust you a lot more, anyway. But I can. I don't want to leave you alone more than I have to, though."

They. I knew it meant the sadists he'd told me to treat so politely. The white-jacket man I'd threatened to murder. Our hosts in this damned place.

"Why would they trust you?" As soon as I said it, I knew it was a dangerous question.

"Let it go for now, Kezz. Please? Let's go wreak some havoc."

And in fact I wanted to. I wanted to smash whatever I could. I pulled away from him and walked to the wall unit, opened the cabinet door, and took down the blue vase with its twitching glass bouquet. Josh started shoving Emma's beige chenille recliner across the room; it had wheels but they squealed and dragged through the dark-gold carpet. I held the front door open for him as that hairy lump of a chair came heaving toward me, step by step. It reared as Josh maneuvered it over the threshold, then went crashing down the cement stairs and spilled onto the walk.

The stars tonight seemed impossibly bright, pink and pale green. They throbbed as if they were trying to communicate. Sending us waves of awkward conversation that never quite made sense. There were lights on in some of the houses up and down the block. I understood that it didn't mean anyone was home. All the signals flashing in on me seemed incoherent, but I was still caught up in the dialogue. I stood there receiving light, receiving dark, glad to forget everything else, as Josh jumped down the steps and kicked the recliner with a triumphant whoop.

We were really doing this. We were naked in the opal night, about to torch our foster mother's favorite chair. I didn't know what I was feeling; an alternating current of doubt and dizziness flowed in me. Still, I helped Josh shove the recliner as far as the street. It fell in a wide gap between two parked cars, dust sighing from its upholstery.

He grinned at me. "May I please have a flower, Kezzer? Though really, you should go first."

I pulled out two flowers then set the vase on the curb. Handed one to Josh. He beamed and raised his flower in a toast, and we clinked bobbing glass petals. Yellow on red. The flowers looked spastic with worry, like they knew what was coming.

"You're not your mom, Ksenia Adderley," Josh announced in ritual tones. "Oh no. Not even close!"

And then I felt it: savagery, the longing to crush and wound, as if that was what the stars had been transmitting all along and I'd finally taken it in.

I closed my eyes and swung my flower viciously against the nearest car. Just the way I should have swung that bottle of champagne earlier. I heard the tinkle and scatter of glass, and I heard my own shrill howl. I threw back my head and keened. Josh was laughing so hard he gagged a little, and his flower smashed down after mine. He bent for the rest of the bouquet and slipped another wire stem between my fingers. I whipped it down. My thoughts, my movements were glossed with delirium. Crunch, ring, and scatter, that was the refrain. That was Josh feeding stems into my blind hands while I screamed and danced around the parked cars, that was the cry of the flowers' impact, that was the singing of the shards. I opened my eyes in time to see Josh hefting a decorative faux-stone turtle and winging it through the nearest windshield, just for good measure.

I recognized the car; it was a steel-blue Toyota that belonged to old Mrs. Hixson next door. Josh had always been so sweet to her, helping her with errands and small repairs. She'd beam when she saw him and leave bags of homemade cookies on our doorstep—never suspecting that Josh wouldn't eat them because she'd used real butter. But if she wasn't here—if she was in some other where that only happened to resemble this one—then I guessed she didn't need her car anymore.

Still, I found myself missing him, the Josh who would have been furious at anyone who'd harmed anything of hers.

And besides, I was out of flowers. I was out of screams and breath and darkness to hold inside my closed eyes. All around me was the glint of shattered glass in flat preschool colors, the dark hatching of wire stems I'd cast aside. Now I felt way too sober for what we were doing.

But Josh obviously wasn't. He was still shrieking at the night, gasping with laughter. "Oh, we forgot to bring a lighter! Wait, wait, wait, Kezzer, I'll go get one!" He turned and sprinted back toward the house.

And then I was alone, naked and pale in the darkness. The fractured windshield held a cat's cradle of light. It was so silent that the electric whine of the streetlamps grew loud and tinny and rhythmic in my ears, like some kind of lifeless incantation.

So much quiet and emptiness had the effect of making me doubt I was alone. I scanned the street, the mica gleam in its asphalt so bright it looked like tiny perforations seeping sun. The breeze stirred my skin. There was an instability that might have been just in me, or might have been in the scene: a sense that the bland, low houses had been pasted on the night, not quite perfectly, or that they were slipping on glue not yet dried.

And then Josh was running back, and once again I felt his warmth and nearness as a huge relief. I needed him too much, now. I knew that but I wasn't sure what I could do about it.

He flicked the lighter in his hand. "Destructive rampage, part two. That chair is an abomination. It should be wiped off the face of the earth!"

Off the face of the what, *Josh?* But I didn't say that. *Really, is* that *where we are?*

"Let's get it away from the cars," I said. And Josh gave me one of his searching looks. He knew, maybe, that I wasn't with him in the madness anymore. Just along for the ride. Still, we got hold of that chenille lump and shoved it farther out, right into the center of the street. Set it upright again. Josh held the flame to its skirt until it started first to smolder, then to run with amber light. Soon its polyester stuffing was shriveling into hollows of tangerine flame and we had to step away from the chemical stench. Josh wasn't crowing anymore either. Instead he held my hand, watched the fire in silence. It cracked like a shotgun. Spat up plumes of poisonous black smoke.

This frenzied dependency that you and Josh feel for each other—that doesn't look like love to me, Kezz. Mitch had said that to me just two weeks ago, when Josh was out of earshot, naturally. *Real love isn't based on mutual desperation.*

That's easy to say when you've never been desperate. I'd actually said that to him. Really, what other kind of love did Mitch imagine would be possible, ever, for either of us? If he was right, then Josh and I were both damned to permanent loneliness. Desperation was what we had to work with. It was what we had to give.

But when you've always been as smug and safe as Mitch, that's not something you can understand. That's what I was thinking as I watched Emma's chair transformed into leaping heat. The flames peeled back the darkness, revealed what had been burning inside it all along.

I thought I'd try to explain it to Josh: that was us. That was the way we loved each other. That was why I could never blame him for anything he did, no matter what it was. "Baby?" I tried. "I've been thinking about something Mitch said. Don't take this the wrong way, okay?"

But then I didn't get to finish, because they were around us: those beautiful creeps from the gorge, the ones who didn't trust me, the ones who did trust Josh. White Jacket and Peacock Leather, Pink Dreads and Mink Head, and others I recalled, or didn't. Just the way I remembered them, except with a jagged distortion that canceled their beauty. More of them now, maybe thirty or so. And they were taller than last time too. I'm nearly six feet and the shortest of them was half a head above me.

Josh pulled me closer, wrapped an arm around my waist. I checked his face. He had his chin up, but I saw a flash of apprehension. Josh tipped his head at White Jacket, looming very near us now, and smiled with deliberate charm. "Hi, Prince."

"Good evening, Joshua. And of course the lovely Ksenia. How delightful to see you again so soon."

Prince smiled at me from his overhang of a head. We both knew: I'd let him kiss me. I'd done nothing to stop him. The humiliation of that kiss sizzled in my cheeks, leaked down my throat. I couldn't even spit. Everyone was staring at Josh and me, at our bared skin, though they didn't seem to think it was worth mentioning.

"So soon?" Josh asked. He cocked his head at me. "Kezzer, you didn't say—"

"I met Ksenia in town today," Prince said. "We discussed my murder. How bright the roses would bloom, that fed on my blood. Your sister is adorably brutal, Joshua."

"Kezzer!" Josh said, and then froze. Because the man he'd called Prince was reaching out for me, both hands sliding along my jaw and into my hair. Behind him Emma's chair was a mass of tumbling flames.

do tell

At first I stiffened, and then I moved. All I knew was that my skin rejected Prince's touch, spewed it back. Without even understanding what I was doing, I lunged at him. I registered the blazing chair behind him, but a plan to shove him into it—I don't think I had one. Instead I had his kiss still coiled and flexing in my cheek, and I had Owen's seventeen-year-old bulk pinning me down. Owen's voice whispering that, if his parents knew, they'd send me away again. He'd been right, it turned out; he was their bio child, after all, and I was just a stray dog. And I had what I couldn't name, whatever was happening to Josh. Some kind of unbalancing in who he was, like the rage in him was getting the best of his gentleness. All the times I'd been too shocked, too scared to react at all—it turned out now that those moments were still with me, and they were tensile, and ready for violence.

My hands shot up and forward, catching him at the base of his throat, and my legs sprang. I was screaming again, yowling, like I had when I'd smashed those flowers, but more loudly. And Prince gave way. Even if he was nearly seven feet tall, tonight, he was light, airy. Decayed inside. One naked, skinny banshee of a girl was enough to send him flying.

Into Emma's fiery chair. And I was airborne too, winging after him. I'd shot myself into nothingness, that was how it seemed, until I landed on my knees on the asphalt. My head, horribly, fell on Prince's thigh. I reared back and saw him, in his shiny leather tights and white bubble of a jacket, sitting enthroned in flames.

His stance was lazy, comfortable, both arms spread on the armrests.

His followers stood silent, but Josh didn't. He cried out and came after me, wrapping me in a soft embrace. Pulling me back and away, and the whole time the terrible thing was that Prince didn't scream, although he must have been burning. He'd seemed as dry as tinder. He didn't respond at all, just lounged in the blazing recliner, his head tipped slightly to one side. The brilliance around him singed my vision, and it was hard to make out the look on his face—but at a guess I would have said he was bemused. Toxic whorls of smoke caught in my throat and sent me stumbling back, still tangled in Josh's arms. Prince didn't seem to care.

If anything, the black scarves of smoke wrapped him lovingly. He stood up, in no hurry at all, a few small patches of blaze still clinging to his hair and clothes. A girl I'd seen that first night, with a dress of silver snails, jumped forward to pat the flames out. Was that all there was to it? I'd committed the most violent act of my life, tried to burn a man alive, and he barely deigned to notice? He advanced on me and Josh, head still tilted, smile at a slant. Josh was opening his mouth, ready to babble who-knows-what in my defense; maybe that I hadn't known what I was doing. Maybe that I was too traumatized to be touched.

"Your sister is such an enlivening presence, isn't she, Joshua? I suspect the tedium of court life exhausts a man more than hard labor ever could. Ksenia flings herself at me, strives to do me bodily harm, and I find myself wonderfully refreshed."

He reached out and patted me on the cheek, and again I was openmouthed but helpless, my throat thick with a wobbling mass of what felt like heat and pus and tears all at once. Because the violence in me had finally broken free.

And it had been useless.

Josh relaxed, though. He didn't care that I'd failed, only that Prince didn't seem to be angry with me. "I like her too." At least there was an edge in his voice. "Oh, Kezz, you're bleeding? Why don't you go inside and get cleaned up? I . . . this might take a while."

Crimson was running down my shins. I'd hurt myself, not Prince. That made it even more shameful, somehow: that no matter what I did, the wounds would rebound into me, or straight through me and into whoever I loved. I couldn't cry, not in front of these people, but the tears I was holding back turned the stars into dandelion bursts of light. I would have given anything to run into the house and escape.

But I'd already let them steal him from me once. "I'm staying with you, baby. Whatever they want from you, they're going to have to take it from me too."

Prince grinned at that, and beckoned the mink-head girl closer. "Of course. You needn't worry about your sister, Joshua. We can attend to her scratches for her here. No trouble at all. Unselle, dearest?"

"Kezzer!" Josh said—and it was in the new, weirdly authoritative voice I'd noticed earlier. "Please go in. Let me deal with this."

Prince stepped aside and the mink-head girl—Unselle, he'd called her?—rustled closer in her frothing dress. All at once I got the sense that she was a big deal in this place, maybe Prince's second-in-command. She knelt at my feet in a pool of pale lace and arched her chest toward me. Her ruffles engulfed my calves. I had no idea what was happening.

"No," I said. I understood one thing now: there was a price to be paid for being here, for the house and the champagne and our freedom from a world determined to tear the two of us apart. Even if none of this was my choice, I wouldn't let Josh pay for both of us. "I won't lose you. Not any more than I have already."

"You surely can't expect to hide Ksenia away from society indefinitely, can you, Joshua? Not when she brings such grace wherever she goes," Prince said. And now the girl's head was flung back, her eyes closed and her ice-pale curls tumbling backward.

Blood dripped from my knees onto her lace-veiled breasts and she shuddered. It would have been such a perfect face, if there wasn't something sharp and terrible about it. She seemed to have three pairs of cheekbones, raising thin, knobby ridges to each side of her nose.

The stuffed mink head sewn over her heart gave a sleepy little growl, yawned, and swirled a long pink tongue over its jaws. I saw a drop of my blood splat on its jutting lip. Heard it purr.

I almost jumped back, but Josh was still pressed against me and Prince was watching with his acrid green eyes. He'd enjoy it if I panicked. Instead I stood perfectly still while the girl wriggled closer, rubbing me with her chest, and her lifeless mink began to lap the weeping blood from my skinned knees. Its rough tongue dug into my peeled flesh, pausing once to suck out a curl of bright-blue glass from one of those broken flowers. I hissed against the pain, but I held steady. Kept my expression blank and disdainful, as well as I could, though I felt queasy.

The problem was, Prince obviously enjoyed this too. Watching a taxidermy mink slurp down my blood was as good as a porn film; that was what the look on his face told me.

"Kezzer isn't really part of this," Josh insisted. Though there was something hungry in his expression too, watching that dead thing feeding on me. I could feel its whiskers trembling on my skin, feel its freakish hot-cold breath. "She's living here with me, but only because I brought her along. She didn't come for you."

"And does it matter why she's here, Joshua? She's in my realm and she belongs to us, along with the pleasure of her company."

I was starting to feel weak. How much of my blood was that mink sucking down? I raised my foot and knocked Unselle back, and she flopped over in a frilly heap. Eyes still closed, ecstatic smile. Emma's chair now misshapen behind her, a charred hulk drooling stray flames.

"That's not how it works. People only belong to whoever they love," Josh said. I was relieved to find that he was still capable of talking back to these people, and dismayed to realize that I hadn't been sure if he could.

"Is that so? And why don't we enquire what Ksenia herself has to say on the subject?"

It wasn't something I wanted to talk about, because I wasn't sure if I belonged to anyone, not even to myself. I loved Josh, but was that enough to make him own me? Maybe I did belong to a part of Joshua, though: the part that Mitch and Emma didn't want to think about or even believe existed. To the rage and desperation that could make him much more dangerous than he seemed to be. To everything in him that had brought us here.

And I was afraid that those were thoughts that might prove Prince was right, in a way.

I opened my mouth to say something, though I still hadn't decided what. But then I saw that Prince wasn't looking to me for the answer.

He was gazing at my bowler hat, with an air of waiting politely for it to speak.

His arm snaked out, longer than I would have thought possible, and lifted the hat off my head. Held it in front of his face, and gazed into the hollow where my scalp had been, and where the oversized eye had welled up earlier. Of course: that eye had been *his*. Exactly the same bright bile green. And now he spoke into the hat, like someone calling into the depths of a cave.

"Ksenia, my beauty? What do you think of all this? It seems to me that Joshua is presuming overmuch on your affection. So: where do you belong, and by what are you possessed? Do tell."

Then he threw my hat on the ground. Hollow facing up, just the way that Josh had said I should never let it fall. In case there was something in there, something that might try to escape.

There was. They burst out now. There were so many that at first I couldn't make them out; all I took in was a blur of jointed petals, multiplying mothlike wings.

But no: they were all me. Jagged and fragmentary, stunted and squeaking. A legion of broken-mirror Ksenia-imps, no taller than the middle of my thigh. They swung and shook like ringing bells, each one unfolding into more and more leering duplicates. Thousands of them, all as naked as I was. Blond hair like poisonous spines, tiny pointed breasts. They swarmed and bubbled over the lawn, sometimes flat and sometimes bristling with dimensions, their limbs clacking like cicadas' wings. All of them wore black penny loafers, all of them had bleeding knees.

And maybe I'd been in denial about the Josh-imp. I'd managed to believe that it was distinct from Joshua himself, that it was an alien entity. But seeing my own broken, dwindled selves was different. I recognized them, I knew they were more genuinely and completely *me* than I had ever been myself, in all my life. My true image, my sick and garbled being.

No wonder Prince spoke to them and not to me. They were my reality, and they would never lie, to him or to anyone.

But they didn't answer him now. Instead they rolled up the lawn in a rattling, faceted melee, leapfrogging one another, clapping together and then splitting into multiples again. Sometimes they shrieked, and I recognized the high, pitiful voice that had clamored out of my phone right before I threw it down. They piled onto one another and flocked straight up the butter-yellow siding, plastered the roof of the house's low main section.

There was more clattering, more seething. And then Mitch and Emma's bland suburban house had an entire second story, where there'd been nothing but sky five minutes before.

That was it. The night was silent and starry, with only a few stray mousey peeps emitted by the new upper level of our house. All the Ksenia-imps were gone from the lawn and the street. I knew that the second story was made out of little Ksenias, that it was a living colony of my fractured selves, but they were doing a brilliant job of making the addition appear as if it had been there all along. There was the same yellow vinyl, or what looked just like it. The same shingle roof, just one floor higher up. Two windows gawking darkly at the night, both open. The only innovation was the curtains blowing in our new upstairs rooms. There was enough light from the streetlamps that I could see they had red and white checks, brighter than anything Emma would have chosen.

Not what I would have chosen either. Except that maybe I had.

Everyone had fallen silent while all of this was happening. Understandably. Now Prince bent down, scooped up my hat, and handed it back to me with a flourish. It was no lighter than it had been, but somehow I could feel that it was empty in a way it had never been before.

"And there we have it, Joshua. Whatever questions you might have, pertaining to Ksenia's *belonging*—I believe she, and you, can locate an answer somewhere up there. Assuming she'll let you in, of course. And now I think we'll wish you both a good night."

"Kezzer won't go up there!" Josh said. His voice sounded frantic, percussive; was this the first time since I'd found him out in the woods that he'd been truly afraid? "You can't make her. We'll both pretend—that whole floor—we'll just ignore it. I'll board up the stairs!"

We hadn't been here for very long, but I already knew that boarding up a stairway was no kind of solution. Josh should have known that too, especially since he was the one who'd dragged us into this. Those imp things could warp the house to suit their own purposes, open as many ways through as they wanted. I'd seen what the Josh-imps had done with the stairs down to our lower half-story, dilating space and collapsing it again, and why would the Ksenia-imps be any less capable? It wasn't like Josh to be willfully stupid.

"Oh, but I don't suppose Ksenia would have gone to the trouble of building so much new space onto your house," Prince observed. "Not unless it had something to offer her."

That was how it happened. As honestly as I can remember it, anyway. But I can't tell how long we've been here. Every passing second has a trickery about it, and when I try to pin anything down—any word, any hour, any slippage of the sunlight down the walls—I find that I can't. All I can say for sure is that *here* isn't going anywhere.

Part Two

lexi
holden

The king looked round him, to left, to right,
And in sooth he beheld a fearsome sight;
For here lay folk whom men mourned as dead,
Who were hither brought when their lives were sped;
E'en as they passed so he saw them stand,
Headless, and limbless, on either hand . . .
Men and women on every side
Lay as they sleep at slumbertide,
Each in such fashion as he might see
Had been carried from earth to Faerie.

Anon, *Sir Orfeo* (translated by Jessie L. Weston)

every skein of light

If I have to tell this story, then can I whisper the words? If I have to think of their names, over and over, even when I'm drifting through sleep, can I please keep them so soft that they settle like white feathers on my thoughts? I practice in my mind; I repeat the names *Josh, Ksenia,* so lightly that I hardly feel the sharp edges or the pain. When their faces float up in my inner vision, I send them streaming out of focus, fringy and smeared and wet.

But I keep them with me, and that's what's important. They dwell within, and I am inhabited by what once was.

"It wasn't your fault, Lexi," Xand tells me, over and over again. But he says it because that's what you say to your girlfriend, especially when you miss the way she used to be, and you want that happy, peaceful girl back again. When he says it, I don't think he even cares if it's true. "You didn't do anything to Kezzer. She killed herself. It was her decision, not anybody else's, and you really can't blame yourself for that."

There are murders of the kind that everyone knows about, with guns and blades and blood, and then there are murders that are so gentle and secretive that even the murderer has no idea what she's done until much later. She might not realize for days.

The second way, the soft way: that was how I killed Ksenia Adderley, and even if I had no clue what would happen, even if all I did was to say the wrong thing, the consequence was still that she died in my arms. I know Xand doesn't mean it like that, I know he's trying to be kind, but when he tells me not to feel guilty, he's really telling me to forget my own heart and bury it along with my friend.

Because there's no possible way that I can get rid of the truth, not without getting rid of the heart that holds it. I remember what I did.

I might have killed Josh too; no one really knows, and most days I imagine that no one ever will. They never found his body, or even the slightest hint of where he'd gone. Joshua Korensky seemed to have evaporated, turned into sky and clouds. At least he would have liked that, to be high and windy and blue.

"Lexi," Xand says, and takes my face in his hands, "are you listening to me? I feel like nothing I say gets through to you anymore."

"I'm sorry," I tell him. "But Xand, it doesn't help me. What you're saying doesn't help. It's not about *blaming* myself. It's just that it's actually better for me if I take my share of the responsibility. It's the strong thing to do, and I wish you could see that."

The curtains glow through a mesh of blossoming shadows, and the petal-pink crystals of the chandelier shiver out their almost inaudible singsong over our heads. We wouldn't be having this particular conversation in the living room if anyone else were home, but my parents are still at the college and Marissa is at her cello lesson.

Xand sighs. "It's been more than nine months already."

Why should he bother to say that? How could I not know? "It doesn't really matter to me how long it's been."

"It matters a lot! You just got into *Brown*, Lexi! You need to let the past go, so you can focus on your future."

Need to. Do I need to? Is crushing my own emotions really such an essential activity?

"I can have a past and a future at the same time," I tell him. And there's an image inside me, as fine as a sliver of the moon: Ksenia next to me, listening to Xand telling me what I *need* to do; how the turn of her head would reveal a gaze cold, and sharp, and stubborn. Then her profile dissolves; still, for half a moment, I can sense her indignation on my behalf. "Just watch me."

Xand's brows pucker in his handsome face. Green eyes, brown curls; he's one of the most beautiful boys in our whole school. But what used to seem like his sunny, positive outlook feels false and intrusive to me now; maybe I've changed too much. "Are you getting mad, Lex? I'm trying to be supportive!"

I stand up, leaving Xand alone on the billows of the velvet sofa. "I know you are. I think I need some time by myself."

The pucker deepens. "You mean—just today? Or—"

I don't answer that. What can I really say?

"Lexi!"

"I don't know," I tell him. "I'm—you can let yourself out. Just make sure the door locks when you close it."

He chases me into the foyer, though, and I feel like he should know better. He should understand that, even if I've only gone twenty feet in terms of my physical body, my heart is already far away; it's falling beyond his reach, a silent avalanche. Just as I reach the front door he grabs my upper arm, taking unfair advantage of how much bigger he is than me, how athletic and tall. First he felt entitled to tell me what to feel, and now he's trying to control where I go?

"Lexi, you're going to make me say things I don't want to say. Josh and Kezz—they were my friends too, and I don't want to bad-mouth them. But you're not leaving me any choice."

"You do not have my permission to hold my arm that way," I tell him. I wince a little at the sight of Xand's fingers, freckled and milky pale where they compress my dark brown skin. It's insensitive, at least, for him to play at having power over me. It's also delusional. How much patience does he think I have?

"Will you listen to me, if I let go? Just for a minute?"

"My freedom is not something you can bargain with." I'm compact, petite; Xand towers over me. Words are my power. "Let go."

And he does, though his eyes are wide and his breathing comes quick. I turn to leave. "Have you considered that maybe Kezzer made the right choice? For herself, I mean. Like, what would have happened to her, if she'd lived?"

I stop with my hand on the knob. "There would have been many different possibilities for her, Xand. That's exactly the point."

"As messed up as she was? Kezz at thirty would have been a junkie in a trailer. She *saved* herself from that. Lexi, that's what you need to see. Neither of them was going anywhere, and you're going everywhere, and I can't stand to watch you tearing yourself apart over these trashy kids."

"Trashy," I say. "You just called them your friends." People said cruel things like that about my dad too, when he was young; that he was just another ghetto kid, that being brilliant wouldn't be enough to rescue him from the destiny they'd mapped out in their minds. But he kept fighting through it all, and he became a professor.

Besides, whenever you belittle other people in that way, it's yourself you make smaller.

"That's why I didn't want to say it. I mean, it wasn't their fault or anything, but Josh and Kezz were both screwed no matter what."

What point is there in arguing over the potential of my lost friends, the one who died and the one who vaporized? Why should I say that they were smart and talented and brave to Xand, who apparently didn't learn any of that by hanging out with them through long, black-satin nights by the gorge? I knew them, if he didn't. I know them still in the whisper-story that runs along my days, and I know that their story keeps on unscrolling in ghostly spirals, in countless possible lives they'll never get to live, long past the point where Ksenia's spiky blond head stopped beating against my arms and her shattered heart came to a standstill. She had a real future, and she would have defied Xand's vision of her.

Xand's life has been easy, comfortable; his family's not exactly rich but they've never been hurting, either. And even if my situation is similar to Xand's, I can say truthfully that I never regarded Ksenia and Josh as anything less than my equals. Was Xand just *slumming*, hanging out with them?

If he was faking being their friend, he did a good job of it—but that just makes me feel worse.

I walk out, my pulse racing at the thought that he might follow me again and try to stop me from getting in my car. I don't allow myself to run, though I really feel like it. My Mini Cooper, a gift for getting into Brown, even custom-painted in my favorite peridot green, is right there in the driveway.

I get in and start the engine; I don't look back, and I drive away.

He'll tell himself I don't mean it. He'll say that I'm just being sensitive—or, oh, excuse me, so terribly *oversensitive*—in my adorable-but-exasperating way. That I'll calm down and come around and be coaxed back into sweetness and tenderness, because we both know I have before. But this time I think it's distinctly possible he's wrong.

I turn onto a dirt road through the woods until I reach a hidden hollow, deep in the viscous glow of the honeysuckle. Then I park and flop my face onto the steering wheel and cry.

Ksenia? Did you know, or at least suspect, that I was the reason Josh ran away? Is that why you timed your suicide just right, so that I would see it? It would have seemed almost preposterous, you poisoning yourself over Josh—like some kind of overblown small-town Shakespearian tragedy—if only you hadn't actually died.

I think you did arrange things for my benefit, so that at least a modicum of your pain would be visited on me. You of all people must have known that that's the kind of visitor who never goes away.

I met Josh and Ksenia when we moved here at the start of my sophomore year. They weren't the kids I was supposed to be friends with, more or less for the reason that Xand just rubbed in my face again. As a daughter of two professors, I instantly found a clique of the other professors' kids and the children of lawyers and architects, just waiting to welcome me in. A pair of scrappy, furious, pretentiously alternative kids whom everyone knew were in foster care—I should have smiled at them in the halls, just to show that I was the *nice* kind of popular, but I also should have kept my distance. Those were the silent rules that tinted the atmosphere in our classrooms: stick with your own kind.

I'd only been there a week when I first encountered them. I was sitting with my insta-clique, a dozen mixed boys and girls, on benches in the quad, when someone I thought was a tall blond boy walked by, in black cutoff jeans and a flowing black T-shirt. I thought, *If he wasn't so scrawny, he'd be drop-dead gorgeous.* I suppose I didn't make much of an effort to hide the way I was staring, because the guys with me burst out laughing.

"You swing that way, Lexi?" one of them—I think it was Derrick—asked.

I don't care to respond when people refuse to say what they mean. I tipped my head and waited for someone to come out with it.

"Not that I've got anything *against* it," a boy named Dylan added, with just enough emphasis to be offensive, "but you really don't look like a dyke!"

Now I understood. "That's a girl?"

Another peal of laughter. Now that they'd said it, it became clearer to me; her face had a masculine sharpness and definition under the peaks of light hair, but as I kept looking an unexpected delicacy seemed to come out of hiding. She'd sat down on a bench at a distance from us, alone, and fixed a faraway gaze on the trees. She held a book, but she wasn't reading.

Of course I wanted friends at my new school, and I wanted everyone to accept me. But something about the laughter made me feel hemmed in, breathless, and hopelessly lonely. Why should that girl be any different from how she was, right at this moment? I said, "She's beautiful."

There was a round of scoffing noises.

"I'm into it," Dylan announced. "Can I watch?"

I wasn't about to answer that. I raised my eyebrows.

"Don't be disgusting," a girl named Lila said, and I looked at her, hoping she might support me and tell him off for making such obnoxious comments. But that wasn't her intention. "Ksenia doesn't even shave her *legs*."

It occurred to me then that I didn't really know any of them, these kids who were pretending to be my friends only because I dressed well, because their parents had met my parents at parties. I wasn't so certain anymore that I was interested in knowing them any better.

"Kezzer could be hot if she tried," Dylan said, defensively. "Tall, skinny blonde? Hell, I'll shave her legs for her. Or her . . . you know."

"Not a tit in sight, though," Derrick observed, in a tone that implied Ksenia had personally cheated him by being flat-chested. "And she wouldn't have any friends at all, if she didn't come with Josh."

"Is Josh her boyfriend?" I asked, and everybody howled again.

"He's her foster brother," Lila explained, taking condescending pity on me. "Just a freshman, but he has a lot of older friends. There are kind of weird rumors about him and Ksenia."

"Kezzer!" Derrick yelled across the quad. "Hey, Kezzer!"

She looked our way. Even from this distance, I could see her disdain.

"Lexi is new here! She wants to meet you!"

For a moment I thought she would ignore him, but then she got up off her bench and sauntered over, with deliberate slowness. It gave me time to dread what might transpire once she reached us, but it seemed like anything I did would be interpreted in ways I didn't mean. Lila giggled nervously.

Ksenia stopped eight feet back, barely bothering, and met my gaze. "Hi, then," she said. Her eyes were dirty gray, with hazel rims. She had acne. It was strange to think of this androgynous, pimply girl in cutoffs as *elegant*, but that was the word that floated into my mind.

"Hi," I said. My voice came out so soft that I wasn't sure she'd heard me.

"Lexi was just saying how you could pass for smoking hot," a boy named Adrian put in. "And she was wondering why you ruin it by, you know, pretending to be a guy."

"I didn't say that!" I said, but Ksenia had lost interest in me. She was *examining* Adrian, that was the only word for it, with a look of drawn-out, casual contempt that sent a wave of fidgeting through the group. My cheeks were burning.

"Tell her it's like how you could pass for human," Ksenia told him at last, in a voice of perfect neutrality. "If you didn't ruin it by, you know, acting like a little bitch."

Then she was stalking away. "Who's calling *who* a bitch?" Adrian flung after her, but his face was blotchy red and there was a sweaty, heavy glaze to his eyes. And it came into my mind, as lightly as a breath, that this was a moment of decision for me; that if I left them now, Adrian and Lila and Dylan would never welcome me again, never wave me to their table at lunch or act like I was meant to be one of their number.

I also realized that it mattered more to me what Ksenia thought than it did if these kids cared about me one way or the other. I stood and walked after her. Lila called, "Lexi?" once, and then someone hushed her.

"Hey," I said, to Ksenia's black-and-blond back. She pivoted, not rushing a bit, and hit me with the same look of chilly inspection that she'd turned on Adrian. "Hey, I really didn't say that—what Adrian said. I would never talk that way about anyone. I wouldn't demean myself with that kind of ugliness."

The way she was gazing down at me made me wonder why I'd gone to the trouble of chasing her. Who was she, to put on so much attitude?

"Okay," Ksenia said. Even her voice was low and smoky enough to be a man's. There was an awkward lull in which I was terribly aware of birdsong and gray eyes and shimmering trees.

"What I actually said was—a compliment. Adrian just distorted that." Why was I still trying?

Ksenia shrugged. "He would." She gave me a kind of half nod, turned, and walked away again. Her long, knobby legs were covered in ivory down, just like Lila had said. She was poised, blade-sharp, and merciless, and I was bitterly sorry I'd left my group for her—even though, if I was honest with myself, I didn't like them at all.

Before she'd gone five steps a chubby boy with a frizz of blue-streaked black hair came bouncing up, flung an arm around her, and sent her spinning. She laughed—who knew she was even capable of such a thing?—and I realized this must be Josh. Then he caught sight of me and beamed. "Hey. You just have to be new here, right? Because I know *everybody*."

"I'm Lexi," I said. He was plastered in sparkly makeup, and his halo of black and blue tufts fluttered absurdly. Did he think he was auditioning for some '80s glam-goth band? "I like your hair."

That was all that was necessary, as I discovered, for Josh to adopt me as his new best friend—especially once the gossip reached him about how I'd stood up for Ksenia. Xand heard the story too; we'd met in passing before, but we only really talked when he approached later that day to tell me I'd done the right thing. "Derrick and Dylan are kind of my friends, but I know they can be immature jerks sometimes. I just wanted to apologize for how they were acting." Maybe it wasn't so much, in retrospect—but since Xand was the only one of the *popular* kids who made an effort, it felt like a lot at the time.

After that, it was always Josh beckoning me to sit at his table. Always beaming and enthusiastic and so delighted to see me that it took a little getting used to.

And just as Derrick had said, Ksenia came with him, as a kind of bonus, though I could never quite shake the impression that she was my friend—how should I put this?—*indirectly*. She hugged me when we met, and she was loyal enough to cold-shoulder anyone who annoyed me, but she never revealed the slightest vulnerability, never once cracked her facade.

It got old.

"You can't blame Kezzer," Josh would say, whenever I brought it up. "It's seriously harder for her than anybody knows but me. She *totally* likes you, Lexi."

I finally lift my head off my crossed arms, and gaze around at the dense emerald glow under the vines. I can't go home, not when Xand might still be there waiting for me; I might need a few days, or a few weeks, before I can bear to speak to him again. One thing I'm sure of: I will never again allow anyone to tell me that I should not feel this ache, this regret. Even if Josh and Ksenia had more reasons to be angry at the world than I could ever understand, they never seemed to take the view that Xand does: as if it were improper, *indecent,* for a girl with my luck to feel anything negative. They had a way I liked of not making any assumptions about who I should be, or what I was supposed to feel. Both of them would have met my grief with a natural, easy acceptance, and neither would have ordered me to get over it.

First I call my dad, tell him I've broken up with Xand, and ask him to let me know if the coast is clear when he gets home. I trust him: he'll leave all the metaphoric windows open for my words to blow through, but he won't pressure me to confide in him before I'm ready. I know he won't ask questions or say anything except "Of course, sweetheart." And that's what he does.

Then I drive again, heading into town, into the golden plunge of the sun. I want to find somewhere so quiet and remote that no one will glance my way or try to speak to me, where I can let my thoughts sail away on the streaking colors of the sunset. I stop once, pulling over at the Bagel-Fragel for a fragel—a cinnamon-raisin bagel fried like a doughnut and rolled in cinnamon-sugar—and tea. I can't go to the gorge, because that's one of the first places Xand will look for me, if he's looking, but maybe I can find a corner to myself in the university's rose garden.

I turn the corner onto Grand, and that's when I see something that should be impossible. Though on reflection it's not *entirely* impossible, even if I'd come to believe we'd never see him again.

Joshua Korensky.

At least, someone with a shape like his is walking along, a block ahead of me—a figure with those wandering curves that you could only really describe as voluptuous—and hair layered platinum over dark brown, the way Josh's was when he disappeared, though knowing Josh he would have changed his hair at least three times by now. Someone who's wearing a hoodie with black stars that I could almost swear I remember. But whoever it is, I'm looking at them from behind. Probably I should assume that it's a stranger, even a woman; maybe a university student, one who happens to have Josh-like hair and similar taste in clothes.

Should I be comforted by the thought that possibly, imaginably, it could be my lost friend? I'm not, at all. Because if I have every reason to dream of Joshua alive and well, to see my dreams reflected on the mirror-bright streets—that would take *one* of them off my conscience, at least—in a way it's even more terrible than it would be if he had died.

If that is Josh, he let everyone go wild searching for him, and he let everyone despair of finding him again. He let the Delbos and his best friends weep themselves sick for over nine long months, when he could have just picked up the phone. And he let Ksenia die.

There isn't much traffic. I coast along at the speed of sleep, keeping pace with that Josh-ish figure, and watching for the moment when he, or she, will turn and betray an identity.

Whoever it is, they're twisting from side to side, staring in the faces of passersby who never seem to return the look. If that's Josh, then why aren't those people staring, crying out and reaching for him? In nine and a half months, has everyone forgotten how we all searched for someone with precisely that hair, that shape, that height?

I think I understand, or at least I imagine an explanation, as I slide up the sun-lacquered streets: it's him. He's come back to our town looking for Ksenia, because knowing how he felt about her, it just isn't possible that he could have stayed away forever, not if he was still on Earth. He has no idea what happened, and he's waiting to see her at any moment. He's unraveling every skein of light, sure that the shining thread will lead him straight to the one he loves.

Of course, if she'd lived, she would have been long gone by now. What would hold Ksenia here without him? But maybe that hasn't crossed his mind.

He stops at the corner, turns and looks both ways—almost, though not quite, at me. Round brown eyes, glitter-rimmed; creamy cheeks; full pink mouth; a slightly hooked nose. And I can say that I have positively identified Joshua Korensky, who should be ashamed to show his face within a thousand miles of this place, where his every step tramples Ksenia deeper into her grave.

I roll down the window. Honk and shout his name. He ignores me.

So he came to find her, hoping he wouldn't be recognized. Then shouldn't he have made some effort at disguise, put his hood up, at least? Nothing is making any sense.

He crosses the street and heads up—of course, I see it now—Whistler Drive. I've avoided this street ever since Ksenia died, but now I turn and follow, scanning for a parking place as I go. I'll chase him down on foot, and we'll see if he can keep pretending I'm invisible once I'm directly in his path. There's a spot free almost immediately, but to pull into it I have to look away from him.

Just for an instant, I swear it.

But an instant is too long, because when I look around Josh has vanished all over again.

Right in the middle of a peaceful block of low houses with flat, bare lawns stretching down to the street. It's completely devoid of tunnels, of dense shrubbery; anywhere at all that someone playing fugitive could hide.

I get out of the car and stand there, watching the emptiness of the evening. Sprinklers toss their shredded rainbows in midair, someone laughs in the distance, and the shadows stretch like webs across the light. "Josh?" I call. "Joshua? It's me."

But there's no answer, and why would there be? How can Josh reply, when Xand is right and I've driven myself half-crazy by convincing myself that I'm responsible for everything that befell the two of them? I'll probably see Ksenia next, shrugging and speaking in bitter monosyllables; Ksenia, refusing to let anyone get close to her except for Josh, her one and only true exception.

I climb back into my car, and sob my way in circles around the block.

an orchestra of breaths and bells

It isn't until I'm in bed that night, watching the dusty pink haze of streetlamp light on my ceiling, that my feeling of airless, gasping insanity recedes enough that I can think at all clearly. I turned off my phone earlier to quiet the chiming persistence of Xand's texts, but now I turn it on, just in case there's a message from someone else. If I really saw Josh today and not some wafting mote of delirium, then I'm certain he saw me too, and he heard me yell his name. But no, of course not; there are a dozen texts from Xand, and three voicemails, and that's it.

Through my vent I can hear Marissa acting out different roles in her current daydream, her soft little voice leaping into higher and lower registers as she switches characters: a girl pirate, a talking octopus. It's a lovely sound, Marissa playing out her fantasy theatre in the quiet of her lilac room, though sometimes I find it just a touch disconcerting. I try not to listen, so that she can have her privacy.

I spent hours today thinking I'd lost my mind, but then a memory I've silenced for months began murmuring to me while I was loading the dishwasher. And now that I'm alone in the rosy night, that memory is getting louder, as if an orchestra of breaths and bells and marching steps were steadily approaching me. At the time it was all so utterly bewildering, it made such a havoc of reason and emotion, it was as if the whole town silently agreed to pretend it never happened. We conspired to brush the memory of it out of all our minds and never mention it again. But the fact is, this isn't the first time that there have been inexplicable occurrences in connection with Joshua Korensky.

He disappeared over nine months ago; that, everyone can agree on. The town threw itself into a frantic search for him; that, too, is part of our accepted history.

The part that nobody likes to talk about is that bizarre interval when we all believed—was it only for twenty-four hours, or less, or more? In any case, it wasn't very long—that Joshua had been found.

It was the third night after he'd vanished, when everyone had started to give up, when there was a low rustle of insinuations that Ksenia must have killed him, that it must have been a crime of passion, and it seemed I was the only one convinced she was innocent. That the guilt, such as it was, belonged to me, or at least that it was shared between me and Joshua.

For almost everyone, though, it seemed to be very, very easy to believe that a brusque, chilly foster-care girl like Ksenia—one taken from a mother who was approximately a prostitute and certainly an addict, one eventually raised by bighearted pillars of the community who should have known better—would have turned out to be a homicidal, compulsive liar.

Xand knew how worried I was, so he didn't wait to call me. My phone's ring broke through my sleep at five in the morning. "Lexi! They found him! He's—not totally fine, I guess, but he's alive! They brought him to the hospital a few hours ago!"

Maybe this was where the feeling of restless, relentless craziness began—when Xand's voice scattered those words through my fading dream. Or maybe it had started earlier, on the night Josh went missing? Had everyone's behavior not seemed just a shade unstable, distorted, in the days since then? Even halfway drowsing, I knew immediately who Xand meant. "Who found him?"

"Kezz did! She called 911. He was back in the exact same place where they ran into that party, is the freaky thing, right where we searched a million times."

The day before Xand had said that he didn't believe in the party, didn't believe in those strangers Ksenia claimed she and Josh had met under the trees; there would be *some* kind of evidence, necessarily, if she were telling the truth. Apparently Josh's return had made Xand change his mind.

I breathed out. My sense of relief kept coming, unspooling like a thread; as Xand explained how the news had come to him, through Derrick's mom, who worked in the emergency room, then through Derrick to Dylan, and Dylan to him, I kept feeling more and more that I had barely escaped from a horrible fate. So much tension slipped out of my muscles that I thought I might fall apart.

I interrupted. "Can we go see him?"

"Visiting hours aren't until noon," Xand said. "Noon to three. I'm going to head over there as soon as they'll let us in. And maybe you could make those vegan brownies?"

I remembered something. "I promised I'd go see Grandma Claire. She bought matinee tickets in the city for me and Marissa, and then we're all supposed to go shopping." At that moment, it didn't seem so urgent anymore to reach Josh as quickly as possible. He was back, he needed rest, and he would be around from now on. More than that, I was still just a touch ashamed of what I'd done, even now that it seemed we'd been spared the consequences I'd been dreading; I wanted to see Josh, I truly did, but since I had such a good excuse . . . maybe not right away. "I'll send you the brownie recipe. You need coconut oil. And could you tell Josh I'll come see him as soon as I can?"

"Sure," Xand said. "And Kezzer too? Now that you don't have anything to feel bad about, you're not going to keep avoiding her, right?"

I hesitated, just for a moment. "And Ksenia. Yes. Tell her I'll call."

I never liked calling her Kezzer, though almost everyone, even the Delbos, had picked up the nickname from Josh. It sounded so harsh to me—and even if she seemed like a harsh person sometimes, it didn't feel right to *emphasize* that sharpness and roughness over all her other qualities. She was also luminous, precise, and fragile, like frost-flowers vining up a windowpane in January. And my mom's mom, Grandma Claire, is the only other person I've ever known who can look so perfectly elegant, so composed, no matter what she's wearing.

Ksenia's real name captured more of her personality, I thought.

Marissa and I got up half an hour later and took the train into New York, and spent the afternoon with our grandma; we always followed the same program, lunch, the theatre, sundaes, shopping, then a late evening of movies and takeout at her condo in Brooklyn Heights. My dad comes from a poor background, but my mom's parents are driven and very successful, even a bit snobby, and some-times refer to themselves as African-American aristocracy, with just the lightest touch of irony. They would have been appalled to know that I had a friend as low-class as Ksenia, and I had never mentioned her to them, because how could I describe her without lying? "What are her parents like?" would have been their very first question. I love Grandma Claire far too much to listen to her call Ksenia *trailer trash,* and I knew that was the phrase she would use.

Josh's parents had at least had the good taste to die, the front half of their car crushed in a rockslide while their four-year-old son wailed, barely scratched, in the backseat. So it was safe to allude to him in passing, now and then.

Once that afternoon Xand texted me: *Brownies came out great! Josh says yum!*

Marissa and I got through the whole day without saying a single word about the drama that had swept through our town—my little sister is exceptionally sensitive about knowing which top-ics to pick, and which to leave alone—and the next morning we got back on the train and went home. It's a long ride, but I thought if I rushed I could make it to the hospital for the very end of visit-ing hours. And that I really should show up, even if I only had ten minutes, or Josh would be terribly hurt.

My mom met us at the station, but she agreed to drop me off at the hospital. "I don't think that boy is there, though."

"You mean he already went home?" I said.

She hesitated. "I've . . . been hearing different things, sweetie. Why don't you go ahead and check? If you don't find him, it's not much of a walk back." She let me out at the corner and I turned up the wide front walkway.

Xand was sitting on a bench just outside the entrance, a row of red and saffron lilies blooming just behind him. There was a look on his face that I had trouble sorting out, because it seemed to be mixed from too many emotions, with a morose crumpled mouth and pinched, angry brows and a glaze in his eyes almost as if he were drugged. Whatever it meant, it couldn't be good.

He saw me, jumped up, and rushed to catch me in his arms. "Lexi, Lexi, Lexi," Xand breathed out. "Please don't go in there! It's not safe!"

"It's not safe in the *hospital*?" I asked. "Xand, what's wrong? Are you okay?"

He leaned back to look at me, one hand curled on my cheek. His gaze seemed to clear, to gust like sideways wind, to cloud again.

"I didn't mean that," he said at last, though his voice sent shivers down my back. There was a wavering frenzy to his tone, a madness that stirred my perception of the flowers, the broad glass doors, the reception desk's tan lip. "I just mean—that Josh isn't here. Don't go in."

"You mean they released him?" I asked, but from Xand's awful, flickering agitation I knew it couldn't be that; something terrible must have happened. God, had Josh died in the night? "Xand, tell me what's going on!"

"Nothing," Xand insisted. "Nothing is going on. It's just that— they never found Joshua, after all. He's still missing. They said Kezzer was here overnight, but she went home this morning."

"What do you mean, they never found him?" I asked, and there was a trembling unreality to the view, as if I could see every molecule in those red lilies shaking loose and wandering into hysteria. "But you saw him, Xand! You texted me!"

Xand hitched up his shoulders and looked away.

"Josh wasn't actually here. I just asked at the desk, and they said there's no record that he was ever admitted." Xand delivered those words with what I can only describe as a desperate finality, like he hoped they might settle everything.

"But—look at me, Xand! You *saw* Josh, right? You talked to him? You said he liked the brownies!"

Xand kept his gaze stubbornly averted. He was hyperventilating and I could feel his legs vibrating against mine.

"Xand!"

"I *thought* I saw him, Lexi," Xand croaked at last. "I thought—but he was never here, okay? When I said Kezzer found him, I was—just wrong."

"So why was Ksenia here, if Josh wasn't?"

No answer.

"I'm going to ask the receptionist myself, Xand. If you thought you were watching Josh eat brownies, then that means he was here. Maybe they just—mixed up his records somehow."

Xand tightened his grip on me and his gaze finally flashed into my eyes. "Please don't, Lexi. Don't go in that building!"

"But why not?"

He stared down again. His cheeks were bright and hot.

"You think, if Josh could vanish from the hospital, then anybody else could too? That if I walk up to that desk, you'll see me melt right into the floor?"

Xand heaved a deep, tremulous breath. "Joshua was never in there, Lexi. Kezzer never actually found him. Maybe—that was just a lie she told 911. Or maybe she's having some kind of mental breakdown, and she really believed it."

"But *you* believed it!"

"Please, Lexi. *Please*. Let's just get out of here."

Maybe I should have refused; maybe it was a moment of weakness on my part, that I didn't wrench myself out of Xand's arms, march up to the desk, and demand to know what had become of my friend. But Xand's madness was sliding into me; I took in his shivers, and the rush of his fear made my blood course faster. How did I feel such dread on a sunlit walkway in June? The incoherence of it all shimmered on the pavement and turned the bright petals into monstrous flicking tongues.

I let Xand lead me away. I let him hold me and caress my hair while I cried my eyes out on his bedroom floor. I was grateful for the comfort then. On some suppressed level, I was even relieved that Xand had been there to protect me, though I didn't know from what. Somehow the amazing perversity of what had happened— that Josh was found and unfound again, seen and unseen—deepened my sense that he must have died. When I imagined staring down at Josh's empty hospital bed, an icy shiver crawled through me. I had the irrational impression that, if Xand hadn't stopped me outside, I might have caught some ghostly infection of the mind.

And I wasn't the only one who suspected that Josh had appeared after his death. Later that night I talked to Eleanor Leigh; she thought she'd visited Josh in the hospital too; she thought he'd seemed almost fine, even if his face was bruised; he'd eaten chocolates with her, laughed at her stories of the search.

"But he was never even there, Lexi. That whole time? How crazy is that? So you know what I think? I think what we all saw was Josh's ghost."

So was that what I saw earlier today? Did I follow a *ghost* onto Whistler Drive?

If Josh is nothing but an apparition now, then I suppose that would explain why he hasn't done anything new with his hair in so long.

It's already after two, and I know I'll never sleep tonight. I watch the mauve dusk, how it suspends cloudlike above me. So shapeless, so smudged, as if someone were hard at work erasing everything I know of reality.

And then I lean out of bed and reach for my phone, and touch a number that was disconnected months ago. It rings, and it comes to me that his number almost surely has been assigned to someone else by now; it might belong to anyone, anywhere, in the quiet of their own private night. I'm about to embarrass myself by waking up a perfect stranger, just because I felt like indulging an impulse that I have to admit is insane. I shake myself and move my thumb to hang up the call.

"Lexi!" Josh's voice bursts into my ear. "I am so, so happy you called! Oh, you have no idea how much we've missed you."

"Josh?" Am I dreaming? "Is this real? Did I actually see you today?"

"I—didn't have time to stop and talk. I knew once we started there would be way too much to say, is the thing, but I still felt terrible about leaving you hanging like that. But you know once we start talking for real, we'll just go on for *years*."

It's really his voice. Isn't it? Has unreality braided itself into the radio waves streaming through my phone?

"That's what you're worried about? I thought you were dead!"

A pause. "I don't know if you can understand this, Lexi. But there were so many choices that I *didn't* have. I know I probably hurt people, but please—remember that you don't know everything. Try not to blame me!"

"Do—have you told your foster parents? That you're all right?"

Silence.

"If you haven't told them, Josh, then you know I have to!"

"Don't do that." Quickly. "At least, don't tell anybody yet, Lexi, okay? Because you might change your mind once you see me!"

"Once I *see* you." Will Josh warp the fabric of the world again, be found and unfound, witnessed and obliterated, the way he was before? Because even if he's begging me not to blame him, I think I do. Why did he stay silent for so long? How could there possibly be a legitimate reason for his wounding everyone this way? I'll still take my share of the responsibility—it's a point of pride with me to own my choices, both good and bad—but now I'd say the lion's share of the guilt belongs to him. "Do you know about Ksenia?"

"We really shouldn't discuss this on the phone," Josh says, a bit fretfully. "Lexi, just come talk to me in person. Today at five? But you have to promise you'll come alone!"

I give up; whatever is happening, however unsettled my mind might be, there's nothing to be gained from resistance. "Where?"

Silence. Did Josh hang up? Did I talk to him at all? Then I hear him sigh.

"Meet me at the gorge."

a velvety, minuscule death

"Lexi?" Marissa says in the morning, when our parents are out of the kitchen—and how wide and deep her eyes are, watching me, and how shy is her hand, reaching for mine. "Did something happen?"

"It's okay, Mar-Mar," I tell her. "Just—I had an argument with Xand. I think I don't want to be his girlfriend anymore. These things happen when you get older, and it's not anybody's fault."

She nods. "That's what Daddy said. He said I shouldn't say Xand's name unless you mentioned him first. But I meant something different."

You have to watch out for this one; she's small even for eight, and quiet, and wistful, but there's no telling how far she's seeing into you at every passing moment. "Why do you say that?"

"Because it's like you're not seeing us. You're looking at something else."

I'm looking into the shadows of my own room last night, into that moment where Josh's voice came gushing out of my phone. The call was there in my phone's history when I checked earlier, it certainly went out, but possibly I sleep-dialed and only dreamed up the conversation that followed.

"I don't know," I tell her. "I think it was just a nightmare."

She comes over and nestles against my side, rests her little head on my shoulder. Just for a moment before my mom calls us, and we have to leave for school. I'm tempted to ask if I can skip, which is not something that usually would be tolerated in my family—but at this point class for me is just a formality, and what difference would one day make?

Then I pull myself together and go—more than anything so I can watch and listen. If anybody else sighted Joshua, or heard his voice where it shouldn't be, then the gossip will be all over school.

I pause once in the quad, and call the same number that conjured up Josh last night. Three harsh tones, and then once again there's the old recording saying that the number has been disconnected. That seems to be solid evidence for my theory that what I heard last night was only in my mind.

And then what about what I saw?

Xand corners me once, all too predictably. "We need to talk."

"You mean, *you* do," I say. "And I believe the verb you're searching for is *want*, Xand. You *want* to talk to me, but you're not going to until I decide I'm ready. Acting pushy won't make that happen any sooner."

"Why are you treating me like this? I've been so completely loving and supportive—and I knew you were still upset about Kezzer—but I really thought with us everything was fine." His voice is rising. I've always thought of Xand as basically one of the good guys, maybe with some issues but generally considerate, generally kind. He's always been a bit too judgmental for my taste, a bit smug, and there've been things I let slide before. Maybe too many. Now I'm wondering if I'm going to wind up with a stalker.

"I'm not ready to talk to you, Xand. Your job for now is to work on respecting that." I can see the struggle in his face; he truly means to be sensitive, to do the right thing, but at the same time—he wants what he wants, and he expects to get it.

At last he manages a nod, almost in tears. "Let me know when you are?"

I soften enough to give him a hug. He's trying. I've hurt him and he really doesn't understand why.

A few people overheard us; I couldn't avoid it, not when we were right in the hallway. Soon the school is going to be humming, because we were supposed to be the ideal couple. I can't control it, and I'm not sure how much I care; what matters for now, for today, is Josh's voice still flowing in my head, telling me not to blame him. As far as I can tell, I'm all alone in knowing that there's a chance, however slim, that Josh has somehow come back.

What matters is what I'll see, or not see, at five o'clock by the gorge. I think, once or twice, of just not showing up, but how else can I test the truth of what's been happening?

The seconds drift down, as slow and frail and murderous as chipped-glass snow.

I make myself go swim laps after school, to do something, to transform my anxiety into weariness, but I brush off my friends afterward and get a sandwich to go at the diner. I park near the gorge and eat in the car, watching the dashboard clock in its impossibly drowsy advance. Four thirty-seven, now. Josh used to be the late-running type, and I wouldn't expect that his ghost or his double, or even the complete negation of his being, would be any more punctual.

I catch myself biting my nails, and I quit that a year ago.

At a quarter to I climb out of the car and wait for a moment at the side of the road. What am I doing? Listening? Trying to analyze the components of this particular quiet, with its ordinary warbling birds and the stroke of leaves on leaves? Then I turn in, walking through the pale unraveling birches, the maples' chartreuse claws. Over moss and lichen-scabbed rocks, then to the clearing where we always used to go on warm nights. No one is there, so I sit down on a stone and watch the freckling light.

I try calling Josh, just one more time.

He doesn't answer, but I don't hear the robotic voice explaining that the number I have dialed is no longer in service either. Instead I hear a peal of bells, guttural and piercing and lovely all at once. A terrible sound.

I hang up as quickly as I can, but I can't avoid the suspicion that I didn't hang up quite fast enough. The impression made by the quiet woods has altered, as if something in those tones affected my brain waves somehow, dosed me with some slippery sonic drug.

I check the time. Five exactly. And all at once I think I'm not willing to wait any longer, not on the slim chance that the real, living Josh will show up.

When I stand to leave I see something moving through a scrim of trunks and sparse spring leaves. It's not in our clearing, that is, but in the next one farther on, and the detail seems significant to me, though I can't remember quite why.

There's a yellowish fluttering that can only be bleach-frizzed hair. I start walking toward it, waiting—hoping, perhaps?—for it to disappear.

But he's there, he's really there, and the moment I part the branches he turns to see me, grinning at me as if not a single day has passed since we last met.

"Lexi!"

He jumps forward and catches me in a big, warm hug, and I don't know if it's habit or relief or genuine happiness that makes me hug him back just as hard. Or maybe it's pity, since after all I have to tell him something that's going to destroy him. Because as long as I wasn't sure if he was real, I could refrain from anticipation of just how it will feel to break the news to him, about Ksenia.

"Josh, I am having some trouble believing this. But it's really you." Those round brown eyes, rimmed in charcoal and lilac glitter, that big soft-lipped smile. He hasn't changed at all. "Where the hell did you disappear to?"

Maybe there's one tiny possibility that I don't have to blame him: if he was taken captive and somehow just escaped.

"I know it's been a while," Josh says, letting go of me. "It's so completely awesome to see you again, Lexi."

"You—couldn't you have called, Josh? Emailed, done something? In nine *months*? What was stopping you?"

For a moment his eyes go wide, though I can't imagine how

that could come as surprising information. Then he grins. "You'll think I'm a raging asshole, right, if I say I lost track of time?"

It shouldn't be funny, but it nearly is—at least, it might be if it wasn't for *her*.

"Josh, listen, there's something I have to tell you. I'm really, really sorry. Right after you left, Ksenia died. It was ruled a suicide."

Josh just looks at me. It comes into my mind with a breath of horror that I'll have to hammer and hammer at him, beat him with words, to break through his denial. He might be genuinely incapable of believing in a world without her. I think he could accept any story at all, any wild science-fiction planet I could invent for the occasion, as long as I told him Ksenia was living there, and that she missed him.

"Lexi? I wish you'd never had to think that—any of it. But Kezzer is totally fine."

I stare. It might be even worse than I thought. "She's *dead*, Josh. She's been dead for a long time. I can understand why you wouldn't want to believe it. I wish I didn't have to believe it, either. But— Ksenia took poison, and she died right in front of me. I was holding her."

Josh's mouth rounds for a moment, then shuts again. "That must have been so horrible for you, Lexi. I'm so incredibly sorry you went through that."

That's all he has to say?

"It's the worst thing that's ever happened to me." Before, I wanted to be gentle with him and spare him the pain of it as much as I could, but his blank, smug, imperturbable face is getting under my skin. How can he possibly care so little? "But it was infinitely worse for her. She was suspected of your murder, Josh. Of *course*, and you really should have known she would be. She couldn't face it, I guess, all the blame, everyone whispering about her, coming right on top of losing you. You know Ksenia—as tough as she pretended to be, none of it was real. You broke her heart."

I wait for a reaction; wild sobs, crumpling features. The kind of sorrow that will spare me from having to despise him. But he smiles instead of crying.

"Oh, Lexi. You, um, you might have to suspend disbelief for a while, okay? But it's really not that bad. Kezzer is living with me, and she's fine. We're basically married now." He delivers that last sentence with a defiant lilt, because we both know what I think about that—though what I think can't possibly matter anymore.

"I *saw* her die, Josh. I thought I just explained that?"

"And I just saw her drinking coffee, and she just kissed me! So maybe what you saw doesn't matter as much as you think it does."

Dots of sun sway across his face with the wind, and he's still wearing that maddening smile, but now to go with it there are tears in his eyes. Either he's certifiably insane, or else there's some extraordinary explanation here.

"Are you saying Ksenia faked her own death? So the two of you could run away together?" For half a breath it seems almost possible that she and Josh could have come up with a scheme that wild, if it meant they wouldn't be separated. What *wouldn't* those two have done, if it would let them take control of their own fate at long last? But that's just the effect of those terrible bells still ringing in my mind, and after a little more thought I understand how absurd the idea is. The dress she wore in her casket didn't hide the incisions, or not completely. "Josh, they did an autopsy. Ksenia was cut to pieces. They took out her heart. Nobody could live through that!"

"Lexi," Josh says, with ostentatious patience. "Why don't you just come see her?"

For a slow moment all the functions of my body, breath and pulse and brain waves, suspend together: a velvety, minuscule death, there in the woods, before my life resumes.

"Go see *Ksenia*?" Only two weeks ago I left daffodils on her grave, but I suppose she could have been exhumed since then. I imagine her greenish white, clay-cold, and dappled with decay: a walking corpse, leaning in to hug me.

"Oh," Josh says, and grins. "Then you'll believe me! When you see Kezzer walking around totally happy, and totally, completely free of all the crap everybody put her through. And anyway, I know she really misses you. You know how you used to complain that Kezz would never open up to you, and everything intense that you knew about her came from me? But I think she actually misses you more than anybody. She really might—be different now."

"Go *see* her," I say again. "Josh, if this is a joke, it's unspeakably evil."

"Of course I wouldn't do that, Lexi! You—it's awful you were hurt so much already, because of us. But maybe seeing Kezz again will help make up for that, and then you'll forgive me?"

He has to be insane.

But at the same time, I have to see for myself.

"You mean right now?" I ask.

Josh bounces a little and squeezes me again, quickly. "Sure, now. I knew you'd come!"

"Where is she?" I guess, if this were real, they'd be hiding out together in some cheap motel twenty miles up the interstate.

"At the house," Josh says, as if that should be obvious. "Um, Mitch and Emma aren't there right now."

I gape at him, trying to absorb that; but of course, when Joshua ran off, there was no reason why he wouldn't have taken his keys with him. "You're staying in their *house* while they still believe you're dead? Josh, that has to be the most perverse thing I've ever heard in my life. You know how much they loved you."

Josh scowls. "If they'd really loved me, then they would have loved Kezzer too, and not acted like she was some creepy wild animal. Kezzer and me—anybody who loves us has got to love *both* of us. And if they don't, then it doesn't count."

It's just a few miles away, their old house on Whistler Drive. "We can take my car."

"We can't," Josh says. "We have to walk. But I know a shortcut."

He holds out his hand, and it's warm and firm when I take it.

"Josh," I say. Walking through the woods I feel almost ill, and there's still a hint of those bells lingering in my ears like tinnitus, only more terrible and more exquisite at the same time. I feel like there are infinite questions, infinite ramifications to explore. Where has he been all these months? "When you disappeared, and then—there was this strange time where we all thought that Ksenia found you—"

"Yeah," Josh says. "Lexi, God, did you know that Xand tried to make your awesome brownies? And they were totally not as good as yours, but I had to pretend. I don't know how he got them so leathery."

"Then that was real," I say. "Ksenia didn't lie about finding you. You were really in the hospital."

"Of course I was. I mean, until Kezzer took me home."

Nothing makes sense, but as we walk deeper into the woods, in what I think must be the opposite direction from the Delbos' house, I start to adjust to behaving as if it made sense, to taking the impossibilities almost for granted, as if they were light, trivial, ignorable things. One thing that must be true: Ksenia didn't take him *home*, not if home means Whistler Drive.

"Lexi? You haven't told me anything about you. Like, how've you been? What's been going on?" He's not looking at me; instead he's peering ahead at the trees, as if the path were almost too subtle to make out.

"Oh," I say. For a moment it feels hard to remember. "Well, I got into Brown, and my parents are totally over the moon about it, naturally. And—don't say anything about this, okay? But I think I just broke up with Xand." Josh's eyebrows shoot up and he glances at me, but he's tactful enough to keep quiet. Alexander and Alexandra, how could we not be meant for each other? "Oh—and there's been this bizarre epidemic that none of the doctors can figure out; I mean, they haven't been able to identify a pathogen or anything. Seven kids have died so far and all the parents are panicking. We're sending Marissa to stay with Grandma Claire this summer, just to make sure she's safe."

Josh stops walking and turns to me. "I hate to think of that. How sad everybody must be. But Lexi, the important thing to remember is that those kids are in a better world now. No one can ever hurt them again."

The look in his eyes is wounded and serious, even urgent; it's an astonishing statement, coming from him, but he obviously means it. "I didn't think you were religious."

"I don't have to be religious to know that this is the worst world *ever*. Anytime anyone is happy, or in love, or amazing here—people will try to crush it, Lexi. And mostly they succeed! Every time I see Kezzer, I remember what people did to her. Just because she was beautiful and, and *vivid* in a way they could never be, so they had to try and destroy her. And she can get better, kind of, but never completely."

He's close to tears, so it would be insensitive to point out that for me the world has been mostly pretty great—and also that he's just contradicted what he said before, about how happy and free she is now.

"It's the only world we have going on, Josh. So our only option is to work as hard as we can to make it better for everybody. Help build each other up, make each other stronger." I hesitate. "Love each other."

He smiles and touches my cheek. "But you're one of the really special ones, Lexi. For every person who thinks like you do there are at least three of the bad kind. And maybe ten of the kind who just don't care or feel anything."

I'd like to tell him that's not true, but he wouldn't believe me. He turns and starts walking north again, along a path that must run roughly parallel to the gorge, and I follow.

"Lexi? Do me a favor? When you see Kezz, don't mention that thing about it being nine months since we saw you? It's just—

she's been having some memory problems, since everything, and it might confuse her."

I've accepted that we're walking in the wrong direction, and I've accepted that he's back, but the casual, lazy way he talks about *seeing* Ksenia: that still gets to me.

"Since everything?" I ask. "You mean, since she died?"

"You'll see," Josh says. "We're getting close now." He points at a thicket of what I think are blackberry bushes, just starting to form moist new leaves. "We go through there."

"Through the thorns? We'll get completely scratched up!"

"Yeah," he says. "Sorry."

I look to both sides; it would take us a minute out of our way to skirt the brambles, up through some rough areas off the trail, but nothing too bad. "So why don't we just go around?"

But Josh is already down on his hands and knees, practically burrowing into the blackberry bushes as if he were some kind of rabbit. And it crosses my mind that it'll be easier to get through if I'm close behind him, while his body pushes the canes apart.

So I drop down and follow him, straight into the thicket, trying not to think about what the thorns will do to my lace shirt. Josh squirms and thrashes just ahead of me, and I keep my face turned so it won't be as close to his backside. A thorn scores a wicked streak along my neck, and my shirt snags at the shoulders.

And then we're through. "Lexi Holden," Josh informs the air. "Alexandra. She's like the sweetest person ever, and really cool. I bet you'll love her."

He's already up and he reaches down a hand to lift me to my feet. "You were introducing me to the tree trunks, Josh?"

"You know how I hate to be rude!" Josh grins. "Lexi, come on! I don't like leaving Kezzer alone for this long."

I glance back, and I still don't see any reason why we couldn't have circled the thicket instead of scrambling through it. We've come back to the edge of the woods without my noticing, and to my left the trees are thin enough to let through a view of houses and parked cars.

We walk out through dreamily deserted streets, and turn a few more corners, and then I'm looking at Whistler Drive. It bears repeating that it isn't supposed to be anywhere near here, or maybe I've just gotten that disoriented. And while most of it looks just the same as I remember, there are a few details that seem definitely out of the ordinary, like for instance a charred recliner sitting in the middle of the street with its steel framework poking through blackened clouds of stuffing. It's right in front of a house that looks just like the Delbos', the same yellow siding and the same magnolia tree, except that theirs was just a single story, with a half-level down on the left, following the uneven ground. This house has a second floor above its entire main section, with two open windows framing perfect darkness.

But that's the house Josh heads toward, his steps picking up speed. "Josh? Is that a new addition? The upstairs floor, I mean."

He fires an irritable glance at the upper story. "Yeah. That's new."

"It seems weird that the Delbos added all that extra space, *after* you and Ksenia were gone. Wouldn't most people decide to downsize, then?"

Josh doesn't answer, and I lose all interest in the question, because I've just noticed something in the window, where the curtain is pushed aside.

There's a head with short, spiky blond hair just visible over the back of the sofa. I can make out a curve of cheek, a hand, the top of a book. I'm still telling myself that it can't be Ksenia, but if it's not then Josh has found a remarkably convincing impersonator.

Josh is already at the door, and I run to catch up with him.

"Kezzer? I brought somebody to *see* you," Josh singsongs, and I have to restrain myself to keep from just shouldering him out of my way. And then I'm in, and she's scrambling up off the couch and gaping at me, with her dirty gray eyes saucer-wide and her jaw hanging; obviously, she's every bit as shocked to see me as I am to see her.

"Ksenia?" I whisper.

She comes stumbling toward me, all her movements jerking and unhinged and so zombielike that I almost shy away. She's wearing black cutoffs, a flowing black T-shirt, just like she was the day we met.

And then Ksenia—brittle, guarded, withholding Ksenia, who never seemed to care about me half as much as I cared about her—collapses in a pile at my feet. "Oh, Jesus, *Lexi,*" she moans. "Lexi, this can't—you *can't* be—"

I don't know what I'm doing, but all at once I'm on the floor too with my arms around her, feeling her heart race and her breath shaking. And she is warm, warm, warm, and very much alive.

"Ksenia," I say; I can't seem to lift my voice above a whisper. "Is it really you?"

She leans back a few degrees to look in my eyes, and grazes my cheek in the rapid, nervous way that you'd touch a friendly wolf. "Lexi. I don't know."

not a single one of them reaches my voice

Josh laughs, as if that were a joke, or as if he'd give anything to convince himself it was a joke, and lands on the rug next to us, and then for a while we're all squeezing the air out of one another in a big cuddle puddle. After a moment Ksenia starts laughing too, a little breathlessly, and I follow, crashing into the laughter as if I had tripped on my own relief and bewilderment.

"I watched you *die*, Ksenia," I say, and her nearness and vitality make the words hilarious, in an awful, dizzying way. "Right in my arms. I watched you die. And then they took you away and cut you apart!"

"Don't be sad, Lexi," Ksenia says, and her words gasp out wildly; she's still half laughing, but I don't believe she's kidding about this either. "It's better that way. I was never meant to live in the first place."

"I dumped Xand for saying basically that," I tell her, and then realize too late how hurtful it must be.

"Is that why? I didn't want to ask you, Lexi," Josh says. "But then oh my God did he have it coming! The nerve of that guy!"

"He just wanted to persuade me to get over it," I explain. "Get on with my life. But I didn't appreciate him acting like he was some kind of authority on what was best for me." I realize that I'm wandering onto thin ice, conversationally, and then I'm cracking up afresh at the idea that there could be any ice thinner than discussing Ksenia's own death with her. But I don't want to approach anywhere near the reasons that I had, for feeling so haunted—and now it turns out that Xand was right, and I didn't even need to. "Ksenia, how—I don't know, how can any of this be happening?"

All at once the two of them seem to have exhausted their laughter, and Ksenia extricates herself from our tangle and scoots back a foot. She shoots a glance at Josh that just screams *unspoken significance*. "I don't know," she says again. "If I died, it wasn't my idea!"

That's not what the coroner said, but I decide to keep that to myself.

Josh struggles to his feet. "Do we have any of that amazing strawberry lemonade left, Kezz? Or did you drink it all?"

"I think there's some," Ksenia says, and he heads for the kitchen.

"Good," I say, and I'm about to add, *I'm incredibly thirsty*, but Ksenia grabs my wrist so hard it hurts and shakes her head, eyes wide.

NO, she mouths at me, silent and emphatic. *No, Lexi.* Then she lets go and stares down, almost as if she were ashamed.

I hesitate, because it seems so preposterous; Ksenia can't suppose that Josh would try to poison me, could she? But there's no mistaking the fear I saw in her eyes, and already Josh is coming back with frosty pink-brimming glasses in each hand, ringing with ice. Why does everything sound like those bells to me? He holds one out to each of us.

"Actually," I say, "I'm fine for now."

Josh looks at me reproachfully. "It's *homemade*, Lexi! Did I smush all those strawberries for nothing?" I can smell the fruit and the sweetness, somehow brighter than other scents, and Ksenia's gulping hers like there's no issue. I almost take the glass, but then I see the warning way that Ksenia is staring at me over the pink fluid lapping at her lips.

"I'm really doing my best to stay off sugar," I tell him. "Fruit juice is the worst. Don't be sabotaging my diet with your *homemade*, Josh." He pouts. "You drink it."

"Oh, fine."

I watch closely while he raises the glass, but he's clearly swallowing down the contents, so they couldn't possibly be dosed with anything. When he tips his head back to drink the last of it his eyes close, and I seize the opportunity to mouth *What the hell?* at Ksenia.

She shakes her head in response, and I suppose this kind of dumb-show signaling isn't the best way to communicate anything terribly complicated. I feel more intensely by the minute that I need to find a way to speak to her alone, if she can't come out and say what she means in front of him. Honestly, as snappish as she can be with people she doesn't care about, she's never been much good at standing up to Josh, and that has been an ongoing problem.

Josh's glass thumps down on an end table, and now that I'm calmer I notice the place is a mess, with dishes and books strewn around, and spills left to congeal, and candy wrappers under the furniture. All of which would be out of character for their foster parents, certainly, but what concerns me more is that it's also odd for Ksenia, who has always been tightly controlled and something of a neat freak, making such a performance of being perfectly responsible that I think if anything it just made the Delbos even more uncomfortable with her. I think they kept waiting for her to behave like a kid.

"So," Ksenia starts. "Lexi . . ."

Then she falls silent, and her face conveys confusion and possibly a sluggish kind of panic. I remember what Josh said about *memory problems,* and I wonder if she's sick somehow—though in fact she's looking more beautiful than ever, clear-skinned and shimmering. *Crystalline* is the description that comes to mind. I might have infinite questions for the two of them, but suddenly asking a single one seems unbearably painful. I stand up and reach out a hand for her.

"Why don't you show me the new addition?" I say, to say something—and also on the off chance that we can get a few minutes without Josh watching us. Which is what he's doing right now.

Apparently that was an awkward thing to say, because it provokes a fresh crossfire of meaningful looks. "We haven't actually been up there yet," Josh explains. He glances over at the dark mouth of those brand-new stairs; it's on the kitchen's back wall, just to the left of the dining table.

"Cool," I say. "Then we'll go exploring together. Ksenia? Are you coming?"

And maybe I'm getting out of patience with the situation, because I tug Ksenia over there a shade too assertively—as if I were playing, but not really. Josh comes right behind us. The stairwell is so shadowy that you'd think there wasn't a single window up there, but I don't see a light switch, and I decide not to let it bother me. I run up the first three steps.

And then they drop out from under me. My heart plummets, and so does the rest of me. Josh catches me by my armpits right before I hit the floor and helps me back onto my feet.

"Would you like to see the backyard instead?" Ksenia asks, and even in the middle of my shock I'm glad to hear the sardonic rasp back in her voice. Josh laughs.

"See, that's why we haven't been up there, Lexi. At first I thought I'd just board it up, but then I decided it was better if I knew what we were dealing with. But neither of us can climb those stairs. They won't let us."

"What is going *on* here?" I say. The stairs look perfectly normal again: dusty, honey-colored wood, with a cheap aluminum handrail on the wall.

There's a grayish, shineless patch in the center of each stair where the finish has worn through, as if people had been going up and down a *lot*, for years now. I prod the bottom step with my toe, and it feels solid and as real as anything: a well-defined feature of the material world.

"I'll show you," Ksenia says, "if you get out of the way."

I do, and she moves in. "Hi," she says. To the *staircase,* and it reminds me of how Josh introduced me to a bunch of trees earlier. "It's me, Ksenia Adderley. Kezzer. You can't pretend you don't know who I am." She jumps straight up onto the second step, and it—what? It folds away from her, it recoils into the void, it furls itself out of existence? In any case, it drops her without ceremony, but since she knows to expect it she lands more or less gracefully, and somehow right beside me. "See? Same thing happens with Josh."

"Not exactly," Josh says, sulkily. "It's meaner with me. At least it lets you down so you don't hurt yourself! It has to know how much I love you, so it's totally unfair that it has it in for me!"

I'm listening closely, trying to make sense of a nonsensical conversation. "Are you saying that this staircase—cares about Ksenia, somehow?"

"Maybe it only cares about the real Ksenia," Ksenia says. "Maybe she's the one who died, and I'm just nothing." There's such a rough, wounded sound in her voice that I stare and almost hug her again, but now there's a defensive hunch to her posture that discourages me.

"Oh, Kezzer!" Josh says. "That is so completely not true! Of course you're you!"

"You're real enough that you're still my friend," I tell her firmly. "You're real enough that I still love you, no matter what. I don't know what I saw die, but you're the one that counts for me now, and it means more to me than I can even tell you, Ksenia, to see you alive again."

The light around us fades a little, gives a quick purplish swoon, and then comes back full strength.

Ksenia turns to hide her face from me, but I can tell she's crying. "I'm so sorry, Lexi," she says. "I was a rotten friend. Josh told me how you complained about me."

Of course he did, just like he told me everything about her. "You weren't," I tell her. "I just wanted you to trust me enough to tell me things yourself. I felt like Josh was your official translator, or something."

And then, impulsively, I climb back onto the bottom step.

It holds me. Josh catches his breath, but Ksenia isn't looking.

"I know," she says. "I actually overheard you talking with him a few times. Like when he told you the story of how I got put in foster care, and I was scared shitless you'd be—just repulsed by the whole thing."

"I didn't think you cared what I thought," I say. I go up one more step, waiting for the plunge, but it doesn't come. Another, and another, and the darkness starts to shuffle softly back around my eyes.

"But how could I have told you something like that, Lexi? That the cops caught me waiting in the car while my mom was off screwing the guy who paid our rent, and then they found her drugs in my sock? With your pretty house, and your perfect family? Your parents actually *love* each other."

She delivers the word *love* venomously—but it's the kind of venom brewed from envy and longing and heartache, and I don't blame her at all.

"But you never judged me for any of that," I tell her. "At least, I thought you didn't. You never assumed I was too spoiled or prissy to hang out with you. So why would I have judged you for something your *mom* did?"

Ksenia has never, ever revealed so much of herself to me, and I'd like to comfort her—except right now I know that climbing these stairs is more important, and I can't begin to guess how I could know such a thing. I feel the scrape of their wood under my shoes, and I climb two more. I'm getting high enough now that I start to feel a kind of trembly anticipation, sensing just how much it will hurt when they let me fall.

"Because you'd know I was shit," she says. "Coming from a shit background like that, where everybody was always out of their minds, and you couldn't believe a single fucking thing they said to you. My mom even lied to me about who my *dad* was."

"Do you know how much it hurts me to hear you talk that way? What were you, eight? Like *Marissa*? Listen, I will only ever judge you by the choices you make, here and now, not for things you can't even help. That's a promise, Ksenia."

"Nine, actually," she says, and finally turns. I hear the whisper of her bare feet and her gasp when she sees me halfway up the staircase.

"I *know*," Josh says. "It's totally crazy."

"Lexi? Can you see anything?" Her voice jumps with anxiety, but my eyes are so flooded with shadow that I could be climbing into a cloud of black moths, brushed and obscured by their wings. I'm not that far from the kitchen but none of the light below seems to reach me, and my pupils can't dilate enough to expose anything ahead.

"I can't. It's too dark."

"I feel like I really need to get up there. It's been driving me crazy that I can't."

"Well," I tell her, "maybe you just haven't introduced yourself properly." And I'm hoping she'll guess what I'm referring to; we had a terrible fight, once, when I tried calling her by a different nickname than Kezzer, a softer name. She almost hit me. It was one of those strange moments where somebody's rage reveals just how deeply you've reached inside their heart: that name *mattered*. But with all the incomprehensible secrecy that's going on in this house, I feel like I shouldn't let Josh know what I'm thinking; it's private, just between me and Ksenia.

I'm not looking her way, but I swear I can *feel* her stiffen. Did she understand me? I've made it almost two-thirds of the way up now, but I stop with a shudder of foresight, almost positive I know what's about to come.

"What are you talking about?" Josh asks.

"Oh, you know," I say. "Maybe if *Ksenia* isn't doing the trick, she should try giving the stairs an alias. Maybe there's some kind of hidden code."

Ksenia snorts: one of those rare flashes where she seems like her old self again. "I am Wilford B. Hogsworthy the fourth," she informs the stairs. "A gentleman farmer from Lancaster. Gonna let me up now, or what?"

She stomps onto the bottom step, and the entire staircase implodes beneath us. It crumples like memory, it swoons like unconsciousness, and for a tiny sliver of time I'm gripping the handrail and swinging in the abrupt nothingness. Then I drop, and even though I was well forward of Ksenia on the steps I somehow crash down right on top of her in a tangle of limbs. And I am almost positive that the stairs deliberately arranged for her to break my fall, and maybe even take some extra bruises as a consequence.

They didn't care for her sarcasm, that's obvious.

"Well, *that* worked," Josh says, and helps us to our feet. "But it's phenomenal that you got so far, Lexi. Kezz, why do you think they let *Lexi* go up, and not me?"

"Maybe because Lexi is the best friend I've ever had, even if I didn't deserve her," Ksenia says, surprising the daylights out of me. "Maybe the stairs are smart enough to get that."

I don't think I've ever seen Josh look quite so hurt, with his brows up and his mouth draping. "Kezzer! Then what am I?"

"You're insanely important to me, Josh. You're my whole world. But you're—not that."

It's a statement that I would consider open to a variety of interpretations, not all of them positive, but it seems to partly mollify Josh. He kisses her fervently on the mouth, and I look away. Has she really stopped thinking of him as her brother? She used to be pretty clear about it.

"Then why don't the stairs let you go up, Ksenia? I mean, by that reasoning, you wouldn't be your *own* friend!"

I think I meant to be funny, as if saying that might defuse the tension, but I'm discovering that words have a way of transforming their meanings when you say them in this house.

I look back at her and her eyes are on mine; whatever Josh thinks, *happy* is not the right way to describe her now. She looks savage, arctic.

"Jesus, Lexi. Have I ever been?"

Sometimes at moments when everyone has said just a little too much, there's a special kind of silence that flows in and makes it hard to say anything else. This would be one of those times, because I know how sharply, how seriously, she meant it, and the part about not knowing if she's real, and the part about not deserving me. She's alive, certainly, and being alive is mostly allowing her to feel a whole spectrum of suffering.

Josh snaps out of it first. "Lexi, you're staying for dinner, right? I'll start cooking. Maybe like a pasta primavera? Is cream sauce cool for your diet?"

Ksenia bites her lip, but I don't even need her anxious gaze this time, because there's enough of a warning in Josh's voice: unless I am gravely mistaken, his tone was a shade too casual, but with a stealthy eagerness just below the surface. I don't know why it would be such a big deal to stay and eat with them, but there's a whisking alarm in my veins, and I don't have to know.

"I can't, actually," I say. "I have to pick up Marissa from her cello lesson."

Josh puts on one of his looks of wounded innocence. "Lexi, can't somebody else get her? You haven't seen us in ages!"

"I know. But my parents both have meetings, and I promised. I can't just leave Marissa waiting! Anyway, you know, you're both here again, right? At least for a while? So I'll just come back and see you soon." I expended a few too many words for such a simple message, and if Josh has a sharp ear, he'll know it means my nerves are shaken. But of course I would have more than enough reasons for feeling that way, even if I weren't suspicious. I mean, those stairs alone would suffice.

He heaves an exaggerated sigh, but Ksenia looks relieved.

I start shifting back into the living room, and they both follow. Am I really not going to find one second to speak to her privately?

"Soon, then. You promise? I know you were upset by, by the way we left, but you forgive us now, right? We seriously just did what we had to do to hold on to each other!"

"I know that," I say. "You two were in a corner. It was cruel that you had so little choice about your own lives."

"Lexi," Ksenia says abruptly, "it's getting cold out. Why don't you borrow a sweater?"

I look at her. "Sure. Thank you." I don't mention that all her sleeves will hang down past my fingertips.

"Come pick something," she says, and grabs my hand. I suppose that following us to her room seems just a breath too awkward or too blatant even to Joshua, because he drags along at a short distance behind us. Ksenia yanks me down the half-flight of stairs to the hallway and then into her old room, and Josh comes along far enough to hover on the steps. Ksenia leaves her door wide open, and I'm positive she does it out of calculation, playacting innocence in her turn.

The moment we're out of Josh's range of vision she bends to get close to me.

"Lexi," she whispers against my ear, and I can almost feel my neurons bristling, receptive and alert. "Run. Get out, and never come back here. No matter what Josh says to you."

She grabs a black fuzzy sweater off a chair and shoves it into my hands. It's made of thick, expensive cashmere, much nicer than anything I can remember her owning before.

I wish I could ask what she means, demand all the details, but the awful fact is that I actually don't need an explanation. What matters is that she means *something*, and she's obviously doing her best to protect me—my God, from someone she loves. It only takes a flash before I decide to trust her.

"What about you?" I whisper back. My photo of her and Josh

together at the gorge still hangs above her dresser. It looks as if the Delbos never touched a single thing in here.

"You saw me *die*, Lexi. Just go with that." She kisses my cheek, softly and quickly, but there's an intensity to the kiss that startles me. I feel a tear brush from her lashes, and a hard, stifled gasp against my skin. "And don't blame Josh. He's—not right. Get out!"

There's a terrible moment where a thousand replies and arguments and questions rise up in my mind like a roaring wind: like, Get out of what, exactly? Why does everyone keep telling me not to blame Josh? What's this *not right* you're talking about? You know he always used to tell me not to blame *you*? And: Ksenia, I can tell you're miserable, but pretending that you're dead is not something I could ever do, not now that I've seen you again. And: Ksenia, why don't you run with me?

A whirlwind of things I desperately want to say to her, and not a single one of them reaches my voice, because Josh has appeared in the doorway. There's an inquisitive quality to his stare that I don't appreciate.

Ksenia smiles at him, warm and bright and carefully composed. "See, baby, now Lexi *has* to visit soon, so she can bring back my sweater!"

"Jesus, Ksenia. Of course I'll visit you. Nothing has been the same since we lost you two," I say, keeping up my side of our conspiracy, and pull the sweater on over my head. If Josh guessed what Ksenia just told me, what would he do? It's unimaginable that he would try to stop me from leaving, unless maybe he would? My heart is pattering and my mouth fills with a hollow taste, dry and gray, while Josh's brown gaze surrounds me.

Ksenia sidesteps around him and heads back toward the door, trying to pull us after her with her personal gravity, but for a moment Josh and I stay staring at each other. I just want to relax, to breathe deeply, to believe he's still truly my friend, but when everything else seems to be changing its shape and warping its meaning, maybe he is too.

"I've got to get going," I say. "I'm already going to be late."

"Okay," Josh says, and smiles. "Get home safe."

We shuffle together up the short flight back to the kitchen, past the yawning shadow of the new staircase, and then meet Ksenia at the open front door. She's staring out at the feathers of sunset streaking the lawn, her look abstracted and sad, and she jumps when we come up behind her. I hug her, and one realization becomes clear to me through all the senselessness of the day: this might be the lasting goodbye that we missed before, when I watched her die.

"You remember the way?" Ksenia asks lightly, and Josh flinches.

"Josh showed me a shortcut," I tell her, and then I hug him too—not *right*, she said, *he's not right*, and I'm still wondering about possible meanings that phrase might have. And I walk away from them, across the lawn.

When I reach the sidewalk I look back to see Josh standing with his arm around her shoulder, both of them watching me go, and it gives me an awful impression as if I had been to visit Ksenia in some sort of institution, maybe a mental ward, and Josh was there as her nurse, her guard, her keeper.

As soon as I'm around the first corner, out of their view, I hear light footsteps coming just behind me.

just enough of the truth

I suppress the impulse to run, to draw attention to myself, even as my pulse starts to race and my hearing shivers with a residue of the bells I heard when I called Josh's number. It could easily be a coincidence that someone is back there, or by the sound of it, two or three people; it might have nothing to do with me. I place each step with false serenity on the sidewalk, though tiny spasms grip my muscles and urge me to charge madly up the block. I can't give in to dread, can't allow panic to blur my vision and make me miss my path; my mind is full of an inexplicable certainty that I have to return by precisely the same route we followed here. Why is that idea so clear to me?

Well, if it didn't matter, if I could take whatever streets I chose, then why would Ksenia have asked me if I remember the way?

I turn the next corner—it was just here that Josh and I came around the bend, wasn't it, by this house with the green shutters, the swan in flight painted on the mailbox? The footsteps stay directly behind me, crowding closer now, with a muttering, soft-soled sound. And I shouldn't look back, I know it, but for a moment fear defeats my self-possession and I glance over my shoulder. There are three of them: a pale girl in dragging lace with some kind of animal head sewn as a decoration on her chest, a softly brown girl in golden scales that reflect the sunset like dazzling tangerine brushstrokes, and a boy in tight, silver-glazed gray with a fountain of snow-bright hair.

The pale girl catches my glance and smiles at me, with a dainty curl of her rosebud lips. "Josh," she murmurs, "can she get away?"

The voice coming out of her mouth is *Ksenia's* voice, low and plaintive and worried. My knees waver and I glance again, unsure which I should distrust, my sight or my hearing; did I hallucinate Ksenia speaking, or could it possibly be that Ksenia is trailing after me, and I somehow imagined a different face in place of hers? The girl is tall and blond like Ksenia, but with a torrent of whipped-cream curls, and her face has a doll-like, simpering prettiness, nothing like Ksenia's knife-edged beauty.

She catches the bewilderment in my look, and leers. Prickles course down my back. Her cheeks appear oddly peaked, as if they were crowded with too many tiny bones. I keep stumbling, haphazardly, my head still twisted over my shoulder; I can't make myself look away.

Her companions titter, then the brown girl in the goldfish dress rolls her eyes at me. "I don't *know*. I mean, she's not all the way here yet, just the first couple of steps here? But I don't think Prince will be super excited about Lexi just walking out. I don't know what they'll do."

It's Josh's voice. Unmistakably. As if that girl's lips were opening, and a radio broadcast were pouring through them. They all grin broadly and I finally tear my eyes away from them and focus on the sidewalk in front of me, *just keep going, just keep going,* though at every step I feel as if my calves are about to collapse. They're only a few paces behind me, and all three of them are taller than I am, longer-legged, almost certainly fast enough to chase me down if I run.

"You should have gone with her," Ksenia's voice says. "Or let me." I won't look again, I refuse to, but from the voice's position I think it must be the boy who spoke this time.

"Oh, Kezzer, you know that wouldn't help! They'll do whatever they decide to do. Anyway, Prince is so weird about you that they'd probably mess with Lexi more if you were there, just to watch you freak out. You know, he thinks it's *cute.*"

That was one of the girls, I can't tell which, pouring out Josh's warm timbre, and I stumble a bit from the breathless understanding that everything I'm hearing is what Josh and Ksenia are saying to each other right now, this moment, in what they must believe is privacy. I'm eavesdropping, not because I want to, but through the mouths of these freaks. Where on earth am I, and what is happening to me? But I can't think about that, not yet; all I can do is concentrate on getting away.

The trio behind me bursts into giddy laughter. I've arrived at the next intersection, and the asphalt glimmers citrine and bronze, and the trees sway like an illusion of calm while I stagger to a halt. Because I know we turned repeatedly on the way here, turned at every corner, but now as I gaze into rippling blue shadows and elongated light I can't remember which direction is the one I need, to get back to the woods. To Josh's special shortcut.

I can hear them breathing, those people, those *creatures* who are following me, and I almost expect to feel their hands seizing my body, but nothing happens. I gaze left and right, hoping to catch sight of something I remember, something that will reveal the way home, and they wait at my back.

"Josh," one of them says, channeling Ksenia, "Lexi has to get home! She—I know you did it for me, baby, and I'm grateful, but this place isn't right for her. It's only for people who don't make sense anywhere else. Like us."

"I just hate for you to be lonely, Kezzer. I thought you'd be happy!"

"I know. I know you were trying to take care of me. But we can't do that to her family." A pause, a dimple of silence; did we pass that red car half a block away on my left? I'm almost certain that we did, and that just around the next bend I'll find the woods. A flash of that precise scarlet seems to rise up in my mind, beckoning and persuasive: a color that reverberates like a bell. "Josh, *please* help her!"

"Oh, Kezz, you know that's not a fair thing to ask!" Josh's voice sighs inches from my right ear now, and lace billows, dry and airy, at my ankle. I gaze straight ahead but milky curls lap in the corner of my eye, and then the golden-scaled girl starts sidling up too, hemming me in on that side. A single slim, pale finger caresses my jaw, and the blonde leans so close that her frothing hair nods across my cheek. "Did you *say* something to her, Kezzer? Is that why she wouldn't stay?"

Trembling cascades through my limbs and my throat feels thick and choked, but I understand what they're doing, jostling up on me this way. They want me to bolt in the opposite direction and lose myself forever—and it will be forever, I know it, I can *feel* it, if they drive me from my path. How I know it, how these creatures can carry my friends' voices into my ears—none of that matters. What matters now is listening to what I know, paying close attention to my own heart and the memories impressed on my mind.

We never passed a red car.

Something warm and wet and slippery probes my collarbone and I do not permit myself to look. Something furry nuzzles me.

I lunge right, bowling straight into the lacy blonde; she topples down in a cloud of her own curls and I leap over her. And, my God, that animal face on her chest is snarling at me as I fly above it, its teeth bared and shining. I land in the spill of her ruffles and the fabric slides beneath my foot and sends me wheeling forward. Needle-sharp fangs rake my left shin as I stagger; just before I crash facefirst into the pavement I catch hold of a lamppost, pull myself upright, and run.

I can't tell if they're chasing me. All I can see is the blurred street, the swimming trees, but for a sustained moment my ears are so glutted with that bell-toned resonance that I can't hear anything else; I can't hear the sound of their feet and I don't dare to glance behind again. My lungs feel on the verge of bursting. I'm almost positive that at the next corner I'll see the woods, the wavering green, and then the path back to that blackberry thicket.

If they know everything Josh and Ksenia were saying to each other just now, if they can catch their voices and release them again like birds into the air, then they also know everything Ksenia whispered to me. They know she told me to run. Will they punish her somehow? But I can't think about that, not yet, not yet; I can only think about reaching the next street, about the houses rushing past and my pumping legs and the way out of here, wherever and whatever *here* might be.

I reach the intersection and the woods loom high and vein-blue with the sun dropping down behind them. One more block to go—though for all I know those creatures might follow me in there, or there might already be more of them, dozens, lurking in ambush among the trees. I don't believe they're precisely human, those girls in lace and scales, that spume-haired boy—but that's another thing I can't think about. *Get out, and never come back here.* That's what she told me, and now there's no more question as to why.

I can see the path's opening into the woods, a blue-black mouth. And standing directly in front of it is Ksenia, somehow looking even taller and paler than usual. She stretches out a hand to me, her eyes wide in appeal, and staggers forward on her bare, heron-thin legs.

All I can think is that she made it this far, *how* doesn't matter. Wherever this place is, whatever strange distortion swept her here, we can escape together, and Josh will just have to catch up with us. He knows the way.

I race toward her, ready to grab her, ready to pull her along with me. She doesn't look well, and maybe they've already injured her somehow, but we don't have far to go—assuming that blackberry thicket marked some sort of transitional zone, and it did, I know it. I know it by the way Josh announced my name on its far side. Once I get her to safety I'll call for help, and then she'll be alive again, really alive, where anyone can see her and talk to her, where people's voices stay put in their own throats.

"Ksenia!" I shout. "Come on! I know the way out of here!"

We're only a few yards apart now and she seems to be having difficulty staying upright. Her stilt legs poking out of black cutoffs seem to be growing, hinging into new joints, growing excess knees that bend in abnormal directions. Her skin looks faintly gray as she lurches toward me on those inhuman limbs, each step slicing the air into weird polygons. She's at least seven feet tall.

"Lexi!" she croaks. "Lexi!"

Not her, not her, not her.

Momentum nearly sends me crashing into her, and it's only at the last moment that I manage to pull myself up short, to rear back before her fingers touch me. I retreat a few paces, gaping in disbelief.

"I don't want to die, Lexi! Don't let me die again!" Her arm is still reaching toward me, sagging with impossible elbows she can't quite control; even her fingernails are growing at terrific speed, clawing the air in their eagerness to reach me.

I have to get around this tottering thing, whatever it is—*not her*—but God, that's Ksenia's face, her hazel-rimmed gray eyes, and maybe those are truly Ksenia's tears streaking down, stolen from her the way they stole her voice before. How much did she risk, trying to save me?

"You were going to abandon me," the Ksenia-thing wheezes, pitching on its spidery legs; they're so grotesquely long now that they zigzag out to either side of her, with her torso swinging in the middle. "You were going to leave me to die again. *I can't think about that,* that's what you thought. Isn't it? Isn't it?"

The real Ksenia wanted me to escape from here, at any price; she wanted me to leave her behind. Even in this labyrinth of false voices and mirages, that's how I know it was truly her, absolutely my friend, even if she wasn't sure herself. But still this thing's wounded Ksenia-eyes, its tone of raw accusation, catch at my heart, because what it's saying is true.

I feel something scraping my chest; it's those nails, jutting a foot from fingers just as long, scratching at my sternum like a cat at a door. The thing cocks its head at me, blond hair twitching, gray eyes as senseless as they were when Ksenia sprawled dying on the ground.

"It was mostly my fault you died before," I gasp, still out of breath from my wild dash, and I don't even know why I feel the need to confess to this monster. The endless pale legs and arms pleat like a fence across my path now, but they look weak and brittle; possibly I could crash my way through, snap this sick, sad thing into twigs. But how could I do that to something that might be—not really Ksenia, of course, but that might contain some trace of her? "I told Josh—things I shouldn't, and he completely flipped out. I didn't trust your capacity to speak for yourself, was the reason for it, and because it made me so angry that you couldn't seem to be direct with him. But that still didn't give me the right to speak for you, Ksenia. I'm sorry."

The Ksenia-thing can't exactly walk anymore, not with so many of its knees grazing the pavement while others poke at strange skyward angles, but it shuffles closer, and now even more than fear the most complete and killing pity takes over my heart. This thing isn't her, it's not the true Ksenia—but it's also more than an illusion, I think, it's partly and imperfectly my friend. And I'm almost positive I recognize the part of her I'm talking to, now that it's come out of hiding. Its pallid face gleams with tears and snot; like a heartbroken child, it doesn't even move to wipe its cheeks.

And its name is not Kezzer.

"If you're so sorry," it rasps, "then *stay* here, Lexi. Don't leave me!"

All at once I see that those multijointed limbs are still extending, bending into a kind of cage around me. I'm surrounded by bars of thin, white, wiry flesh, by bulging elbows, more and more of them at every moment, and all those bars are covered in ivory down. My heart leaps with the understanding: this thing has kept me mesmerized until it's almost too late. The violet mouth of the woods shows through the gaps in this fence of skin, and in the descending light the tree-shadows have slipped into a darkness nearly black.

"The real you would never ask me to do that, though. Maybe

you were never your *own* friend, Ksenia, but you're mine, and you care too much about me to want me to be some kind of sacrifice."

Its pale face bobs and jerks only a foot away from mine, now. Just for a moment, it looks confused. "That's what *she* says," it sneers. "But you know how she never says everything, and anyway it's all mixed up with lies. She can't tell a whole true thing, not ever."

"You're wrong. Ksenia can tell just enough of the truth," I insist. "She always finds a way to say *enough*, even if it's hard for her. As long as you're actually paying attention, you can understand what she means." I force myself to lean closer, to wind an intimate arm around the thing's neck, while its sweat clings to my skin. It shudders at my touch. I bring my lips up against its ear. In the midst of all this horror, where has my confidence come from, my conviction that I know exactly what to do? "I'm sorry," I whisper. "But you have to let me go now, *Sennie*."

my voice becomes vapor

It reacts to that name just the way *she* did the one time I tried it, with a sharp spasm and muscles knotting tight, a kind of rictus distorting her face. The only difference is that its limbs are so tangled that it can't yank back a hand and hold it poised to strike me. I take my arm away from the thing's neck, its tendons jumping now, and hold myself away a few inches: far enough to watch its eyes.

"Did you *talk* to one of them?" it snarls, and its voice could be a recording of Ksenia from almost two years ago, played back into this unnatural twilight. Not a single note, not one flex of her breath, has changed. "If you did, you'd better tell me."

"What do you mean?" I ask it; I may not know where I am, or what precisely I'm speaking to; oh, but I still know my lines. That conversation made a terrible impression on me: I'd never seen such an awful look, like a bubbling wound, on anyone's face before, and at the time I shrank into myself, frightened by what I'd evoked. "Are you asking if I talked to somebody about you? 'Cause if that's it, just Josh, and you already know that."

"Then why did you call me that?" A pause. "Even Josh doesn't know they called me that. Are you telling me you just *made it up*?"

Just two soft little syllables, but already I knew better than to repeat them then, and I don't repeat them now; once was enough. I'm trying not to glance to either side, since it feels important to keep my stare fixed on this thing's gray eyes, but in my peripheral vision I can see the slither of its limbs retracting.

"I just thought it sounded nice, Ksenia. I've never really liked

Kezzer as a name for you." I paused back then, giving myself a moment to master my fear while we sat alone together near the gorge, Josh off pissing in the woods; I pause now. "You might want to put that hand down, before you do anything completely stupid."

"I don't believe it." Ksenia's voice echoes from the past and emerges from that thing's mouth; but oh, its legs are buckling, shrinking, dragging back toward its body in white wormlike trails through the dusk and mud. Two years ago, this was the moment where her hand dropped back onto her leg, and I saw that she was shaking, violently. "I don't believe that just came out of nowhere. Don't think you can mess with me, Lexi."

"If I say something," I told her, "then that means it's true. And if you can't accept that, and I mean *absolutely*, then you're not worth being my friend."

That's what I snapped at her then, so I recite it now, and I barely remember which time I'm in, which place; ever since I first glimpsed Josh through the window of my car, I've been so hopelessly swept up in dreams. But I remember that I felt just a bit cruel, speaking that way to Ksenia, because I knew in my heart that she wasn't secure enough to say such a thing to anybody herself, not really. I knew she wouldn't be able to withstand those words, coming from me. She was the one who'd raised her hand to me, ready to land a blow, but from the look in her eyes I had delivered that blow straight to her. She couldn't even speak.

That poor pale-limbed monster has folded itself almost to nothing now, twisting into a tight rope of arms and legs, with Ksenia's shocked face perched at the top. It looks away from me, just the way Ksenia once did, using all her strength not to sob, and I walk around it, slowly, carefully. The woods are so close, so *close*, though I can hardly see anything of them now but frayed darkness against a violet-gray sky.

The Ksenia-thing is at my back now, and I can hear it starting to whine, in a slow, sour, piercing drone. I can't risk looking at it, can't bear to feel so sad for anything; instead I pace as evenly as I can toward the opening between the trunks. The whine grows louder, creeping up the scale.

"I'm sorry," I tell it, calling over my shoulder without letting my gaze turn. "I hope you'll be okay." And then I push my way into the darkness of the path.

It lets out a kind of shriek, and at last I look back. Just for an instant, I swear it.

Four figures are standing in a shaft of moonlight that seems to have come out of nowhere, and the Ksenia-thing isn't one of them. A heap of old straw, of broken sticks, sprawls where the spider-Ksenia watched moments before, and instead I'm looking at the trio that followed me, lace and scale and seafoam. I'd forgotten all about the bite on my calf until I saw them, but now I can feel the pain of it, a dull, steady throbbing. The boy with the foamy hair is holding a small brown girl by the hand, and at the sight of her yearning little face I nearly forget myself, nearly scream and go charging back to them.

Because I know her. I've read her stories before, bounced her on my knees; I've chased after her, growling like a monster, while she screamed with laughter.

It's Olivia Fisher, the daughter of my parents' close friends. And she died six months ago, still just five years old; died of a disease that no one has been able to identify. She's buried not far from Ksenia, swathed in the same dewy grass; I only have to wander a few steps to share my flowers between their two graves.

Oh, so this is the *better world* Josh talked about; this is where no one, so he claimed, will ever be wounded again.

The impulse to run to Olivia fades with a new understanding: how close I've come to joining her, and how close my parents are, even now, to weeping by a stone with my name on it, and I suppose with some awful mimicry of my body just below. If I ever thought before that I knew what terror is, I was wrong: it's an electrified cloud, blindingly white, that steals my breath and my vision, disintegrates my bones, fills my throat until I feel sure I'm choking. I have to turn, to race up the path, but my legs won't listen to my mind.

"Lexi?" Olivia whimpers, and then my paralysis shatters like a windowpane, my body spins away from her, and my fear turns from stillness into speed. I pound through the woods, guessing my way in the darkness, half-convinced I'm lost, but then I see the blackberry thicket like a mass of black teeth. I throw myself onto the ground and scramble through, not caring how the thorns tear at my face. Ksenia's sweater snags and I thrash so hard the sleeve rips.

And then I reach the far side, and even though I'm still in the night, the woods, something in the atmosphere eases and my breath glides smoothly from my lungs again. I only really understand the oppression I felt in that impossible place, that travesty where Josh and Ksenia are living, now that I've left it behind.

Now that I've left *them* behind, along with little Olivia Fisher—and of course, of *course*, those other children who've died of the same unknown ailment in the past nine months. I lie on the dirt and twigs, letting the tremors slowly drain from my limbs, letting my breath gradually descend into something resembling normalcy.

I escaped, and that was all Ksenia wanted. She practically begged me to go. What can I possibly tell everyone—that I saw her alive, and Josh, and Olivia? Saw them captive—because isn't that what they are?—in a world that I could hardly distinguish from ours—because isn't that right, too? It was like a perfect simulation of here and now; at least, it seemed the same until I provoked it.

My phone is ringing, and I hesitate to answer—just in case I'm wrong, and I never got out after all. In case it's Josh, his undertone rolling with bells. But no, the screen says *Mom*.

"Hello?"

"Lexi! Sweetheart, thank God! We've been beside ourselves with worry. Are you all right?"

I try to answer, but my voice becomes vapor, becomes clouds, and instead I burst out sobbing. Because how can I ever expect her to believe in the reality of what I've seen?

Because how can I tell her that I left my friends trapped, just so I could save myself?

once you've been to nowhere

I've been gone for more than a day, I discover next. The whole town has been searching for me, and the police brought Xand in for questioning; it's all so dreadfully familiar. How perfect it is, how flawless, this script that we all keep acting out, without ever guessing that that's what we're doing. The police with their suspicions, the doctors with their useless tests, the parents weeping by their children's graves, and now me as well: we say the words those creatures have slipped into our mouths.

"I have no idea," I say. "The last thing I remember, I went for a walk by the gorge, and—I must have lost consciousness somehow. I came to lying by a blackberry bush." I say it, knowing that there are no other possible lines for me, and knowing that they—whoever and whatever *they* are—have put me in this position, where for the very first time in my life I can't just tell the truth.

I assume they're perfectly aware of that. I assume that they've quite knowingly manipulated me, by leaving me in possession of a truth that anyone would mistake for insanity.

I spend a day and a night in the hospital, being tested for everything the doctors can come up with: epilepsy, date-rape drugs, brain tumors. The teeth marks on my calf excite concern, and I'm informed that I'll have to receive a series of shots for rabies, just in case. The first injection is horribly painful, but I find I don't care in the slightest.

I care that those creatures—who really *can't* be precisely human, considering what they can do—have effectively bullied me into lying to my own family, simply because of how distraught and frightened my parents would be if I told them what actually happened. As I float on my back in the clanging tube of the MRI, that's what I'm thinking: that those creatures have compelled me to behave in ways I despise. I have a low tolerance for anyone trying to control me, much less succeeding.

I'm thinking of something Josh told me: that Ksenia was raped repeatedly, when she was only eleven years old, by the biological son of the couple who fostered her just before the Delbos. That those earlier *parents* gave up their plan to adopt her and sent her away again, hoping to keep what had happened a secret, hoping to protect their boy from facing any consequences. She never even told her social worker, Josh said; she'd never told anyone but him, because she hadn't actually said *no*, not out loud, and because she hated herself for choking on her own silence. Now, again, her right to make her own choices has been ripped away from her, I'm sure of it. I saw the despair on her face, and I know she can't just leave that awful nowhere.

I'm thinking of her, and myself, and Olivia, and my anger hums along with the machinery. I'm also thinking that if those creatures could have stopped me from leaving with physical force, they probably would have done so; instead they relied on psychology, on blasting me with guilt and grief and horror to trick me into staying. I gave way to fear, but possibly, if I'd just fought back, I might have caused some real trouble for them. By the time I leave the hospital, a single thought blots out the whole of my mind.

I will not let this vileness stand.

Quite uncharacteristically, my parents want to keep me home for a few days; all my efforts to shelter them clearly aren't helping, because they watch me with mournful anxiety. I have to insist on going back to school, but when I get there I find I don't have much to say to anyone, and after a few halting efforts at conversation most of my friends seem to be avoiding me as well. I suppose I seem changed; I suppose, even if I look just the same as ever, people can barely recognize me.

Everyone but Xand, when he finds me alone on a bench. He stands there, too nervous to try to sit, light wobbling on the tears that fill his eyes. "I know I'm not supposed to talk to you yet, Lexi. But can I just say I'm worried? I'm really worried. Did—if somebody hurt you, you know you can tell me, right? I—no pressure. I heard you before, really. Just let me know if I can help?"

Once again he's the only one making any effort at all, and there's a shattered sweetness to his voice. If I weren't so changed by what I've been through, I might melt completely. As things are, though, I get up and hold him, and tell him I appreciate it, really. And yet the whole time I feel infinitely far away, and Ksenia's kiss is closer to me than Xand's arms.

I have to give him credit, though: he still recognizes me, if imperfectly, even now that I'm on the other side of the veil.

When I'm at home I feel a compulsion to check my reflection over and over again, just making sure that *I* can still recognize the girl in the mirror. All of five-foot-two, curvy and compact, with glowing brown skin, and natural hair worn in long twists, and uptilted, jet-black almond eyes; she's pretty and sweet-looking, with a dangerous intelligence in her gaze, but I feel a certain detachment from her that I've never experienced before.

Once you've been to nowhere, I discover, a trace of it clings to you, and it fundamentally alters who you are. At night, in the silence, I can still hear the shimmer of those bells.

On the third day I get in my car after school, and drive through our bland, placid streets, under our cresting trees, up Grand and as far as the intersection where I watched Josh cross in front of me. Rounding that corner is almost beyond my capabilities, and my hands shake on the wheel; they try to jerk back against my will when I start to turn. But I'm not going to be bullied again, not by the creatures who stole my friends, and not by my own fear, either.

I think I know what I'll find, but I have to know for certain; I have to take it in, accept its reality with my own eyes.

Two miles farther and I'm looking at 32 Whistler Drive.

It has the same creamy yellow siding as ever, the same magnolia tree, a few blooming azaleas in an almost exaggerated shade of pink; those shrubs weren't in bloom, not in Josh's *better world*. And, just as I almost knew would be the case, the house's main section is only a single story high, with its split-level wing stepping downward on the left. In other words, that whole *addition* that I saw, that whole second story, was—what? An artifact of nowhere. Not of this world, in any case.

I pull up just in front and stare at the house, absorbing it as it is now, and remembering it as it was when Joshua led me to its door. That upper floor, those stairs Josh and Ksenia couldn't climb—they must have some kind of significance that I can't quite put my finger on.

Emma Delbo comes around the corner of the house, a pair of pruning shears poised wide open in both hands as if she were contemplating using them to commit a murder. I haven't seen her—*since everything*, as Josh would say, since the funeral for that Ksenia I'm now convinced was as fake as a string of glass pearls—and I'm shocked at how aged Emma is, how her face is crumpled with bitterness and her body slumps forward. Of course the Delbos got in trouble—they weren't really supposed to go off and leave their foster kids unsupervised, not even if Ksenia was just a breath shy of eighteen at the time. And coming home to find one of their kids dead, the other gone: that came as a crushing shock to them, since another feature of the oddness then was that not one person had thought to tell them what was going on.

Now that I think of it, I'd bet those creatures arranged it that way; I'd bet they somehow reached into our thoughts, bent and tweaked them out of shape, and hid the ones that said, *Mitch and Emma need to know about this.*

Emma's curls are still light brown, but even from here I can see that her roots are three inches of pure gray. The bags under her eyes are slate blue and so puffed that she seems to peer over them with difficulty, and with suspicion.

She looks at me and doesn't smile, though we once saw each other fairly often.

I almost drive off, but it feels too callous. She's a husk, an emptied thing, and even if I can't come out and say what I know, maybe I can still find some way to comfort her.

I turn off the engine and climb out, then walk across the wavering lawn, its grass the electric green of new spring growth. "Hi, Mrs. Delbo. How are you?"

The look she gives me is utterly hostile, in a slow, oozing kind of way. "Alexandra. You must have some reason for coming around again? You wouldn't have bothered just to see how *I'm* doing, now that my son is dead."

I nearly snap at her that she's hardly the only one who's grieved over Josh and Ksenia, but she's too pitiable for that. "I—had a dream, Mrs. Delbo. It might sound strange, but I'm nearly certain that Josh is still alive. I thought I should let you know."

"I dream about Joshua every night." She practically snarls it, and I make a note to stay well out of range of those garden shears. "Has that brought him back?"

I'm sorry for her, but anger is also rising inside me, and not on my own behalf. Because there's one terrible fact of the case: if the Delbos had decided to adopt Ksenia as well as Josh, then the two of them never would have been so desperate, never would have feared the separation that was coming. Josh and I never would have said the things we said to each other, and maybe Josh wouldn't have gotten into whatever bizarre kind of trouble he's in right now. If the Delbos had only been able to open their hearts, just a bit more, to my brittle, frost-flower friend, then maybe all this suffering could have been avoided.

All right, it's only a *maybe*. But the possibility is with us, along with those shaking azaleas, that single-story yellow house.

"I didn't say I could bring him back," I tell her. "But I thought— maybe you'd be glad to know that not everyone has given up hope."

"If anyone's dreams were going to bring Josh back, mine would," she pursues resentfully. Emma Delbo was never my favorite person, but I really can't remember her behaving like this, with such self-absorption, such a tainted heart. "That girl killed him out of envy, because of how dearly we loved him."

I've heard more than I can stand, no matter how soul sick she is. "What Josh said in my dream was that you didn't love him. He said if anyone couldn't love Ksenia too, then it didn't count."

She gapes at me with her tired green eyes and her shears veer up to point straight at me. I take a step backward, toward my car.

"*No one* could have loved that girl," she says. "It wasn't possible. What Josh thought he felt for her—that just showed how badly he needed our help. Imagining he was in love with that cold, ruthless, cunning little—"

"*I* loved her," I interrupt. "I'd say that proves it could be done. And she never hurt anyone, especially not him. Mrs. Delbo, Ksenia was a beautiful, caring person; if you couldn't see it, then that's on you, not her."

And I turn to go home, because no matter how disturbing, how dangerous Josh and Ksenia's new nowhere is, I'd actually rather be there than here, talking to this woman who can't seem to muster the smallest compassion for a girl she once called her daughter.

I notice the strangest sensation as I slide back into the car—as if something silky, crisp, and barely there were clinging to my leg.

now we're all living under a spell

I had enough sense to hide Ksenia's sweater in the trunk of my car right after that phone call with my mom, and to smuggle it up to my room later; now I put it on, feeling the infinite softness of the cashmere spilling past my fingertips. The fabric is still covered in bits of bark and dried leaves, but I don't pick them off, just like I'll never try to mend that rip in the sleeve. The dirt, the tear: all those things are parts of the truth, and all of them recall Ksenia's voice in my ear. How she warned me to run, how she told me to consider her dead and never return.

It's difficult for me to think about my own part in this disaster, and about that conversation over nine months ago that might have been its origin; that is, I know what happened, and what was said, but I prefer to let my thoughts glance off the memory, to avoid dwelling on the specifics. But since everyone but me believes Ksenia is dead, since I've been to a nowhere that should not exist at all, shying away from that conversation feels too cowardly. I let the memory rise up, let it take over my mind.

Tonight I'm sitting cross-legged on my bed; at the time, I was sitting on Josh's. Xand sometimes got jealous of how close Josh and I were, but we had an understanding: that even if Josh fooled around with some of his other friends, he was absolutely not allowed to lay a finger on me. I told Xand that his only two choices were to trust me, or leave, and after some complaining he had the sense to go with the first option.

Even if I'd been single, I never would have kissed a guy who loved someone else, and it was no secret who filled Josh's heart.

Sometimes it seemed as if half of our friendship was me listening to Josh obsessing over his foster sister: the usual *When she said X, do you think she meant Y?* routine that people perform when they aren't getting what they want from someone. Because even if Ksenia gave more of herself to Josh than she did to anyone else, she still held a lot in reserve, and he would worry over every nuance of her speech, hoping for some sign that she was finally coming around.

It got old.

I suppose I started to feel impatient with the whole thing, and why shouldn't I? But what I should have said, of course, was *Talk to her. If you don't know how she feels then ask her, and just make sure you're really listening when she answers.* And that wasn't what I did.

"Josh," I said that night, "think about it. Ksenia always refers to you as her brother, and I don't think I've heard you call her your sister once."

"Because she's *not* my sister, Lexi! To me she's just Kezzer. She could never be—just one thing in my life, like a sister or a friend. What we have is way bigger than that." He was leaning sideways against his bedroom wall, a chaos of unfolded laundry all around him, and his hair was platinum layered over deep brown, with garnet-red bangs. Because this conversation occurred just two weeks before he disappeared, because it was the damage done, the unbearable revelation from which Josh decided to escape.

"So why don't you say something to her? The next time she calls you her brother, why don't you let her know that you don't see it that way?" I pulled my legs in and sat with my arms around my knees; it was a warm June night, that much I remember, with the windows open and a subtle stir of wind getting into everything. We had just finished finals.

"Lexi! I could *never* do that to her. I'm the only family she has in the whole world. Her real mom hasn't even remembered her birthday in, like, three years." His eyes were wide with outrage.

"Well, I don't think you can be both," I said. "I mean, her brother and her lover. I think that when she keeps calling you her brother, she's giving you a message, and you're just not hearing it." I paused; I knew my opinions were going to upset him, but I didn't yet grasp how seriously. "If you're her only family, then it seems pretty harsh to expect her to put that at risk. What if the two of you get together, and then it doesn't work out? She'd be losing way too much."

"Kezzer can't *lose* me," Josh said. He was sitting straight now, his knuckles paper white. "That is not a possible thing that could happen. We need to stay together forever. Everything else in the world keeps falling apart, and this is the *one thing* we can both count on!"

After his parents died, I knew, he'd gone through five homes in four years before the Delbos took him in. Even his own grandparents gave him up after a few months, saying that they were too sick to cope with a child. So I could see a bit of where he was coming from, but I have to admit, now, that I didn't see it clearly enough.

"She's going to have to move across the state," I pointed out. "She'll probably start college, at least part-time. What if she falls in love with someone else, like somebody she meets in school? Can you promise that she wouldn't lose you then?"

The shocking whiteness had spread from his knuckles to his face, and he was biting his lip. "You don't know what you're talking about. Kezzer can't fall in love with anyone else! It's always been about me and her, ever since we were kids! I'm the only person in the universe she could ever love that way."

I guessed even then that he wouldn't be delivering those words with so much vehemence if he truly believed them. While I'd seen Ksenia kiss both boys and girls at parties, there was something kind of going-through-the-motions about it. I wasn't sure whom she actually felt attracted to, if anyone, and I wondered if that had crossed Josh's mind as well.

"I'm not sure that's true. Josh, think about it: Ksenia can't afford to be honest with you—maybe not even with herself—because she knows how you feel and she's terrified of losing you if she doesn't give you what you want. Why don't you try backing off, and let her come to you, if that's what she decides? Because maybe you don't mean it that way, but right now you're basically taking advantage of how vulnerable she is."

In retrospect, what I said sounds rough and blunt, but at the time I was proud of my restraint: because I *didn't* say, *You know Ksenia was raped, and now the absolute last thing she needs is to have some guy pressuring her again. Especially you.*

"You're saying she's never going to be in love with me." It was the closest I'd ever seen Josh come to snarling; his face was seething, its white abruptly flooded with scarlet, and there was something in his look that made me pull back. "Did Kezzer *say* something to you?"

"Not really," I admitted. "You know Ksenia doesn't exactly go around baring her soul to me. I'm just—reading between the lines."

"Then you're just wrong! And it's a good thing you're wrong, Lexi, because if I believed *anything* you've been saying—I'd disappear forever. I'd jump right off the edge of the planet!"

Even in the moment, I was pretty upset; I'd never seen such rage, such menace in Josh's face before. I didn't entirely dismiss what he was saying, but I mostly put it down as dramatics, as an outburst of passion that would subside once he thought about it.

I was able to go on telling myself that Josh would calm down; that is, until he vanished, and then I understood how big my mistake had been: that I'd been treating Ksenia like a child by speaking on her behalf, without ever asking if she wanted me to do that. The fact that I felt protective of her was no excuse. Ksenia was old enough to find her own truth, and to voice it. I thought that Josh had made good his threat by running off with the strangers from the gorge, and that, if I'd only kept my mouth shut, he wouldn't have been so reckless.

I thought maybe the strangers had murdered him, and I was the one who'd set it in motion. When I saw Ksenia during the search, shame weighed down my eyes; I couldn't bring myself to tell her what I'd done.

And when she died, or when that very convincing illusion of Ksenia died, it seemed clear enough that I had killed her.

The story is different now; that's how it goes. You think you have a good hold on the thread, you think you can follow it, but then it twists and winds and knots in your hands and suddenly you're on a path you never even knew existed. But there's one thing that's still the same: by saying what I said to Josh, I had a lot to do with everything that's happened.

Josh jumped off the edge of the planet, just as he warned me he would. And he pulled Ksenia along with him, and some other people too, and maybe he thought it was only fair to make me share their fate, since I'd been there in his room that night, and I'd forced him to hear a truth he couldn't tolerate.

I was the one who said the magic words, and now we're all living under a spell.

All this time I've been sitting in the darkness; I'm in no mood for light tonight. Only shadows are tender enough that I can bear their touch against my skin, against my raw and throbbing heart. My calf still aches where that dead animal raked me with its teeth, even though the wound has been salved with antibiotics and painkillers and wrapped in soft bandages. I've been so lost in my memories that I almost forgot the pain, but now I'm returning to myself, to the glowing mist cast by distant streetlamps and the sweep of passing headlights on my sky-blue walls.

I'm returning to a sound, and I can't say how long it's been going on before I noticed it. A kind of crisp rustling, maybe like the whisper of a taffeta ball gown, maybe like an autumn leaf learning how to speak. What is it? It's a bit of a cool night and I closed the windows hours ago; that noise can't be the result of wind.

I reach to switch on my bedside lamp—and catch a blur of motion. *Something* darts to hide behind my nightstand before light blossoms in the room, but I saw enough to know that it's perhaps two feet tall, pale and spindly and strangely flat.

Something, I'm sure at once, from *there*. My heart is in my mouth as I stare at the spot where I saw it brush past. The apricot-gold glow of the lamp hovers in a cloudy sphere, dreamy and serene, and I clench my fists and breathe as deeply as I can.

Once you've been to nowhere, who can say what might follow you home?

"I saw you," I say softly. "You might as well come out. Do you have something you'd like to say to me?"

A tiny pale hand—human in shape, but so small, so frail—folds around the edge of the nightstand. And then a delicate, pitiful, broken-looking thing edges out into the light; even with my heart racing and my breath stilled, I can feel its shyness, and see the mixture of dread and quivering hope in its single, dirty gray eye. A miniature, fractured Ksenia; it would be completely naked, apart from its tiny black shoes, if it hadn't swathed itself in a washcloth. It has ruby blood trickling down its knees and not a trace of my friend's attitude.

"Sennie," it pipes at me, in a thin, shrill, barely audible voice that sends shivers creeping across my eardrums. "You know Sennie?"

"I do," I say, as well as I can with no breath. And after a moment's silence: "I think I know her really well, in fact."

The poor little thing nods gravely, with its head that sometimes seems as flat as a paper doll, and sometimes more complex, more dimensional. "You—maybe you *help* Sennie?"

Longing sends its voice even higher, into a squeak that I feel more than hear, but I know what it said.

"Yes," I tell it. "Help Sennie. That's exactly what I'm going to do."

I think Marissa has some old doll clothes she was going to throw out. I'll find this little Ksenia-beast an outfit in the morning. In the meantime, I reach down my hand, palm-up so it won't feel threatened.

"Your knees are hurt," I tell it. "Come sit on the bed, and we'll get you cleaned and bandaged, okay?"

Part Three

joshua korensky

Where the wave of moonlight glosses
The dim gray sands with light,
Far off by furthest Rosses
We foot it all the night,
Weaving olden dances
Mingling hands and mingling glances
Till the moon has taken flight;
To and fro we leap
And chase the frothy bubbles,
While the world is full of troubles
And anxious in its sleep.
Come away, O human child!
To the waters and the wild
With a faery, hand in hand,
For the world's more full of weeping than you can
understand.

W. B. Yeats, "The Stolen Child"

the only way to break them open

You are just you, Kezzer. That's the most important thing of all to understand, but nobody besides me ever realized it. It isn't just that you're not a girl and not a boy, though that's obviously part of it. It's bigger than that. You're also not a tree and not a horse and not a doorway. You are not *anything* that ever existed before you, because when you were born it created a totally new phenomenon. The past snapped off and fell away in crumbs. I knew it the first time I saw you, like you were a fundamental shift in what was even possible, and with you I'd be able to walk straight up the walls, and my footprints would scorch the paint.

Okay, so maybe sometimes other people sensed how new you are. They got it a tiny bit, in their half-assed way, but only enough to want to hurt you. And I'm worried that maybe that's what you don't see: that *never* would have stopped. I told you someone would murder me because I didn't want to scare you. But in reality it would have been you, someone would have killed you, back where we were before. You don't do it on purpose, but just by existing you make normal people obsolete. You screw with their whole reality. You make it so they don't *count* anymore, and they can't stand that.

This is all true. These are the true, the truer-than-true things I couldn't say because I knew you wouldn't believe me. You don't know what you are either, Kezzer, is the problem? Like, they've all trained you to hate yourself so hard that you can't see yourself any better than they can.

Or, okay, so you're a person at the same time. A person, but also something *not* and something beyond and something that needs a whole new world to live in, just so it won't die. And what do you know, I got you one. A new world. It's a present, and it was seriously expensive, because another true thing is that they don't just sell new, impossible worlds on the sale racks at Target.

I'm the only one who ever understood any of this, and that proves I'm the only person who could ever deserve you.

I had to get you out of there, Kezz. I *had* to. Like, if you'd heard everything Lexi told me, about how you might fall in love with someone new, maybe you would have thought I was just jealous. But it wasn't like that at all. While Lexi was talking to me all the vague dread I'd been living with sucked into these hard, sharp lines, and I could *see* it. How vulnerable you would be once you left. How you would basically set yourself up to get murdered, by trusting the wrong people. Maybe even by duping yourself into thinking you loved them.

Everybody goes around saying they do what they have to do, but they seriously have no idea. Because our new world, that dazzling, crazy, magnificent world where we're creating our future together? I'm still paying for it.

I know, I know, Kezz: you wouldn't understand. Do you think it doesn't hurt me, knowing how you'd *look* at me if you realized what work I'm doing for them?

The dizziness is starting. Not bad, not yet, but I still hurry and eat one of the berries Prince gave me. They hold off the world-sickness long enough that I can do my job here.

"Hey, Luke!" I call. At the edge of the park, and he's just unlocking his bike to go home. Which is a miserable place to be going, and I know all about it from Derrick, and no little kid should ever have to deal with that kind of garbage, not ever again. "Luke, you remember me, right?" He looks up, red-haired and confused.

Okay, so their parents maybe don't haul off and punch Luke and Derrick right in the face, and they don't fling them into dungeons full of gibbering spiders, but no one ever hugs them or talks to them except to be cruel. Their dad's entire vocabulary is literally *Shut up* and *Stop whining* and *Nobody cares what you want,* from what I've seen, so if you think about it, part of my mission is educational. Maybe he'll learn how to say some new things, thanks to me.

"Josh?" Wide blue eyes. "But you were gone!"

"I'm back now, though. Want to come find Derrick with me? I'm on my way to meet him."

Luke is seven, and this is what his whole life has been: waiting for someone to ask him to come too, instead of scowling at him for tagging along. "Derrick will get mad if I come. He always yells at me."

"Oh, I know that, Luke. It's horrible that he has to act that way. The thing is, this is such a sick world that the sickness burrows into people, and then they *do* crap like that. Like yell at the kids they should really be keeping as safe and happy as they possibly can."

He gapes at me. There are a few people in the park, but none of them will notice me unless I want them to. It's not actual invisibility, it's just a way Prince showed me of choosing how I present myself. I can make myself seem *here* or *not here,* on a case-by-case basis, even if I'm pushing through a crowd.

"So—I don't want him to yell! Even if he's nicer in front of you, as soon as you leave, he'll start!" He's trying to keep it together, but his face is squirming from the tears that want to get out.

"Oh, Luke. You think I don't understand, right? But I actually understand better than anybody in the whole world! Do you know why I came back? I mean, I completely despise this town. It's cold and depressing and brutal, and almost nobody here knows how to love anyone. I would never set foot here again, for one second, if I didn't have a serious reason!"

"But—what *reason*?"

"Because I couldn't leave things the way they are. So I came back to make everything better." I hold out a hand. "Are you coming?"

I mean, of course he is. Something else true: anyone who's been hurt enough knows, or at least suspects pretty hard, that the regular world is a scam, a fake, and that there just *has* to be a better, realer, more vital one: a world that blazes and jumps, a world that's hard to see because it's so brilliant that it's like it burns your eyes, at least until you get used to it. So when you finally get an invitation, there's no way you're going to turn it down.

Okay, Lexi ran out on us. And obviously Lexi is amazing and I don't mean that she's shallow, but maybe she's such a positive person that it's made her delusional? She's been protected all her life and it's almost like she's never had to learn what it means to *really* feel anything. Like, she used to say she loved Xand, but that meant something utterly different from what I mean when I say I love Kezzer. We could be speaking completely separate languages.

"Okay," Luke says. Then, "Do you have a bike?"

"That's not how we get there," I tell him. "See, if you want everything to be new and different, then it's up to you to make it change. You have to try doing ordinary things in new ways."

Another stare. "Like *how*?"

"Oh, you know." I'm smiling so wide it hurts, because I'm really so happy for him. He's getting out so much *younger* than I did—though then I guess I never would have found Kezzer. "Magic. But the way we have to go is also really close. Um, you can just leave your bike locked up here."

There's a new way through, because Prince is always opening doors and then after a while they drift closed again, and how fast depends on what they're made of. This one is gorgeous to look at but it obviously won't last for more than a few minutes. It's the reflection of the sunset in the Bagel-Fragel's plate-glass window, right across the street. It's hard to describe, but you kind of slide in between the reflection and the glass, and then bam, you're across.

Derrick might be sad, maybe even their parents will be sad. And I'm sorry, up to a point, but honestly I'm a whole lot more not-sorry overall. Luke's family grieving is actually a good thing, because they're all people who need a major lesson in giving a damn.

Luke's replacement will be along soon to hop on that bike and ride home—totally instinctively, like a salmon, because most of those decoy things aren't all that bright. It'll get sick in a day or two, then die, and Luke's family will never imagine that he has a new life a million times better than the one they gave him. And even if they grieve so hard they explode, that would be better than how they live now.

When people are closed, sealed up, then sometimes the only way to break them open is to break their hearts. I'll be teaching them what it means to care, even if it's going to be too late for them to fix anything.

That's another thing I can't stand about this world, the one that Kezz and I ditched. You can go up to people on the street, and ask them the time. Or you can check your phone's clock, and see the numbers. But there's only truly one answer, here, to *What time is it?*

Too late. It's just too late.

And Lexi seriously thinks she gets to judge me, for rescuing the person I love from that?

We step through into music. Unselle is singing in her metallic, buzzing voice—like a swarm of cicadas, kind of, but still horribly beautiful. She's right in front of us, shining in her cloud of white lace, her arms outstretched toward Luke.

"Home it is now, dearling, prettyling. What are you, poppling, but the child in my song?"

He gawks, staggers. I know she's putting on her act extra hard for his benefit, the way she does with kids. Her mink purrs on her chest, and Unselle reaches in her sleeve and pulls out a peach for him. Fat, humming like a bee—the fruit itself, I mean. The smell is so luscious you can *hear* it.

He takes the peach, because that's how it goes. None of them resist Unselle for more than ten seconds, ever. There's a flowering tree like another cloud of lace behind her, and she sits against the trunk and pulls Luke onto her lap while he eats. That's it for him being scared, or lonely, or worrying about his horrible family. Just like a flip in the air, like his memories do a somersault, and then whap, he's done.

It's not like it was with me and Kezzer, or even Lexi; we're old and complex and ornery enough that for us the whole process is a lot more complicated. Little kids are really simple and straightforward, and they don't know how to keep the magic out at all. See why I don't feel bad, even if Kezzer might not approve?

You can't just sit around and wait for every single person to agree with you, before you do anything.

I feel it too, actually. The song and the smell of that peach, like they set off sparks in my brain. A glittering web, pulling me back in. Unselle notices it and smiles at me over the top of Luke's head.

Which—nobody has to remind me, okay? But I can't watch Luke eating the peach without remembering about Kezzer, and how she must have said something that freaked Lexi out so badly that she ran off and wouldn't stay for dinner with us. I don't like thinking negative things about Kezz, but there's no other explanation. Imagine if you gave someone the most incredible present anyone had ever seen, a brand-new *planet* where even the trees are covered in infinite glittering possibilities, and then they just tried to smash it? I have to be very, very conscious so I don't start resenting Kezzer for that.

So many people tried to destroy Kezz that the destruction is still in her body, like the way you can carry around an electric charge, and then it shocks the next person you touch. Except infinitely worse than that, obviously. It's not her fault. None of it has ever been her fault.

I just worry that Prince might not see it that way.

the land of not too late

Prince has a way of showing up; all his people do. At our backs, or looming into our faces, or just standing around on our lawn and waiting for us to do something entertaining. The one thing they don't do is come inside the house, unless you count Prince's eye bubbling up at the bottom of Kezzer's hat, or the way they seem to know an awful lot about what happens in there. So I've been away too long already and I'm starting to get that sick, doubtful ache that comes over me whenever I have to leave Kezzer by herself, but that doesn't stop him. He's there, and that means I have to deal.

Have I mentioned that I do a really amazing, huge amount for her? Including all kinds of stuff that she doesn't even suspect, much less appreciate?

"Dear Joshua!" Prince says, right beside me. He has his usual look, the white puffy jacket and tight black pants, and it's getting pretty boring.

"Hey," I tell him. "I really need to get home."

"Of course you do. The lovely Ksenia is waiting at the window, so eagerly that the thought of you has stolen the breath from her lungs. Her lips are tinting azure, and she asphyxiates in the midst of endless air, all of it hers for the taking, if only she could remember to inhale. But how can she concern herself with anything so trivial as breathing, while the one she adores is far from her?"

One thing about Prince: he likes to watch us react, like our most extreme emotions are just delightful to him, and it would be best if I could keep the things he says outside of my skin, and outside of my brain. But he has this way where whatever he tells me beams onto my thoughts like a movie. Like, I *know* that Kezzer is probably just reading on the couch, but I still see her the way he described, pale blue and suffocating where she stands, and there's a crack of adrenaline that makes my legs jerk because they want to run to her so badly.

It doesn't matter if I know it's all a trick. It still takes over. I have to actually remind myself to see the ordinary things, the sidewalks and houses and trees.

"It's just—I don't think it's good for Kezz to be alone too much."

"Indeed not. Ksenia's blood is by now so depleted of oxygen that she's beginning to see things that aren't there. Her vision is full of failing light, of spots in unknown colors. Some of those spots take on the aspect of faces." A pause. "And are those faces yours, Joshua?"

Another trick. A game. But I actually *see* the inside of Kezzer's mind, I see her thoughts twitching around like bright balloons in the air, and so I know exactly what Prince is talking about.

"Lexi?" I should shake it off, but I can't, not when it's right in front of me. My mouth starts to get that electric crawl that happens around him, and it makes my whole skull shake, almost like a bell ringing. "Kezz is thinking about Lexi?"

"It's strange, isn't it, Joshua? I was so sure Ksenia's final dreams would be of you! But it appears that Alexandra is very much present to her now."

Present to her. Lexi ran away, okay. But suddenly I see it in Prince's words: that's no guarantee she'll *stay* gone. My thoughts go leaping in a million directions, scratching and grabbing for what that could mean. Is Lexi going to start some kind of trouble? Would she really do that to me?

"I thought—it would make Kezzer happy. Having more friends around." I say it because I have to say something. "I'm sorry it didn't work out."

Prince rests a hand on my shoulder and turns me to face him. Bright green eyes and that crest of dark brown hair, all way too close.

"How generous of you. You only sought Ksenia's happiness, and never once thought of how it might come at your own expense." A pause. "You have such a beautifully trusting heart. It pains me more than I could ever say, to see how ready Alexandra is to take advantage of your innocence."

What do you mean? The words slide into my head. I can feel how they're coming from Prince, and I totally resent it. But it doesn't matter, because after a long beat I still hear the echo bouncing out in my voice. "What do you mean?"

I know what he means, though. I see it. He smiles and the movie blasts all over my brain: Jesus, Lexi is sneaking into our house right now, tiptoeing down those stairs that held *her* up, but that always drop me. And Kezzer—the whole image of her blue and suffocating has vanished. Now she's smiling up at Lexi, like she's been waiting for her this whole time, and Lexi is bending close and running her fingers through Kezzer's jagged hair. Closer.

I was a sucker. I thought Lexi would respect my relationship with Kezzer and leave us to be happy together, but apparently I was wrong. And it was my own stupid mistake, trusting Lexi and letting her see Kezz *alive,* letting her in. But God, I should have known better! Lexi never understood how me and Kezzer feel about each other. Those awful things she said to me—they were crawling with ulterior motives. She tried to sabotage us before, I *see* it.

Is what I'm seeing real, though? I can't tell. It seems like there's a problem with this movie. A plot hole. Then I hit on it.

"Lexi is straight," I tell Prince. "She's totally not interested in girls."

"Examine the taxonomy arrayed in your heart. Have you ever made such a shocking mistake before? Ksenia Adderley—do you class her in the genus *girl*?"

I don't, but doesn't Lexi think of Kezzer as a girl? Maybe it's not safe to assume what Lexi thinks. *Right, right, right.*

Prince smiles; I see his smile sort of bobbing up through the movie where it's paused in my head, Lexi's lips floating two inches from Kezzer's. I hear him talking.

"How I pity you now. That first flush of understanding, the dawning comprehension of how profoundly your erstwhile friend means to betray you—no one can live through such a moment without it changing them forever."

Ten minutes ago the whole idea would have seemed ridiculous, but now it's—how do I describe it? It's like a comet burning its way from bullshit into clear reality. Lexi came back to steal Kezzer from me, and she's in our house right now. But is that a possible thing Lexi *could* do? How would she even get in here, when the entrance we used together is gone?

How doesn't matter. I have to get home. Now. I'm springing with panic, but there's one more question that has to come out first. *Is it too late?* come the words in my mind, and now there's hardly any delay before they rebound out where we can both hear them. "Is it too late?"

But no, *no;* that's the whole point of being here, of opening up a planet full of new possibilities. It's the Land of Not Too Late. It has to be.

"Why, no. Not yet, I think. You'll find that our lovely Ksenia is still with us, and you'll be very sure to bring her along to our gathering tonight, won't you?" Prince says. I calm down the tiniest bit, but I'm still tensed to run. He smiles, but there's so much glimmer in my eyes that I can barely see his face. "And besides, my dearest Joshua, it's never too late for revenge."

so what's to trust?

Okay, what Prince said helped a *little*—it's not too late, not yet—but that doesn't mean I have time to waste. I break away from him, from his shine and the visions he sends blinking through my eyes, and run like hell the rest of the way home. That movie that I saw before, that moment where Lexi was about to kiss Kezzer and then coax her away from me: is it happening? The image snapped. I can't see it anymore, I can't tell. *Kezzer, please, you should know by now who really loves you!*

There's the yellow burst of our house with its weird dark upstairs windows glaring into what should be *our* dreamy afternoon, Kezzer's and mine. I pound up the walk and fling back the door, then practically throw myself into the living room. That's where they were before, that's where I saw them. My mouth is open to start screaming.

But, um, no. Nobody's here. Which could mean the absolute worst has happened and Lexi has already snatched her away, but didn't Prince promise I would find her? "Kezzer?"

Something bangs at the kitchen window. I rush to see what it is.

There's a ladder back there, one of the jointed aluminum kind. Which is crazy. Why?

So I dart out again, and around the back of the house, and then I see her. Kezzer, I mean, but it's so different from everything I was *supposed* to see, from that movie that bombarded my brain with its pictures, from Lexi's dark hand in Kezzer's pale hair. I'm having a hard time catching up to what's actually in front of me. At first I'm too startled to call up to her, and I just stand there trying to take it all in.

That horrible upstairs addition, those rooms that built themselves right in front of us out of a million broken little Kezzers—it has a window in back too. How come I never noticed that before? Or did it just appear today? It's wide open and full of jet-black darkness that the brightest sunlight can't seem to penetrate, just like the windows in front.

Kezzer is wobbling around on what must be the tallest ladder she could find, and she's trying to climb into our new upper story through that window. The stairs won't let her up, so okay, she's trying something different. Which instantly bugs me, once I understand it, because why did she wait until I was out?

Lexi. I get this nauseating feeling that that's it, that Lexi is *in* there, that Kezzer heard her calling. What I saw wasn't quite right, but close enough—oh, and maybe this isn't the first time, maybe whenever I'm away Kezzer runs for the ladder and crawls up to Lexi, and she's lurking up there all the time, just *waiting*, even when I'm cooking Kezzer dinner or resting with my face on her shoulder.

But as I watch—my new theory doesn't hold water either. Because Kezzer can't get in.

She lunges forward, up on the second-highest rung, and grabs for the sill—it's the way she's jerking around that's been knocking the ladder against the kitchen window. So she must have tried this a few times, already? But when she reaches out, the windowsill ruptures under her hands. I know the addition is made out of those mini Kezzer creatures, but normally they disguise themselves as walls and stairs so well that you can't see them at all. Not individually.

But now as Kezzer grabs they all come bursting out, and tiny flat fists pop out by the dozen and pummel her back, and little scissory mouths snap at her. Where there was what looked like yellow vinyl siding and a window, suddenly there's a freaking mob of squeaking, flailing cardboard Kezzers. So many of them that I can't make out the real Kezzer from the waist up, though I can tell she's thrashing as she tries to beat them off her.

"Damn you!" Kezzer yells at them. "You know me. So why? Why are you keeping me out? I just need to *see*—"

I almost think it's funny, and I almost think she deserves it, except that the way the ladder is pitching is starting to make me nervous. It almost looks like the addition is caving in on her, except instead of boards and plaster crashing on her head there are those jackknifing copies of her, slamming her in the throat with their bony knees. She can't hold on much longer and I leap forward, because even if I still have that cold, hard lump in my chest— Kezzer *betrayed* me, even if what I saw wasn't true she still betrayed me by whispering secrets to someone I obviously can't trust—I don't want her to get hurt for real.

Sure enough, she's falling. Before I can get close enough to catch her, I see Kezzer sort of dangling in space. The swarm has her by the ankles and they're just letting her twitch around, head downward and struggling, with a rosebush scraping at her scalp. One of them slithers down her body and literally folds itself around her head.

"No!" it jabbers. Right in her ear, but still loud enough that I can hear it too, and it wallops me that I've never heard identifiable words from those things before. "No, no, no!"

"Why the hell not?" Kezzer asks. The mini-Kezzer is bent across her eyes and she still hasn't noticed me. "If you're part of me, why aren't you on my side? Unless I'm just the bullshit copy?"

"Try," the thing babbles.

"What do you *mean*?" Kezzer barks at it. "How am I not trying?"

"Harder!" it squeals, so sharply that her eardrum must quiver, and then they drop her, all her little ziggity copies drop her. But pretty softly, and they're careful to chuck her free of the rosebush. She lands on her back in the grass, and it probably didn't do anything worse than knock the air out of her. Which—I wouldn't want to say this out loud, naturally—but I'm an eensy smidge disappointed that they didn't teach her more of a *lesson*.

Because really, if she wanted to try climbing in there, why didn't she tell me? There's been a little too much of Kezzer going behind my back recently.

She lies on the grass and gasps with her arms flung over her face while all the cardboard half-hers go clattering back up and patch the dark scribbly hole they just made in our house. They slap themselves into place and go back to being vinyl siding. Good as new.

"Kezzer?" I say. It sounds pretty cold. "You okay?"

She pushes up onto her elbows, slowly, and looks at me in a way I don't like much, anxious and super-focused and—intrusive, like she's trying to read the future in my entrails. Just because she's a miracle, it doesn't mean she never gets on my nerves.

"You were talking with Prince," she says. "I can tell."

"Which is your problem *why*?" I snap. "Kezzer, just stop worrying."

She sits up and her gray eyes keep hanging on to my face. "They're really getting to you, baby. Every time you're with them, you come back—less yourself. You think I can't *see* that?" Her voices pitches up. Like, it turns into this mosquito sound, when it should be a low, fuzzy rasp.

"What about what *I* saw?" I say. "Just now? Why do you keep sneaking around and doing stuff I don't know about?"

From the way her stare gets even sharper, I know she knows the rest of what I mean. She just plain lied to me to help Lexi get away, and it's not reasonable for her to expect me to forget that.

Kezzer gets to her feet, moving kind of stiffly, so maybe she's at least bruised. For an instant her face is so hard I almost step back. "I thought I heard something. Upstairs."

"You—" Okay, I guess that changes things. As long as she's telling the truth, which I can never count on. "You heard *what*?"

She hesitates, and brushes herself off in this half-assed way, not actually caring about the dirt and grass all over her. She hasn't even been washing her hair much.

"Footsteps." I guess my mouth falls open at that, because Kezzer half smiles. "Actually, I know I heard them. Somebody was walking right overhead. Maybe you can see why I'd want to investigate?"

A stranger, just bumbling around in our house, spitting on the floor and putting their feet up in those rooms we can't even get to ourselves—it's the worst thing I've ever heard. Total and complete outrage. And if it's not a stranger?

That's double-worse. *Lexi, it's Lexi,* says the buzz in my head, but if Kezzer hasn't already figured that out I'm sure as hell not going to be the one to tell her. *Lexi's found some way in that I don't know about, and she's here to steal Kezzer from me.* I know Lexi didn't agree with everything I did, but still, we were close for years. I trusted her. And now it's like I see what was there all along, all the distortion and smudging and sweet-voiced teasing is torn away, and I *get* it. I was a fool to think Lexi is my friend.

She's the enemy.

It's never too late for revenge, Prince said. Right, right, right. Hey, maybe there's even time for preemptive revenge, before Lexi manages to destroy everything I've fought so hard to create?

"Just because we can't get *upstairs,*" Kezzer says, and it's really hard for me to dial back in and hear her over all the ruckus my thoughts are making, "that doesn't prove they can't come down. Like, while we're asleep? It's creepy as shit."

Right. "So what did you *do*? I mean—whoever it is—did they try to talk to you?"

She shakes her head. "I yelled up. Nobody answered."

If she's telling the truth for once, then I can deal with this as an explanation—but, God, she's lied to me before. Because if Lexi saw her chance to get Kezzer alone, why wouldn't she *take* it? All at once words are bubbling up into my mouth, jumping up and smacking on my teeth, and I'm not even trying to hold back. My heart is spewing lava.

"That's what you want me to think!" I yell. Because I'm seeing it; the glitter and the specks are swarming into pictures, and I'm watching Lexi hiding up there, waiting in the dark, and Kezzer sneaking up the stairs to her whenever my back is turned. "You—I bet you're lying. I bet you know *exactly* who it is, hiding in our house!"

I guess I can see how, to Kezzer, it might seem like all of this is coming out of nowhere. She looks so bewildered that for the sharpest little blurt of a moment I almost feel like I'm the one being an asshole. But then I get over it.

"Josh? I'm trying to tell you that we have a problem. You are not helping."

"Well, what am I supposed to think? You already totally betrayed me by saying whatever you said to Lexi, and now—oh, Kezzer, how am I supposed to know you won't do something even worse next time? I just want to be able to trust you!"

Maybe nothing I'm saying is true, maybe it's all some crazy noise that slipped into me when I was with Prince, maybe I'm the one who's being cruel—but I believe all of it, I see it, it's all over my vision and my heart is beating out Lexi's voice, and I can *taste* Lexi kissing Kezzer, like the kiss is jumping around in my spit. I'm trying really hard not to cry.

"Josh!" Kezzer says. And oh, *that's* like it should be. If Kezzer sees I'm upset, she comes to me, always and forever, and she does now. She comes and wraps her arms around me and tries to squeeze the shaking out, and it helps, but not enough. "Okay, so I shouldn't have lied to you. I'll admit that part. Lexi—she has a *real* life out there. Don't you see? She has the kind of family we never had. I couldn't stand—but I'm sorry I wasn't honest about it, baby, okay? Are we good now?"

No. "You let her climb the stairs. They're *you,* Kezzer. Those stairs are made of who you are, and we both know that! The whole floor upstairs is you. And Lexi just started walking right up, and you have *never* let me in that way."

Kezzer strokes my hair, and I nuzzle close. "You—try not to take this the wrong way, baby, please? But you've just been talking to Prince, and he messes with your head. It keeps getting worse."

Is she actually *trying* to say the most infuriating thing imaginable? "Why do you keep making this be about Prince?" And then I'm shoving her away and screaming, and I didn't plan to do it. I'm full of words and sounds and impulses that came from I don't know where, but they still boil out. "It's got nothing to do with him! You're the one who fucked up, Kezzer, and *you're* the one who has to take responsibility, and stop trying to pretend—that you can blame everything on—that Prince has got some kind of remote control he can use to jerk me around! It's totally crazy!"

Tittering, musical and harsh. We have an audience. I don't even look around, I'm so used to it by now, but I think Prince's people are up in the trees, watching us and laughing. I can tell by the hike of Kezzer's shoulders that she's just noticed too.

"It's got nothing to do with him?" Kezzer asks—flat and hard, but she's raising her voice, obviously for their benefit. She has to know they'd hear her even if she whispered, but I guess she's making some kind of point. "Yeah, except that I was trying to save Lexi from becoming one of his damned toys in this shithole."

I'm so shocked I can barely speak. "Kezzer, you're talking about our *home*."

She actually hisses through her teeth. "We're nowhere, Josh. It's the void with some houses slapped on top of it. We're so pathetic that we can't even function in the same *world* as other people."

"We don't live in the same world as *other* people, Kezzer," I say, and I'm really making an intense effort to stay calm, "because those are the same people who kept trying to crush us." People like *Lexi*. I never used to think of her that way: as one of the bland, empty, evil ones, one of the people who use boring normalcy as a cover for how vicious they are inside, but now I see the reality I missed back then. "I got you out of there so they couldn't keep *hurting* you."

Kezzer stares at me, breathing hard, and then she shrugs. "I don't think it matters where I am. You talk about wanting to trust me, but the real Ksenia—probably she's what Lexi saw die. So what's to trust? But just because I'm disposable, it doesn't mean *Lexi* is."

"Kezzer!" I say, but she's turning on her heel—she's turning her *back* on me—and stalking away over the shiny green lawn. And the giggling trills all around us, like some garbled mixture of a sitcom laugh track and a thousand manic birds.

why did you send me to die?

By the time I get in the house Kezz has vanished—probably in her room, slumped on her bed and scowling into empty space—and the bitch of it is, we *still* need to go to their party tonight. We should probably eat dinner first, and I should really try to clean her up and get her into some kind of cuter outfit. Even though Kezzer just said the meanest, most destructive things possible, as if she'd spent weeks refining the calculations for how to maximize hurting me. Even though she's in a vile mood too, and she'll bring all that attitude along with her. Which, okay, Prince and them won't mind, because they think that Kezzer's worst tantrums are adorable, and they probably even prefer her in a rage. But she can still ruin *my* night.

You know what? I'm not cooking for her. I'll eat by myself.

I'm just dumping some leftover stew into a pan when I hear it: footsteps, sounding really definitely human, creaking across the ceiling right over my head. Would I recognize the sound of Lexi's steps? I listen as hard as I can, and I try to call up one of Prince's brain-movies so I can see what's happening, but it doesn't work. It *could* be her. But I'm not positive. And either way, it is just grossly, horribly not-okay that somebody is violating our space.

I storm to the foot of the stairs. There's nothing but darkness up there, same as always. "Hey!" I yell. "This is private property!"

The footsteps stop dead, but that's the only answer I get. I don't usually believe in violence, but sometimes you have to make an exception, and all at once I'm ready to literally kill whoever it is up there—if I can get my hands on them. It's a tricky thing to do,

though, when the stairs will throw me halfway across the room if
I try anything.

"Why don't you come down and talk?" I call up. "This doesn't
have to get ugly. Are you hungry?"

No answer, but I get the sticky, draggy sensation of somebody
listening hard, and wondering hard, there in the dark. Maybe I
can make out the sound of breathing, right at the top of the staircase?

God—I didn't even think about a weapon. Now, *that* was an
oversight. I slip back to the kitchen and get the biggest, sharpest
knife we own, hyperalert all the time for any tiny groaning-floorboard
sounds, then dart back to the stairs. I keep the knife behind my back,
because whoever it is—*Lexi, Lexi, Lexi, or, well, probably*—can see
me, right?

"So, are you coming down, or what? Because this is getting
ridiculous."

Silence, or maybe a faint shuffling. And—does it even make
sense to say this? But I'm getting less sure that it's *Lexi's* silence.
Like, the tone seems wrong. It's meek and sad and pitiful, and
maybe I don't know Lexi as well as I thought, but I know some
things she *isn't*.

Then, really softly: "Joshua?"

Whose voice *is* that? It's so quiet it's hard to tell, but I'm pretty
sure the Lexi hypothesis is wrong now. Which actually, maybe,
makes this extra horrible after all? "Yeah? If you know me, why
don't you come downstairs where we can see each other? No offense
or anything, but the way you're acting is pretty disturbing."

A pause. A snag in the breathing, up there? "Joshua. Why did
you send me to die?"

I'm going to go out on a limb, here, and say that this is not a
question anybody passionately wants to get from a creepy stranger
lurking in their house. My heart slams in my chest. "What's *that*
supposed to mean? I don't even know who you are."

"I know I'm not whole-me," the voice keeps on, in this whimpery, nagging way. "But I'm enough-me! Enough that I thought—maybe you could love me a little? Enough that you wouldn't—"

"I never did anything to you!" I'm screaming, out of the blue, out of my mind. But I shouldn't, I should stop, because it's really better if Kezzer doesn't hear this. Oh, except she must have by now. So why doesn't she come stick up for me? "I never hurt you, or anybody, and I am so, so sick of these—these insane accusations, when they're the last thing I deserve!"

A sob. If this ghastly *thing* invading our home comes down here, I swear I will kill it repeatedly.

"I didn't die, though," it says. *She* says? "Not for long. But I don't know what they did with my heart. Am I allowed to miss it? And then I crawled through all the cold and the mud, for so, so long. Joshua, you never, ever should have hurt me that way!"

God. It almost goads me into trying to run up the stairs to take *care* of this freak, but I put the brakes on. The thing is, those stairs are nasty, vindictive little jerks, and every time I step on them they throw me back harder. I don't need a broken spine.

But the way I'm feeling, I have to do *something*. My body is full of this spastic energy and my hands aren't totally under my control anymore, and I'm still holding the knife. I'm screaming and it's not even making words anymore, and—is it even on purpose?—I stab one of the stairs, hard.

The knife jerks out of my grip and sticks trembling in the wood. For a second I just stare at it: the steel blade jiggling with light.

Blood starts oozing out around the blade. Because of course that's not wood, not really. My own voice rings in my skull, repeating something I said—*when* did I say it? *They're* you, *Kezzer. Those stairs are made of—who you are, and we both know that!*

I get one more second to wish I could take it back before the staircase erupts in my face.

Millions of them, it must be millions, like they've been breeding and replicating all this time. Pointy elbows shove into my eyes and guts and I'm covered in pinching teeth, like a school of paper piranhas. I must go staggering back, but I only know it when I hit the floor and feel the mini-Kezzer-things crumpling under me, then snapping back so my whole body jumps around. I shriek and slap at them, but there are just so *many,* and everywhere I see those pieces of Kezzer's face like fragments of a smashed LP. An eye in a zag of half nose, a half mouth full of razor fangs.

And they aren't all *her,* either. A brown eye with glitter liner glares an inch from me, like I'm looking into a mirror, and I hear this sick, thin version of my own voice growling at me. They jump on my face with jagged heels and the back of my head bangs the floor again and again. I'm shrieking so loud my throat feels torn. Where *is* she?

"Kezzer! Help me!"

Teeth pierce my ankle. I can feel my skin rip free: a hot jolt of pain, and the sickening *sound* of it, the moist shredding *kah-kah-kah.*

"Kezzer!"

Is she really not coming? Doesn't she care? Another patch of flesh tears off my neck and there's that rusty blood stink and I'm crying, not even from the pain, or because my own staircase is going to eat me alive, but because Kezzer is *abandoning* me. She's in her room, listening to me die.

Then I hear something banging back—oh, the front door? And Kezzer's running toward me. "Get off him! Get off!" She must have grabbed the broom from somewhere, because I see it swinging just above my face, scattering mini-Kezzers in a jagged cloud. She drops the broom and seizes them by the fistful, yanking them off, and they scrunch like tinfoil in her hands. "You *will not* hurt him! You will—freaking—not! I don't care what he's done, I don't care. You know he's not right!"

The horrible little paper-cut teeth slide out of me.

They all let go and scatter, some of them cheeping in this bad-dog kind of way.

She crumples over me, smoothing back the hair from my face, and bursts into tears. "Oh, Jesus, baby, you're bleeding."

"They were going to kill me, Kezzer." The pain in my ankle and the side of my neck feels cold now, this weird icy singing, and I must be bruised all over. "You weren't here, and I swear—they would have just ripped all my skin off! You weren't *here!*"

Kezz scatters little kisses on my face. Oh, I guess this counts as making up? She wipes her tears on her sleeve and gives me about as sweet of a smile as she can ever manage. "Baby? Can you walk, if you lean on me? Because I need to get the first-aid kit, and I don't want to leave you. Not this close to—"

She glances over at the stairs. They're back, just the same as before, except for the blood still oozing from the fifth step up. The knife is there, stuck in the wood. Does she see it? Maybe she'll assume the blood is mine, from one of those bites.

How long until she asks me what happened? Kezzer learning—about what that thing upstairs said to me, about how I stabbed—anyway, she *can't* find out about that.

But then she looks from the stairs to me, and her expression is suddenly a lot harder. This look of knowing despair, and—that can't be *loneliness,* because it's impossible that Kezzer could feel lonely with me! Without a word she stands up and walks over there, yanks the knife out and drops it on the floor, then takes off her hoodie and uses it to blot up the blood.

"I can walk," I say, to make her pay attention to me again. She comes back and slides her arm around me, biting her lip, and helps me up. Maybe I hang on her a little more heavily than I technically need to. "Where did you go, Kezz?"

"Just for a walk. I was—" Oh, now she's not looking at me. "I needed to get out for a minute."

She gets me to the bathroom, sits me on the toilet's lid and carefully peels my clothes off, and wipes me down with peroxide while I yelp. I have so many minuscule wounds that there's no realistic way to bandage all of them, but she gauzes up the two big ones where those vile munchkins actually chomped my skin off. She keeps her eyes fixed on what she's doing and doesn't meet my gaze much, or talk, and it's starting to bug me.

But then she kisses my forehead, and it feels like it always does: like another wound, but the best kind of wound, full of rustling softness instead of pain.

Just like the first time I saw her. Just like the first time I took her hand, and felt how the glow of her lit my whole body, opened up my guts. I didn't care that she wasn't talking, because I knew right away that, no matter how messed up everyone else was, we could stay in that glow forever.

"Kezzer?"

"Let's hope those cuts don't get infected. What the hell do we do if you need a real doctor?" She's still looking away, and all at once I get it: she's been crying this whole time. She doesn't trust me enough to let me see that?

"Kezzer?" *I'm so, so sorry,* I almost say. *I've done something horrible.* Where is *that* coming from? Somewhere deep, the words gagging up just when I don't expect them. I swallow them back down. "Um, we still have to go out tonight."

Kezzer grimaces and I get a nanosecond glance from her before she slumps down to kneel on the bathmat and leans her head on the tile wall. "One of those stinking parties? You're not in any shape for that."

"We *have* to though! You know how touchy they get when we don't show up." If we stay in, the house will be surrounded by midnight. They'll bang on the walls, make hideous noises. Every window will be full of their faces, and they'll distort and ripple their heads in the freakiest ways you can imagine, chittering at us. "It's seriously better if we just go. You, um, you kind of need a shower." Kezzer just stares at the floor. "I'll help with your outfit."

"Fine," Kezzer says at last, but harshly. "We'll party our asses off." She gives a sick laugh, then finally looks up at me. She's still freaking out about what I did to the stairs, I can tell. Tears smear her flushed cheeks. Her accusation prods me right in the eyeballs, even without her saying a damn thing, and my vision turns sparkly and warped. I almost get mad again, but then something inside me sticks out a foot and trips my anger before it can get going. Because I really don't want to blame Kezzer. I don't want to look at her like there's something gumming up my eyes and I barely recognize her anymore. I just want to love her and not worry about anything, not ever again, and dance with her and belong to her where no one can ruin what we have together. And I want her to relax and trust me enough that we can finally be lovers for real, because she *still* doesn't; her muscles seize up every time I touch her. Why does it have to be so hard, just to be happy?

"Kezzer? You know how much I love you?" Why do I sound like I'm begging?

"I love you too, Josh," Kezzer says—but, God, her hard-ass stare is saying something different. "If you're still in there."

I think it's best if I try to ignore that last part. She doesn't know what she's talking about.

what is a grave, if not a doorway?

So she's not paying much attention, and she lets me wash her hair and choose clothes for her in this numb, withdrawn way. Still, by the time I'm done, Kezzer looks phenomenal, absolutely as unique and gorgeous as anyone in Prince's retinue. She looks like one of them, all the way. It just goes to show how totally she belongs here, even if she hasn't completely accepted that yet.

I dressed her in a white tuxedo shirt, with a hem that I sliced into dangling ribbons as high up as her rib cage, and over that a black satin jacket I cropped two inches below her arms, and black glittery shorts that show off how long her legs are. Then she has pointy black boots that would have cost a fortune if we'd actually had to pay for them, instead of just snagging them from a storeroom in the abandoned mall. She even let me make her up with thick cat's-eye swoops that cover her entire eyelids. I kind of swirled up her hair with some gel. And maybe I'm biased and everything, but I swear she could walk in anywhere, into any club in Paris or New York or Tokyo, and the doorman would gasp, and step out of her way, and not even ask to see ID.

No hat, not when I've spent so much time getting her hair right. Besides, I've noticed that her bowler hat makes Prince and them kind of skittish, like even they don't trust it much.

I just wish Kezz would notice—and hey, maybe *appreciate*—how outrageously cool and striking and dangerous I've made her look. Like, okay, it was dumb of me to stab the stairs, I *get* it, but maybe now it's time to stop obsessing and at least try to enjoy our lives? But when Kezzer is dressed she just flops onto the bed and stares at the ceiling while she waits for me to get ready, and she never even checks the mirror.

I pull off a look for myself that's pretty good, but not as good as hers—pajama bottoms with spaceships on them and a big vintage old-lady sweater with sequin planets and crescent moons. My skin is still stinging everywhere, so I have to stick to soft, loose clothes. I haul Kezzer to her feet, and that's when she finally sees her reflection in the mirror hanging on her closet door.

"Gawd." She stares for a second, and the look on her face could stand some *improvement*. "Well, I guess it doesn't matter."

"Kezzer! What do you mean?"

"I look like such a poser. I mean, whatever. But still!"

It's hard not to get hurt. Over and over again, until sometimes it starts to seem like that's all I do these days: drive Kezzer's words away, push them off, before they can sink their teeth in me the way her nasty hobbit-things did. Besides, we've already had one fight today, and it seems too awful to start another one.

"You look *amazing*, Kezzer. It's, like, a deconstructed Marlene Dietrich thing? You could totally pass for a rock star."

I guess she hears the pang in my voice because she turns to hug me—lightly, because I'm so cut up—and it feels like my skin is jumping to get even closer to her arms, which is how it *always* feels. Even if there are moments when I think she's being insensitive, or even sometimes moments when I really, really wish I didn't have to love her so much, the reality is that this is who I *am*: my whole body is made out of love for Ksenia Adderley, and it's not like I can change that.

"You're the one who could have been a rock star, Josh. I mean, for real. You're the one with the voice. I've never heard anybody who can sound—as *moving* as you do." She's gazing at me now—wistfully, maybe?—and stroking my hair.

"So, I'll sing tonight," I tell her. That might cheer her up, I hope. "Any songs you want. Prince always likes that too."

"Yeah," Kezzer says. "But I mean—where it would count."

"Oh, Kezzer, don't start that again! Please? It counts here. It counts even more than it would if I was singing for a bunch of jerks who don't deserve it."

"You still could," Kezzer says. "Run like hell, next time you're out. And I'd be happy, knowing you could be—really yourself again. In a lot of ways, they've shut down your heart."

I don't want to bitch her out for saying this stuff, even though I actually would like that—bitching her out, I mean. "Let's *go*."

"Okay," Kezzer says, but she doesn't mean it. I have to catch her hand and drag her to the door, and out into the night.

The funny thing is that, even though they never tell us where their parties are going to be, we can always feel it as soon as we step outside. Like all the surfaces are slippery, curving to funnel us where we need to go, though the streets look as flat as ever. We roll with it, and it's like we're rolling with the whole planet, letting it spin us through a slow, sparkling trance—how can Kezzer not love it here?—until we touch down behind the middle school. It's the big back building, where the swimming pool is, and the fire door is propped open.

We can hear them inside. Singing, and laughing, and there's that quality the voices here have; it's like they echo all the way to infinity, and pick up scraps and radio waves and twinkling bells on the way back. That's another thing Kezzer doesn't see, like what an *honor* it is that they even want me to sing for them, when their music is so super magical. I pull back the door and we walk in.

I mean, they aren't *human*. That's not something Kezz and I talk about, but we both know it. And when they want to, they can make their beauty flare up to such an extreme that you get kind of wobbly, just looking at them. They're putting it on hard, tonight, and there are more of them than I've ever seen in one place before. But I still swear that Kezzer is the prettiest one here, and that is *something*.

They're clustered all around the pool's brink, dancing through veils of minuscule lights like floating stars. The air is this pale blue-violet, like it's been tinted with some kind of glassy mist. We're not close enough to see down into the pool, but even the glow coming off the water is lilacy. As we step deeper in the humidity goes up my nose and bogs all over my skin; there isn't the usual chlorine pool stink, more like rotting flowers and salt.

I guess I should be used to Prince's crew by now, but I still gawk; some of them are riding ghostly horses that must be made of the swirling mist rising off the pool. The horses go prancing in circles around the high ceiling, hooves clapping on the tiles, and their manes streak the shadows with long blurs of iridescence. Other guests are waltzing, like a dream version of a Victorian ball, except of course that their outfits are crazier and the drifting lights catch in their hair, lights that burn peach and white and blue through the softly purple atmosphere. Some grow their legs so long that they look like built-in stilts, and sway above us; they sprout feathers and bird faces and wade through the pool that way, like huge half-human flamingoes in shiny top hats. The music is a babble of broken whispers and little trails of melody and soft bells, and it seems to come out of invisible speakers that flit around the room, always changing location. Okay, so maybe Prince can be jerky sometimes, but he knows how to throw a *party*.

I don't get to keep staring, though, because Prince is on us pretty much instantly, clapping his arm around my shoulder, chucking Kezzer under the chin. "Joshua! Ksenia! The fairest of all my company. Welcome!"

The whole huge space pops and quivers with echoes; Prince's words hammer in from all sides. Kezzer stares straight over his shoulder and doesn't react at all—but I know he thinks that's adorable too. He loves how rigid she goes when he grabs her, and how she'd obviously claw his throat out if she only believed it would change anything. One thing I'm sure of: Kezz would be thrilled to die if she could take Prince with her, she hates him that much, and he knows it too. It's part of her charm.

"Heya, Prince," I say—and I see his hand curl on her wrist, and

her effort to keep her face blank while she's obviously screaming silently inside her own skin. I can't help it, I'm still in the habit of
trying to protect her, so I say the first thing I can to distract him.
"Um, you know Kezzer heard some stranger walking around in our
house earlier? We might need help getting them out."

I'm not about to mention what *I* heard, that totally repulsive
conversation I had while Kezzer was out on her walk. I'm worried
that she might think too much about the stuff the intruder said to
me, maybe even take it seriously. But Prince probably already knows,
and all at once I'm worried he'll blab it all out in front of her.

Prince grimaces. "Ugh. They're such vermin, really. We do what
we can to seal the cracks, but they still worm their way back here,
now and then. It's thoroughly distasteful."

That gets her attention. Her eyes snap to him. "You know who it
is, then?"

"Why, Ksenia!" Prince says, and strokes her jaw. I really,
really wish he'd keep his hands away from her. She looks sick. "It
was *you*, darling. That is, it was your poppet, the brainless simula-
crum of you that was buried with such wailing and free-flowing
grief. The one that *died*, as you're so fond of observing, except of
course that its death didn't take. They're ever so much harder to kill
than you might think. Still, they fret continually about dying, in
the most tiresome way you can imagine. I suppose it's all they
know."

That's enough to send a jerk through her whole body. "Lexi
said they hacked that other Ksenia to pieces."

Prince smiles. "A thing like that? Its organs were purely for show.
The doctors seem to expect them."

I don't like where this is going. Kezzer's eyes are way too wide,
too glittering and frantic. And, um, really? *That's* what I was talking to earlier?

"That fake Kezzer was *buried*, though," I say. Quickly. "Nailed
up in a coffin! Prince—I know this is your idea of being funny—
but there's no *way* it could get here."

"Ah, Joshua. What is a grave, if not a doorway?" Unselle comes up behind him and it's like her whole lace dress is alive, frothing and hissing like the sea. She plucks at Prince's sleeve, her head leaning over sideways and her mouth in this twisty red ribbon. She's beautiful and everything, but all the surfaces of her face look so off-kilter and unnatural. "And now, if you'll excuse me? There are myriad steps to pour into the dance."

Kezzer is breathing hard. "Is he lying, Josh? Would you even tell me?"

"Lying about what?"

"The one Lexi saw die—or she *thought* she saw die—it was the copy?"

Oh, right. She's been hung up on this fantasy that she's not the real Kezzer.

"I've told you a million times, Kezz! Of course you're the real you! So what got chopped up—it was just like a decoy Prince sent back. So everybody wouldn't stress too much over what happened to you."

She stares. "And you knew that? Since when?"

And it's still upstairs in our house; I mean, according to Prince, anyway. What the hell does it want with us? Why can't anybody leave us alone?

Everyone is watching us, peering through fans made of giant dragonfly wings and twisting their heads around the way owls do, so they can keep gawking while they dance. I see Unselle looking over her shoulder, leering in this way that I swear bends her mouth until it's almost vertical, like a grasshopper's. There's a lot of half-stifled giggling.

I'm not even going to try to explain things to Kezzer, not when she's giving off such accusing vibes. I grab her wrist and tow her out into the dance, and for a while we're caught in the current, our minds giving in to the music the way ice yields under your shoes in spring. It's the kind of thing you have to roll with here. The world tumbles and sets you in motion, and your legs go by themselves, and your head feels like it's bobbing on the sea. And you go with it, because every movement is bigger and wilder than you are.

Kezzer and I swirl toward the pool, clutching each other for balance, while a pair of stork-people teeter overhead. They're doing this awkward high-stepping dance, bending their knees in all kinds of weird directions, and it looks like they're trying to keep from tripping over things down in the water. One of them curls a wing over her face and grins at us coyly through pearly feathers, and except for the beak her face looks pretty much human. She's laughing, fluttering to beckon us closer. I'm not even trying to head that way, but still I stumble along in Kezzer's embrace, until we're right on the blue-tiled brink.

And then I see what's *in* there, down under the water. As fast as I can, I spin Kezzer so she's facing the other way, because after what happened earlier she really, really does not need to get upset again. But I guess she realizes what I'm doing because she twists to look over her shoulder—and God, there it is again, her crazy stubbornness, like why won't she just let me *protect* her?

But she won't, even though it would be so much better for her if she'd just leave it up to me to deal with the hard parts. She sees what I'm seeing, and she lets out this terrible, slow moan.

please don't think this is me

Okay, so there are a lot of them, just kind of fidgeting around under the surface, rolled in the fetal position at the shallow end and standing or leaning where the water is deep enough to cover their heads. And they're not just kids, though there are plenty of those; one of the first faces I pick out is Lexi's little sister, Marissa, cradled in their mom's arms, with her dad standing beside them. But I also see tons of teenagers we both know, like Xand and Derrick and that horrible, catty girl, Lila, and adults too: sweet old Mrs. Hixson from next door, and our friend Hadley from the bookstore, and a couple of cops who look vaguely familiar. I mean, it's not the whole population of our old town, obviously, because they'd never fit in one swimming pool. Just the college has maybe ten thousand students. But it's enough that they don't have a lot of personal space, like maybe two hundred people or something, and most of them seem to be people we've met.

Except that they're not people, of course. Fakes. Living decoys, like the fake Kezzer that died in front of Lexi and then came here and wriggled through our house. They're all completely submerged in the lavender water, just gaping around or looking up at the ceiling with their eyes reflecting the fluorescent beams overhead. Random scribbles of liquid light dance around on their skin. Kezzer is shaking and I wish she'd calm down, because it's not like anyone is *drowning*.

Though—is Prince planning to bring that many people here? That's usually what it means when you see one of these puppet-people; they get the replacements ready to go first. But if that *is* what Prince has in mind, it was outrageously rude of him not to discuss it with me. I never said I wanted to share this place with a whole horde of evil idiot humans, after we came here specifically to get *away* from them. I'm scoping out the faces in the pool, and I'm recognizing way too many that I would have preferred to never see again. You know, if anyone had bothered to ask me.

The stork-girl wobbles and her foot—which still looks kind of human, but with these long, knobby, birdy toes that end in hooked claws—comes down right in the phony Marissa's face. We've stopped dancing, and Kezzer is just sagging against me, so we both see how those claws gouge long stripes in Marissa's soft, brown cheek. I know it's not actually Lexi's sister, but it still makes me wince.

The fake Marissa coughs up a single, fat air bubble, and looks dazed.

Kezzer lets out this choked, furious sound, and bursts out of my grasp. The whole room feels like it's rocking, water pitching out of the swimming pool, and by the time I get my balance Kezzer is already too far away to catch, barreling her way through Prince's people, lashing out at them with her fists and elbows when they get close. Not that they care, really—they mostly look vaguely entertained, even pleased that Kezzer is making a proper effort again, though Unselle's mink head snarls at her—but it still makes me worried about what she'll do next. It's what they enjoy about her, okay, the outrage and dramatics, but is it possible for her to go too far?

When she gets to Prince, for instance. Because of course that's where she's heading, and there's already a thin scream leaping out of her throat. I'm going after her as fast as I can, but I guess Prince really got to me just now, because the whole world is freckling with black and burning specks. The air warps and shoves me around. I see him grinning as Kezzer gets close, and one idea cuts through the mess in my brain: Yeah, *this* is why he insisted she had to come tonight, so she would see those fake people down in the pool, and realize he's planning something. Something big.

So she would get in his face. Kezzer's been kind of quiet recently, kind of withdrawn, and probably Prince was starting to get bored.

She's really a sucker when it comes to falling for these games of his.

"What the hell is this?" Kezzer is inches away from Prince, yelling her head off, and she grabs his jacket in a big wad of fabric just under his throat. "What do you think you're doing? Jesus, all those people . . . Lexi's *family*. You really think that Josh and I will let you mess with them?"

He just smiles at her—because seriously, what does she think she can do to stop him?—and pats her cheek. "My little Ksenia. What on earth has put you so out of sorts?"

"You're going to kidnap everyone, and send those things in the pool back to die in place of them, and then—all those *people*—they'll be stuck in this damned half-life with me and Josh. But I won't—" Oh, and here her voice starts faltering, because the whole what-can-she-do snag is maybe dawning on her too. "I won't let you. I—we'll find a way to fight."

I've finally shoved through the craziness until I'm almost next to her. She sees me and grabs my hand—and maybe for the first time in my life I resent it. Like, she's just *assuming* I'll fight Prince? Because she takes it for granted that I'll do anything she wants? *Kezzer, hello, I'm not actually insane.*

"Ah, well. That's one use for changelings, Ksenia. It's certainly traditional. But an inventive ruler can think of *other* ways to deploy them. And they needn't always be made of rotten wood and straw, ready to collapse at a touch. These are far sturdier. Fit for battle, you see."

That's a relief. And: *changelings?* That's what he calls those things? Okay.

"Cool," I say. "I was afraid you were going to clutter up the place with a bunch of douchebags."

Kezzer shoots me a pretty rude look.

"So—what *are* you going to do with them?" It's surprising, but now her voice sounds calmer, flatter, than it's been for a while. And Prince grins like this is the question he's been dying for all night.

But then it gets too loud for anyone to talk; there's a hard, clacking drumbeat coming from near the ceiling. We all crane back—it's a pretty tall room—and see that two of those misty horses are in a race around the top of the walls, totally horizontal and galloping with their riders sticking straight out like coat pegs or something. We all turn in circles to follow them, and Prince waves in excitement. One of the riders is Mallora, the girl I met that first night, with her blue-black skin gleaming against the cheap white tiles up there, and her long pink dreads lashing at her horse until they tear little cloudy chunks from his back. She's laughing so hard you'd think she would suffocate.

The other rider is the boy in peacock leather, as rainbowed as an oil spill. I've never learned his name, I don't think, but I remember him kissing Kezzer at the gorge. It didn't bother me at the time, but now I feel this hot, thick hatred, watching him smack at his horse. He and Mallora are both shrieking, roaring, beating their mounts into shreds—they're only made of water vapor, after all, and they're totally not solid enough to take it. Both horses are pounding so hard that their hooves start to break apart, and for a while they keep galloping on the stumps. Then they're down to their knees, hobbling pathetically along the walls above us, while the crowd screams them on.

Seeing those poor horses, even if they aren't real animals—for a few pulses, it's like something is coming back to me. Something I'd forgotten. All at once Kezzer's voice rushes into my head, saying, *In a lot of ways, they've shut down your heart,* and I know that somehow I couldn't really *hear* her, not while she was saying that to me. My mind feels so much clearer, and my eyes cut through all the glitter and bewilderment, and I turn to watch Kezzer, where she's watching the horses, her face tight with grief.

For a few more beats I want to hold her, and cry, and tell

her—how sorry I am? Is that it? I feel my mouth opening, I feel words like slippery pearls on my tongue, and these aren't from Prince, but from somewhere else, somewhere that aches so bad I could cry. *Kezzer, you're right, this isn't who I'm supposed to be. Please don't think this is me!*

Prince is looking at me in a way that cuts off the words, though. A hot sickness floods my skull and my vision swarms. And then there's a howl of frustration from Mallora, and I look up to see her leaping off her crippled, broken cloud of a horse—she has no problem standing on the wall twenty feet up, her body poking out sideways—and kicking it in a rage. The horse gives a pitiful *whuff*, like dying wind, and skids down the tiles, still thrashing. It hits the floor and kind of spills along, oozing around everyone's legs and losing its shape by the second, until by the time it reaches the pool it's a vaguely animalish blob of fog.

Then it spills into the water and dissolves with a hiss. I feel Kezzer's nails digging into my palm.

I was going to say something to her, wasn't I? But I can't remember what it was now, so it couldn't have been that important.

"You were just asking me something, Ksenia. Weren't you? Oh—you wondered why I felt the need to create such a large assembly of changelings. What use I thought to make of them." Prince is gazing at her affectionately, and I don't see why she can't just get along with him.

Kezzer is staring at the spot where that cloud-horse sucked into the water, but now her head snaps back toward Prince. "Yeah. I *am* wondering about that."

Icy sarcasm whips through her voice. Haven't I asked her to be more polite? Like, repeatedly?

"I'm sure you have no suspicion of it, Ksenia. But the fact is that one of the residents from your former town recently offended me. She behaved with such unforgivable insolence that I see no choice but to avenge myself. My changelings will assist me in making my wrath felt, in ways those human wretches could never anticipate.

Direct and physical damage to your world is largely beyond us, you see. But I've designed these newest replicas to be capable of attending to such matters on our behalf."

Lexi; by the person who offended him, he obviously means Lexi. The *unforgivable insolence* he's talking about must be when Lexi ran away. That, and maybe what Prince said before, that Lexi is scheming to steal Kezzer from us? We can't let that happen!

And there's what Kezzer did too. How she betrayed me and Prince both, whispering information to our enemy. *Unforgivable,* Prince said, and the word bangs and echoes until my head feels huge and hollow and full of nothing but bat-winged syllables: *un, for, giv, able,* all wheeling through space.

I watch Kezzer's face as she takes it in, what Prince just told her—I mean, as well as I can through the stars and the little void-colored grains drifting around. Pinched, contorted, barbaric. It's not her best look.

"You think we'll stand for that? An assault on our old friends? Do you really think, for one second, that Josh and I won't *stop* you?"

There she goes making assumptions, like her mood swings can pick me up and throw me around, wherever she wants to send me.

"Oh the contrary, Ksenia, I believe Joshua is ready to take on greater responsibilities." Here I start hoping he doesn't mention how I've been helping with the kids, because Kezzer doesn't know about that part, and she'd probably refuse to understand that I'm doing the right thing for them. "He'll be leading the charge. And really, if you think about it, Joshua is ideal for the job. He has such great insight into our foes! After all, he was once a human knight."

as any artist does

I'm having trouble understanding exactly what he means, because the glitter is getting deeper in my head now, not just in my eyes. It's like his words wink and rotate the way sequins do, and sometimes they beam back the light, sometimes they don't. My mouth crawls like a hive of bees. But I can tell from the catch in Kezzer's breath that whatever Prince just said had a pretty big impact.

"Once?" Kezzer snaps, and now I really can't take the way she's looking at me, even if I can only halfway see her eyes. But before I can do anything about it she turns back to Prince. "You've destroyed him! The selfishness and the emptiness, and how callous he is now—none of that is *him*. He tried to trick our best friend and trap her here, and Josh—he still doesn't see anything *wrong* with that."

Wait. Kezzer can't be saying those things about *me*, can she? She said my name, I heard her, but it doesn't connect. I'm just now catching up to what Prince said earlier: that I'll be *leading the charge*. And Kezzer called it *an assault on our old friends*. Okay, maybe I can see why she would disapprove, but I'm having trouble feeling anything except this hazy anger at her. She needs to start respecting my decisions, whatever they are.

"I've only worked with the materials at hand, Ksenia," Prince tells her. "As any artist does. Such ferocity, and loss, and longing, and desperation, all in one youth—it made for extraordinary potential. I had only to brighten certain colors. To enhance what Joshua brought to me. And oh, his rage against your world, and even at you! It's been a great pleasure to shape him to my ends."

Kezzer gasps. At first I think she's reacting to what he just said, but then she looks down and I follow her eyes, to where the knife I used earlier is stuck just above her hipbone. Her white tuxedo shirt is stained with spreading crimson. How did *that* happen?

Casually, Prince plucks the knife out and drops it with a clang. "Such rage," he continues, like nothing happened, "that he was ready to wound you, earlier. He knows perfectly well that those stairs are composed of a person he purports to love devotedly, and yet he drove the blade home without a pang. And how touchingly you rushed to his defense, not to your own!"

Kezzer is clutching her side and her fingers are bright with blood. I don't know what to do. "Kezzer?" I try. "I didn't mean—" But it's too hard to finish the sentence. I stare at the red seeping through her sliced-up shirt.

"Oh, it's only a flesh wound, Joshua. Don't start with any bothersome qualms now. Not when you'll be riding forth this very night with your troops behind you, to make your old world suffer as it deserves."

"Tonight?" I say. I'm having trouble saying much. Kezzer's blood is dripping on the tiles, but her focus is on me.

"Alexandra will be moving against us at any moment," Prince explains. "She has a traitor assisting her, one who will help her invade our territory. I mean to attack first."

That makes sense. Won't Kezzer have to admit that that makes sense? But she whirls on Prince with her upper lip hiked.

"Lexi will *never* come back here! She wouldn't throw her life away for no reason! And Josh won't have anything to do with your *attack*."

"Oh, Ksenia. For *no reason,* you say? You may be a very small and inadequate reason, but are you no reason at all? Alexandra bound herself to you, and so her return here is as inevitable as night. And then there are the children, of course; she means to steal them from us as well, if she can. As for Joshua, he'll do as he's told. Unselle has gone to fetch his steed. Dearest Joshua, are you ready?"

Things have gotten really quiet, except for a few snickers. Can't she see that they're trying to make us argue? Why does she have to let them manipulate her so *easily*?

If she was as smart as I've always thought, she'd just start kissing me and throw them all for a loop.

"You can fight this, baby," Kezzer says to me so softly that it's hard to hear her. "Please. I *know* you can."

We're all waiting for so long that it's like there's a break for commercials before the program resumes, and the whole time Kezzer keeps gazing at me, I can feel it. But I'm not in any mood to look at her.

"Oh, for chrissake, Kezzer," I finally say, and it comes out harsh, and cruel, and caustic. "Would you please just stop *bitching*?"

Around me faces break out in crooked, congratulatory grins, like the walls are made of gleaming teeth. Kezzer buckles a little, then catches herself, and I hear the sob snag in her throat.

They're clambering out of the pool, all of them, those changeling people: hoisting themselves over the tiled lip, clawing their way up the ladders. They're dripping wet and maybe a little bloated from being underwater for so long, and there's still a soft lavender glow clinging to their skin—but yeah, apart from that, they'd fool anybody. And—it's just sinking in—they're here to follow my orders. For once in my life, I'm going to be in charge of something.

From the corner of my eye, I see Prince wrap an arm around Kezzer's shoulders, and I see his hand dig into her with a tight, iron pinch, but I guess I can't always be jumping up and down to protect her.

"You see," he croons confidingly in her ear, but loud enough that I can still hear him just fine, "it's only natural that Joshua would hate your other selves, Ksenia, and even want to murder them: your personal changeling, for one, and all those squealing, splintered little replicas of you that have displayed such an interest in, ahem, architecture. He hates any aspect of you that remains outside his grasp. To put it another way, he's enraged to find that so much of you will not answer to the name *Kezzer*."

She doesn't answer, but I can feel her. She's brittle enough to shatter at a breath, staring after me. I don't look at her directly; instead I turn to where Unselle comes riding on another of those cloud-horses, stepping gracefully around the pool, with a second horse trotting along behind her.

"And that," Prince continues, "is why Joshua is ready to become truly one of us. Very soon, he will complete his transformation, and join us forever. Like us, never-contented."

"But not me," Kezzer growls, low enough that I barely catch it. "You can't be bothered to change me."

"Not so much that I can't be *bothered*, my lovely Ksenia, but that there is far more piquancy in keeping you as you are."

My horse is almost here, and it's a real beauty. I can see coils of mist spiraling inside its head like smoke inside glass. Rainbow fumes where the light hits it. I hope Prince had the sense to make it tougher than the two racehorses that just fell apart.

"And even if Josh does manage to fight—what you're doing to him, you've still got me as a hostage. He's screwed either way." I think Kezzer's voice just set a world record for bitterness. I guess on some level I was aware of that, the hostage thing, but it still seems obnoxious of her to come out and *say* it.

Unselle hauls back on the reins—and it's kind of literal-minded of them, but I see that the reins are *rains*, lines of silver droplets stretched across the air. She looks fantastic, though, with her billowing lace dress spreading over the swirling white vapor of her horse, all that white accented by the bloody writing on her skirt and the ruby twist of her mouth. I've never been that into her look before—too girly—but now it seems fascinating, scintillating. She gives a flick of her hand, and my horse comes trotting up and stops right in front of me.

Unselle smiles. All at once she's the most gorgeous person I've ever seen. The changelings are crowding in behind her, their mouths gobbling fishily at the lilac air.

"My knight?" Unselle says, and gestures for me to mount.

I've got no idea how you're supposed to get on a horse, like my life hasn't been much for sitting on anything higher than a sofa, but that doesn't matter, because as soon as I think about it I'm up, perched on the cloudy saddle.

"Shall onward we be?" she says, and strokes my cheek. All the pain slides out of my skin, so she must have healed my cuts. I feel myself start to go, and *where* really doesn't matter at all.

Somewhere behind me, Kezzer screams. And hey, I didn't even say goodbye to her. Do I need to say goodbye? But I'll be back soon, and Kezzer will get over her freak-out. Everything is going to be fine.

But I promised I'd sing for her. That's the last thing in my mind as we ride off, up the wall and then straight through the ceiling, with the changelings shuffling behind us: I never sang for Kezzer tonight, and I *told* her I would. I even told her she could pick the songs.

Part Four

lexi holden

When she sees four azure wings
  Light upon her claw-like hand;
When she lifts her head and sings.
  You shall hear and understand.
You shall hear a bugle calling,
  Wildly, over the dew-dashed down,
And a sound as of the falling
  Ramparts of a conquered town.

You shall hear a sound like thunder,
  And a veil shall be withdrawn,
When her eyes grow wide with wonder,
  On that hill-top, in that dawn.

Alfred Noyes, "A Spell for a Fairy"

the particular shapes of
her silence

My fragile, fragmentary, two-foot-tall Ksenia and I can't plot strategy in my bedroom: the vent carries a drowsy ribbon of echo between my room and Marissa's, and she might overhear us. Instead we sit together in my car, going over the plan, and how could I ever have understood what I'm up against without her? I can't call her *Ksenia,* since she's only a shattered, wounded fraction of my friend, so we've settled on Kay: a name that alludes to her origin, but that I can say aloud without my heart breaking.

Kay kneels on the passenger seat, peering at me from the single gray eye in her broken face, wearing the yellow eyelet doll's dress that I found in Marissa's discards. It fits her absurdly, stretching and contracting in strange places as she shifts between two and three dimensions like a paper parrot in a pop-up book, but she adores it. And I've come to understand, from her peeping, eager voice and enraptured stare, that she also adores me.

The real Ksenia is endlessly gifted at hiding her feelings, or perhaps more precisely, lacks the slightest idea of how to reveal them, but her fragment has the transparency of a child. And what Kay feels—doesn't that show me something of Ksenia's truest heart too?

"Lexi," she squeaks, "Lexi, there's only one way where they can't stop Sennie from leaving! Remember, remember!"

"I know," I tell her. "We've been over that." At least twenty times, actually.

"But she has to think herself! No you to tell her! You say, and the way is ruined!"

"I won't say it. Ksenia's smart enough to figure it out on her own." And she is; I'd say that she's fiercely smart, but she might have secret obstacles in her mind that will prevent her from thinking through this particular problem. I'll just have to hope that she's had enough time to consider the puzzle confronting her, in her miserable captivity. Enough time to change.

Because, as Kay keeps pointing out, there's no other possibility if I'm going to save her.

Kay chirps at such a high pitch that I feel her voice more than I hear it, as an eerie, seismic presence in my ears.

"Smart enough!" she pipes, beaming with her half mouth; she's a sweet little thing, she really is, but she's taken quite a bit of getting used to. "You say Sennie is smart!"

It's both exhausting and touching, this ravenous need for affirmation, but I understand it. Kay is frantic for all the approval Ksenia never received while she was growing up; she craves the same support that my parents showered on me. *That was such clear thinking, sweetheart! I love how carefully you constructed your argument.* Did little Sennie ever hear that, while her mom lay passed out on the floor?

"We'll go in tomorrow night," I confirm, since Kay never gets tired of hearing it. "First we'll get Ksenia to safety, and then I'll go back for the kids." It's a statement that doesn't begin to address the heavy dread in my heart, though; namely, that Ksenia will simply refuse to leave without Josh. That she'll choose to destroy herself, abandon all her own hope and potential, as some kind of sacrifice to a boy who honestly doesn't deserve it in the slightest. Not after the way he stole her from her own life.

But I can't believe that. I *won't* believe it, not unless Ksenia screams it in my face. And even after that, I'll still do anything I can to persuade her.

"Us too! We go with you!" It isn't always simple to decipher Kay's squeaks, but I've gathered that there's a vast throng of other shard-

Ksenias just like her, and really, what I'm attempting is sufficiently terrifying that I'm ready to accept any help they can offer me.

If I'm honest with myself, there's no compelling reason why we have to go tomorrow, instead of tonight. No reason at all, except that it takes time and concentration to gather enough courage to return to that place, where even the trees exhale a soft despair, and battle whatever nightmares I might find there. I'm going to do it; I've made that promise to myself, and also to Ksenia and Olivia, although they have no suspicion I'm coming to reclaim them. I remind myself again and again, that, as far as I know, the inhabitants of that nowhere have no physical power over me; I should be okay, as long as I don't lose my nerve. Even so, the fear that I might never return to my own world is so hot inside me that I almost imagine my body is glowing with it.

"Let's go home and get some sleep," I tell Kay. "We need to be strong for tomorrow."

Once we've parked I slip silently through the door and tiptoe up the stairs without even turning on a light, Kay hitching a ride on my leg; no one would notice her, but I still can't face my parents. Just the fact of what I'm planning feels like an immense and terrible betrayal of them, and it doesn't help a bit to assure myself that I'm doing the right thing; no, the only thing a decent person *could* do. *How could I possibly leave little Olivia Fisher to spend an eternity in nowhere?* I ask them in my mind. And they reply, *But Lexi, you're not even eighteen! This is a mission for specialists, sweetheart. For professionals. It's much too dangerous for anyone else.*

But well, when it comes to understanding Ksenia Adderley, to breaking the code of her rescue, I'm convinced that I'm the best-trained specialist there is. How can I know her so well, when she always worked hard to conceal her deepest self from me?

I know her through everything she never said, that's how. I know her by the particular shapes of her silence; my ear is keen enough to sound out Ksenia's evasions, her terrors, and to mark all that she contains. If I never recognized that truth back in the days before all the madness descended on us, well, it's become clear to me now.

Once we reach my room Kay scrambles up the dresser and goes to sleep in my sock drawer, with an old sweater as a blanket. Predictably enough, though, I lie awake in a darkness so charged it seems to bristle. And I suppose Marissa can't sleep either. I can hear her voice sifting through my vent and out into my room. She must be playing one of her daydream games, performing all the characters in some sweetly fantastical drama, because her tone keeps alternating between two extremes: sometimes gentle and cautious, sometimes brusque and demanding.

I really try not to listen to what she's saying; even little kids deserve to have their privacy treated with respect. But it's so quiet apart from her voice, and I'm so tense that my attention turns to barbed wire, snagging on everything.

And after I've heard the first few words, there's no hope of tuning out again.

"I've been here for hours, waiting for you. Why won't you come play?" It's Marissa's voice, inflected by some imaginary personality much coarser than her own. I almost smile, but something in its tone pulls my lips out of shape.

A soft hesitation. "I'm not allowed to do that. My parents say it's not safe." She sounds like herself again. I know it's only a game she's playing, but I feel a quick rush of relief that the tender girl I know is back.

"Oh, but you don't care if it's safe for *me*? I guess you don't. You think I should just go away and die!" Marissa replies to herself, the rough voice taking over. And of course, every drama needs its imaginary villain, but I'm almost certain I detect genuine resentment, so unlike my sister that it startles me. Maybe it's only that Marissa is developing an impressive gift as an actor?

"I didn't say that!"

"Then why don't you give me your room? I count too! Don't you think I deserve a chance to live, as much as you do?"

"Everybody should get to live," Marissa answers, once again restored to softness. "But I don't think it's right that you want *my* life. I was already here!"

"But Marissa, don't you see?" The harsh-voiced character is making an effort to croon, but it sounds false and treacherous. "There's only one. Only one life for the two of us, and you've already had a long turn!"

Every hair on my arms, on the back of my neck, stands alert. If this is a game, it's a singularly disturbing one.

There's a long silence. The dusk in my room seems to swell, like a caught breath straining to escape my lungs. Then the softer Marissa whispers, "But my family would miss me. I don't think you could fool them."

"That's not true!" The brutality of the tone is nothing like the Marissa I know, with her velvety introspection. "I'd make a way *better* daughter than you do! You're just weird and boring, and everybody knows your sister is the smart one! Your parents will be so much happier with me!"

I slide out of bed, the white noise of terror obscuring my thoughts. If she's working out issues I never suspected she had through this uncanny dialogue, then there's no way I could justify bursting in on her. I scramble for excuses, for anything I could say: *I thought you were having a nightmare.*

There's another pause. My blood roars in my ears, crests, and strikes against the night confining me. "I *know* Lexi is smarter. But . . . I think they love me anyway?"

"One of us has to die! If you won't do it, I will! I'll jump right now! Is that what you want?"

"No! Please, please don't!" There's a creaking sound I can't make out—but, even though Marissa's voice is clearly raised, she's also abruptly much quieter.

As if she's moving farther away from the vent. Where?

"Then *you* have to!"

I've given up on evaluating the situation, on second-guessing what I should do. I throw back my door and sprint down the hall-way, past the scalloped fans of luminance cast by the nightlights. I can't hear Marissa's voice anymore, not now that I've left my room, and my mind spins frantically at its limits, at everything I can't know until I see my baby sister, catch her tight in my arms. *What's happening right now? What is that* voice *doing to her?*

Time skids under my feet as I run; every minuscule instant carries me closer to the fatal one where I reach Marissa's room too late. *What's happening, what's happening* . . .

I've just seized her doorknob when her voice comes back.

A thin, short scream.

And then I'm crossing her threshold, my hand slapping the light switch as I leap past, ready to grab her, ready to *fight*.

Soft incandescence floods her bedroom, terrible in its emptiness. And on the left, the maw of an open window gasps; even the screen has been raised. An old, solid oak stretches close enough that Marissa's curtains catch in its twigs.

"Marissa!"

"Lexi! I'm right here!"

And then I see her, out in the tree. Or actually, I see what I must have expected, on some level too painful to fully accept into my awareness: Marissa doubled, Marissa twice over and tangled up with herself, both versions wearing pajamas printed with purple elephants, both with adorably fluffy pigtails.

And I understand in a flash: it's a false Marissa, just like the false, pitiable Ksenia I saw die, after Josh spirited away my friend to his *better world*.

But from everything I've overheard, stealing Marissa isn't the goal this time. And something about this mimic feels *different* from Ksenia's; it's palpably nimbused in evil, in an atmosphere like an icy sweat.

My beautiful, deep-hearted little sister is grappling with her vicious double in that oak, the leaves pitching desperately with the struggle. And the branch she climbed out on is almost certainly too thin to support me.

The calculations surge through my mind too fast for me to consciously follow: if I race down the stairs and out of the house, if I try to reach Marissa from below . . . God, too long a time, that will take too *long* . . .

Then, the flowerbeds under the tree, all hemmed in by lines of large, round stones. If she falls, if her head strikes one of those rocks . . .

If I dangle from the open window, then let go . . .

The false Marissa seizes my sister by the throat and slams her brutally against the trunk. I hear her stifled shriek, see the tears glistening on her small face.

And with that I stop calculating. Necessity, inevitability, take possession of my body.

I climb onto the sill and leap as far as I can, to grab the branch where it's thick enough to bear my weight. I fly forward, my hands outstretched for so long that I'm sure I've missed the bough, and missed my chance to save my sister.

Then bark scrapes my wrist and my hands contract, grasping wood that pitches and sways, trying to throw me to the ground. Marissa's sobs, the roughness on my palms: that's all I can absorb. From this angle I can't even glimpse her through the cascading leaves. I hear the branch creak ominously as I swing my body back and forth, gathering momentum, and finally manage to hook my legs around it just as the section in my hands cracks and elbows sharply downward. I barely miss taking a blow to the face.

More twisting and I've pulled myself up so that I'm straddling the branch. And I can see her again, ten feet ahead in the crook of bough and trunk. She's managed to get one bare foot in her double's stomach, her hands tight around a stub above her head, driving that loathsome not-Marissa back; the mimic thrashes and reaches for my sister's face with a hand suddenly sprouting six-inch claws. Oh, but Marissa is *fighting*, and it looks like she might be holding her own.

I shimmy forward as quickly as I can, ready to grab that thing and fling her from the tree, away, anywhere *away* from my sister. Nothing else matters.

But then the false Marissa stops struggling, and pivots to stare at me. Lamplight from the open window washes her in golden clarity. Her neck twists unnaturally far, her face reversing until it's positioned between her shoulder blades: Marissa's lovely heart-shaped face, but with a grotesque sneer deforming it into something that I wish beyond words I'd never had to see. Deep scratches disfigure one brown cheek. Did my *sister* do that? Behind her, my true Mar-Mar is weeping, her foot still wedged in the mimic's guts; she could almost certainly shove that thing off the branch, but she's too compassionate to do it. Even now.

"Al-ex-*and*-ra," the mimic snarls. Her eyes flicker with an inhuman, washed-violet light. "Why didn't you just fall and *die*? But even if you do get Ksenia back, it won't matter. She's bound into that world, and she won't be able to stay away. And anyway, Unselle can find her anywhere. Just like she can find *you*."

"Get away from my *sister*." Mar-Mar shouldn't have to kill this thing; I'll do it gladly, I'll spare her the trauma of hurting this creature with her face. But a dreadful suspicion breathes into my mind: if the fake contains even the *smallest* seed of Marissa, lost among all that alien evil . . .

The not-Marissa grins. "Unselle has tasted your blood, you know. Ksenia's too." The fake's arm abruptly extends, and with a rapid swipe those nails score a set of scratches across Marissa's cheek; identical marks, making their faces indistinguishable again.

Then she writhes sideways, her body slipping into impossible, liquid shapes, like molten wax poured in cold water. And drops from the tree with a cat's lightness, disappearing as she hits the grass.

Whatever ideas I had, that those creatures couldn't harm us physically? For all I know that might be the rule in some circumstances, but there are clearly exceptions. Those ruby welts on my sister's face make that all too apparent.

nothing essential is safe

How I reach Marissa at last, how closely I hold her, and she holds me, while the foliage, immense and tidal, rides the wind all around us. How we're both trembling from relief, bitterly cold where our backs graze the night but so warm in each other's closeness, and how she cries and cries; all of it comes to me in a trance. No one is made to contain so much feeling at once, such blasting cross-currents of relief and gratitude and sickening apprehension of what might come next. And then, of course, there's the half-stifled, whispering awareness that the false Marissa could come back at any moment.

"You can't stay here, Mar-Mar. You have to go to Grandma Claire's, okay? Right away. I'll talk to Mom and Dad." What will I tell them though? What *can* I say, without giving my own plans away? But that doesn't matter. I know I'll sacrifice Ksenia, if that's what it comes to, for my sister's sake. I just hope, with all my heart, that that won't be necessary.

"We all have to go!"

"I . . . can't yet, Mar. There's something I have to do here."

"You mean, what she said? About getting Ksenia back?"

Marissa heard it for herself, and she's too quick for me to misdirect her; if I try, it will only make things worse. "Yes. I have to do what I can, Mar-Mar. You understand that, don't you?"

"Ksenia didn't really die?"

She's so ready to accept it, and I shouldn't be surprised—I know the lightness, the sensitivity of my sister's mind—but I still am. I remember my own incredulity, and how I couldn't begin to absorb the truth until I saw Ksenia with my own eyes.

"Ksenia didn't die. It was one of those horrible fakes that died, like the one—the one that just came after you." I squeeze her tighter, thinking of it. "We can't get you away from here fast enough. How could I ever let you out of my sight for one *second*, after what happened here?"

It's really sinking in, now, and my blood surges with a single, repeating thought: *How dare they go after Marissa? If they want to assault me, that's one thing; I'm ready to do whatever it takes. But how dare they try to hurt Mar?*

"I knew there was something wrong." She's silent for a moment. "But you *saw* Ksenia? And she talked and everything?"

"We talked. But I didn't know then what I could do to help her, and—honestly, Mar, I got too scared to do the right thing. That's why I have to try again."

"Did she seem okay?"

"No. She seemed really, really sad."

Another moment of hovering quiet. We should climb out of this tree, go inside, bandage her face and maybe make cocoa. Her little arms are so chilled and shivers trickle through her back. Oh, how could she ever have concealed such aching doubts—that she's not as smart as I am, that somehow our parents might love me more—doubts that left her vulnerable to that mimic's trickery? And how did I never once suspect she might believe anything of the kind?

"Then I bet they stole Olivia too," Marissa finally says. "And Felix! Whoever took Ksenia has them too."

"You're right, they do." I kiss her forehead. "I can't promise to rescue all of them, Marissa. I don't even know where to look. But I'm going to fight as hard as I can." I tip back slightly to look in her deep eyes, and I know I can't ask her to lie to our parents. Not even by omission. Now that she understands what's at stake, she might decide on her own to preserve her silence, just for a few more days, but I won't be the one to insist she compromise her honesty. It's bad enough that I've compromised my own.

I try to smile. "Are you ready to climb down? I'll go first, so I can catch you if you slip. Okay?"

I release her and swing my legs over the branch, then drop to a slightly lower perch. For the last eight feet, though, I'll have to shimmy down the trunk as best I can.

"Lexi?"

"Yes, Mar?" Never in my life have I loved anyone as absolutely as I love her now. A spiny, delicate pain seizes my heart.

"You're so brave! You're like a great hero. I don't think I'll ever be like you."

"I'm the one who should be more like *you*," I tell her, and slide down the trunk to the lowest branch that looks strong enough to support me. "How brave were you tonight? You fought a monster that looked just like you, and you didn't even panic."

She was *too* brave, actually, letting that false Marissa lure her out into the tree.

Then I hear something inexplicable, and freeze with my arms wrapped tight around the trunk.

A muted, rhythmic clopping: the unmistakable sound of horses walking at a stately pace through the garden just below us. But I can see the expanse that emits the sound, and it's completely vacant; just predawn blue clinging to the grass and a row of midnight irises. Marissa must hear the horses too, because she squirms to face the other way and then leans out, far enough to make me nervous, with one hand still curled around the trunk.

"Josh?" Marissa says, her voice soft with wonder.

A sensation like frozen oil saturates every inch of my body. And at the same time, there's a deep, pooling sickness inside me, from the awareness that I feel this way at hearing my old best friend's name.

"Marissa!" I hiss. "Stay where you are." And I slide down the trunk, gripping with my legs but descending as fast as I can. Dew soaks my feet as I alight. The hoofbeats have ceased, but I still can't see anything there except the twilit lawn. Mist scrolls through the tufting grass, binds the flowers in milky tendrils. I glance up at my little sister, amazement brightening her eyes as she peers at something invisible to me. "Mar? I can't see him. Is he alone?"

She shakes her head. "There's a white girl with him, wearing bloody lace. She's horrible. And their horses look like clouds with legs."

"Listen, Marissa: you can never trust Josh again. I'm not sure if he can help it, but he's—become part of something evil. If you ever see him when I'm not with you, you have to run away."

"Oh, like *you* get to talk about trusting anyone!" the emptiness proclaims. And then Josh—how should I put this?—he phases into the world the way a dream brightens against the dimness of sleep. Only a few yards away from me, he sits on a marvelous horse sculpted from eddies of fog. He's dressed incongruously in pajama bottoms and a truly absurd sweater featuring a gaudy sequined starscape, and a few fine sparks hover in the glitter smeared around his dark eyes. His hair is an appalling mess.

I still don't see the girl Marissa mentioned, though I do believe I've met her before. I'm careful to keep my back to the trunk.

"In that case, Josh," I say, "I assume you had nothing to do with the attack just now on my *sister*?"

A quick rounding of his eyes. A suppressed flurry of guilt on his face. I see. The situation is even worse than I thought—and after his awful, uncanny attempt to entrap me, I thought things were unspeakable already. I've cherished a hope that possibly I could save Josh as well as Ksenia, but now I understand; he's just too far gone.

I can remember a time when Josh was wonderfully kind and playful with Marissa. When she was in the hospital from a burst appendix he visited every day, made up songs for her that had her laughing to the point of tears. But it seems that time is done. *Not right,* Ksenia said. *He's not right.*

"You didn't leave us any choice! Lexi, we *know* what you're planning!" His head turns toward Marissa, and his eyes are full of innocent appeal. "Marissa, can you imagine if one person was your whole heart? Practically your whole body? You couldn't just let somebody steal that from you, could you? One heart is all you're ever going to get!"

"*Steal* is a verb that only applies to inanimate objects, Josh. The one I had in mind is *rescue*." My voice is so hard that I think it could cut glass.

Even after all the horror, after what he's done to Ksenia and all those children, after what he's tried to do to my family, Josh still has it in him to look astonished at the concept. To look indignant, hurt, and deeply affronted. "Kezzer is *happy* with me."

"When I saw her, she seemed like she was dying in slow motion." At that a girl's metallic laughter splits the rising light, and though I still can't see her I notice four faint impressions in the grass, dimples where the blue dawn thickens into ink. A kind of buckling passes over Josh's face; his eyelids narrow and his gaze flinches away. Oh, so he knows *exactly* what I'm referring to, no matter how he denies it.

"What-*ever*," Josh snarls. "Lexi, I hate to say it, but I think you're full of shit." He turns his horse, ready to gallop away from here. The four small hollows that reveal his companion's presence, though—those stay where they are.

There's a line of trees and flowering shrubs along the back of my parents' property: the golden wands of forsythia, poplars lancing into green. And all at once something I didn't see before comes into focus: tucked among the trees there are at least a hundred faces, all of them gazing at me.

Among them, the false Marissa. Xand. Lila. My favorite English teacher, Ms. Briggs. The more I look, the more familiar faces seem to rise up from the ranks, and yet I know not one of them is real. I'm looking at an army of duplicates, churned out by some infernal Xerox machine. What on earth is Josh up to? And if each of these doubles targets its original, the way Marissa's double just tried to kill her . . .

We'd be looking at a massacre. *Why*, though?

"Are you really planning to murder all those people, Josh?" I ask. His horse stops, though his back is to me now. "*None* of this was my idea, Lexi! I just wanted everyone to let me and Kezzer be happy. And anyway, you're the one who offended Prince!"

God—it's to get back at me, then? For escaping, and for wanting to help my friends?

Josh digs his heels into his cloudy mount, and it leaps up and then levitates, floating clear of the shrubs and the neighbors' garage, before he and the horse both vanish in midair. There's a new, clanking round of laughter from the unseen girl in the bloody lace—*Unselle*, that was what the false Marissa called her. She must be the one with the whipped-cream curls and the animal's head that raked my calf with its teeth; that's the only thing those comments about my blood could mean. I can tell by the dents in the grass that she hasn't gone anywhere. I look around for Marissa, still in her perch in the oak, and from something in the fixity of her gaze I'm certain she and Unselle are facing off in silence.

"Mar-*isss*-ah!" the voice comes at last—a voice that can only be from nowhere, abrasive and inhuman as it shreds the blue air. When I met Unselle before, I only heard her speak in borrowed tones, in voices pilfered from Josh and Ksenia. Her true voice is hideous. "It is your sister's blood I have sipped, drippy-drop on white teeth. Alexandra comes sneakitting to our realm, and I will taste her nearness there, as anywhere. You dream she will be spared? Your dreams are poisonous lies!"

The shadow-prints on the lawn deepen for an instant, and then vanish. I know her horse must be flying away from us, probably following Josh.

When I glance back toward the forsythia, every one of those familiar faces is gone. Where?

"Lexi?" Marissa calls, and comes clambering down the tree. She dangles from the last branch and I reach for her, catching her as she tumbles into my arms. The first rays of dawn gild her soft brown cheeks, drenched in tears. "Lexi, I know you want to help everybody. But I don't want you to go to—where that girl comes from. I'm so scared, and you won't be safe!"

Of course it won't be safe. I've been kidding myself, believing that it could be relatively easy, and that Ksenia and I will make it home unscathed.

Until Josh visited me from his nowhere and tried to drag me into it with him, *safe* was precisely what my life had been; for the most part, at least. I broke my arm, once, in a fall from a skateboard. I came down with a pretty bad case of pneumonia when I was six. On my ninth birthday a policeman clapped my mother in handcuffs, in front of me, for absolutely no reason, and my heart almost burst with the terror of what he might do to her; he only let her go once she threatened, in very exact, legal terms to sue. But really, that's all I've known of danger before this nightmare descended on us, and it seems like it's about to get much, much worse. How can I possibly warn our town of the creatures invading us now? What language could I use to describe them, that anyone here would be able to understand?

I've never had to make such a choice before: to willingly place myself, my future, and my family's happiness in jeopardy. And yet, within the past hour, that choice has only grown more urgent.

"Nothing essential is safe, Mar-Mar," I tell her, and pause to kiss the tears from her cheeks. "You shouldn't have to understand that yet, but someday I know you will."

The sun is rolling up through the shrubbery, and I know today is my day to understand that particular truth. Because how many people will die, and how many others will be lost forever, if I don't?

minds slap shut like books

I carry Marissa into the house, where our mother is just coming downstairs dressed for the gym. And what possible lies, what evasions, are left in me, as I watch her register her two daughters, both of us in pajamas made filthy by clambering around in the oak, and Marissa with her clawed cheek, tear-streaked as she clings to me? My face must give away a whole novel's worth of grief and dread.

"Lexi," Mom says, with terrible emphasis, and runs down the stairs to hug Marissa and me. For a flash I almost wonder if it would be easier to live like Ksenia, without the weight of so much love and expectation; then in the next breath I know it's a cruel thought, and that Ksenia was ready to die, if she had to, so that I could keep a life she envied bitterly. This much I know: when she told me to run, she didn't give a damn about the consequences for herself. Only for me. And probably those inhuman creatures, her captors, understood that perfectly.

"We saw Josh," Marissa tells our mom, through a fresh wave of tears. "But he might be bad now."

And there it is. Once my parents grasp the truth—if such a perverse and distorted truth is something they *can* grasp—I'm fairly certain they'll go to any extreme to keep me from tumbling deeper into that nightmare. Did I just sacrifice Ksenia forever, only because I was too proud to ask Marissa to keep quiet?

"Josh? You mean, Lexi's friend who vanished? Joshua Korensky?" Mom asks. Her mouth tightens; almost everyone in our town adored Josh, but my mother regarded him with a certain skepticism. *Anyone who tries so hard to be charming is worth watching closely;* that was her answer when I asked why she didn't like him. "Lexi, is that really what happened?"

I try to respond, but for a moment it's like it was when I answered her phone call in the woods, when I had just returned from nowhere; my voice evaporates before it can shape words. And what can I say?

And anyway, you're the one who offended Prince! That's what Josh told me. Whatever those creatures are up to, it's personal. Until this instant, I've been holding on to a last trace of denial, but it's gone now.

Anyone I love is a target. They'll hurt my family to destroy me, and they'll destroy me to shatter Ksenia's resistance, once and for all: a waterfall of wounds. By warning me, she showed them the best way to crush her. They won't hesitate to take advantage of everything she revealed.

"Mom, you're all in serious danger." *This* is what I have to say; it's the only thing that matters. I hesitate. "The whole town is. Please just get Dad and Marissa out of here!"

"Sweetheart, slow down! If it's really *Joshua* you're worried about, I'm sure your father and I can handle anything he gets up to." She gives me a little shake, but her expression is full of anxious tenderness. "This isn't like you."

"It isn't like how I used to be," I agree. "But I've changed recently. You've seen it, and you've been worrying."

She catches her breath. "Yes."

"Then please just believe me when I tell you that I've changed because I *had* to. I—" *On a leafy street, in a drowsy yellow house, I stumbled onto something monstrous. My spirit had to swell, and it had to change its contours, to meet the enormity on its own terms.* All right, saying that to her would go poorly. But that's the truth spelled out inside me. "There's a lot I haven't told you. But right now we're facing an emergency."

She looks sharply at me and I can see all the objections in her eyes: the classes she's supposed to teach, the graduate students she has to advise, Marissa's school. Spring break is still three days away, and how can she possibly go anywhere before then? "Do you think Joshua might—what, start *shooting* somewhere? Do you know something? If you do, we have to call the police."

I almost laugh, or sob, but in a way she's not so far off. Calling the police won't help anything, but maybe it won't hurt much either.

"It's not just Josh," I tell her—and then I give in. I'd rather not think of it as lying, so hopefully it's fair to say that I *translate* the truth into something she'll understand. "Those people Ksenia saw him with are real. They're a really crazy, sinister cult, and I think he's been brainwashed."

He's not right, Ksenia said, but all at once I understand that *brainwashed* isn't the correct word for it. Something in him warped when he disappeared; it's as if a hand reached in and twisted just where he was weakest, most vulnerable. I'm so startled that I almost drop Marissa, and she slips down and lands lightly on the floor.

Joshua Korensky is *enchanted*. Enchanted! Even Marissa is getting too old to believe that such a thing could be possible, but I find that *I* do. I've seen too much recently not to believe it. It's contrary to my upbringing to think in such irrational terms, and until now I've avoided the obvious conclusion—but what is Kay, and what was that flying horse made of condensed fog, if not magic? God, what *are* those creatures keeping my friends imprisoned?

My mom is talking to the police, and I can't even hear her over the whirlwind of my own thoughts. And that's when my mother's voice and my own astonishment are interrupted by a series of piercing screams; they're coming from just outside.

My mom and I stare at each other. "Marissa," she says, "go up to your father. Right now!" Mar nods and runs up the stairs, and I move for the door. "Lexi, you are not going out there!"

"I am," I say. "I'm the only one who has enough information to deal with this mess." If anyone should stay inside, it's her, but I know she'll never accept that. Before she can do anything to stop me, I slip out and race across the lawn, my mother following just behind me. The scream has subsided into a terrible, childish keening, coming from just around the side of the house, where Marissa and I climbed down from that oak tree fifteen minutes ago.

The sun is higher now, enough to streak the lawn with deep blue bands of shadow, enough to spark the dew with minute prisms. The oak's bark looks like countless tiny, golden islands adrift on midnight rivers. And there on the bark is a child's soft, mauve-brown mouth, and that mouth is crying out.

Nowhere has followed me home in more ways than I ever could have imagined. Nowhere has seized control of every molecule, of the living substance of my world.

I can hear my mother panting to a stop just behind me, and the shocked intake of her breath.

"Lexi!" the mouth in the tree wails. "Lexi, I know you saw me! But you just ran away!"

I recognize that voice now. It's little Olivia Fisher's voice: the daughter of my parents' friends, who died at just five years old, devastating her family. Except that of course her death was a charade, and she's still alive in that not-place.

Where I *saw* her, just after I encountered that not-Ksenia with the spidery, pleating limbs; that's when Olivia showed up, holding hands with the creatures who had followed me, and I heard her call my name.

Where, as she's just reminded me, I panicked at the sight of her, understanding that her fate could so easily be mine. Where I bolted, and left her trapped. Heat rages through my cheeks, my eyes weigh me down, because the mouth in the tree knows the most shameful moment of my life so intimately.

And even worse, my mother just heard what it said.

"That's why I'm coming back for you," I say at last. I have to fight to lift my chin, but I do. "I admit I behaved like a coward, Olivia, but I'm going to make it right."

My mom grabs my arm. "Lexi, get inside and pack. As soon as you've spoken to the police, we'll drive out to the cabin." The cabin is my grandparents' vacation home in Cape Cod; really, it's more of a small, elegant, modern beach house, all glass and silvery wood, but that's what we call it. When I glance at my mom, she's staring straight at Olivia's mouth on the oak, its tiny teeth biting a wet, pink tongue. But that's the thing, it's all so mad, so impossible, that my mom can't even acknowledge what she's seeing.

Just like how no one could quite acknowledge it when Josh returned and then disappeared again. Minds slap shut like books to protect themselves from the havoc confronting us.

"It's too late," Olivia's voice whimpers from the oak. "Lexi, maybe you could have saved me then, but now it's too late, and it's all because of what you did! You should just give up. I'm lost forever."

All at once it hits me that, even if this voice is truly Olivia's, even if this isn't just a welt of dream opening in the world's skin, she might be under the same uncanny influence that's consuming Josh. She could be reciting the lies they've imposed on her. *I'm lost forever* strikes me with a whiplash of certainty, and I know that nothing the mouth says can be trusted.

"Like hell you are," I tell the tree. "You can let Prince and Unselle know I said so."

At that, the mouth stops pretending to be sad. It wrings into a fierce, unsettling grin, and when it speaks again all the childish sweetness is gone from its voice, replaced by a harsh rasp. "Oh, Alexandra, they can hear you just *fine*. And they can hear Ksenia mumbling to the air, pleading that you *won't* try to save her. See, *she* knows she isn't worth it! You have to admit that Ksenia understands more than you do."

My mom yanks on my arm. "Lexi, in the house! This instant!"

Unselle can find her anywhere. Just like she can find you.

That's what Marissa's mimic said, and for all I know it was a bluff, just another mirror in their maze of falsehoods—but something tells me that maybe, just maybe, that particular statement was true.

Even if it weren't for the mission I've taken on, there's no way I could go with my family to Cape Cod, and risk bringing all this evil after them. And it's awful, I know it is; I've worked all my life to be the daughter my parents deserve, but now I have to hurt them terribly.

I pull my arm from my mother's grasp and leap away from her, spinning to face her once I'm out of her reach. "Mom, I can't. You have to go without me."

It was a mistake to look at her; her dark eyes are huge and over-flowing, and her mouth has fallen from shock. "Sweetheart, *please.*"

That's even worse. My mother doesn't beg.

"Making you and Dad proud has been the single most important thing in my life," I tell her. "But right now—there's something that matters even more."

"Lexi!"

"I'll meet you at the cabin if I can," I say. "But if I don't come back, please try to forgive me." And with that I turn away from her, and run as fast as my bare feet will fly. I can hear her chasing after me, but I'm carried by fury, by a kind of wild, bitter exaltation that I never knew could be mine. I'm borne up by the coronas of tear light in my eyes, until I barely feel the ground.

Before too long, I know she's fallen behind; that she'll turn back to get her car, and that, by the time she drives through the dawn-lacquered streets, I'll be nowhere to be seen. I was counting on hav-ing Kay's help, but as far as I know she's still asleep in my sock drawer; there's nothing for it but to do what I have to on my own. I swing right at the end of the block, heading up the grade that leads to the cemetery.

In every tree I pass, children's mouths babble and yowl at me. "Alexandra," one shrieks, "they missed Marissa, so who will they try now? If you go after Ksenia, who will you leave behind, here, in this town? Who will you leave to die?"

I'm still running, but my steps falter just a bit at that. Realiza-tion knocks the breath from my lungs.

Xand.

even dreams consume

They have me cornered, so that no matter what I do I'll be responsible for the next gust of tragedy. Can I truly abandon Xand to them? In the initial shock of the false Ksenia's death, he stayed with me constantly, rocked me in his arms for hours. I haven't forgotten how sweet he was when I needed him most. And even when we fought, even when I left him, he was *trying*, just trying in the wrong way. But on the other hand, they're so clearly determined to divert me from reaching Ksenia; they'll play any trick to twist my steps away from her. And that can only mean one thing: they're afraid. Of me, and of what I could do once I find her again.

I hesitate in the midst of the sidewalk. Dawn like saffron paint spatters the gray cement. Ksenia has been the focus of my grief, of all my longing to mend the fissures running through our world. But isn't Xand's danger more urgent than hers?

For all I know, they could blockade my way through to her, if I don't go right now. They must realize that I've been heading for the cemetery; they must grasp what that means.

All around me, mouths with curling lips still gibber from the tree trunks. The spring foliage nods with somnolent heaviness, and my ears echo with their taunts. "Oh, Alexandra, whatever will you *do* now? Do you really think it will make the slightest difference either way? We'll take them all from you, take whomever we like, and grind them down into one blur, one boiling formlessness: the raw matter of *our* reality. Alexandra, even dreams consume, and children such as you are their food. Is that what you want for

Alexander, or would you rather watch him die? Run, run and you'll arrive in time. Maybe we'll be generous, maybe we'll let you choose. Hurry, now. We'll *wait* for you."

Whatever these creatures are, they're made out of lies; they're built of deceit and illusions as surely as I'm composed of living cells. And yet they might still mix in fragments of the truth, if only to make our pain and confusion even worse.

I finally turn right, to run the mile to Xand's house—I'm still in my satin pajamas, still barefoot with my soles stinging from how I raced up here, but there's no way I can risk going home for my phone. I'm not even choosing him over Ksenia because I want to, but because it seems like the only decent thing I can do. I'll have to take the chance that, by the time I can return to the cemetery, the passage Kay told me about will be sealed.

I've gone a block downhill when I notice that someone else is keeping pace with me on the opposite side of the street. I should have known, I should have anticipated that this would be a gesture that Josh's new friends would find especially amusing, but I still swerve and nearly smack a lamppost.

Because, of course, it's me.

They've made no effort to simulate my outfit, my torn pajamas with trails of dark grit where I shimmied down the tree; far from it. She's dressed beautifully, that imitation Lexi, in a flowing, wine-red sundress that billows at her ankles as she runs, clings sinuously to the curves of her legs. Delicate gold gladiator sandals wind up her dark calves. And she's wearing more makeup than I typically would, unless I was going to a party. Her eyelids shimmer with blue-violet iridescence and her lips are ruby-bright with gloss.

She glances at me from the corners of her almond eyes, not bothering to turn her head, and smiles as if her mouth were filled with secrets as plump as cherries. A blue shadow longer than a night streams behind her heels.

"Alexandra," she calls, with venomous sweetness, "wasn't it such a terrible mistake I made, leaving Alexander? Oh, but now I understand; the two of us just can't keep *away* from each other. Do you think he'll take me back? I'll shower him with kisses, I'll wrap myself around him like a vine. And then . . . I'll do whatever I decide."

"Stay away from him," I shout back, my voice thinned by breathlessness. We're both running at a pace I know I can't sustain much longer, a near sprint. I can't help hearing the contrast with how she sounded, her tones oily and insinuating and not even faintly winded.

She grins at me and leaps forward with unnatural grace; her sandals snap at the pavement. Then, while I stare in disbelief, she doubles her speed, her wine-colored dress whipping behind her. She's me, but also not; a sheen of beauty, of killing sensuality, high-lights her strong swimmer's arms and the nape of her neck.

She's me as I might appear in Xand's fantasies, at the moments when his longing sharpens its teeth: absurdly alluring, more goddess than girl. I drive myself faster, even knowing how impossible it is that I could outpace her, and for a while I can still watch the garnet and brown of her diminishing under the trees. I'd like to tell myself that Xand won't be fooled, that he'll notice at once that there's something wrong, something *exaggerated*, in the Lexi writhing against him—and at the same time I recognize how little faith I have, that he can tell the false me from the real.

If I could trust Xand to see through her, then maybe I wouldn't have had to break up with him. I can't see her anymore, and pain radiates through my chest. I slow down, my legs weakening with the knowledge that I'll never get there in time to prevent whatever it is she's going to do. Then I stop completely, breathing hard.

They're going after Xand because of me. I can't ignore the responsibility implied by that. But if I have no realistic chance of saving him, then wouldn't it be best if I reversed course and tried to reach Ksenia?

Then I remember what the tree mouths said: they'll *wait* for me.

I'm the audience they require, and until I get there, they'll linger, drag out the preliminaries. Only once I arrive will they raise the curtain.

Unless they know I'm not coming. In that case, I have to assume they'll slaughter him offhandedly, if only to get back at me for their disappointment.

I've returned to the same conclusion, that I have no choice but to go on, to seize whatever chance I can, however slim, that I can stop the worst from happening.

I gather my strength and take off down the hill again, the cold pavement scraping my feet.

There's a loud snap, a cracking and creaking, and a snapped-off pole supporting a power line crashes inches behind me. The ground vibrates like a drum against my naked soles. I spin around instinctively and see that the sky at my back is full of those horses, a cavalcade of steam gnarled and spun into rearing bodies, lashing manes. Even their whinnying sounds different, like moaning wind. And on their backs are riders: ghastly and beautiful, dressed in concoctions of scales and impossibly colored silk, their faces with odd tweaks, unusual ridges and planes, that suggest just how inhuman they must be. They prance and swirl above me and I can see their colors shining through their half-transparent steeds.

Some of the horses have a different kind of rider, I see it now: what appear to be ordinary people but which are certainly replicas instead, in band T-shirts and jeans, or tweed blazers and slacks. I recognize a few faces from around town, and they look both drab and surreal scattered among those horribly lovely beings.

But it's the dull, false humans who are doing all the damage.

A man I've seen at the gas station rounds back and darts at the branch of a tree just above my head, splintering it with a single kick. The branch plummets and I barely sidestep in time. Above me, the unearthly riders leap. An inhuman girl pivots in midair to catch my eye, her long pink dreadlocks whipping at her shoulders, and gives me a confiding smile. As if their attempt to kill me were a friendly gesture, something that might bring us closer.

In their world, I had the impression that these creatures were incapable of physical violence, and maybe that's why they've brought this legion of imitation humans with them; it seems that the same restrictions don't apply to these mimics. They're like weapons made all the worse by the bland familiarity of their faces.

I leave the sidewalk and sprint instead down the center of the street, to be as far as possible from falling wreckage. The rising sun throbs in the leaves, and around me the town is waking; I race through the whirr of coffee grinders, the twittering of alarm clocks.

What kind of world are all those people waking up to?

Not one they've ever seen before. Not one they have the faintest idea how to cope with. The cloudy procession runs in midair behind me, heels smashing windshields, snagging laundry lines; a woman steps outside in her bathrobe to see what's causing the tumult.

Before I can yell to her, two fake-human riders blow by, a cable tangled around their feet. It catches the woman by the neck and drags her a dozen yards before she's smashed headfirst against a truck. Even from a distance, I can see how her head is at an angle, which can only signify one thing. She's not stirring even faintly, and I know there's no point in trying to help her.

She didn't have time enough to scream. How deluded must I be, or how arrogant, to imagine that I can defeat this madness? Pausing, even long enough to glance at the murdered woman, gives them time to launch another branch at me. This one catches the edge of my shoulder and sends me staggering; it's pure luck that it missed smashing my skull.

The riders laugh. As for me, I run, run through a fragmenting town. The serene morning sounds of frying eggs and rushing showers are now mixed with scattered shrieks and the shrill tinkle of falling glass.

As I race at least a dozen of the riders stay close behind me, now and then lobbing projectiles just behind my heels. As if they're herding me, because the course I'm on was their choice all along.

I hope to God my mom has given up searching for me by now, and made the decision to get Marissa and my father out of town. As long as my family is safe, I'll face whatever comes next with all the courage I have.

there are lies that have some truth in them

By the time Xand's house rises over the curving ground, the drama is already under way. From a distance, I spot the garnet sweep of her dress in the wind, its color even more vivid against Xand's white house with its neat black shutters, its shrubbery trimmed boxy and severe.

He's with her, of course he's with her. She stands on tiptoe to twist around him, her brown fingers deep in his hair, his pale cheek lowered to press against hers. So far from seeing through her, he's yielding utterly to the illusion of this sultry, sweet Lexi who wants him back and raced to him at dawn just to tell him so. Even though I'm still too far away for her to catch the rush of my footsteps, she seems to feel my eyes on her instantaneously. I notice the slightest rotation of her head toward me, and a smile that seems to glide in my direction. *Oh, Lexi, I thought you'd never come!*

She pulls his lips to hers and kisses him, deep and ravening. Xand seizes her by the hips, and now my steps have carried me close enough that I'm nearly certain I hear him moan. What makes it even more unsettling is that I can see the theatricality of her gestures, even if Xand can't; her passion is overblown, insincere, as artificial as she is herself. With my revulsion and my fear for him comes anger; how can he possibly imagine that that creature is me?

In my mind's eye, I already see the scenario that artificial Lexi is planning. I'm supposed to cry his name, tell him to step away from her; she's supposed to croon into his bewildered face, and then grin sidelong when he accepts her, new and improved as she is, in preference to the frazzled girl in ripped pajamas. I suppose it's hard to see any alternative to doing just what she expects of me, but I still search for one; for anything at all that I can do, besides simply following her script.

For a start, I approach in silence, my steps slow and so soft that I'm within ten feet of them before Xand's head jerks in my direction. His mouth rounds, and then he tries to cover his dismay with a smirk—how did I imagine that I was in love with him, I wonder? I still say nothing, and my mimic starts to pout, clearly annoyed at my failure to recite my lines.

"Okay," Xand says, with desperate jocularity—still *trying*, but now he's trying to fool himself. "Good one. What are you going to tell me, that you two are long-lost twins?"

He has to see it for himself; I don't think I can save him if he doesn't. He has to look in my face, and recognize that the true Lexi is the one who doesn't want him. I've changed so much since my foray into nowhere that now I can scarcely remember the Lexi who *did* want him. I loved him, and I still care—but wasn't there always something missing?

Besides, it's beneath me to plead for my own identity.

My mimic lets him go and spins toward me. "Why don't you tell him, Alexandra? Does it mean nothing to you, if I kill him?" She leans in, uncomfortably near, and for a moment I see our confrontation through Xand's eyes: my double looming so intimately I feel a jolting fear that she intends to kiss me. Our two heads with their dawn-brushed twists of dark hair must take on the disquieting look of a dividing cell.

Xand's smirk is turning into a bent crevice of panic, as if understanding might at last be opening inside him, and with it the beginnings of fear.

"Xand," I say. "Go inside and lock the door."

"Lexi?" And there it is; he can still escape, if he'll only pay attention to what he truly knows, and what he wishes he didn't know. He hesitates, his gaze fluctuating between us. "We have to be together. I knew that if I waited, you would come back. I *knew* you couldn't just stop loving me so easily!"

Even he doesn't know which of us he's talking to.

"I'm never coming back to you. But I love you enough to want to save your life, Xand. Now show me you have the sense to listen to me, and run away."

No. He still wavers, and my mimic smiles, her tongue flicking the air like she's tasting his weakness. She swings back to him, her skirt lofting thigh-high in a gust of wind, and runs one silky finger down his cheek. Her nails are perfectly manicured to match her outfit, I notice, the same wine red as her dress, with bright golden tips. I've been biting mine again, ever since I saw Ksenia.

"You see, Xand? Love is truth. Love is all that matters. So if you want to know which of us is the *true* Alexandra, protect your heart. Choose the one who loves you."

Xand gawks at her, blank-eyed and mesmerized. "You're right. Oh, *Lexi* . . ."

"Is that me, do you think?"

"Yes."

"Oh, Alexander. Is it really?" She kisses his throat, a soft acknowledgment. Where her slim hand rests on his chest, I notice that her red-and-gold nails are at least an inch longer than they were only moments ago.

I have to do *something,* and there isn't much time. I rush her, meaning to throw her to the ground, to give Xand the barest chance of breaking free of her spell.

A tiny flick of her hand, almost too quick to see, and I'm stumbling backward with a sharp pain in my sternum. Her gaze never left his face, and he doesn't seem to see me anymore at all. Overpowering her isn't an option, then.

It's taken me this long to notice that the riders have stopped pursuing me, presumably because they want my full attention on what's happening here. Only a few white streaks like jet trails linger in the sky.

"Do you know what I learned from Joshua Korensky, Alexander?" Her voice is changing, barely resembling mine anymore, its tones hollowed out and only a weary sibilance remaining. "Joshua taught me something interesting."

Xand opens his mouth in surprise, then closes it again. "What?"

"He said that one heart is all you're ever going to get."

And then the hand on Xand's chest snakes around to rest on his back. Xand gives a little anxious jerk—he *knows*, on some suppressed level he knows what she means to do—but he doesn't have the presence of mind to tear himself away. I just have time to see an unnaturally long, sharp, gold-tipped nail sprouting at terrific speed from the false Lexi's forefinger. A scream of warning drives up from my throat just as my double slides her nail, with a casual *pop*, straight between Xand's ribs.

Xand gasps, his eyes rolling back, and the double wriggles its finger: twisting the nail, opening a wider hole.

A moment later the nail glides back out, and Xand's heart is skewered on the tip like a bloody peach. My mind rebels, rejects everything I'm witnessing with my own eyes. Something in me insists that it's all a hallucination, and that they've tainted my perceptions to the point where I can't trust anything I'm seeing.

"I had no idea," my double muses, "that it worked like that. For all I knew, you might have a limitless supply."

Xand falls, a slow, simple folding-up. Apart from a ruby blot on his shirt, there isn't any visible blood, and I could almost convince myself that it's all another trick, a hideous sleight of hand. That Xand will be just fine, oh, in an hour or two.

But then I see the way the false Lexi is smiling at me: an *It's all for you* look, and I know I'm doing the same thing my mom did: closing my mind against an intolerable reality.

"You see, Alexandra? Ksenia's changeling was made just to die in your arms, and apart from that she was worthless. Nothing but rotten wood and old straw, dressed up so prettily. But not me. I was designed especially for this occasion, as a weapon to wound you. I'm strong and I'm fast, and I've never had a heart at all. Until now, that is."

She stands over Xand's unbreathing body, his beautiful, pale profile framed by the lush green grass, and holds his heart up where she can admire it.

I try to speak and feel my words bursting into silence.

"*You* murdered him, you know, Alexandra. This only happened because you tried to interfere with your betters. Joshua agreed that we had to show you what a terrible mistake it would be, to try to claim things that don't belong to you."

By *things* she means *people,* and for a sliver of a moment I'm consumed by outrage that she would dare to describe Ksenia and Olivia that way. Then the rest of her statement strikes home.

"Josh agreed to this?" Even after our appalling conversation by the oak, after everything Josh said himself, it's still so hard for me to believe the worst of him.

"He said Xand deserved to die. And that you needed to see for yourself what you've done." Another of her sly smiles. "He thought it would encourage you to take *responsibility.* Don't worry, though. I'll tidy up before Xand's family sees him. This isn't meant for them."

Then she bends. With her heart-free hand, without the slightest appearance of effort, she grasps Xand by one elbow and heaves him up over her shoulder. Even his spilled blood lifts up from the grass, scrolling after his corpse like crimson ribbons. Not a trace of him remains behind.

The cruelty of it stuns me. Will Xand's family ever know what happened to him? Though if they knew, they wouldn't be able to comprehend it; all they would see is that I've murdered him, just as my double said.

Still, I move forward to stop her, although I know perfectly well that stopping her isn't something I can do. My hands reach forward as if I could pull Xand away from her, and she leaps airily, landing a dozen feet back. And then I hear something: a stifled rustling, a torrent of whispers, coming from farther up.

They're here, they're all around us; maybe they've been watching this whole time, only veiled in invisibility, and only seen fit to reveal themselves now.

Cloud-horses perch awkwardly on the crests of the trees, their legs drawn together like the stems of some wispy bouquet. I see Unselle on the garage roof, her frothing hair and dress blurring into the cumulus-dotted sky behind her. Her horse's hooves drum anxiously at the shingles, and she actually lifts a pale hand to wave to me, smiling sweetly. The sight of her brings back the sickening, ashy sensation of her breath against my ear, her lips disgorging a stream of Ksenia's voice. I have never before in my life felt such acute loathing for anything or anyone as I do for her; she affects me like decay incarnate, like rotten meat dressed up in snowy frills.

By the time I can pull my gaze away from her, my double is gone, and Xand's corpse with her. And yet, to my disbelief, I see Xand himself—could his death have been an illusion after all?— walking toward me in a dappling of leaf shadow. His smile beams toward me, warm and bright and eager. He looks even more handsome than usual, with his chiseled face and green eyes, his dark hair waving over his pale forehead.

Of course Xand's murder was no illusion. I know exactly what it is stalking me across this shimmering lawn. *Not him,* I'm thinking, *it's not him,* when he seizes hold of me and kisses me fiercely on the lips.

Being kissed against my will by Xand would be bad enough; coming from this pseudohuman thing, this replica, it's so revolting that I gag and shove him away with both arms. To no effect; I might as well be shoving stone, and the false Xand keeps me bound tight in his embrace.

"No one else will care that Alexander is dead," the creature whispers in my ear. "No one else will even notice. Why should you?"

"You will let go of me, *now*," I snarl back. "I don't belong to any of you."

A wave of giggling comes from the treetops.

"Are you sure that's true? You're bound to someone who belongs to us. She was properly introduced, she pledged herself to our Joshua, she ate our food. And *you* pledged yourself to her, such a lovely promise, such sweet words. Prince hadn't even made me yet, but oh, I was already listening! We *all* were. *You're real enough that I still love you, no matter what.* And after that, we knew . . . we only had to wait to claim you. You see?" His hands start wandering, greedy to take in more of my form. "So why not start with me?"

"Ksenia *doesn't* belong to you, though. She defied all of you when she warned me not to eat anything, and when she told me to run. She protected me and my future without caring what you might do to her because of it. She proved that her mind is still free, and her mind is all that matters. And since she *isn't* yours, then whatever I said to her—it just isn't relevant."

It's quick, subtle, almost undetectable. But for the first time, I swear I see a flicker of discomfort on his face. He tries to cover it with a sneer and releases me with a little push.

Even the watchers in the trees stop snickering, and there's an audible note of consternation in their sudden quiet.

"Don't *be* like that, Alexandra," the false Xand says. A brilliant, entirely empty smile rises on his face like an artificial sun. "I brought you a present. See?"

I'm ready to tell him that there is nothing I would accept from him, not under any circumstances, when I see what it is, and my thoughts turn in a silent revolution. My hand stretches out before I have time to consider what I'm doing. Because pinched between the not-Xand's fingertips is the black felt brim of Ksenia's bowler hat, unmistakably hers, with the same scuffs, the same slight sheen on the crown. It was already battered when she found it at the thrift store, and then she wore it constantly.

My first instinct is that she must have sent it to me, as a kind of message. And even once I cast away that thought—I can't imagine that she would have used this creature as an emissary—I still can't stand to see him holding it. They will touch nothing of hers, and nothing of who she is, not if I can help it.

I seize the hat and pull it close against me, and he grins. A hundred smiles break out around me in a palpable wave, and I shiver as I sense their excitement. Did I just make a mistake?

"Be careful how you hold that thing, baby. It's tricky. It could be dangerous, especially if it gets hungry. Keep the brim up, okay? Unless you want to find out what it can do, of course."

He turns and walks toward the house, and I'm just processing that—this vile thing means to take Xand's place, impose itself on Xand's family, and if I try to warn them there's not the faintest chance they'll listen to me—when a windy rustling floods the yard.

They've all vanished. The cloud-horses, the creatures on their backs; I can't see the snowy trails their departure left before. Some of the highest branches are pitching, though, as if they had been relieved of a burden. They even left the entirety of this block intact, without a touch of visible destruction.

The scene looks disconcertingly normal now. Just that false Xand strolling toward a two-story white house with black shutters, a random middle-aged neighbor getting in her car. From the glance she jabs at me, I realize that to her I'm the most jarring element on view: a pajama-clad black girl holding a bowler hat, standing barefoot on the grass for no apparent reason.

But given how those creatures seem to have the trick of slipping in and out of visibility, I can't assume that all of them are truly gone. There must be at least one of them hovering nearby, waiting to see what I'll do. And as for that, well, there's only one viable option: to run back the way I came, to reach the graveyard, and to follow Kay's instructions. That is, if the way hasn't been closed to me. If I still can.

The imitation Xand stops, almost at the front door. I have to admit he's an impeccable copy, without any of the telling, off-key elements I noticed in the false Marissa: no lilac phosphorescence, nothing blatantly evil in his expression. Even though I know the truth, I still feel a shiver of temptation to believe that Xand never died and that this is truly him. That's how these mimics work; they play on our denial, and on our longing for those we've lost, until we're willing to overlook the aching disharmony between the true one we love and the false one we see.

He meets my gaze, and with that the illusion fails, because his look transmits a shock; something calculating, chill, predatory.

"You know, Prince will hurt you all he can for thinking you can steal Ksenia. But that doesn't mean he doesn't want you to *try*, because that's how he'll catch you too. A bite of our food is all that's left, you know, it's the last thing we need, and you'll get *hungry*. Alexandra, you'll be so much happier if you just forget everything you saw there, and belong to me. I'll keep you safe. I'll tell Prince you're all mine, and that he shouldn't bother your family."

"You're a walking lie," I point out—though everything he just said gets to me much more than it should. My knees quake and my head chimes again with that unearthly resonance, that singing echo. "Every hair on your head is a lie. It would be absurd for me to listen to you."

"There are lies that have some truth in them," the pseudo-Xand fires back. "Are you sure I'm not one of them?"

I'm not sure; I've consistently gotten the sense that these imitations are—how should I describe it?—*seeded* by their originals. Even that spidery Ksenia had a touch of genuine Ksenia-ness about her, and this creature conveys a trace of something truly like Xand. The resemblance comes from something deeper than just their matching features.

"I know I'm not whole-him," the fake continues, "but I have enough of him in me that I'm in *love* with you, Alexandra. They let me have that much. Enough that I want you more than anything, and now that Alexander's out of the way . . ."

A wave of revulsion crashes through me at that. I left the real Xand, and yet this nothingness, this deceit wrapped up in Xand's appearance, thinks that somehow I'm his for the picking? That coldly and calmly exploiting Xand's death is an easy way to win my heart? I spin on my heel so quickly that I almost drop the hat.

"Watch how you hold that thing!" he shouts after me. "I'll call you later!" Just like Xand himself, he doesn't seem to comprehend that I've rejected him. And I'm not about to waste any more time explaining what should be so very obvious.

I know I'll mourn the real Xand for a long, long time. I still loved him, even if it wasn't in the way he wanted—maybe it was *never* in the way he wanted, even if I didn't recognize that at the time.

But you don't have to love someone perfectly for their loss to tear through you.

Now is not the time to let myself dissolve into grief.

nothing of great matter to her

I turn to run, though by now my naked feet feel raw.

And that's when a silver car squeals into Xand's driveway, so fast that it nearly rear-ends his parents' SUV.

My mom, her gaze bright with longing, her usual composure replaced by a disordered blend of fear and outrage. Of course she would look for me here. Why won't she understand the desperate necessity of getting far away, of saving whatever she can?

There's a line of woods behind Xand's house, and I could run for it again, if only it weren't for her car's *other* passenger. He's on the car's roof, and I'm nearly positive she has no idea what's up there. A cloud-horse, its legs splayed slightly, hooves skidding awkwardly on the metallic surface. And on the horse, a rider.

Joshua Korensky.

"Hey, Lexi," he says, far too casually for someone who's helped leave a trail of corpses scattered through our town. *This* is what they've done to him: he can't feel the reality of other people anymore. It's as if they've severed the nerves that reach to connect with all the rest of humanity, that receive living waves of emotion. Xand was a friend of his, but if Josh knows Xand is dead—if he *authorized* Xand's murder, the way my double said—then he clearly doesn't care in the slightest.

Josh notices the hat, still brim-up in my hands, its black bowl turned to the sky. "Ugh. You know that thing is dangerous, right? You should give it to me."

"I'll give it back to Ksenia," I snap. "Just as soon as I see her. And anyway, it's a *hat*. How can it be dangerous?"

"It's not just a hat anymore, though. Not after everything. It's like a gun that shoots changes instead of bullets, Lexi. And you don't even know what it's *loaded* with." He reaches for it again, and I ignore him.

If it's really some kind of weapon, then obviously surrendering it would be ridiculous.

Why hasn't my mother leapt out of her car yet? I can see her leaning over behind the window, clearly tugging hard at the handle. The door doesn't seem to be yielding, and her face is tense with suppressed fear. I can't bear it, and I run to open the door from the outside.

"That won't work, Lexi," Josh says. He's looming over me, his hair a slanting cascade as he bends above my head. "I'm keeping her in there for now, okay? She'll just be in the way."

I try to stay calm. "You will let her out this instant." My mom is banging on the glass, gesturing to me, but Josh is right; I'm yanking on the door, and it doesn't budge.

"Yeah, no. I really won't. Trying to smash the windows won't work, either. Jesus, Lexi, do you even get that all of this is your fault? You're messing with Prince, which you should seriously know better than to even think of doing. You've made yourself into a problem, when you could have just left us alone. So what do you expect us to do? Just *take* it, because you feel so righteous about dishing it out? It doesn't work like that."

Us. So he sees himself as truly one of them, now. I used to be ready to share the responsibility for the disaster that's overtaken us. But while Josh keeps talking, I feel that change.

Yes, I said things that set Josh off, and he was fragile and hurt and desperate beyond my comprehension. He's suffered so much loss that the thought of losing Ksenia too was enough to unbalance him. And I shouldn't have spoken for Ksenia. I'll own that much. But Josh's descent into cruelty, and the fact that he thought kidnapping Ksenia to another world was a reasonable response to his pain: those acts are not mine, and I refuse to take on the faintest breath of guilt.

"So why don't we just *ask* Ksenia what she wants?" I say. The words fill me with lightness, with a sense of liberation. "We'll go together. If she says she wants to stay in that nothing of a place forever, I'll respect that."

That doesn't address the problem of the stolen children, of course, or of Xand. I can't avoid the dreadful recognition, either, that it will be almost impossible for Ksenia to bring herself to the point of abandoning him, no matter how utterly he deserves it. It does nothing to help the dead, or ease the grief of their families. But it strikes me as being a proposal that Josh will find hard to ignore. Even now, after all that's happened, his love for her remains his justification for everything.

And maybe, just maybe, I can persuade Ksenia to put herself first for once in her life. To honor her own potential, her own future, and leave Josh to the fate he's made for himself.

Josh gapes. He wavers, perched high up on his misty horse, but his expression now reminds me of a frightened child.

"We both wanted to find a way to stay together, Lexi! That was the whole *point*. So we had this huge problem, and I'm the one who solved it. I honestly don't see why you think you get to criticize that."

"Because consent doesn't count if you don't know what you're agreeing to," I say. It's only an intuition, of course, but I'm nearly certain that Ksenia didn't grasp what Josh was up to. She must have gone through the process the false Xand described, and it's easy to imagine how she could have been coaxed into saying something that would count as *pledging* herself. She must have eaten their food, but did she understand what doing that would mean? It's not as if Josh warned *me*, when he tried to trap me there. "And it doesn't count if you have no way to change your mind. If you really love her, Josh, why don't you give her a chance to do that?"

The glass mutes her voice, but still, faintly, horribly, I can hear my mother shouting inside her car. I press my hands on the pane, so she'll feel that I'm with her.

But that's all I can do for the moment, because something in Josh is weakening under the impact of my words. His enchanted numbness wavers visibly, splits, like rents spreading through a veil. And behind it I see such grief that, in spite of myself, I nearly reach out a hand to him. "Josh . . ." I say.

And then it's over. A distant coldness seizes his face again, with such brutal abruptness that I can hardly accept he's still the same person. He glances down, bending over to scowl at my mother's frantic face, and tugs on the glittering reins; I hadn't taken them in before, bright ropes of crystalline tears with nothing supporting them. The horse taps the car's roof sharply, and my mother slumps against the glass, eyelids fluttering shut. But her chest still rises and falls; Josh really has enough power now to bring on a magical sleep?

As long as it's temporary, it's better for her than helpless terror.

"You just want Kezzer for yourself," Josh snarls. "You think I don't know that? You'll trick her into thinking she's in love with you, and then you'll move on to your fabulous life without her, and she'll be completely destroyed!"

I can't even react at first. Where on earth did he get this idea? Or—does he have an actual reason for suspecting that Ksenia might have feelings for me? It's a startling thought, though I can't rule it out—not when I remember the soft fervor I felt in her kiss on my cheek.

But if Ksenia's sexuality has always seemed more than a shade ambiguous, mine is supposed to be simple, straightforward. I'm supposed to like boys. It's only now, hearing Josh's accusation, that I realize Ksenia Adderley's existence might represent a complication for me. The truth is, her poised androgyny has always struck me as a very beautiful and compelling way of being.

But it's hardly the moment to wonder about this. "I want Ksenia to choose the direction of her own life, whatever that is. I want her to have—the full range of possibilities. And if you *don't* want those possibilities for her, I'd say your love isn't worth much."

Another rip in the veil. They've murdered his empathy for everyone else, it seems, but where Ksenia is concerned he still has a residue of conscience. On some repressed level, he knows perfectly well what he's done to her.

Something in what I'm saying hits home.

"Alexandra is without understanding you, dear Joshua." That grating voice, like a rusty chain dragged across a church bell; it comes from a spot to my right, but higher up. "Nothing of great matter to her, has she ever lost. Even her Alexander dies on the tipsy of a fingernail, and does she weep? So how can she feel for one like you, who loves to the core of your being?"

Unselle. I don't see her, but I can tell from the piercing turn of Josh's gaze that he does. She doesn't have to be visible. Bile still rises in my mouth as her image wafts into my mind: a cloud-white girl with cheekbones like broken ice, with lips like spilled blood, and with a snarling, snapping beast in place of her heart.

"Lexi and I were so *close*," Josh complains in her direction. "Like, maybe I shouldn't care so much, but it still eats me up that she just doesn't get it. How can I get her to understand that what she's asking me to do—that it's way too horrible?"

"If you wish Alexandra to understand, then she must lose as you have lost." A single, delicate hand appears in midair, high enough that I know Unselle must still be on horseback. From her fanned-out white fingers to the frill of her cuff I can see her, but the rest of her is still invisible. Those long fingers squeeze shut all at once, with a wringing motion as if she were snapping a bird's neck. "I grant you the power, Joshua. You are still enough human that I can slip the magic through you, to do what I cannot. Make it so."

I don't understand what the gesture means, but Josh clearly does, because his eyes go wide. He looks down at my mother's car, and back to Unselle.

She must lose as you have lost. Understanding comes as if I'd inhaled fire.

Josh's parents were crushed to death inside their car.

a vast and hollow darkness

Awkwardly, like he isn't fully aware of what he's doing, Josh slides off his cloud-horse and thumps onto the car's roof. His gaze keeps flitting around, from Unselle, to the car, to me—though whenever it brushes in my direction, he looks away in a hurry. I can hardly breathe; disbelief and dread suffuse the atmosphere like poisonous gases. I don't dare to speak, not at first, because when I don't know who Josh is anymore, or how deeply they've corrupted his heart, how can I guess what will set him off? Any words I say might be fatally wrong.

Incredible as it seems, I can't afford to doubt Unselle's assertion. She can grant Josh the power to compress metal and glass, with no more than a curl of his fingers in the air. He can squeeze the car like a rag, without even touching it, and he can crush my mother's life inside it.

I missed the instant when Unselle slipped fully into visibility, but I see her now. She sits astride her horse, and her dress and face recall a childhood memory I'd nearly forgotten: an explosion of white feathers and blood in the snow, where a hawk had ripped a dove to shreds. She smiles at Josh encouragingly.

"We did not *wish* so much suffering to her, Joshua," Unselle croons. "We thought the dying of her Alexander might be enough to undo her will, once and for all. But it was not, because she refuses to believe in her guilt. Her eyes must make her accept what she has wrought. Do this, and Alexandra will be no more worry to us. You must make her weep until the tears drain all her essence, so that she does not dare to fight again."

The animal head on her chest yawns and licks its snout with a pink, pointed tongue—I hadn't recognized its species before, but now, irrelevantly, it comes to me: it's a mink. Josh stands on the car, looking lost and hugging himself. Unselle inclines her long neck and waits for him to answer, but he doesn't.

"Josh," I finally say. Then I pause again, my blood throbbing so that I can barely hear my own thoughts. If I make a mistake, if I choose the wrong words now, my mother will die in front of me. "It's not just me and my family you'll destroy, if you do this. You'll also destroy yourself. You'll kill everything inside you that Ksenia has ever loved."

Words are my power; I've made him really *look* at me again, wet-eyed and gasping.

Unselle snorts dismissively. "Alexandra knows nothing of feeling herself. But oh, Joshua, she will play at *your* heart, as if it were hers to strum. Who is she to speak of what your Ksenia loves?" She raises her hand and wrings out the air again. "*Now*, Joshua. It must be done, or we are never to have peace again."

"I . . ." Josh says. "Lexi, I didn't want any of this." He lifts his right hand, plump and pale and dimpled, and gawks at it as if it has nothing to do with him.

"What you *wanted* doesn't matter," I tell him. My voice comes out with a softness, a stillness, that holds back the tumult inside me. "All that counts is what you choose to do, here and now."

"Listen to Alexandra, and she will gain you nothing but sorrow. Listen to me, dearest Joshua, and become truly one of us; then you will live forever, on the brightest dreams that can be wrung from their sad lives."

Josh stares at me, openmouthed and helpless, and his fingertips curl in just a few degrees. Instantly a metallic crunch shreds the air, and huge dents appear in the sides of my mother's car; my God, dents in the shapes of enormous fingerprints.

I spring forward without meaning to; my mother's head rocks against the window as it shifts position, but other than that she doesn't stir. A few cracks streak through the glass, thin sketches made of light. But there's only one thing that matters: those dents aren't yet deep enough to have hurt my mother seriously. And Josh stops, his eyes starry with shock, as if he can hardly believe himself what he's just done.

A tiny, fractured face peers at me from the backseat. Kay is in there. Can't she do anything to help?

"Why so laggard, Joshua? Is it that you are lazy? Is it that you are too weak of spirit to be one of our company? Do you care nothing who slips into your chest and robs you of your heart? Do it!"

Josh isn't looking at her, though. My gaze and his are locked, and all of our old friendship, all our moments of closeness, pass between us: a transfusion of light and longing. His hand floats on the air, the very ends of his fingers still bent slightly inward, but unmoving. *Josh,* I want to say, *it's my mother in that car, but it's also your humanity. It's everything of worth in you, and it's Ksenia's love for you. If my mother dies, all that love and worth will die with her. Be the person Ksenia believes you are.*

But I don't have to say it. Joshua still *receives* me, and the flow of my emotions enters into him. I can see it happening; the fog of enchantment tears from his face and leaves him exposed, and raw, and more human than he's been in a long time.

Unselle must see it too. I can hear her mink growling.

Josh's hand goes slack. It drops to his side like a falling tear.

"Unselle, I can't." It's barely a whisper. "Even if Lexi is my enemy, now. I can't do that to her. I—it was easier to think about *revenge* when I wasn't looking right at her."

"And yet you belong to us, Joshua." Unselle's voice is even quieter than his was. "Would you live always as the plaything of those you have betrayed? Do what you must, this instant, and I will let your weakness pass into forgetting."

"No." It's more a creak, the protest of an old hinge, than it is a human voice, but I nearly weep from the beauty of it. It's the painful sound of consciousness opening inside him. "No. I'm not going to be—the person who *did* that. Lexi is right. Kezzer would hate me."

I suspect that's part of what they wanted: they'd gladly grant Josh an eternity with Ksenia, but one consumed by her hatred and despair. He'd live forever, suspended in a cloud of Ksenia's destruction, in a suffering that she could never quiet. And Prince, and Unselle, and the rest of them? They'd savor every moment of it.

Unselle's horse rears and Josh jumps down off the car, almost falling, in a very human way, when he hits the lawn. And in his face, I see my old friend: wounded to the quick, but with a genuine warmth and even innocence again.

"Lexi?" He hesitates, as if he's stunned by coming back to self-awareness. "I think I might have done something terrible."

Quite a few terrible things, if we're going to be clear about it, but there will be time for that later. I never should have given up on him; I never should have let these monsters make me despair of someone I loved. To give them *anything* of mine is to give far too much.

"You have. But it's not too late to fix that, Josh."

Except for Xand, except for the other dead. *Save as much of yourself as you can, Josh, even if you can't save everything.*

"Am I . . . like, a huge asshole, if I ask you to forgive me?"

"You're less of an asshole for asking than you would be if you *didn't* ask. But Josh, you're going to have to do more than that."

"Right," Josh says. Still glazed, still baffled, but trying. "You tell me, Lexi. I'll trust you?" Then he glances at Unselle, rigid on her cloud-horse, the mink head spitting on her chest. "But I mean, they'll kill me."

He throws out the last line like it's an afterthought.

"Far worse than that, Joshua," Unselle hisses at him. "Far, far worse. You will not die, but we will slowly render you, still living, into the substance of our world. Such pain it will be, shattered and remade and forever silent." She reaches out, her arms extending impossibly, and curls her hand around the back of his neck. Her nails spurt longer, piercing his flesh, and Josh gasps with the pain. Bright beads of blood roll down his skin. "And as you are ours, I will take you now, to live in all that proceeds from your failing us."

"You can't have him," I tell her. "You can't have any of us." That's what I didn't grasp before: our refusal has to be absolute, and even Josh's slide into complicity isn't enough to change that. "Nothing *human* will ever belong to you."

She smiles at me, her face not human at all now; it's something like a fissured iceberg, with blood running through the cracks. "Ah, Alexandra. Behold what you cannot save."

Effortlessly she heaves Josh into the air, with nothing but her talons piercing his neck; she's going to sling him across her horse, and then it truly might be too late. Bizarrely, a bright azure dragonfly, with elongated wings, chooses this moment to circle in and perch briefly on the fingers clutching Josh.

But I'm holding a weapon: *a gun that shoots changes instead of bullets*. Change, any change, seems like an improvement over watching the destruction of my friend. Can I trust myself to use the hat properly? The black felt seems to hum in my hands, quivering in me with deep waves of warmth. I'm careful not to glance at it, or I'll give my intentions away to Unselle.

"Lexi, will you remember that I was so, so sorry, even though I screwed up? Will you tell Kezzer? I know I did everything wrong, and now I'll never get a chance to make up for it." The tears on Josh's cheeks look unnaturally radiant, beaming like dissolved stars. He's trying to be brave, but I can see he's on the verge of breaking down completely. "What if they hurt Kezzer too?"

And I step toward him, the bowler hat still in my right hand, as if I meant to embrace him. He's kicking in midair and the neckline of his sweater is sticky and wine-dark with blood. I don't know if I can save him, but I have to try; to do nothing is to abandon Josh to endless suffering.

And it's to let them win. Unselle is heaving him higher up and I have only a sliver of time to act.

I stretch as high as I can, the black hat like a negative moon against the bright sky, and at the meridian of my reach I flip it over, right onto the top of Josh's head. I can feel a quick *whuff* of suction, as if Ksenia's hat were eager to seize him. Josh lets out a startled shriek.

Unselle laughs hideously and retracts her claws, so that Josh crashes back onto the grass. And then I see that half of him is already missing, sucked into the black hole of that hat; he's vanished down to his waist, the bottom of his sequined sweater bulging out below the brim, his compressed wrists still twitching. His hands clutch rhythmically at the grass.

"And now, Alexandra, what is it you have happened to do? Have you done our labor for us? Have you given over Joshua, to be consumed by dreams?"

How could I have imagined that any good could come of a gift from one of them? But of course, of *course*—if they gave me a weapon, it was because they trusted that I would use it to hurt myself.

I drop down and grab hold of Josh by his legs. At first I think I'm trying to pull him back, but almost at once I feel how deep and how relentless the drag of that hat is, how it could swallow even light, how it feeds on our world to disgorge into another.

This isn't what I meant to do. It's not what I wanted to happen, or how I intended to travel to their *better world*. But I won't let Josh go alone, not now that he's finally himself again. Are we going through to that nowhere I've already seen, or to an even deeper and stranger realm than it is? Is this my last chance to reach Ksenia and the lost children?

All these thoughts flash past, so quickly I can hardly track them. They flicker like broken lightning on the brim of that hat, now sliding past my eyes: a vast and hollow darkness, prickling with unknown force.

Part Five

unselle

And ere a man hath power to say, "Behold!"
The jaws of darkness do devour it up.
So quick bright things come to confusion.

William Shakespeare,
A Midsummer Night's Dream

but still enduring

Ah, pretty Joshua. What a fool's choice it has made, who might have been petted and dandled, immortal and bright and ever-ravenous for all that feeds us. Our dream is a starveling one, always empty and unsatisfied, but how it waxes glimmer-hot on such sustenance as you are! Your every little weeping, your every fit of passion, hastens the steps of our dancing, raises thick and green our trees. And if you became one of us? Ah, then the boil of your exploding heart would fuel us through a hundred of your years, and the children you brought us for perhaps a hundred more. For one of them in turn might grow to be a knight of ours, and transform himself into the substance of our world.

But no. You, our Prince's favorite plaything, failed where you might have burst.

You failed us saying *Kezzer, Kezzer,* who was the first gift you gave to us, though you still thought, silly poppling, she was yours. Had you become one of us, oh how in the heat of changing your poor love would combust and go cold, ash flung upward from the fire!

And then, our Ksenia's sobbings, her gnashings, once she understood? More sustenance, more lightness and grace for our waltzes, more radiance for our speaking stars! We would gather around the house, and admire her grieving through the walls. We would applaud and send a rain of delicate birds to die against the windowpanes wherever she watched for you. And you, dearling Joshua, you would applaud with us. You would suckle down her bitterness like so much milk, then take her in your arms, and care nothing how she broke.

But *no*. Prince perhaps spoiled you, overfond and overkind lord that he is. You grew stubborn, wicked, a horror of ingratitude champing at your lips. A little curl of your fingers, a drizzle of blood to seep out, at my request? Such a small thing, dearling. Such a trinket, no more than a necklace of ruby to wind upon the ground. And you would not oblige me!

Kezzer would hate me. Why, yes. Such a pleasure it would be to taste that hate that I can hardly bear the loss of it. When she has been so obdurate in her love, how that love would blaze in its destruction!

Well, then. It is slower, it is less savory, in this way that you have chosen, Joshua. It offers less delight. But still you will be consumed, with your Alexandra beside you, though you will never see her. We will bury you both in light that will not touch your eyes. And soon enough, your Ksenia too, once she accepts my gift and uses it to go pursuing you. Now I stroke the black felt with my fingers, I whisper incantations down into its darkness, just as I did before I sent it to Alexandra. Ksenia must take it from my hand, tame and eager, and she *will* do so. As foolish as her friend, who accepted the same gift from us. Ksenia is already on her way to me, thinking she tricks us, thinking she escapes us.

Even Ksenia's thinking of it is naughty, naughty, no matter how untrue. We will tend her suffering with exquisite care, to punish her for such rebel thinkings as she has now, while chirping to her stairs.

Her scrap, her bit, her broken-offling, no wiser than its parent. It was there, watching you and Alexandra and the hat she popped onto you. It will mean to help Ksenia, oh, it will intend the sweetest it can! And so we will make it her undoing.

This way is slower. Your tears will flow as glaciers do. Our trees will sway in a breeze lethargic with your tedious grief, but sway they will. My mink will hang his tongue, ever so sleepy, yet now and then he will lick his lips. Slow and dull, but still enduring, for did we not promise you *forever* with your Ksenia? To you, dearling Joshua, your life will seem longer than death's own rule.

And then, we still have the children for our playing. But they grow numb, and only rarely weep.

Part Six

ksenia adderley

Dim vales—and shadowy floods—
And cloudy-looking woods,
Whose forms we can't discover
For the tears that drip all over:
Huge moons there wax and wane—
Again—again—again—
Every moment of the night—
Forever changing places—
And they put out the star-light
With the breath from their pale faces . . .
Its atomies, however,
Into a shower dissever,
Of which those butterflies
Of Earth, who seek the skies,
And so come down again
(Never-contented things!)
Have brought a specimen
Upon their quivering wings.

Edgar Allan Poe, "Fairy-Land"

that makes two of us

I've thought about it a lot, how we wound up here. It's not like I've had a ton else to do, brooding around in time so shapeless that even the concept of a day seems like a sick joke. It's gotten to be a habit, obsessing over the exact blue of the air that caught us that night. Over how Josh's eyes blurred when he called me *Keyshaun*. It was all I could think about until Lexi showed up here, and her presence hit me like a wind that said, *Come back to life. Come back.*

It changed everything, Lexi's visit. She triggered a lurching shift in perspective, and the realization that I still have something to fight for.

And when Prince sent Josh after her? That changed everything again.

Now I've got to turn my concentration to just one thing: how the hell to get *out* of here, before Josh does something so destructive that I can't stand to look in his face again. Before he loses his humanity, once and for all, and becomes just another of our—whatever they are—our glittering, empty, foully seductive *hosts*. Whether I can stop him, I don't know. I don't know if he's beyond the point where he'll listen to anything I say. But I definitely can't stop him while I'm stuck here.

None of them prevented me from staggering back to the house, my tuxedo shirt mashed in a bloody ball against the wound in my hip, the scraps of my chopped-up jacket wagging with each step. Nothing I've done so far has changed a damn thing, so why would they worry now? I step inside and flip on the lights. It's all creepy enough here without hanging around in the dark, thanks. Go sit cross-legged at the bottom of those stairs, ass on the tile floor. Stare up into that corrosive darkness. Dried blood clogs the gash Josh's knife left in the wood, and my matching gash burns at the sight of it. I reach out and touch the step, like I can comfort it. The stairs are practically all I have left, now that Josh is gone.

Maybe Josh is out happily destroying our old world, but it's not like I'm alone in this place. There are the stairs, which are aware of me even if they don't like me much, and there's someone else too. The air has that elastic feeling it gets when someone is listening, like they're tugging on the other end of the silence and stretching it. I know what's lurking at the top of the steps, in those rooms where I can't go.

"Hey," I call up. "So, Prince tells me you're my personal changeling? Is that enough of a connection to get you to talk to me?"

Prince said some interesting things, actually. Stuff about how that other Ksenia got here, for a start. But I don't expect her to respond.

"Why don't you talk to *me*?"

I jump at the sound of that voice, because it's exactly like an echo of my own, emerging from the blackness up there. I knew that would be the case in theory, but hearing it is something else.

Then I get myself together. "Sure. So, tonight, Prince told us that you came through my grave? But you ended up here. That means there must be—some kind of door—from the upstairs rooms. Back to the real world, I mean."

What is a grave, if not a doorway? And doors cut both ways, as a rule. It stands to reason, though it isn't much help if I can't get up there.

The other Ksenia, the *changeling*, since allegedly I'm the one who's a real person, she doesn't answer. Sullen pain in the ass that she is.

"So it would be helpful if you had some tips on how to get to it. You know, before everything goes to complete shit? Who else is going to warn everyone?"

Silence. Then, resentfully: "I don't even know who you are."

Oh, doesn't she? All at once I hate her, the way you might hate a piece of broken glass in your throat—though I guess this is an improvement on all the people in my life who've been so sure they knew all about who I am, when really they've had no clue.

"I'm Ksenia Adderley."

"Oh, you are *not*."

"Yeah? Because you think *you're* the real Ksenia? I hear they hacked out your guts and left you as empty as an eggshell." Then, experimentally, I try the same thing I've done a million times already. I stand up and step onto the lowest stair.

The way the stair drops me feels almost sarcastic. A dismissive flick, like we both know how stupid it was to bother. It doesn't make me feel like being any nicer.

"Newsflash. That shit kills humans. There's really not a lot of wiggle room."

Silence again. And I can tell—though how can I tell?—that this time I've hit a nerve.

"Why do you think these stairs stayed put for Lexi, anyway?" I ask. Not that the changeling's going to tell me anything. I'm getting the impression that those things might not have a lot of brainpower; she seems as dumb as a plank. "Actually, I've been thinking about it. What Lexi was saying, when she started going up. It was a lot of heavy emotional stuff. All about how much I suck, though you know Lexi would never put it like that. She'd find a way to make it sound *gracious*."

I've given up on getting anything useful out of the spare Ksenia in the attic. So it comes as a surprise when she gives a plaintive cry. "Lexi? You mean Alexandra. She was the one who *held* me. I didn't want to die, but she *held* me."

"You call that dying? You did a crappy job of it."

"I *did* die, though. It just didn't last. But they took my heart, and now I'll never find it again."

I can't let myself get distracted. "Lexi said I should try giving the stairs a different name. Not Ksenia. Do you know what she had in mind?"

Because I might know. I've suspected what Lexi meant from the second she said it. But if my changeling would just contradict what I'm thinking, I'd be ready to like her better.

A pause. "I'll know it when I hear it."

Okay. I've never wanted to do this, but Josh is out there. If he hurts Lexi's family, or even if he *lets* anything bad happen to them, how am I supposed to forgive that? And he won't be able to forgive himself, either. Not if he ever gets his mind back. Getting up those stairs is my only option.

Even before I open my mouth, just the thought of that name slams me with a freezing blast of panic. My breath turns to solid ice, blocking my lungs. Then I concentrate, and exhale, and the name comes with it.

"It's me," I tell the stairs. "Sennie."

I lift my foot. The staircase looks exactly the same, way too boring for how tricky and perverse it is. But now it *feels* different. Still skeptical, maybe, but like it's open to at least having a conversation.

And then I'm standing on the bottom step, and it's holding me.

Maybe I've screwed up everything else in my life, but I really can't blow this. I have to reach the top if it kills me.

"It wasn't fair to Lexi, what I said before. When she started going up, she was just being really honest with me, and I was being honest back. Is that what you want me to say?"

I can hear the changeling shuffling around, now. Feet scraping nervously at the wood floor. Then: "Sennie? It's you? I'm supposed to hate you."

"That makes two of us," I tell her, and laugh. Pretty nastily. "Like, I can stand being *Kezzer,* most of the time anyway. *Sennie,* though—I feel sick saying that name at all. I almost hit Lexi once, just for calling me that. Do you know why?"

I climb onto the next step, convinced it's going to throw me. It doesn't.

God—I think I get it. I think the stairs want to hear the rest of the story. They want me to cough up all the miserable details, even if I choke.

There's a new silence, a new mix of air and expectation. But I go up one more step without getting slammed back down. It's something.

"It's because both of them called me that. I mean my mom, and the guy I thought was my dad. And then when he found out he *wasn't*, he kept repeating it. *Don't cry, Sennie. You'll always be my little duckling, Sennie.* Of course, that was the last I ever heard from him."

It's getting darker. Lexi made it farther than I am now, and I'm wondering how she didn't freak out. Already it feels like the black air is eating all the light right out of my eyes, and I'll never see again. I find myself clutching the handrail so viciously it feels like I could splinter it. The stairs can go on acting like they're ordinary, nothing but plain wood, but I know what they really are. I can feel them thinking under my feet, feel them considering me critically. It's enough to send vertigo jolting up my legs. Maybe the stairs are just messing with me, letting me get this far, and when I'm almost to the top they'll rear like a snake and bash my brains out.

The one I'm standing on twitches and a shriek leaps out of my throat. But once I've caught my breath, I'm still a third of the way up.

Right. That twitch was just a warning. I've got to keep giving them what they want. *Feeding* them. That's their price.

"So, what my mom said, when I asked her why she'd lied? She said, 'Aw, Sennie. Don't be sore. I just figured he was the best one who might believe it.' And maybe he was, but he wasn't fucking good *enough*."

She hasn't said anything for a while, my changeling. But I can hear her more clearly now. She's making this ghastly, hollow wheezing sound. "So . . ." she whispers, and then hesitates. "So, why would that make you hate Sennie?"

I can hear her unspoken objection. *Sennie* wasn't the one who lied. She was just a kid, her life knocked sideways again and again by all the screwed-up games the adults kept playing with each other. It's the kind of thing Lexi would say, and for a moment I'm at a loss how to explain. When you've been living with the same hatred all your life, it seems so obvious that it's not even worth thinking about.

"Because," I say, and then I have to stop. The damned stairs, my changeling: am I really going to let them squeeze everything out of me? I'd rather rage, smash all the windows, set the whole house on fire, than say the words that come next. But then I do, because I have to. "Because Sennie was the one who got left."

I get another stair out of it. It's not going to do me much good if I collapse on my face and scream. All the blood drops out of my head and I don't think I'd be able to see anything, even if I wasn't standing in absolute darkness.

They're all waiting for me to go on, the stairs and the freakish other Ksenia, but suddenly I don't care anymore what they want, because the story's taking over. The words lunge up on their own.

"Sennie got left, because that was all she was good for: being lied to over and over, then ditched for being a fake daughter. Once it finally sunk in that my dad was never coming back, I started pulling this catatonic act every time someone called me that. I'd curl up in a ball and rock and refuse to move or say *anything*. It worked eventually. My mom hated the name *Ksenia*, though. Too fancy and too weird, for people like us. She hated every single time she had to say it. Letting my fake dad name me after his mother was just another part of her scam, but then she was stuck with it."

I'm at least halfway up, still clinging to the handrail. It feels like the gravity up here is unstable, malicious, tugging me from different angles. Maybe it's the gravity of my old world, reaching for me through the cracks. Any minute now I'll probably puke. And my face is wet with tears, slick and cold, but not cold enough to stop my skin from burning.

"Josh said Ksenia means *stranger,* though. If that's true, it makes it the perfect name for me. What the hell else have I ever been? Even with my mom, I felt like she must have picked me out of a gutter somewhere. Except that she never would have bothered. She never seemed like she wanted me, and honestly I'm not sure I wanted her, either."

Silence, and silence, and silence. Except I can hear all the words in it, coiled and waiting to spring.

Then she comes out with it, her little wheedling voice creeping out of the darkness. "But you loved your dad. The man you *thought* was your dad. You thought he was the most perfect person in the world."

I can feel the stairs waiting for my answer. One wrong syllable, and they'll throw me so hard my body will shatter the walls. I'll be lucky if I can crawl away from the wreckage. And then I'll never reach Josh, and I'll never stop all the evil he's about to inflict on people who have no idea what's coming.

But for way too long, I just can't say it. I must be near the top now, but I can't see a thing.

My legs halt, along with my voice. Because I know the stairs won't let me go any farther, not until they've ripped all the truth out of me, just like my changeling's organs got ripped out of her. Who was I calling *empty?*

I saw that fake Marissa, down in the pool. Even if I don't know exactly what they're going to do with her, I can guess that it won't be anything good. And Lexi—she wasn't here long. She didn't really say that much. But it was enough to make me feel like I had a shot at being a person again—or maybe not *again*. Maybe for the first time ever.

For that, I'll fight anyone who tries to mess with her. Even Josh.

"I loved him," I say, and then something gives way. At first I don't know what, though: the stairs, or my legs, or what's left of my heart. All I know is that I'm tumbling forward.

My hands smack down on ashy, unvarnished wood. My knees. It's too wide to be a step. And after a breathless moment, I know what it means.

I've made it to the top, but that doesn't mean I've made it far enough.

they stole me from myself

For a while I can't make myself move. The darkness is so profound that it turns every sound, every movement, into another spike of unreality. I hear my changeling still wheezing somewhere, her breath whistling like wind through a cracked window. I only really know I'm still here from the nagging tick of my heartbeat, the dull, deep burning in my hip.

But kneeling on the landing won't do anything to help Lexi. I force myself up, still half-convinced I might plummet at any moment. Maybe keep falling forever. I lean on the wall, for reassurance more than anything.

And feel something poking into my arm. A switch. "You know, you could have just turned on the light?" I snap. "You've been up here in the dark for how long?"

It's easy to tell her that, but it's harder to flip the switch myself. I have a feeling I might not want to see what's up here, in the forbidden second story. As badly as I've wanted to get up to this floor, still, now I don't want to know. So maybe I'm not rocking the rationality—but it's always easier to want things before they're in your face. I saw all those broken-mirror Ksenias go writhing out of my hat, jumble and stack themselves and build these rooms. Whatever is up here is made out of me, out of who I am. And that's always been high on the list of shit I prefer not to know about.

Then I do it. Ordinary-looking lamplight floods a less-than-ordinary room.

It's long. Sloping ceiling with exposed beams that cradle saggy pink-fuzz insulation, those two windows with the garish red-checked curtains. Gray wood floor, scabby in places with ancient paint. All of that seems fair enough, like a decent effort at normality.

Less normal is the row of pint-sized beds made of pea-green metal; they're like you might see in some movie set in a Victorian orphanage, but smaller. Maybe a yard long at most. They might be about the right size for the shattered Ksenia-imps, assuming those things ever sleep.

Still more unsettling is the avalanche of dirt that spills at an angle from the far wall, half-engulfs a few of the beds, and scatters crumb across the floor. It's been there long enough to sprout a few gaunt weeds.

But as I look around I fail to see anything that could pass for a doorway. Was coming up here a total waste? If it was, then how will I ever get over letting Lexi down?

Someone is sitting on the bed nearest to me, doubled over between her spread knees so that her spiky blond hair bristles in my direction. Her legs are awkwardly long for the low bed, jutting up like mountain crags. The fact that I'm standing ten feet from her isn't enough to make her look my way. She's wearing a bland, stiff, navy-blue dress printed with these horrible little flowers, definitely nothing I ever owned, and after a second I realize: Mitch and Emma went out and bought it at some bargain basement, just so they could *bury* me in it. So that my death would at least have the advantage of making me look respectable. I guess they decided they should get what mileage they could out of it.

It's harder to keep hating the other Ksenia now that I see her, but I wish she wouldn't act so pathetic. "Would you sit *up*, already?"

She does. Her hideous dress is unbuttoned to the waist, and as she straightens the ragged red suture bisecting her torso streaks into view. A second crosscut below the clavicle, so the stitches form a capital *T*. Even now that her body's unfolded she keeps her head bent, staring down at it.

"Sennie? I don't know what they did with my heart."

"Realistically? They probably burned all your organs to a crisp.

Medical waste and everything. I don't think they're super precious about the crap they yank out in an autopsy." It would be good to settle this issue. I feel sorry for her, but that doesn't mean I want to listen to her mooning on and on about her lost entrails.

That makes her look up at me. A perfect copy of my gray eyes, sharp cheekbones, pale skin. Fine. But that wide-eyed, helpless, wounded look is not something I ever would have allowed to go crawling onto my face. Is it? "Burned it? Then I can't get it back? Sennie? Can't you make them give it back?"

I wish she'd stop calling me that, but if I say so I'll probably find myself dropping through a brand-new hole in the floor. It's not just those stairs that are made from the Ksenia-imps, it's this whole upper level, and *Sennie* is the only version of me they'll tolerate here.

"I can't get your heart back, no." I stare at her. "It's not like you were using it anyway. Did it even beat? Prince made it sound like he just slapped it in you for decoration."

Prince. He must know I've made it upstairs. They always seem to know everything we do and say, like they can spy on us straight through the walls. The eye in my hat was the least of it. So why didn't they stop me?

The changeling breaks out whimpering. God—that whistling sound I heard before is coming through the gaps between her stitches. Of course, they hacked her lungs out too, so there's nothing inside her to hold in the air when she tries to breathe.

"But—I liked it! I knew I wasn't whole-me, but I could *pretend* better with a heart! And it did beat, Sennie, it did! Just in case anybody listened!" Her mouth crumples piteously. "It did at *first*."

I wouldn't call it a nice thought, but it occurs to me that I should stuff a cheap watch or a can of Spam or something in there. Just to shut her up. And then a sharp recoil of pity hits me. She can't help what she is, not any more than I can. Prince made her and used her for his creepy schemes, and then he ditched her like so much trash.

I consider bullshitting, of course; it's the strategic thing to do.

Tell me how to get back to the real world, and I'll get right to work on tracking down your heart. But the cruelty of it gives me pause, and so does the thought of where I am. Those Ksenia-imps have made it clear enough that they put a premium on the truth. I doubt they'd let me get away with an outright lie.

But going by what she's said, there's another angle I can use. "You said Lexi held you. Lexi was kind to you, and nobody else was. Right?"

So she didn't put it quite that dramatically, but I guess the exaggeration is passable because I don't go plunging into some spontaneous abyss.

"Lexi held me in her arms. I knew dying was my whole job, but I was still so scared! And Lexi kept begging me *not* to die. I couldn't tell her how angry Prince would be if I didn't."

"That's what Lexi is like. Other people maybe talk a lot of crap about doing the right thing, but Lexi just does it. She doesn't even know she's being brave, or kind, because to her those are the obvious things to be." I let that sink in. "But now I'm the one who has to help *her.* You know what a vindictive scumbag Prince is, right? He's going after Lexi, back in our old world, and there's no way I can do anything about it unless I can get there."

It's all true enough, but there's still something cold, flat, and numb in my voice—even though cold is the last thing I feel. The chill now is thin, a skin of ice over something inside me that's roiling. My changeling just sits there looking at me, with her long neck sloping over and her fingers absently running up and down the gash in her chest. I get the distinct sense that she doesn't trust a word I'm saying.

"You're just worried about Josh," she finally observes, snidely. "And Josh wanted me to drop dead too. Even though I loved him so much! So why would I tell you anything, Sennie?"

Because if you don't, we'll see how many times you can die. Saying that probably won't help, though.

"Of course I'm worried about Josh. Prince and them are

chewing up everything that matters in him, and he doesn't even know it. He doesn't stand a chance in hell of defending himself! And now they're using him to hurt people, so he'll be wrecked once and for all. They said it themselves. They're going to rip his humanity out of him." I pause. That didn't sound cold. It sounded like the fire is finally taking over. "I can care about Lexi too. You've always just been a thing, a shell, so you don't get it. But I felt like— like they'd made me into what *you* are. I felt like they'd stolen everything real inside me, when they trapped me here. They stole me from myself. And Lexi—I don't even know *how* she did it, but she gave me back—who I really am. I even thought *I* might be the changeling then. That the real Ksenia was dead. But Lexi made me feel like maybe I could choose reality anyway. I'd do anything for her."

It's one of those things you don't know is true until you've said it.

She looks at me, lamplight skewered on her spiky hair. There's something in her gray gaze that makes it seem to take forever, crossing the air between us, as if her thoughts were enough to slow light to a crawl.

"Who did?" The snap of her voice makes me jump.

"Did what?"

"Stole everything inside you."

Right. I just said *they*. I have my reasons for preferring not to be too specific.

"Prince and all his sadistic creeps."

The floor cracks at my feet, with a sound like a machine gun. For a moment I grab at nothing, expecting to crash all the way to nowhere. It wasn't the whole truth, and I should have known—I *did* know—that it wouldn't fly.

But then the crack stops, its edge toothed in long splinters. Just another warning, then. Still, it's clear enough that I have to say it.

"And Josh too. But he didn't mean it."

They let me get away with including the excuse, at least. But the jagged blonde in the flowery dress just sits there, gawping and stroking her stitched-up wound, not telling me anything I need to know. I'm ready to start screaming: *What the hell do you want from me? Are you going to keep dragging this out, until Lexi and her family are dead?*

But then I see that she's pointing. Straight at that pile of dirt.

"You mean, the doorway's under that heap?" I look it over: dense, heavy, with a smell like turned clay. I don't have time to excavate the whole thing. "Are you going to help me dig?"

"Not *under* it." God—if I really look at people the way she's looking at me, then it's no wonder I make everyone uncomfortable. "That *is* it. Sennie, see? That's the bottom of your grave."

they didn't make everything

The bottom of my grave. I wasn't prepared for the doorway to show up in such a messy form. So I'll start burrowing, and find myself in my own coffin, considerately vacated by my changeling here. And then—what? I'll be buried alive with no way to escape, no chance to fight through the crushing pressure of the earth above me? Maybe all I'm doing is setting myself up for an especially gruesome suicide.

My changeling just keeps pointing. Triangles of light perch on her sharp cheekbones, her spiky hair casts needles of shadow across her forehead. "Sennie? They made me. Prince made me, just so I could die in place of you, and dying was the only reason I mattered. And I wanted Josh to protect me, but he didn't care; he wanted me to die for you too. Even though I loved him! I *had* to hate you for that."

I hate you too, I almost say. Except that's not true anymore. It would be hard to put a name on what I feel for her, exactly. It's some queasy hash of pity and aversion and—ugh—recognition. "I don't blame you for being pissed," I tell her. "You got screwed over pretty hard."

She shrugs that off. "But you need to remember: they didn't make *everything*. Not everything that looks like you."

I hadn't thought about it quite this way. I've been duplicated in such bizarre ways since I came here, and I hadn't really bothered to distinguish between them. But I know right away what she means.

"You're talking about those imp things. This whole second story." She doesn't even nod to confirm my guess, but it's more than a guess. I can feel it. "*I'm* the one who made those."

She's still pointing at the dirt, her pale, bony arm stretched as far as it can go. "You didn't send me to die, though, Sennie. That wasn't you. But I don't know what they'll do to me, for helping you come back to life."

That hadn't hit me either, until she says it. She's betraying the entities that created her—unless it's all another lie, designed to trick me into burying myself alive.

Though there's no point in wondering. It doesn't change what I'm going to do.

"So I just shove my face in there and start digging?"

She nods. "You just go through."

I cross the room, heading deeper into the dank, somber stench of that dirt. It's wet when I touch it, as muddy and inescapable as dreams. I'll be lucky if I make it as far as my coffin before I suffocate. If it weren't for everything that might be happening on the far side of that heap—Josh riding around in a trance, Josh maybe murdering the people he ought to defend with his life—I'd stay right where I am, thanks. Roots jut through here and there like malformed bones, and the ends of worms probe at the air. A gray-white larval *something* drops, wriggling at my feet.

But for all I know, Josh might be about to murder Lexi, or Marissa, while Unselle eggs him on. Compared to that, what else matters?

I reach forward with both hands, ready to plunge in up to my elbows, to push and slam my way into the muck. My changeling is behind me, now, and I can *feel* that she's turned to watch. I can feel her gaze like claws hooked into my shoulders.

She's right, though. However much a thing like she is can suffer, Prince will make sure she goes right to the limit for this.

I twist around. Maybe it's got something to do with how she was copied from me, but I swear I can feel the way our stares meet and tangle in midair, gray and slippery and full of longing.

"Hey," I tell her. "Thank you."

And then I turn back to the dirt, and push in. There's not a lot of resistance. I feel a bubbling, an oozing, more liquid than solid. I was expecting to claw away at the muck for hours, but almost instantly I'm stuck in it up to my shoulders. My knees buckle, dragged against the slope, and my feet skid out from under me. Sludge shoves at my throat and I rear back instinctively, trying to keep my mouth and nose clear of it.

That won't be happening. I'm being engulfed in some kind of freakish vertical quicksand. My muscles jerk with contradictory impulses, part of me still determined to dig deeper, the other part desperate to fight my way free. The combined result is panicked, pointless spasms. Chunks of mud fly loose as I thrash.

And then I'm inside the pile, my eyes clenched tight. I feel the cloying, gritty pressure of dirt grinding across my face, but I can't tell if I'm doing anything to propel myself forward.

It doesn't feel like I'm moving myself at all. More like the muck is swallowing me. I could be inside the Earth's own throat, constricted by its slow, wet hunger. It grips me hard around the ribs and all my air bursts out with a hiss. Now I'm struggling for real, but it's useless. I'm clammy with dirt and terror, my limbs flailing at random angles. Once my shin bangs against something that feels like planed wood. My lungs burn and my diaphragm jerks, ravenous for air. If I give in, though, I'll fill my lungs with this living filth.

And then, just like that, the earth spews me out. I rupture into air and gasp, and gasp again, crumbles of dirt dropping onto my tongue. My mud-slimed hands paw wildly to clear the muck from my encrusted eyes, my choked mouth. I'm not free all the way, only as far as my waist. Shivers dart at violent speed through my back and arms. Blood roars in my ears.

It takes a while before I'm together enough to risk opening my eyes again. I must have swum straight through my coffin— probably that was the plank I knocked against—and on to the surface, because I'm in the cemetery. I recognize it by the old Methodist church where Mitch and Emma used to go on Easter, with its scaly white paint. The light is yellow and streaky, but I have no way to guess if it's evening or an hour after dawn.

And right beside me, there's a very small, plain stone with my name on it, and dates that claim I died a few days short of my eighteenth birthday. About how I'm not so dead after all: I haven't thought about it much, because I probably don't care that much, but seeing me is going to come as a terrible shock to a lot of people.

Also, about not being dead: I need to get the hell out of this dirt, pronto, and go find Josh and Lexi.

The dirt was eager to shove me along before, but now it's behaving more like dirt usually does, grasping my legs in its chill grit. I'm fighting to loosen it enough that I can pull myself out, when I see something running toward me over the dew-speckled grass.

If running is the word for it. The thing coming at me is low on dimensions, so that at certain angles it's a barely perceptible black line, jarring up and down. Sometimes a third dimension pops out of it, though, and I see a recognizable hip, or a bony shoulder. Sometimes it turns enough that I get a glimpse of its cracked-plate face.

But parts of it are a little thicker, fluffing out in weird bulges, and as it gets closer I see why. It's wearing *clothes*. A puffy doll's dress that in this light is nothing but a yellow smudge.

I don't much like having one of those things come at me while I'm still trapped, and I thrash harder. But then it comes back to me, what my changeling said.

So Prince made her, a living object with a single, sad purpose. But he didn't make everything that's running around with my face on it. Meaning that some of them I have to take responsibility for myself.

Meaning that this little broken-mirror Ksenia-thing, with her grin now leaping out at a right angle to her paper cut of a head: she *belongs* to me. She's not Prince's creature, but mine.

Maybe I can trust her.

"Sennie!" she squeaks as she gets closer. "Oh, Sennie! You

thought of it, how to go! You understood! And you see, the stairs stayed for you! They waited, just for you to finally say your name!"

I plant my hands on the grass beside each hip and drive myself upward as hard as I can. Another twist, a fierce thrash, and I start to pull free. My feet peddle at the dislodged soil that drops in beneath me. I make it out as far as my mid-thighs.

I've talked to the stairs a lot, sure: hanging around in the dust-colored light, begging them to give me a break already. Addressing one of these things as an individual, though, feels a lot more uncomfortable. But now it seems like that's what I have to do. "Hey," I say. "What are you doing—in the real world? I thought you didn't belong here."

That *is* where I am now, right? Everything still feels a little off-kilter.

The Ksenia-shard is close enough now that it turns sideways, showing me her whole flat, fragmentary face. It looks kind of sheepish.

"Lexi climbed the stairs. Grabbed her leg then."

Ah. So that's where the dress is from, and the bandages on her knobby little knees. And more important, maybe this thing can take me to Lexi. Another writhing struggle, doubled over so that I can get enough leverage, and I finally pry my legs all the way out. I'm ready to run, hard, wherever she tells me to go.

"Where is Lexi now?"

"Sennie . . . they took her. And Joshua. Took them away!"

They.

The sad little thing is still prattling at me, but I can't follow what she's saying. There's only enough room in my head for the first words she fired off. *They took her.* Those words repeat, hissing like embers striking flesh, and every time I think them they burn.

I can't imagine much worse than going through that crushing earth again, but I'll do whatever it takes. I swore it. I turn and throw myself back on my grave, and even as I'm falling I see that the hole

I came through is gone. The grass is a scarless sheet of green. I smack down, and the ground hits my chest with a brutal, unyielding thud.

"Sennie!" the me-thing chitters. "Not that way! Used it up, that way!"

You don't say. "So what do I do?" The thought of those inhuman creeps prodding at Lexi, dragging her into their dances, kissing her cheeks—it's so nauseating that my muscles seize with rage.

And now the second half of what this thing said hits me. *And Joshua. Took them away!*

Which would seem to imply that he didn't go voluntarily. "Was Josh fighting back?" I ask. And the Ksenia-imp nods its sliver of a head, its single gray eye wide and solemn.

He finally did it. Josh found the strength to be himself again. If the situation weren't so desperate, I'd crack up weeping from sheer relief. *I knew you could, baby. I knew you were still in there!* But there's also the flip side to his defiance: if Prince has Josh, what monstrous things will he do to him, for daring to turn against his masters?

Josh reclaiming the freedom of his own mind: that would be Prince's idea of the gravest possible insult.

"Unselle has the hat," the Ksenia-imp says. I could slap her for picking this moment to blurt nonsense, but then she keeps going. "The hat ate them, Sennie. It ate them all the way through! Josh said no to killing Lexi's mother, and the hat ate him up! Lexi thought the hat would help, they tricked her with taking it, but when she saw what . . . she grabbed on." A pause. "And maybe now, what happens from eating?"

Digestion.

"*My* hat?" The idea opens up some peculiar questions, but there's no time for them. "It *ate them through*? You mean, through to that— other world?" Another nod. "Then could it eat me so I go there too?"

Hope spikes in me: it might be better this way, actually. The hat might take me straight to wherever Josh and Lexi are trapped. If I burrowed back through my grave, how would I track them down?

Another nod. "But Unselle has it! And she is evil, evil, bad."

"Then we'll fucking take it from her." Unselle, with her billowing lace and her bloody script and her metallic simpering. Unselle with the yawning, snapping mink where anyone human would have a heart. Out of all of them she's the one I'd be happiest to kill, except for maybe Prince, if only killing them was something I could figure out how to do. "So can you help me find her?"

Hesitation. "Don't know where. Unselle has a horse."

Right. I should have known that a creature sliced off from me wouldn't be much use. I look away, trying to stop myself from saying something mean. It's not actually her fault.

"Sennie? Lexi calls me Kay! She gave me my own, whole, very own name!"

"That's great," I snap. I'm not paying much attention, just scanning the tame suburban streets, the bloated spill of blue shadows. The sun is up far enough to launch sparks through the trees. Where in all this bland serenity would Unselle be? We're on a hill, so I can see the town rambling into the distance: the hot glitter of cars on Grand, the midnight groove of the gorge.

Even if it's on the dull side, our old town, it's real. It's made of car alarms and trees and vinyl siding, people and cats and sprinklers. Not sick, distorted dreams. I'm standing on real ground, even though it feels weirdly light, disconnected from my feet. Still, if only Josh and Lexi were with me, I might fall to my knees and soak the grass with my tears.

But I've got to go back. Of course I do. How can I deserve a real life if I don't save the people I love?

"Unselle can find you, though, Sennie. She has your blood in her. She can tell where you will go."

The gorge. The clearing where Josh and I first stumbled into them. That's where. Now that I've thought of it, it's obvious: how Unselle will come sidling through the trees on her cloud-horse, her mouth pitching like a boat in a storm, and curl a cold hand on my neck.

We have a date.

this ground i'm lying on

"Get up," I tell the imp-thing—right, Kay. "Hitch a ride, however you do that. I've got to run."

She vanishes, squeaking. I feel the eeriest rustling sensation against my leg, like a parasitic newspaper crawling on me. And then we're off, charging down the hill with spangles of morning sun dashed into my eyes. The green world heaves and tilts. Maybe I'm not acclimatized to reality anymore, because it's rougher going than it ought to be. I've always been a strong runner, but now I'm battered by waves of nausea. Dizzy with alternating light and shade as I race below the branches. My legs aren't pumping like they should.

God knows how they'll torture Josh. And Lexi—I'm picturing her captive, disoriented, maybe in some cage that's even viler because, to glance at it, you might think it was the everyday world.

But if Kay knows what she's talking about, it's even worse than that. *What happens from eating.* What is it, anyway, that powers Prince's realm?

How far is it to the gorge? More than two miles, I think, but even though I lived in this town for years I'm foggier than I should be on how to get there. It's connected somehow to how sick I'm getting. I have this horrible feeling that I'm not all the way here. That my feet aren't quite striking the ground.

Whatever. What I'm feeling is of zero importance. All that counts now is what I do.

The town is starting to look weirdly messed up. Lots of snapped branches, toppled poles, cars with their roofs staved in, as if a violent hurricane had passed in the night. But the sky is blue and golden, the breezes as soft and floppy as dog ears. Sirens wail in the distance, and I get a distinct sense that I'm looking at the trail of devastation left by a legion of changelings—with Josh in the lead. Is his army still here somewhere, now that he's gone? Or did they go home, once they had Lexi?

I'm still racing as fast as I can, but the dizziness is making me swerve as I go. Out of nowhere, a dry heave doubles my body. I keep running, contorted with cramps. The view of our town arches into my eyes and then ebbs into darkness, over and over again. What is *wrong* with me?

But I think I recognize the street on my right. I think it ends at the woody margin by the gorge, so if I can just keep going straight, if I can just not fall on my face before I get there . . .

I pass a street sign, and the name flares up, horribly bright, before it collapses into darkness again. Whistler Drive. It's not where I thought I was, not where I should be. All at once I'm not sure if I'm even heading in the right direction.

A face veers into mine, glaring like a headlamp. I see light brown curls and gray roots and a gaping mouth. Eyes so shocked they look like windows at the exact instant a rock ruptures their glass.

And yet I'm not thinking about who it is, not at first, because all at once I get it: I'm feeling like I'm not all the way here, not truly in this world, because I'm *not* here, not really. I ate their food. I did everything Josh asked me to do. Prince and them, they still have a hold on me.

The woman in my face screams wordlessly and swings a fist at me, sloppily. Misses, so I don't feel the need to punch her back.

Then she starts adding discernible comments to her shrieking. "You ghost! You ghost! You vicious, nasty little ghoul! You bring him back! Do you hear me? Bring back our Joshua! Oh, where did you hide his body?"

She grabs hold of my dirt-smeared vest and then lets go, maybe in astonishment at my solidity.

"Hi, Emma," I say. I was never under any illusions that my foster mother was all that crazy about me, but her reaction to seeing me alive still comes as a disappointment. Then her raving starts making a little more sense to me. Of course, it's all about how much she misses Josh, not that he ever really gave a damn about her. "I'm trying to bring Josh back, actually. Maybe you could give me a ride to the gorge?"

Because with the way I'm swaying, I'm not all that sure I'll make it there on my own.

Emma staggers back a few feet. "You murdered him. And then you came back to torment me."

I don't want to be cruel to her—don't want to be anything except *away* from her, honestly, if I didn't need a ride—but I still crack up at that. In a hysterical, unhinged, knee-rocking way. It's just so preposterous.

"I'm the one who got buried. So, really, it might be more accurate to say Josh murdered *me*? On a temporary basis. At least, that's what I'm hoping." It's true in a way. Josh helped set up my fake death, and he let that poor changeling keel over in my place. But from Emma's glare, it doesn't look like she's buying my version of events. "Listen—I have to get to the gorge. I think there might be a way to get Josh back. But I'm feeling too sick to run."

Not that I have anything like a plan for getting him and Lexi back. But if I can reach them, that will be a start.

I've always been a stranger—here, and everywhere else. I could never make myself love my foster parents, and I know I had no right to expect any love from them. But still, nothing has prepared me for seeing such hate on the face of someone I lived with for six years. I always tried, at least, to do the right thing. To be responsible and decent, even if I couldn't be warm.

Her enraged face is dialing in and out, like a time-lapsed moon. My sense of the ground is getting more remote by the moment. And it's really sinking in, now, that I need her help. Right now, with no more delay. How can I fight Unselle if I can't stay conscious?

"I don't care if you hate me," I tell her. "Just give me a ride already. Then I promise you'll never see me again." I get a quick hit of inspiration. "If you won't drive me to the gorge, I'll haunt you till you die."

A momentary snarl, then she nods at a nearby car. I hear the bleat of unlocking doors. It worked.

I've just made it into the passenger seat when the whole world falls away.

I come to with the door next to me hanging open and Emma yanking on my arm, my limp body sagging sideways into a border of grass and dandelions. "Get out! I did what you asked. Now get your scrawny, murdering carcass out of my life!"

I almost fight back, but then I remember: the whole point was to get here. I let myself topple out of the seat and onto the patchy turf, but I'm not sure I can stand.

"I didn't kill Josh, Emma. I can't tell you he's fine, because he's not. But I don't think he's dead."

Emma is the one who's dead; I see it now. Dead at heart. She used to be an okay person, probably even better than average. But now it's like her insides have been steeped in poison until there's nothing left in her but toxic rot.

That's another consequence of everything we did, Josh and me. And of everything that was done to us too. Poor, pathetic Emma is another casualty of it all.

I see a single dandelion, growing bigger and more blaring than the sun. I hear the car pulling away, feel the gust of its departure. How was I dumb enough to think I could escape, that Prince and his scummy followers would just let me go? My body can't survive in this world anymore. Sweat is pouring off my head and I grip fistfuls of grass to stop myself from plummeting into the sky.

There's no way I can save Josh and Lexi.

Not while I'm busy dying.

"Sennie," a horrible little voice pipes in my ear. "Sennie!"

God, how I hate that name. "Whatever you want, I'm pretty sure this isn't the time for it."

"Sennie, look!" The imp-thing—right, Kay—is waving something in my face. Garish red and yellow, shiny and rectangular, catching the sunlight in unbearable snarls. "Potato chips! From that car!"

The mention of food is enough to send my guts into violent spasms. I've never felt nausea like this before. "Jesus. Just leave me alone."

"Sennie, no!" I hear the shrill crinkling of the bag ripping open; the sound fills my whole head, as if my skull was stuffed with crumpled, metal-voiced garbage. I can't believe a *sound* can hurt so much. "You must eat!"

This dying business should really pick up the pace. My guts are made of sun-glaring tinfoil; the smell of those chips jabs in and turns into a fist crushing the foil. I gag so hard my throat feels torn, but nothing comes out. God, the vileness of that smell: sizzling dust, acidic grease, an ancient, stale wheeze of long-dead things . . .

I realize too late: Kay is straddling my neck. Her little folded-paper hand is shoving that oily, ashy spew into my mouth. I try to spit, and feel the chips snapping like dried spiders. I try to get ahold of Kay, fling her away from me, but somehow she slips through my hand.

And then a few fragments of chip claw their way into my throat. I heave again, my whole body bucking helplessly, with Kay riding my throat like some kind of flattened cowboy. Kay takes advantage of my twisted lips to shove in another mouthful.

Here's the interesting thing: this time the potato chips taste a lot more like food.

I chew them on purpose, and the spasms stop throwing me around. I swallow, and it feels like an okay thing to do. It becomes clearer where I am: on my side, staring toward the woods where delicate spring trees spray up like emerald froth.

This ground I'm lying on: it's my ground. The molecules flung from busted stars, the ones that made this planet? They made me too. The grass is so close to me that I can see the iridescence streaking up each blade of it, the waxy green perfection.

And when Kay offers me another handful of potato chips, I wolf them like a fiend. Because they're *real*.

I almost feel like I can get up. And then I do, with Kay swinging off the ridiculous sliced-up tuxedo jacket Josh chose for me—last night, if that's a concept that has any meaning now. I must have dropped my blood-soaked shirt somewhere.

Kay. As my mind comes back into focus, I realize what she just did. "You got me out. You broke—whatever the hell kind of hold they had on me."

It makes sense; eating on the other side locks you in, eating on this side undoes it—with the savage repugnance I felt for food here as a pretty solid guarantee that nobody would try it on their own. I would have preferred starvation to eating those chips, if Kay hadn't forced me.

She chirps happily. "See, Sennie? I helped you!" Then, wistfully: "Not enough, though."

"You definitely did enough," I say. "You saved my ass." But even as I speak I'm staring into the woods; is that a stir of something white, something bloody? "Hang on to the rest of those chips, okay? I think we might need them."

I walk in—a little light-headed still. But I feel more like I belong on the planet than I ever have in my life. If I'm a stranger, then I'm the one who carries a secret charge, a disguised power, and it doesn't matter if no one recognizes that at first.

But I still have to reclaim the only two people who ever recognized me, years before I recognized myself.

my version of love

Unselle's not in the glade where we used to gather on summer nights, of course. Deeper in, there's that second clearing where Josh and I first heard their music; where their bells shimmered down on us and we danced in their arms. I failed Josh then. I let him dance on, didn't heed the apprehension running through my body. From the moment Prince first said his name they got their hooks in him, and I should have seen it. That his mind was sliding. That he wasn't right.

So this is the day I make it up to him. And to Lexi too, for all the times I was so walled inside myself that I couldn't appreciate how she kept trying to reach me, whether I deserved it or not. It's awful, that I had to go through so much before I could let her kindness cut me to the quick. A familiar, mossy boulder crests out of a green shadow.

Ksenia, trust me. I know how lucky I am, and I'm not complaining, or comparing my life with yours. Lexi said that to me once, on a velvety, endless night when we were perched together on that boulder, a bottle of wine squeezed between us. *But I think we both live with the burden of a lot of expectations. Ones that other people have put on us. So, I'm expected to automatically become an economist or something, and you—*

Probably I'm supposed to wind up in prison for identity theft. I didn't say it gently. I thought I knew what she was doing, and I resented it. She'd been going out of her way to confide in me, to flaunt her vulnerability. I thought it was a game, or a trick: to coax me into opening up in return.

But even positive expectations are limiting. That's my point. We both have to push back at people who think they get to tell us who we're meant to be. She hesitated. *You have such great grades. Why don't you try applying for scholarships? Why just assume that community college is the best you can do?*

I knew she was right, and I seethed. I thought, *I'm nothing like you.* I thought, no matter how vulnerable Lexi pretended to be, in reality she was safe and happy and strong. Even worse, what she was suggesting: it implied that I should be planning for a life away from Josh, which was enough to start up a burn in my guts. *Now who's putting expectations on me, Lexi?* I snapped. And she looked down. I didn't care that I'd hurt her, or not enough.

I cringe now, thinking of it. Because who else ever believed in me enough to give me advice like that? And all I could do was be rude to her. I stagger a little as I walk, just from the sting of remembering. What a lousy friend I was to her. How she kept giving me more chances anyway.

It was never possible to keep track of time on the other side, but I might have guessed it was more like August there. But here it's spring; drifts of blossoms whiten the woods. They offer good camouflage for something else white and waving and full of lace. It's hard to pick out which pale disturbance might be her dress, her cloudy horse. But then I spot a black blotch, pitching against a snow-colored blur. My hat, held brim up in Unselle's spindly hand.

Of course: she kept the damn hat to lure me here. Bait. Kay squeaks and rustles onto my back. I glance around; there's nothing to use as a weapon. Just sticks. I pick up the thickest branch I can find, maybe five feet long and full of leaves as small as sequins. I drag it behind me with my left hand, keeping my right free.

"Ksenia, dearling! Poppling, how our Prince weeps for such a naughty. And you will weep too, for your ungratefulness. Sneak-itting up such wicked stairs!"

I cut through the trees with my teeth grinding. "You know why I'm here."

"Ever so, I know. I can taste you on the air, Ksenia, as you are coming. Why put to the trouble of catching you, when I know you catch yourself? Again, and again, and again you will. Bound to what we own."

She's up on her snarled-mist horse, towering over me. Her horrible, unbalanced grin gleams in the center of her face, but as I get closer it turns into a rictus, her upper lip hiked almost to her tiny nose. The mink on her chest sniffs dramatically, then starts a sustained, rumbling growl.

I don't wonder why. They've just scented it on me, that I'm free now.

She swings the hat down, wobbles it in my direction, just waiting to yank it back out of my reach. I don't bother.

"You don't take, Ksenia? But we wish you to have it, Prince and I! Your own pretty hat, to tipsy onto your pretty head. And be devoured by it, to where we may take of you at our leisure. You think, oh, you are not belonging to us now, you will not eat of our food again? Soon enough you will claw the crawlings from the walls, and eat what you do not see." She pauses. "So will Alexandra."

My back goes tight; I should have guessed that was their plan, to starve Lexi into submission. "Just drop it, then."

"No, no. Perhaps it bounces, perhaps it rolls and flips about. Not for this world anymore, is your hat. Our world, it gives forth; it births and bubbles, goblins and green eyes. Here? One slip upsidesie, and it eats."

Right: Josh said to be careful to keep the hat brim down, over there, so that nothing would come out of it. Here, even as Unselle flicks my hat from hand to hand, I can tell that she's being careful to hold it brim up. It makes a weird kind of sense, that it would have the opposite polarity here. That it would flow in a contrary direction.

She proffers the hat again, smiling as sweetly as she can, which isn't saying much. And I know I need it. Being eaten by my own hat is probably my last hope of rescuing the people I love.

But something tells me, *not like this*. Not as Unselle's docile pet, gratefully taking the tidbits she offers me, and nothing more. Nothing that they don't *want* me to have. Even the mink is trying to look friendly, welcoming.

I told Kay I would take the hat from Unselle, not let her hand it to me like a cookie.

I reach for it, scowling furiously. Anything less would tip Unselle off. She grins and inclines her body, her lacy sleeve trailing past her sharp-clawed hand. Her skin looks phosphorescent, like an ice-colored corpse reflecting moonlight.

Before my fingers quite touch the black brim, I bring the branch up and around with my left hand, swinging it as hard as I can into the back of Unselle's neck.

As far as I know, there's no way to do real damage to these things. But you can take them by surprise. Unselle gives a startled yelp, but—*damn* her—she still keeps her grip on my hat. Off-balance as she already was, she pitches forward, scrabbling one-handed at her horse's neck to keep from falling. And just like a real horse might do, it rears. For a moment I see it high above me, beams of sun piercing its heart, rainbow shimmer jetting out like blood.

As it thuds back down, the hat flies free of Unselle's grasp. She screams: a rusty, grating ribbon of noise, her body lurching off her horse's side as she snatches at the air. The hat spins through the green twilight of the woods, still brim up but angling dangerously. I dart toward it with the full awareness that I'll never reach it in time.

If the hat gets knocked with the hole turned down as it lands, what will it do? Eat a crater in the world? Glut that awful parallel world with heaps of mulch and leaves and stone, until magma boils through and streams in fever-bright rivers through the streets?

That would be fine with me. If it weren't for the risk that Josh and Lexi would be buried alive at the core of it, that is. What's wrong with me, that I didn't think of that in time?

The hat lands in a tangle of vines. Still brim up. Unselle is off her horse now, leaping for it in a smear of frills and crimson.

My fingers are three inches ahead of hers, snatching my old black bowler out of the vines. She's gibbering at me in a voice so warped and metallic I can't begin to guess if it's still human language. But I can identify the emotion gurgling through it.

Fear. Ah, she doesn't like it at all, that I took the hat from her by force. Whatever she was planning, I can tell I've messed it up.

It's the first time I've seen one of these creeps truly afraid, and a hard grin breaks through my face. Maybe I couldn't burn Prince alive, but making Unselle suffer, even a fraction as much as I have? I'll take it.

"You blew it, didn't you? The hat is going to take me exactly where you don't want me to go." I drive my stick into her neck so that she staggers back, hissing at me. She's so light, so brittle. "I'll be sure to tell Prince, if I see him." And I bring the hat down on my head. I still half-expect to feel it touch down, but instead it just keeps coming: a black velvet rain that cancels everything else.

I thought I had a pretty good grasp on what darkness is—from going up those stairs, say—but yeah, not really. Not like this. The void inside my bowler hat devours everything, gnaws even the memory of vision from my mind, and the self from inside my skin. I have a momentary sensation of my body as a rag with all the substance sucked out of it. And then the only definite thing I can still hold on to is Unselle's scream coming from behind me, its terrible scraping-metal echoes.

I touch down. My bowler hat is perched innocently on my head, like it's through with devouring anyone.

I'm in the same woods, but with the faintest glaze of late-summer gold, and the flowers all vanished. With a palpable sense that every leaf is altered, slightly tinged with something false and wrong. Even the birds' warbling sounds thinned-out, tinny and frail. Still, on a superficial level, it's nowhere near as horrible as Unselle was just threatening.

If I'd let her hand me the hat, I'm pretty clear on what would have happened. I would have arrived in this world, but embedded in solid rock, or lost in a maze: someplace where I would have been helpless to find them.

"Josh?" I yell. "Lexi?"

I walk forward ten paces before I remember that I'm not on my own. "Hey, Kay?" I call—softly this time, because now it's occurred to me that there might be things nearby I'd rather not put on alert. "Can you get any kind of read on where they are?"

Kay rustles out of my vest and sort of pleats around my upper arm. I'm really having trouble getting used to it, her dry scratching against my skin. "Sennie? I don't like it."

"Don't like what?" I ask her, kind of roughly. "We have exactly one reason for being back in this place, okay? *Liking* anything is beside the point."

"But—bad things there, Sennie! Where—Josh and Lexi? I don't like it for you."

"I don't care," I snap. "And that means you can't either. If I can get them out, then that's what I need out of life. Whatever happens to me—we both have to let go of giving a damn. Got it?"

Kay is my creature. She better listen to me. She sighs with a shrill, theatrical wheeze. Then: "The gorge. Sennie? In the gorge."

Maybe I knew that, on some level. I can make out the rocks of the gorge's rim through the broken darkness of the trunks, and then a shadowed fall into the depths. Violet-black, and it strikes me now that it's unnaturally dim, considering how bright the day is.

That's what Unselle was talking about, then. The gorge is what they're using as a prison, or maybe something deep inside it. Speaking of Unselle, I'd feel a little better if I knew where she was. I'm sure she'll be coming after me, to fix her screwup while she still can.

Doesn't matter. None of it matters except what I do. In the real world, there's a narrow path that winds down the side of the gorge, if you know where to look for it. I'm going to assume it's here too. I walk over, and as I get closer the shadows down there seem to rise up, gurgling out of the gap in the earth. Once I reach the brink,

I can see a few fitful gleams through the murk, but that's it: not the creek bed that should be a dusty skein at the bottom, not the trees slanting at weird angles from the rocks. A few more minutes of scuffling through the undergrowth, and I catch sight of the path. Thin and slippery, kind of dicey even when you can see where you're stepping.

Ever since I was a kid, people have complained about me: that I'm cold and withdrawn and unfriendly. That I'm incapable of attachment—except to Josh, and then only in a pathologically extreme form. That I don't have the first idea of what it means to truly love anyone. Mitch said that once, to Emma, not realizing I could hear him.

Maybe they're right. Maybe I don't. Maybe being ready to die for my friend and my brother doesn't count as love, not in the way that normal people think of it. I'm even ready to stay trapped here forever as Prince's toy, if that's the price of Josh and Lexi's freedom, and to me that seems a lot worse than dying.

Maybe real love is somehow better or gentler or simpler than what I can feel. But if it comes to that, if I never make it out of here again, I hope Josh and Lexi will think my version of love was close enough.

If it counts to them, then that's all I care about.

"Kay?" I say. "We're going down."

i'll set my own criteria

For the first few steps I can make out the path. It's muddy and eroded on the right side, where it plunges into purplish vacancy. One wrong step, and as far as I can tell there will be nothing to break my fall. Whatever it is that fills the gorge, it's thicker than ordinary darkness. More like a dense vapor, spindling around my legs, hiding the rocks behind heavy whorls. The consistency varies enough that I can distinguish the shapes it makes: lethargic spirals, eddies as sluggish as glue.

My feet and ankles disappear inside it first. I go cautiously, testing the ground at each step before I shift my weight forward. Then there's an unsettling moment where I'm in it past my waist, and my hands seem to float like sickly leaves on a violet stream. A few seconds after that and I can't see anything at all, apart from the murk. I keep my left hand on the dripping wall, though now and then sharp chips in the rock gouge my skin. Kay still clings to my right bicep, sometimes rustling in a dead-leaf way when the wind hits her.

"Josh?" I try calling; my voice doesn't seem to go anywhere. "Lexi?" But I know it's futile. I won't find them until I reach the deepest recesses of this place.

All at once my right foot skids out from under me; my body tilts off its axis. I let out a gagged shriek, sure I'm about to go down—then my left foot catches on something. I wind up splayed in the mud, my right leg kicking into emptiness, my body swinging on the lip between solid ground and the drop. I roll back toward the gorge's wall with my heart hammering, and reach down to feel what saved me. My boot's heel is snagged on a gnarled elbow of wood, probably an exposed root.

I feel for my bowler hat. Luckily it's wedged on pretty well and didn't go hurtling into space.

Fine. I get up and go on. In all this vaguely purple confusion, the sensory deprivation is starting to get to me. Every distant drip of water seems to tap down, muffled and dull, in every direction at once. Each breath keeps rasping long after it leaves my lungs, then goes on muttering in circles around my head.

Soon it starts to sound like more than just breath.

Kezzer, aren't these just amazing? That was what Josh said when he held up the boots that just kept me from plunging into nothing. Shiny, pointy, slick-soled things with lots of weird little criss-crossing straps, not exactly meant for clambering around in sludge. *Remember how I used to get so upset with you for stealing? But now it isn't stealing anymore, because everything here exists just for us! Well, for us and the kids, anyway. Like, there are ten pairs of these boots piled up back here, but we're their whole reason for being! Even the pairs that won't fit! Every last thing in this mall. It all* literally *revolves around us, like we could blast all this crap into space and make it into a new ring. Like Saturn's. Can you imagine?*

The price on the box was upward of a grand. Josh swung the boots by their straps, waiting for me to be impressed. *I like them,* I told him, but not right off. I let him wait, let him feel the grudge in my reply.

I don't mean to say that you don't look awesome in your thrift-store stuff, Josh pursued. *But it makes no sense, where we were before? That all the really cool things go to people who have nothing going on but money. Not to the people who could actually, like, bring out the magic in them. That is so totally unjust!*

I'm wavering into the unreality of our voices, is the problem. Logically, this whole conversation must be just a memory replaying in my head, but I'm *hearing* it. Josh's warm tenor hovers like a breathy ache in my ears. "Baby?" I try, but I know—I think I know—that I'm talking to nothing.

So that's how we know this is a better world, Kezzer. Because everything you deserve, you can have now.

The boots were beautiful, stunning even, like everything Josh had picked out for me. I did want them, with a sharpness like pain, but that only made me pissier. *I'm not sure anybody deserves anything,* I snapped. *Except for maybe a kick in the ass.*

I almost slip again. My heart slams into my throat and I halt for a moment, leaning on the wall and breathing as deeply as I can. I can't let these garbled, chattering memories distract me from the here and now: from step after step after step, placed precisely in the purple blindness.

"Careful, Sennie!" Kay chirps. I almost forgot she's still here.

"Kay?" I say. "Maybe you should keep talking to me. To keep me, like, anchored to where we are? I'm starting to hear things."

And then I hear Josh sob. Tender and openhearted and totally without calculation. The way he used to sound when we were both kids, long before we ever came to this place. Back when we were both—more innocent than we are now, anyway, though I would have spit at anyone who'd called me that. The sob sounds both close by, so close it whirls around inside my skull, and terribly distant. It's really only that, the lack of a location I can point to, that tells me it can't be real.

But knowing that isn't enough to keep longing from whipping through my body. And it's not enough for me to keep my mouth shut.

"Josh?" I shout. "It's me. I'm coming for you."

"Sennie," Kay is babbling, right in my ear, "Sennie, talk about what? You don't be listening to the not-things! Make you fall!"

I totally get that, in theory. But in practice Josh is calling for me.

Kezzer, Kezzer, you came! We're so lost here, so alone. It's like the air is tearing us apart. I know Lexi is here too, but I can't even see her. Kezzer, please hurry!

I *hear* him. Or maybe I know in my heart that the voice is too drifty, too scattered to be him. Maybe even the intonation is a shade off, like a decent imitation of the real thing, but with just a tiny *clang* of wrongness.

Still, even the idea of Josh, of Lexi, lost and calling to me in this dimness: it fires through my body in percussive blasts. I don't make a decision to run. I can't see a damned thing and I'm on a slippery, nine-inch-wide path adjacent to a precipitous drop. Charging blindly into purple-smeared nothing would be too idiotic to contemplate.

I don't decide to run, because I'm already doing it.

"Sennie, Sennie, stop!" Kay is squeaking. "Nice and slow, no hurry, no hurry at all!"

I ignore her, like I ignore the pain where that knife was lodged in my hip. I do have the sense, at least, to keep my left hand skimming along the wall, so that I don't just veer clear off the path. But that doesn't stop the loose, greasy mud from catching me in a long forward slide, horribly fast. My fingertips scrape over the wet stone, but there's nothing to grab, no way to stop myself. I can barely focus on what's happening, though, because I still hear Josh.

Kezzer, I can think now. But they'll steal me from myself again, soon. Please come!

Steal me from myself. Isn't that pretty much what I said to my changeling, up in our forbidden second story? And Prince and them, they always seemed to hear everything we said in that house.

It's almost enough to halt the momentum driving me, because I can't help realizing: it's not Josh at all. Josh probably didn't overhear that conversation, and even if he did, he wouldn't swipe the words out of my mouth that way. He has his problems, he's done some messed-up things. Whatever. But he's not some damned parrot.

The realization *would* be enough to stop me. At least make me think about what I'm doing. If it weren't for the fact that I'm already falling.

I can't tell if I missed the path, or if it just vanished from under me. All I know is that I'm wheeling in midair—not crashing down a steep and ragged slope, which is what I would have expected. I feel my hat go flying off my head and grab for it at random, but I miss it. It seemed important to hold on to it—it was the most powerful thing I had—but there's nothing I can do.

I should be terrified, but I'm not, really. I don't seem to be falling that quickly, and I have time to wonder if the unreality of this place means that we can't actually die here either. It's an experiment I haven't tried, though I won't pretend I didn't think about it, back when it seemed like the only possible way to escape. I just couldn't do that to Josh.

That's the real reason I don't think this fall will kill me. Death is nowhere near cruel enough to keep Prince happy.

Then—in this cloying, obliterating fog where I can't even see my own hand in front of my face—I see someone else. Josh, falling exactly parallel to me, his face vivid and defined and his brown eyes wide open. His garnet bangs flutter in the gust of our descent. He's stretching out his hands to catch mine, and I strain to reach him in return, but the tips of his fingers stay just an inch beyond my reach. It seems so bitterly long since the last time I saw him, when he crawled up on that cloud-horse and turned his back on me.

"Baby," I say, "I found you! I'll do anything it takes to get you and Lexi out of here. I promise!"

Maybe it's a hollow promise, considering the situation. Maybe I'm going to fail him again. But no, I won't accept that as a possibility. I won't even consider it.

"Not him," Kay squeaks in my ear. God, what is *she* still doing here? "Sennie, not him, not him, not him!"

Kezzer! Why do you think we won't die here? Don't you remember what I told you? His smile is sweet but his eyes well with tears. *I told you I wouldn't live that long!*

I'm just not that kind of boy, he had said. But that was literally in another world. That was before the kind of boring, stubborn reality I'd taken for granted all my life became more valuable than life itself.

"Prince wants us to suffer more than that," I say. "And he wants to keep playing with our emotions. *Feeding* on them, I think. Killing us would ruin his fun."

And how could he make you suffer most, Kezzer? Josh says—but *is it him?* Is there something a touch shifty, maybe a touch inhuman, in the way his mouth is curling? *By making you watch me die. And then wonder forever if it was really me.*

A pale hand appears out of nowhere, holding a brilliant silver knife to Josh's throat.

"Josh!" I scream, and lunge to grab that hand. But there's nothing to push against, no way to get traction. I flail pointlessly, shrieking, precisely the same distance from him, while the knife draws a crimson gash across Josh's throat.

And the whole time he's smiling.

"Not him, Sennie! Not nothing, not nobody, not to cry, not to crush your heart!"

Somehow this time I really hear Kay, trilling away in my ear. Even with Prince and them turning his brain inside out, Josh never would have *smiled* like that at my grief.

"You're not him," I say to the thing falling with me. It's not even close to passing now. It looks deformed, inflated, with smears of glitter over painted-on eyes. The blood streaming down its chest has a theatrical cast, like a red velvet scarf dropped in as a prop. "You pretend to be Josh, but you don't understand him at all."

What don't I understand, then?

"You thought you could change him into one of you. And you almost did. But then he fought back, and he broke free of your bullshit. Because he's way too good to be one of you freaks."

I owe Kay another thank-you. I was on the brink of letting my mind slide. Of believing it. How could I have come so close to letting this leering balloon-boy take me in?

Ah, well, maybe. But you're right that we won't let him die. Joshua will live for an eternity, in a tomb of his own making. So will you. Because there's only one way he can be free, Ksenia Adderley, and it's not within your power. And as long as we have him, we'll keep you too.

I'm almost enough of a sucker to ask what the way Josh can get free is, like this thing would ever tell me the truth. But it vanishes before I can speak.

With that, I hit the ground. Hard enough that I go stumbling forward, bent at the waist, with pain shooting up my calves. But not hard enough to break anything. The purple murk is a shade lighter here, enough that I get a glimpse of the dried-up creek bed drumming under my feet, before I trip on something, and fall to my knees.

Maybe it's because I ate those potato chips, but even the ground here looks fake to me. Just because it can bruise me, it doesn't mean I have to believe in it.

I'll set my own criteria for reality, thanks. And nothing Prince can come up with is even close.

i'm not going to let you
take it back

It would be pointless, childish, to keep calling out for them. There's something so stifled in the tone of the silence, like a throat crammed full of mud. I can already tell they won't hear me.

"Kay?" I try, just in case. "Any ideas?"

I can feel her papery little limbs go stiff. "Not here. Josh and Lexi."

"What do you mean, they aren't here? I only came down here because you said Josh and Lexi were stuck in the gorge!" God, I'm on edge. Just like that, my voice cracks from the heat and pressure rising under it. I stumble forward, nearly falling from sheer frustration. "How can I find them, if you keep changing your story?"

"No! They're here, Sennie! But only . . . in the thin lines."

I think for a moment about what that might mean. "You mean, like you?" Could Prince crush all the dimensionality out of them, flatten Josh and Lexi into jagged paper dolls?

Kay hesitates. "Not like me. Like finding the corners."

I can't stop myself from exhaling in an exasperated huff, even though I know she's probably trying her best to explain.

There's nothing better I can do than walk forward, with no clue where to search. My eyes are glutted with the velvet smudge of the air, though at least now I can see the ground in a vague, lumpy way. It's enough that I'm less likely to pitch onto my face. For a while I just go forward like that, each step indistinguishable from the next in the muffling quiet. No birds down here. None of the little striped snakes that used to whiplash through the corners of our vision—in the real gorge, anyway. This gorge is just a cheap imitation. My eyes start to blur, since there's nothing to see. My own footsteps become a hypnotic drone inside my muscles.

And even though I know I can't afford to let my hope flag, *I can't find them, how did I ever think I could find them?* becomes a drone in my head. Not exactly whispering in my thoughts, but even worse than that: on the level just *below* articulate thought. That's where they get you.

Something slices, razor thin, across my peripheral vision. So fast that I don't see it until half a second after I saw it, if that makes sense; the vision doesn't strike my consciousness until it's already gone.

Lexi. Her deep eyes frantic, her hands motion-streaked in front of her, as if she were pounding on an invisible wall. Around her, I think, there wasn't the same somber haze, but something pearly, translucent, hit with waves of iridescence. A background so sickly pale that the contrast made her dark skin look as focused and intense as a pupil.

I jump back, heels knocking on the stones, trying to find the spot where I glimpsed her. "Kay! Did you see that?"

Ugh. I can't get the vision back. I waver, my blood surging until it drowns out all the world beyond this place. I rock ever so slightly backward, forward, trying to catch the precise angle again.

"Thin, Sennie! It's so thin, where Lexi is! So thin you can't get a word in! Too thin to see her!" Kay is whimpering now. Hysterical. It's not what I would call helping.

"But I did! Kay, I saw her!" And she looked terrified: her brows drawn tight, her mouth bent with loneliness. Arms wrapped around her body, like she's bitterly cold. The details are still coming into focus in my mind; Lexi was staring in my direction, but just past me. I don't think she saw me at all. "This is what you were talking about, isn't it? When you said they're *here* and *not here?* They're here—like, stuck in cuts in the world."

I try taking one more step back—and the vision of Lexi tips across my left eye again. There and then gone: a line of revelation that might be a single atom wide.

"Lexi!" I try, though I know it's probably ridiculous. "I'm right here!"

So thin you can't get a word in, Kay said.

What's thinner than a word, then?

I shift left, to get closer to where I saw her. Stretch out a hand, in case I can feel a snag in the air. Nothing.

What gets in where a word can't?

Maybe the feelings that usually skim along deeper than words can reach. Maybe the kind of truth I didn't even know how to feel until Lexi showed up. *You're real enough that I still love you, no matter what.* That was what she said. Words, okay, but the way they wounded me—they were also something more than that. Something thinner than paper, sharper than glass, that got between my skin and the flesh beneath and made me feel myself, outlined in bright pain. Something that made me savagely aware, again, of the Ksenia who had gone numb.

And the light in our house flinched as Lexi spoke to me. Just the way it did in the hospital, when I told Josh how much I loved him.

I think I'm starting to understand how this works.

"Lexi," I say. She's there, inches away from me, even if I can't see her. "Lexi, I have to tell you something. You know I've never been good at saying what I feel, but the thing is, you have to *know* what you feel before you can even try to cough it up. I realize that's not a problem you've ever had. You're so completely yourself, so *aware* of yourself, all the time. So you're just going to have to take it from me: not everyone is like you. I haven't always been able to— tell what my heart is doing, I guess. It just goes on, thumping away, where I can't get a grip on it. Like my heart's at the bottom of a chasm, and I'm standing up on the edge, staring down at nothing."

It's so subtle, so quick, a flicker divided and divided again until it could insinuate itself between a shadow and the wall it rests on. But I see her again. I can't sustain it; there's no possible way to keep my body still enough to hold a vision that fine.

But I caught enough to know that her expression is different, now. Glowing with recognition and longing.

I don't know if my actual words are reaching her, but something is. She knows I'm here. And the fact that she looks this way because of me—it shocks me with a kind of tenderness I can't process.

"Lexi," I try again, but now my voice is alive with hope. "To you, it was probably no big deal—I mean, the things you said to me, when Josh brought you to our house? But you told me I was real, or real enough to be your friend."

I can't repeat the part where she said she loved me, not even here, not even when our situation is so urgent. My face goes hot just thinking of it, with a weird mix of shame and gratitude. Besides, I don't want her to think that I'm expecting her to still mean it, once she gets out.

"I think that you've been trying to tell me that, in different ways, for as long as I've known you, but I couldn't take it in until—until everything was so hopelessly fucked up. Anyway, it was like some kind of spell, like in a story? Because it was like you *made* me real, by telling me that." I pause again. It's a lot of pressure to put on her, what I just said. It would be completely fair for her to be pissed. "Or—okay, like you gave me a chance to make myself real. I don't mean to—none of what I'm talking about is your problem, Lexi. I'm just trying to tell you how grateful I am."

"Ks—"

Lexi's voice, cut off before she can finish a single syllable. But she was saying my name. A hair-fine flash of her beautiful face. I reach toward her instinctively.

A tear. I made Lexi cry.

And then my outstretched left hand pushes into something— like what? Like a peeling-back, like two taut blades of grass bowing outward from the pressure. Just my fingertips squeeze through, but I feel something.

Lexi's warm fingertips curl to hold mine. We're linked. For a moment, that's all we have of each other. "Ksenia!"

"Hey, Lexi," I try to say, but I'm crying too hard. Now that the gap is wide enough for words, of course I can't manage to speak. She slides her palm along mine until she gets a tight grip on my wrist, and I grab hers back. Even if I'm too beside myself to say anything coherent, I can still pull.

Lexi's forearm appears out of the fog. I step back to give her more leverage, and lean my weight as far from the gap as I can. Whatever it is entrapping her, though, it's obvious that it doesn't want to let her out. We're fighting it, but every inch of progress snaps and spasms. The tension keeps its grip on her.

It feels like space is yielding with these paralyzing vibrations that thrum up my arm, set my whole skeleton shuddering inside my body. My teeth rattle like I'm being slowly electrocuted. It's unbearable for me, and probably even worse for her, but her arm emerges past the elbow now.

The buzz gets worse. It's like that awful singing, jangling sensation that took over my mouth that night, but now it's seized my whole body. Lexi and I are both shaking with it now, so violently that it's hard to keep our grip on each other, and harder to order my muscles to keep dragging her out of there.

"Ksenia!" The rattling is in her voice, too, shaking her words apart. "I can see you now! It's been so *dark*."

I saw her framed in pearlescent glow, though. Maybe I'd see her that way no matter what.

Lexi gets free to the shoulder; that's all I can make out clearly. I'm straining so hard against the force quaking through me that everything else turns into a kaleidoscope of fractured light. My vision is ringed in bright, toothy points. The buzz gluts my head, like it did the night they took Josh, and it hits me: if I pass out now, if I fall away from her, Lexi's bizarre prison might snap shut on her again. We could lose each other forever.

I let Josh down, that night. I *cannot* let Lexi down now.

"Lexi!" I call. I can't feel the ground under my feet anymore. All my sensations are limited to her arm in my hand, the pressure of her fingers. "We have to get you out, before—"

"Before we can't," Lexi says. "I know. I'm feeling it too."

She's hauling on me with her entire weight, and it hits me that I could just as easily be dragged in there with her. If my knees give out, if my mind tips, I'll go crashing forward.

I brace myself as best I can, with almost no sense of my body. And at the same moment I feel Lexi driving herself toward me, gripping my arm with both her hands now. The buzzing in my bones is so loud that I think I might disintegrate.

And then I see her face, whole and sustained; I *keep* seeing her. And that's enough to hold on to, enough to keep me from passing out. I drive my heels down and my body seizes, buckles, with the effort.

And then she's standing in front of me. Fuzzy in the dimness, but *there*. She's been through an ordeal, and I should be strong for her. Instead I'm so faint that she's the one who catches me.

"Ksenia." She's shaking, her twists of hair frayed, but she's smiling so brilliantly. "I won't even ask, this time."

"You mean, if it's really me?" I say. I don't want to impose on her, but I still rest my head on hers for a moment. It's that or fall. As soon as I possibly can, I make myself step back, give her some space. "Because I can finally tell you that it is, Lexi."

"That's why I don't have to ask. I can tell just by looking at you."

It didn't occur to me to wonder if she was real either. Not even after that pseudo-Josh I saw as I fell. Lexi is so utterly herself, all the time, that anyone who could be duped by a double of her— that would be somebody who just didn't know her at all.

She's so close to me, but now that she's out of her weird prison the fog blurs us both. And I want to hug her, and I want to tell her how sorry I am that I didn't protect her from getting dragged into this. But I can't. My eyes are streaming loose, sloppy tears, and I know I shouldn't let her see me cracking up. It was so much easier to really talk to her when she wasn't right in front of me.

She's the one who steps close and throws her arms around me.

And maybe I still don't feel like I deserve it—because really, how could I? But I let myself have it: this much, this moment, the warmth of this friend. Even though we still have to find Josh. Even though I'm just going on reckless, stupid faith that we'll discover some way to get out of here again, and back to our own world. All three of us, hopefully, or at least the two of them.

Something tells me there's going to be a price, if Josh and Lexi can get out at all. I don't know what it will be, but I'll pay it. I'll pay for everyone. I won't let the cost fall on them.

"You know, I heard what you said, Ksenia," Lexi murmurs, and squeezes me tighter. "And I'm not going to let you take it back. Are we clear on that?"

If this doesn't count as loving somebody, then I honestly have no clue what people are talking about.

how can everything
become nothing?

"Ksenia?" Lexi says, and I force myself to let go of her and step away. It's not the moment for me to go weak and clingy, even if she'll tolerate it. "I really tried to hold on to him. To Josh. But the way we came here was just so strange and violent, and we lost each other. I'm sorry."

"Through my hat. I heard. I just did that too."

That makes her start and stare at me, though I'm unclear on why. Travel by hat is an established thing, now. "Ksenia!"

"Yeah?"

"Doesn't that mean you were free? You actually succeeded in escaping from this nowhere? Then . . . that means, you must have solved the problem of how to climb those stairs?" I see her scanning the grave dirt all over my limbs. She's putting it together.

Right. There's too much to explain, at least while we're still trapped and Josh is lost. "I *had* to figure it out. Since Josh was leading a freaking army against you. I was trying to stop him, but by the time I made it—you were both already gone."

"You knew all along what the key was, didn't you? But only worrying about someone *else* was enough to make you say that name out loud. Ksenia, am I right about that?"

I'm trying to be more open with Lexi. Be a good enough friend to be worthy of her. But the searching way she's gazing at me now is still enough to make me want to spin on my heel and storm off.

I reject the impulse, though. It feels almost physical, as if my muscles are contracting to shove it out between my shoulder blades.

"Sure. I mean, I suspected. But Lexi, knowing that you were in danger—I couldn't just dick around anymore." That's going to have to be enough of a confession for right now. "Look, I really don't see the point of talking about this. We've got to find Josh, and we've got to—I have no idea what it's going to take to get out of here again. I don't even know if it's possible."

I turn to start searching, but the fact is that my face is blazing and sparks swim in my eyes. I don't know why Lexi's questions feel like needles stitching their way through my skin. And—it's only now I realize it, but I've misplaced Kay. She isn't clinging to my arm anymore. The vapor down here seems to be thinning, but it still feels like walking into oblivion. I stomp forward, feeling Lexi's stare hammering at my back. Looking for Josh is a ridiculous pretense. I'm swinging my head at random, hoping for an oblique glimpse of him, but really—it's that I can't handle looking at Lexi right now.

"Ksenia?"

I just finished crying. I can't break down again, and I can't be that person who knots herself up to keep from lashing out, either. I feel my hands drawing into fists, tightening against my will. No matter how much I love Lexi, I need her to see that it's time to back off.

"Ksenia, we'll find Josh. We're not going anywhere without him, I promise. But first I want to tell you something, and I'd really appreciate it if you had the courage to look in my face while I do it."

A spasm flickers down my arm: the urge to raise my hand, to strike out, to scream at her to just leave me *alone*, already.

And then—I don't know how, but I let the spasm keep going. I let it shoot down my arm and leak out at my fingertips. My hands go limp and my shoulders fall and I'm able, though barely, to turn back to her. The purple mist has lifted enough that the distance between us isn't much help, and I have to see how dark and acute her stare is.

"Get it over with, Lexi."

"It's just that—don't underestimate how happy I am that you did that for me, Ksenia. I know how it must have killed you to have to call yourself *Sennie*." I cringe, hearing that name on her lips, but she ignores it. "I want you to be very aware of how much it means to me, that you fought your way out for my sake. Because then you can keep the next thing I'm going to say in perspective."

I owe Lexi so much, and I know it. But I can't help feeling like she's claiming her debt in blood, making me listen to these things. "What's that, Lex?"

"That it would mean even more to me if you had done it for yourself." Her lips bend up, but I wouldn't call that a smile, exactly. "Do you understand why I'm saying this to you?"

I understand more than I want to.

"I don't expect anything from you, Lexi." Her not-smile wrenches into something fiercer; really, I knew she didn't mean it like that. She probably feels insulted, that I would even imply she's looking for an excuse not to owe me anything. "And I never could have abandoned Josh, anyway. So why would I put myself through that?"

Lexi sighs; not wistfully, more of an aggravated huff. "You just made my point for me, Ksenia. Okay, let's figure out where they've hidden Josh. I was feeling pretty done with him, honestly, but he came through at the last possible instant. He actually put up some serious resistance. I'm not saying I forgive him, because he did too much harm for that. But I can at least consider forgiveness as a possibility."

"I know he fought back," I say. I'm not sure I want to know what she means by the rest of it. "Kay told me."

We're walking side by side now, through a stony landscape blotted by the violet air. It takes the edge off, not having to confront her gaze, not seeing the things she's seeing in me. We go slowly, which makes sense even if it's maddening. I have to stifle the speed and wildness in my limbs at every step. But we're more likely to stumble across Josh's prison by ambling along, searching every inch of the gorge, than we would be if we went charging off like lunatics.

"You met Kay," she says. "So that's what you meant, when you said you heard about the hat. Kay knew where to look for you; she could probably even sense that you were on your way, just as soon as you set foot on the staircase."

"Yeah," I say. "Lexi, we need to concentrate. I barely saw you back there. It's amazing that I found you at all. Josh—you came here together, so he's probably in the same kind of trap they stuck you in. And it looked like a knife's edge in the air, kind of. That thin and hard to catch. Except with your face blurring past."

Lexi stops. "To me, it was just a hole. I couldn't see anything at all before you started talking to me. Ksenia, the bizarre thing? I didn't actually hear your voice, not at the beginning. But I saw images; I can't begin to describe them. They were like colored shadows cast by your emotions, and I recognized you *instantly*. I couldn't hear the actual words you were saying, but I could read the colors like they were a new kind of script. And it was entirely obvious that you were very close, and that you'd come for me."

"That actually sounds beautiful." It does; I wish Lexi would stop saying things that hurt so much. "But Lexi, we have to keep going."

I turn to move on, but she catches my hand. "Wait." Her head tilts; she's close enough that I feel the soft disturbance of her breath. "I bet Josh can sense us the same way. Ksenia, we should go back."

"Back where?"

"Exactly where I was. As nearly as we can identify the spot."

I almost snap at her; something stupid, mean; something to buy myself a little distance from everything I'm feeling. But then I don't. "You—what? You have an intuition about it?"

Lexi shakes her head. One thing she never is, is at a loss for words, but for once in her life Lexi is thinking something she can't instantly smack down in a perfect sentence.

"I think Josh was there. I think he was listening to you *along* with me. They somehow arranged it so that he and I were in the same space, but without being able to perceive each other."

It's no crazier than anything else that's happened. And it should be the best news possible. So why do I find myself not wanting to believe her?

"Okay," I say, because anything else would be too screwed up, even for me. "Okay, we'll go look."

I know why I'd prefer it if Lexi was wrong, actually. Because what must Josh have felt, if he heard me spilling my guts to Lexi like that? He was already getting jealous. And the way she glances at me now, as she starts heading back: I could swear she knows exactly what I'm thinking. She throws her mind out like a net, and it falls through me as if I were water. How did Lexi and I come to know each other so much more deeply, by spending so long apart?

She tosses her head again. Shaking off a thought. "I know I shouldn't tell you what to feel, Ksenia. But seriously, Josh kidnapped you. He tore you right out of the world. And I can *almost* understand why you would keep loving him anyway. Or even if I don't understand, I can respect it. Love like yours is worth honoring."

"I've never asked anyone to understand me," I tell her; it sounds harsher than I intended. One thing for sure, no one ever thought of *honoring* anything I felt before, and I know I should be thankful. "It would be a complete waste of time if I did."

It's a lie, though, and Lexi probably knows it. What's grating on me is that she *does* understand me, just in ways I can't handle.

Retracing our steps looks exactly the same as forging ahead did. The futility is getting to me again. Futility is violet and hazy and slurs on and on like a horizon. Wherever Josh is, we'll miss him. We'll wander back and forth for an eternity, until Prince comes for us, or until we die from thirst.

"The part I'm struggling with, is that you still seem to feel like you have an *obligation* to him. You don't. Not after the way he violated your right to make your own choices." Now Lexi's the one who's having trouble looking at me. Her head hangs, like the dust at our feet requires her full attention. "You owe Josh nothing."

That's not true, I think, but I don't say it. Memory sweeps over me, grasping me inside my twelve-year-old self; how rigid I stood in that drab living room, my social worker fussing at my back. How I deliberately fixed my gaze on an electric outlet in the corner, so I wouldn't have to see my new foster parents shooting each other concerned looks. How my breathing was labored, and the garbage bag containing all my possessions was still slung over my back.

And then how Josh came up beside me and took my free hand in perfect silence. I hadn't said so much as hello to him at that point. He had no reason to expect anything from me but cruelty. In spite of myself, I felt the bravery of what he was doing. I still refused to turn in his direction, but I didn't yank my hand away either. Instead I watched him out of the corner of my eye. A slim band of sunlight swayed, very softly, across his wavy dark hair.

After five minutes of his warm presence I dropped the bag, even though it sickened me to hear the adults murmuring their approval. *Isn't that precious? Josh is working his magic. No, no, don't say anything.*

Owe him nothing? That band of sunlight. The unspeaking tenderness of his ten-year-old hand. How can *everything* become *nothing*, just because someone did something wrong?

"So why are *you* looking for Josh?" I say. "If you think he's so not worth it?"

"I didn't say that. And I think there are extenuating circumstances. But Ksenia, you don't know everything he did." Lexi gives me a quick, sidelong look. Evaluating me. Maybe trying to suss out how much I can stand to hear without freaking out. "I don't know where to draw the line: what he's responsible for, and what he isn't, if that makes sense. But I do think he deserves a chance at redemption."

"Josh hasn't been right since he met them," I say. Defensively, even though I'm shaking inside at the thought of everything Josh might have done. What happened after he rode up the tiled wall at that vile party, and out through the ceiling? "They got in his head."

"And by *not right*," Lexi says, scuffing at the dirt, her eyes studiously averted, "I assume you mean *enchanted*."

I do mean that. My vision smears from the shock of hearing Lexi say it, because I didn't *know* I meant it. I can't help but notice the strangeness of it, too. The most obvious explanation is the exact one my mind repelled, persistently, stubbornly. The wind swells, pecking our cheeks with grit, and in it I hear a kind of humming, or chattering, or the wordless rags of a voice with all the meaning shredded out.

Lexi is right, but I can't shake the impression that she shouldn't have come out and said it.

And then the wind's cries break through their senseless moaning, and resolve into two definite sounds.

Josh's voice, sliced razor fine. Where he is, it's too thin to let a word through, but wide enough to let a stuttering, intermittent note escape. A howl, divided and divided again, broken up by gaps of silence.

The other sound? It's the beat of hooves.

i paid our rent

Echoes splash through the air, drowning our ears in the clatter of horses. Lexi grabs my elbow and we both twist around, chasing the sounds that come out of every facet in the rocks. Above us the mist thickens into solidified dusk, and I can't make out where they are, or how many. But one thing I can tell: there are a lot of them.

"Ksenia! There!" Lexi points, and now I see it. There's a thickening in the shadows that becomes twenty horses, twenty riders, coming straight down the vertical rock face at a gallop. And I know they'll be on top of us before I can reach Josh, I *know* it. But I still pull away from Lexi and leap forward, clawing at the emptiness. Wherever he is, whatever slash in the world is hiding him, I'll rip it open and send him tumbling into the dust. And then Lexi and I will grab his hands and we'll run, even if we're only running into nothingness.

But now I can't hear his voice, not even in that sad, staggered way. The hoofbeats fracture and multiply until every speck of dust jumps with them. "Josh," I yell. "Josh, keep shouting! I'm so close!"

I see Unselle first, rounding on me in midair with her horse's legs at the level of my head. The bloody writing, the phosphor burn of her lace and skin. The mink cackling on her chest.

"Hatless it is now, the poppling. Hatless and helpless! All the way home, how I licked the scent of your blood, Ksenia. Sucked you out of air! Poor sweetling, to think so prettily that you might snatch what we own." She grins, the bright, ragged row of her teeth careening in her face. "You could not even snatch yourself from us, could you? No matter what your eatings."

I'm trying to think up a decent comeback when her horse pirouettes and its cloudy hooves lash into space, with a noise like shattering glass.

And out of the sound, Josh reels and falls to his knees, just ten feet away from me. He rolls into a ball and rocks back and forth, sobbing so hard that I don't know if he even sees me.

I start to lunge forward, to seize him in my arms. But the horse is there, blocking my way. And then Lexi is next to me, close enough that I can feel her vitality like a warm shadow along my side. Somehow her nearness is enough to remind me that I can't just throw myself at Unselle like some impetuous idiot. I need to be strategic. Take some time evaluating, so I can understand what we need to do.

"Try and take," Unselle sneers. "It will be our pleasure to watch you try! He is bound into our world. Stuff him with the eatings of your world like a pig for the banquet, Ksenia. His skin will still be ours, and his teeth, and the soft marrow slinking in his bones, and the dreams that live like worms, gnawing the pulp of his mind. Joshua bound himself here, and cannot be free."

But there was something that hideous mock-Josh said to me, while we were plummeting from the cliff. It told me there was just *one* way Josh could be free. That it wasn't something I could do for him. But a way is a way.

"And then, Ksenia, it is a chain, our havings. Through Joshua we have you; through you we claim Alexandra. All ours, forever, for whatever games might ease our tedium. You think you leave, oh, so pleased with yourself! But it is a false leaving. Because straight back you came, to nestle in our world like a teeny mouse!" Her leer is growing, pitching in her cheeks. Too many damn teeth inside that scarlet ripple of lip. Her mink yawns and rolls its tongue at me. Completely obscene.

"Your fake world is useless to me," I snap. "I only came for them."

While Unselle has been prattling on, the rest of the freak cavalry has come riding in. We're surrounded by billowing horse-forms, snickering inhuman riders. I don't see any of the changelings now. Just our captors, whatever they are, in their vile finery.

"As Alexandra came back for you," a voice says. Reedy and agitating. "That was precisely what Unselle just explained to you, Ksenia. Each of you is bound to the one before. You would have no peace if you abandoned dear Joshua here. Every night your betrayal would sweat through all your pores, until you raced back to us, desperate for relief. No more could Alexandra leave you to such a fate; only a bit of patience, and she would surely return. Ah, all Alexandra's insolence, and her touching belief that she could rescue you! All she did was to bait the trap herself—although, of course, it still behooved me to punish her *intention*. But what would we be, my darling Ksenia, if we could not spin love into webs far stronger than spider silk?"

Prince. Maybe he's partly lying, but there are strands of vicious truth twisted in with the deceit. I just told Lexi that I never would have saved myself if it meant leaving Josh here, and there's no way I can deny that now. Of course, of course, they've used what's best in us as a weapon to bring us down.

But the suggestion that he was never afraid of what Lexi might do, what I might do, that we were always just helpless pawns—in that, I hear a distinct undertone of bullshit. There's something he's trying to obscure. A possibility, a chance. Something he wants to stop us from recognizing.

I don't look at him on principle, though he's sidling up just to my left, while Lexi covers my right. Doesn't stop him from stroking my jaw, of course. He'd love it if I lost control and tried to bite his poisonous green eyes right out of their sockets. He's thrilled by my disgust too, but that's more than I can conceal.

Lexi doesn't have the same compunction I do about staring the creep in the face. She steps around me so deftly I don't realize what's happening until she's right in front of him—though since at the moment he's, like, two feet taller than she is, she has to crane her neck to blast him with attitude.

I expect her to give Prince hell. But she doesn't address him at all, except with her gaze. It's enough.

"Joshua?" Lexi calls, loudly, but into Prince's face. "You heard him. Each of us is bound to the one who came here before. But they didn't say anything about you." She pauses. "And they didn't mention any of the kids you stole, either."

"Josh?" I say. "He had nothing to do with that, Lexi!"

And then Josh comes forward. Actually crawling straight beneath Unselle's horse, as if its legs were a bridge. He looks terrible, sickly pale and battered, his old-lady sweater dangling shredded pink-sequin stars.

Kay is riding on the back of his neck: a parody of all the horsemen around us. She waves to me, her paper-doll hand jerking, and points to Josh's head. Then she folds herself up like a fan and ducks down the back of Josh's sweater. The whole thing was so quick that I'm not certain anyone else saw it.

My black bowler hat slants on Josh's snarled hair. Unselle gives a quiet hiss when she sees it. Like I thought, then. He stops a few feet from her horse and huddles in the dirt—and all at once I know that I *can't* just rush to him, wrap him in my arms, absorb all his pain. He's feeling things he has to feel, at least for now. No matter how much they hurt.

"Josh?" Lexi says again, more gently this time. She finally turns and looks at him. The trails of his tears have sucked up the dust, so his face is scored with mud. Green glitter flings back motes of light when his weight shifts. "You owe me for Xand, and you know it. What are you bound to? From everything they've said, that's the start of the chain. But I don't see how it could have been a specific person who was already here. Not unless there are things I *really* don't know."

"What happened to Xand?" I ask, but it's a stupid question. Because from the broken way Josh gapes up at Lexi, from the way he won't look at me—I have a pretty good idea.

Xand is dead. Josh was complicit in his murder. And even

after *that*, Lexi came here with him. It's an act of such mind-blowing bravery and grace that I stare at her. Like, I might have to reassess my ideas of what human beings can be.

"Lexi," Josh says. And then he stops, words kind of chewing around in his face, like he's just realizing there's nothing remotely adequate that he can say. "Kezzer tried to stop me. She tried to get through to me. And even Kezzer, even with everything she means—I couldn't *hear* her."

Prince, Unselle, their retinue: they all break out in their off-kilter grins at that. As usual, there's nothing they love so much as watching us perform all our charming, frenzied human dramas for them. But that might actually work to our advantage, I think. They're not about to interrupt. Not as long as we keep them entertained. They're so sure it's futile, so sure we're too weak and dumb to beat them, that they can afford to kick back and watch the show.

"She did more than that," Lexi tells him. "She climbed the stairs. She went after you. Do you know what that means, Josh?"

Josh has been refusing to look at me, but now he can't keep it up. I get a single, shame-crumpled glance. "Kezzer? You—oh, you *didn't*—"

"I dug myself out of my own grave," I tell him. "And then I was too late, anyway. It sucked." I hesitate, because I don't like to talk to Josh so harshly, especially not when he's already trashed by grief—but Lexi's right, everything is hanging on getting him to tell us the truth. "Josh? You owe me some answers too. How did you get us into this?"

I see it now, the whole amnesiac act he put on after I found him. Maybe he was genuinely disoriented at first, but pretty soon everything he said was a blind, a deflection. To keep me from asking him precisely one thing: *Josh, what have you done?*

"You made a deal," I blurt, with the jarring sense that I've known all along. Known in a way that I couldn't quite access, couldn't bear to touch. *You sold us both to them, forever, without even asking*—but I still love him too much to spit those words at him. *You knew what you were doing, even if you duped yourself into thinking it would all work out.* "Josh, what was it?"

But don't I know that too? All around us, our *hosts* start tittering. They huff my dismay like a drug.

There's only one way he can be free, Ksenia Adderley, and it's not within your power.

"We were out of options, Kezzer," Josh says. He's trying to look at me, but his gaze keeps shunting aside, or slipping off my face like the fall of a dying bird. My bowler hat slides down and hides his round brown eyes. He shoves it back, reflexively, like he hasn't even registered that he's been wearing it this whole time. "I— everywhere I looked, there were all the choices we *didn't* have. So I made the only choice that was left."

Well—the only choice except the one we both dreaded: to see what kind of lives we could create apart from each other. But I'm not saying that either.

"You didn't pledge yourself to a *person*, did you?" Lexi's voice carries a jolt of revelation. Unselle's red scroll of a mouth puckers in all at once, though the rest of them are still caught up in the show. She jabs a look in Prince's direction, and I can read the worry in it. The pleasure of watching us fling accusations at each other is vying with the risk that Lexi will figure out too much. "You're bound to an *idea*. The idea of you and Ksenia, together forever. The idea of a perfect love that can never end. But God, Josh, what you did for that!"

"I paid our rent," Josh says—for the first time, with a snap in his tone. "Someone had to, Lexi. I never could have asked Kezzer to deal with that."

"Olivia Fisher," Lexi says. Flat, quiet, dangerously controlled. "She was *rent*?"

Josh's gaze darts around. And, okay, I know they've been collecting children. I've seen the kids tagging after Unselle, like a bunch of lobotomized ducklings. Bleary, docile, totally checked out, their tiny hands pawing at her skirt. I've even wondered if there was anything I could do to stop it, and come up blank; I was in the exact same trap with them, after all. But the idea that Josh would have *helped* with that—

He did, though. His cheeks shift in this evasive way, like something rolling over underground. Shame rumbles inside his flesh. That was another part of his deal, then; Prince required more than just the two of us. What am I, that I managed not to see it?

"You've been paying for your dream with other people's grief, Josh," Lexi says. Her voice so soft it burns. "So your dream is what has to die."

what else would i do?

There's a sudden movement as the ring of cloud-horses draws in, and I know Lexi's done it. She's struck their secret like a bell, sent the echoes flying out, until the whole gorge reverberates with an unbearable truth. Josh physically pitches back as if she'd slammed him right in the face, his eyes round with the struggle to *not* understand what Lexi just said. I'm taking it in too. If Josh did what Lexi's asking, if he strangled his idea of the two of us—what would that mean, in practice?

"And that is why Joshua can never be free, Alexandra," Prince says. Inhuman creep that he is, he's enough like us that I can hear the anxiety pulsing under his silky tone. If he was sure we were whipped a moment ago, he's not quite so positive now. "He bound himself to a dream, as you say. And that dream is as essential to him as his own blood. It cannot die while he lives."

Lexi ignores him. "Josh, what happens if you say it? That you let Ksenia go, for all time. Do you know?"

I hear what she's asking. I get it. But vertigo still comes for me, sharp and crackling. My mind stops on the brink of an abyss that extends in every direction at once, and then it pauses. Like it's awaiting instructions.

Josh gapes from her to me, and doesn't answer. But his face gets a shattered look. I see him in fragments, like a dropped plate. And in the space between the shards, I see the void. Waiting for him, just like it is for me.

Those imp creatures are such perfect portraits of us. Living maps of our fractured terrain.

"And why would Alexandra urge you to do such a thing? Joshua, remember my warning!"

For all the attention Lexi pays to him, Prince could be an old newspaper scratching through the dust. That, I appreciate. She keeps on at Josh instead.

"What about the kids, Josh? Since they came here through you, are they . . . also part of the chain? If you can free them, then you *know* what you have to do!"

I wait for Josh to deny it. To say the kids are trapped no matter what, and their freedom isn't something he can make happen. Instead he squeezes his lids tight shut for a moment, wringing the tears out. And avoiding my stare, while he's at it.

Unselle pivots, arching her brows, and the horsemen start to crowd in around Josh in particular. The horses jostle, merging with one another where their flanks overlap. Now and then a misty leg passes in front of Josh's face, fading my view of him into something gray and edgeless, then shifting aside again.

"Lexi," Josh croaks. "Lexi, is it true? Do you love Kezzer too?"

I can't read the look she casts at me. But it's an absurd question. Going by what I saw of Xand—glossy, self-satisfied, stuffed with luck that he did nothing to earn, not to mention a very standard-issue guy—I'm about as far from Lexi's type as you can get.

"I haven't had time to examine my feelings, Josh. And I know I need to do that," Lexi says at last. Gently. "But that's got nothing to do with what I'm saying. You can't use me to evade your own responsibilities."

It's so far from the answer I expected—*Oh, hell no,* or words to that effect—that I can't absorb it. I heard Lexi speaking, but where her meaning should touch me, I feel myself go numb.

"Joshua," Prince says. "The magic that bound you here is spiteful. Reverse it, and it will take its revenge. Do as Alexandra asks, and you will never see Ksenia again. You will never hear her voice. The magic will take pains to guarantee that you do not once pass her in the street, not as long as you live. Any efforts you make to reach her with a single word will be thwarted, and all your longing, your every whispered message, will turn back and shatter in your face. When she dies, no rumor of her death will come to you, and you will know nothing of her life. Do you understand me?"

I understand—enough to know that Josh truly does have the power to free us all, or Prince would never offer up a warning like this. Enough that the stiffness holding me wads up like a rag. I stumble forward through the narrow gap between the horses and drop to my knees—not holding Josh, but near him. Between his face and mine, there's just enough room for all our years together, from the moment his ten-year-old hand first slipped into mine.

We frame those memories where our eyes meet, while the vertigo swells around us. If I look away from Josh for even a sliver of a moment, there will be nothing left for me but the infinite emptiness of life without him.

And is the magic vindictive enough to stop me from ever glimpsing Lexi again too? Probably it is. Probably that goes without saying. That whole *examining her feelings* thing will be totally irrelevant.

"Kezzer?" Josh says. Suppressed sobs ball up his face, so that he looks ten years old again. "Kezzer, do I have to?"

Even if it was just about the two of us, I'd know what I need to say. But there's also Lexi, and there are the kids, all snared in the same magic we are. Just because I never had a real home, that doesn't mean they shouldn't. Maybe helping them get their families back will make up, in a way, for everything Josh and I lost before we were old enough to understand what the hell was happening to us.

"Yeah," I say. "Baby, I'm so sorry. But you do."

So I can't pay for all of us. But at least it's like I promised when Josh and I first came here: I won't let him pay alone. Everything they're going to take from him, they'll take from me too. All I have, and all I love, until I'll live on like my own changeling. My heart hacked out, beating on and on where I can't find it. I picture my

heart lodged in the silt at the bottom of a river, or maybe in a shoe-
box shoved to the back of a stranger's closet. One thing I'm sure of,
I'll stand no chance of ever getting it back.

Fine.

Josh opens his mouth to say it, but he's crying too hard. All
that comes out is a mangled gulping, and he heaves in a breath to
try again. I reach out to hug him tight, knowing perfectly well that
I won't get to. I know what's about to happen. At least, I know
enough to be bitterly aware that I'll never hold Josh again.

Because their arms are already snaking out, impossibly long—
I knew it—to hoist him into the air. Because they're already shoving fish-scaled scarves into his mouth. Raking his cheeks with
their claws in their rush to cram more weird materials down his
throat, so that he retches and writhes in their arms. Anything—*I
knew it*—to stop him from saying those words.

But because I knew it, because it's all like a story I memorized
before I even knew what language was, I've already swung my outstretched hand just as Josh began lifting up.

And I've grabbed my bowler hat off the top of his head.

Not for this world anymore, is your hat.

Yeah, that's what Unselle said. She must think humans are such
hapless idiots that I'd never do the math.

Our world, it gives forth; it births and bubbles, goblins and green eyes.

I turn it over, dark mouth wide like it could disgorge a new sky.
"Hey," I call into the hollow. "Prince didn't create you, and you
know it. You belong to Joshua Korensky. And it's time for you to
act like it."

And then I fling the hat onto the ground. It wobbles on its
domed crown, but it maintains its dark confrontation with the world
above. A small, contained vacancy laughs up at the gorge and the
wild horsemen, the nodding willows, and the whole false town beyond our view.

They've slung Josh across one of the saddles now. He's wrapped in arms as long as ropes, stifled in a skein of multicolored flesh. If nothing comes out of the hat, we're finished.

And nothing does. Maybe I've miscalculated, maybe I'm just as dumb as Unselle thought, because she's tilting halfway off her mount to bring her leering mouth almost to my throat, and her retinue is reaching for me too. I hear Lexi cry out, and twist my head to see her in a tornado of multijointed limbs. Arms the color of frost, of black plums, of blazing sand. "Lexi!" I hear myself screaming, and at the same time I know it's pointless. If I've just failed us all, what can there be to say?

And then I hear something else.

A clicking, a tapping. For half a moment, I think it might be starting to rain. But the sound is too crisp and snappy for raindrops. It's more like the laminated snicker of cicadas' wings.

I turn to see that one of our *hosts*—the boy in the peacock leather, the one with amber skin—is reaching to flip my hat back over. But he's too late.

A geyser of cracked, diminished Joshes spurts out of the hat's black hollow. Thousands of them, unfolding so many paper-thin faces that they seem like a single organism. A vast, gnashing origami dragon, its flanks dotted with glitter-rimmed eyes, its edges ruffling with tiny fingers like cilia. And since the peacock boy is closest, he's the first to disappear inside the swarm.

I can't kill our damned hosts; that's beyond human capabilities. But these imp-creatures aren't human, and it never hurts to hope.

A tendril of Joshes snakes upward, and a dozen scissoring mouths snap in at once, seizing Unselle by the throat. All around me, the horses rear, their misty legs lashing into a froth.

I don't have time to watch the tumult. What counts is using it.

Those sharp little teeth are already at work, gnawing into the arms clutching Josh. Limbs unwind from him like spider legs curling up in a flame, and I leap to grab his shoulders, dragging him back off the horse and onto the ground with a thud. It's a rough fall. Even through the rags, I can hear him groan. I reach down to wrestle him to his feet with my left hand, while my right yanks fist-fuls of mutant silks from his mouth. The scarves writhe in the air like parasitic worms, groping toward Josh's face like they're trying to burrow back between his lips. I fling them to the dust and grind hard with the sharp heels of my boots. He gags and leans against me so heavily I nearly fold.

I hear Lexi shout and turn to see her, fighting against the unearthly flesh binding her. Behind her, riders crash from horses so fear-mad that they crumple their legs into their bodies, as if they're trying to turn back into clouds. The snap and chatter of Joshlings engulfs the riders as they fall. "Josh!" she calls. "Say it now! You know there's no other way."

Josh is clinging to the neckline of my chopped-up tuxedo jacket, staring at me with such longing that I wish I could let him off the hook. Squeeze him and tell him I'll stay here with him forever. But it's too late for that. It's been too late for us, I know it now, ever since the moment when I found him curled up in the clearing.

"Kezzer," Josh says. "If I say it, will you forgive me? I mean, for everything."

I'd like to tell him there's nothing to forgive, but we both know that's not true.

"Baby, what else would I do?" *There's nothing you could ever do, Josh, that I wouldn't forgive, even before you finished doing it. That's the way we love each other, and we always will.*

In the midst of a dozen jagged Josh-ish profiles, I see a single bile-green eye glaring at us. I'm glad that Prince has a good view of what's about to go down.

Josh chokes and gapes around, like something will happen to save him from speaking those words. But there's no reprieve, because there never is. Not from grief like this.

"Then . . . I release Ksenia Adderley. I let her go, for all time. We can't be together, and I know it. The *two of us* is a thing that just doesn't exist anymore." He was right there, fingers twisted in my collar, but by the final syllable he's already standing far away from me, deep in the smudgy purple air. I have no idea how it happened. "Kezzer?" Josh calls.

"Josh," I shout back. "I love you!"

But I've lost sight of him even before the words leave my mouth, and I know he didn't hear me.

the whole bright and whirling world

Hot, staccato red hits my eyes, blinking like some kind of code. I shake my head to make it go away, but it keeps on flashing at me. Awareness picks up enough that I absorb a few more specifics—I'm lying on my back. Something warm and heavy is resting on my shoulder. And my eyes are closed—that red signaling, I realize, must be sunlight jouncing on my eyelids.

I move to sit up, confused, and the soft weight slips off my shoulder. "Ksenia?"

Lexi. She was sleeping with her head nestled against me. She pushes herself up on one hand and we both look around. We're under the half-grown green of spring trees, sun specks darting all around us. Moss and stones and a blue sky shaking through the foliage. The clearing by the gorge.

The real one. The cool damp from the earth blots my back and sun-warmth perches on my hands. As convincing as Prince's fake was, this place has a deeper reality about it than he could ever match. There's a song under the skin of the world here, and it hums inside me too. Like crickets purling *alive, alive, alive.*

"Lexi," I say. I don't have a complete grasp of the situation, but a few memories start to break through the blear. "I thought I could never see you again. I thought that was the deal. The magic was going to get back at us, for getting free."

"*I* didn't say anything about letting go of you forever," Lexi points out. Golden sun and pearl-blue reflections curl on her dark cheeks, and it's impossibly beautiful. She grins at me, sweet and shining.

"Which could be something of a problem, actually. And Ksenia? You didn't say anything about breaking your pledge either. Which might mean—if I understood Prince correctly, I'm afraid you're going to be living with a lot of pain. Missing . . . it's going to be a constant ache for you."

I shrug. What else would it be? And anyway, my mind is already spiking with a new worry.

"Lexi? Did you eat anything while you were there? If you did, we need to get you a candy bar or something right away."

"I knew better than to eat anything, even though it felt like I was trapped for days before you came for me. I'm going to need a lot more than a candy bar." She gets up, a little unsteadily, and half-heartedly brushes off a few leaves. "Let's go to the diner and order one of everything."

I struggle up too. "I don't have any money. And I'm supposed to be dead. Anyone who sees me will freak their ass off."

"My treat. Remember how you just rescued me? And anyway, Ksenia, I'm willing to bet that no one thinks you died now. I'm almost certain that the whole enchantment has just been *undone*, and all those little kids are safe at home. Just as if they'd never been stolen in the first place. For that, I'd say you deserve some breakfast."

"You're the one who kept rescuing me, Lexi. More times than I can count. And you figured out what we had to do. I think— I'm almost positive I was too close to Josh to see it. You did what I *couldn't* do."

"It's my treat anyway." Lexi holds out her hand. "Ksenia, we *have* to go get food before I faint." Then she glances down at herself: barefoot, in torn and filthy pajamas. "Or, okay, we'll swing by my house first. I have a feeling—I bet my family's away at the beach."

I'm looking pretty ragged myself. My boots are thick with dust, my glittery shorts are sludge-gray from all the grime and crusty with my blood. Grave dirt still streaks my legs and crumbles from my hair. And all I'm wearing on top is that hacked-off tuxedo jacket, black scraps dangling. On my hip, a thin pink line threads the skin above my waistband.

I glance down again. Where that knife was wedged in my flesh, there's nothing but a scar.

We manage the long walk back to Lexi's house, both of us staggering from hunger. She fetches a spare key out of one of those fake rocks, and lets us in the back door into quiet so dreamlike and lush that I know at once she's right. No one else is home. I can barely handle the peace of being there, in Lexi's pretty kitchen with its cherry cabinets and Moroccan rugs hanging on the walls. We both slump at the table in a daze, and then Lexi hauls herself up to make coffee and eggs and toast, and we forget all about going anywhere. The antique clock above the sink says it's almost noon, and once Lexi checks the date she tells me it's spring break.

The internet tells us that a tornado ravaged the town last week, inflicting however many millions in property damage, taking lives. In the list of six people dead, twenty injured, there's no mention of an Alexander.

"But you think Xand is still dead?" I ask after a while. We've finished a huge breakfast, and started in sharing a pint of mint ice cream. We need showers, and I can't go around in these clothes forever. Oh, and I'm homeless. But I'm so overcome by the bliss of being here, free from that nightmare, and eating ice cream with someone so awesome, that it seems like I can worry about all of that later.

Lexi's face tightens. "I think so. You and the kids didn't physically die, Ksenia. You were just taken, and your deaths were basically a matter of warped perceptions. They were a distortion, not reality. Xand, though—it was unspeakable, what they did to him. I'll try calling his family, once I'm ready to face it, but I doubt that's something that can be undone." A grimace. "When I left, his changeling had just walked in their door. What if it's still there?"

I nod. "But we don't even know that my death was undone, right? That's just your theory."

Lexi's sorrow reverses instantly into a grin. "Let's test it." And before I realize what she's planning, she runs upstairs and comes back with her phone. What she's about to do—I get it all at once, and it smacks me with panic.

"Lexi, I'm not sure this is—"

"Mom? Hey, how's everything at the cabin?" I'm still trying to talk and Lexi waves to shush me, her smile growing wider by the moment. "I just finished everything I have to do here, so I thought I'd drive out this afternoon. I can be there by dinnertime. Is that good?" I can hear her mother's voice as a series of upbeat intonations, but I can't catch the words. Lexi twists around, perching on the edge of the breakfast table. "Is it okay if I bring a friend with me? Ksenia's back in town!" I almost move to snatch the phone, but Lexi just squirms out of reach and arches her brows at me. More wordless chatter comes from her receiver. I have to admit it doesn't sound particularly horrified. "No, she's just been working up in Buffalo, but she knows she needs to start college in the fall. Mom, honestly? That's part of why I want her to come out. I think she could use a few quiet days to—you know, just contemplate what she wants out of life. Okay, thanks. Pie? Sure, we can stop at a farm stand . . . Love you too." The look she turns on me is giddy with triumph. "You know, if my mom thought you were dead, she probably wouldn't be quite so comfortable inviting you to Cape Cod."

Dead or alive, I can't believe Lexi's parents are willing to let me intrude on their vacation. I'm the one who's always a stranger, always violating other people's everyday happiness. "Why the hell did she say yes? Even before I died, everyone thought I was some emotionless freak."

Lexi shakes her head, still beaming. "You don't understand my mom. To her, you're not just *that disturbing foster-care girl*. It's more like *that disturbing foster-care girl who nonetheless maintained a GPA of 3.9, and read books I recommended to her.* She's a big enthusiast for untapped potential. So we'll lounge on the beach for a few days, and all you'll have to do is cope with some intense dinner conversations about your future. Are you in?"

It's hard to imagine what else I would be. I have nowhere to go.

But it's more than that. I'm so relieved at the prospect of getting to hang out with Lexi for a few more days that my legs go tremulous, just processing the emotion. I've been trying not to think about what she said to Josh, but now it comes back to me, inescapably. Like, that *examining her feelings* thing wouldn't be connected with bringing me out to Cape Cod, would it?

"Thanks, Lexi," I say, because all at once I'm too flummoxed to say anything else. And then I change the subject. She's watching me closely, and I can't completely suppress my old habit of diverting her from seeing too much of me. "You know there's another thing we need to test, right?"

Lexi nods. "If I can talk to—. And especially, if I can talk about you. I'm not ready to try that yet, either, but I promise you I'll get to it soon." She gives a little shake from the shoulders up. "Ksenia? The strange thing is that I tried to say that name just now. And it was like it spilled sideways, right off my tongue. I might be actually incapable of naming—somebody—to you."

I haven't said Josh's name aloud either, not since we woke up in the clearing. *Joshua Korensky,* I think, and I try to force the thought into sound.

It comes out as a kind of grunting exhalation. And with that burst of wordless air, I really feel the ache Lexi was talking about before. I told myself that I accepted the deal we were making. But inevitably there was the wheedling belief, deep in my mind, that somehow we wouldn't lose each other absolutely. That Prince was just lying, or that the magic might be careless enough to leave a few loopholes.

Joshua Korensky, Joshua Korensky, Joshua Korensky. How can I think so clearly what I can't say? I try taking it one syllable, one letter at a time. *Jo—*

No. The magic is onto me. I sound like I'm choking.

"Ksenia," Lexi is saying, "Ksenia, stop!" But I can't stop, not until I get it out. I want to drive my voice straight through the force constraining me. Use Josh's name like a knife, gut the enchantment, leave it bleeding.

Then Lexi has her arms tight around me, squeezing my head against her chest and stroking my hair. I stop trying to say what I *can't* say, and let the impulse drown in her warmth.

We drive out a few hours later. Lexi insists on stopping at my favorite thrift store on the way and lending me the money for a couple of less-insane outfits, no matter how many times I point out that I've got no idea when I'll be able to pay her back. We find two pairs of skinny jeans that fit me, black and gray, and two of my usual ruffled tuxedo shirts, black and lilac. Both of us are giddy in that half-hysterical way you get when you've just staggered out of a nightmare, popping ridiculous hats on each other's heads and gasping with laughter. We buy packs of cheap underwear and black tank tops and a few basic toiletries at the dollar store on the edge of town, and I shove everything into a scuffed backpack that Lexi swears she was getting rid of anyway. Not that I believe her, but I'm too tired, and too grateful, to keep arguing.

Then we hit the highway in her new Mini Cooper. Trees blip past, streaking into a steady chartreuse flux; rooftops wrap up other people's safe, reliable lives. And now that we aren't cracking up, the silence starts to shift its tone. It goes tense, stretched by the weight of unsaid words.

And I should make the effort to say at least some of them. Shouldn't I?

"Lexi," I try. And then it's almost like when the magic throttled Josh's name in my throat, because I completely fail to keep going.

But what's killing my voice now? It's all me, all my own fear, and not some external force. I have to own it.

She gives me a minute, just in case I can hack it on my own. Then: "Yes?"

I pull in a deep inhalation, trying to slow my heart. "All those times when you thought I didn't care, or that I was being distant because I didn't trust you enough—I mean, you see now it wasn't like that. Right?"

Lexi nods, her twists bobbing. All the darkness and the glow of her, framed by the sky beyond. "It was like you kept daring me to give up on you—like you wanted to see how much it would take before I lost interest. But I didn't." Her mouth curls in a wry half-smile, but she's gazing straight ahead. "I think I wasn't ready to truly look at *why* I couldn't give up on you, Ksenia."

Does that mean what I think it means? "*I* don't know why you didn't give up on me! You gave me so many chances, and I have no idea why you thought I was worth it." I have to keep forcing the truth out. Don't I? "I know I'm late saying this. But seriously, thank you."

It feels like something, but also nowhere near enough. Lexi finally glances at me from the corners of her almond eyes.

"Ksenia. What if I'm giving you another kind of chance, right now? Do you want it?"

I can't answer.

"I promise, I will understand *completely* if you aren't interested. It won't affect our friendship at all, no matter what you say. Okay? Because I do know—you've been pressured way too much, and you need—whatever you choose, whoever you love next—you need to make that decision from a place of absolute freedom. So just take this as one of your options." She hesitates. "I'm sorry, Ksenia. I shouldn't have said anything so soon."

Lexi's voice is shifting deeper. Still calm, but smoked by low pain. I'm about to blow it.

"I do—want the chance, though," I manage. "Lexi, I mean, of

course I do. I admire you more than anyone I've ever met. I'm lucky even to know somebody like you. Much less—"

There's a chatter of gravel at the wheels. We're pulling over.

And then Lexi tugs my head down to hers and kisses me, so softly that I'm suspended inside the sweetness of it. A warm dizziness erases the edges of my body, and what remains is her lips on mine, all of me, and all of reality, caught in that contact.

She lets me go—God, too soon—and leans back. Just a few inches, which makes it easier. "Ksenia? There's something I need to make absolutely clear. I'm not here with you because you're lucky. I'm here because you deserve it."

Yeah, right, I almost say. But her eyes stop me. There's something in the depth of them that I can't get across.

"Think about it, Ksenia. Who has *ever* fought through more than you have? You even fought your way back from a world that wasn't the world, and you were contending against creatures that aren't even human. And you didn't just free yourself, either. You made sure that no one else was left behind. What about that says to you that you don't deserve love?" She sounds genuinely annoyed now. "Can you acknowledge what I'm saying to you?"

I messed up a lot, actually. But Lexi has a point. When it was really essential I came through. I ripped the truth out of my heart until the stairs let me climb up, I tricked Unselle, I walked mistblinded down into the gorge. If I heard that story about someone else, I'd give them credit for being almost a hero. So why can't I appreciate the same things in myself?

"I get all that in the abstract," I tell her at last. "It's just hard for me to really feel it."

"Then that's what you have to do next," Lexi says. "Work on feeling it. Can you do that?"

I can do it for you, I want to say. But that's not what Lexi's asking, and I know it. Even if Lexi vanished, even if her car dissolved, and I was left sitting alone by the side of the road—I'd need to learn to feel it anyway. I can't put this on her.

"I can do it, Lexi," I tell her. "I'll keep working on it until I get there."

Lexi smiles at me and starts up the car again. "You've made it so far already, Ksenia. Right? So just keep going."

We don't merge back into traffic just yet, though. She kisses me again first, and this time I let myself pull her close. Holding her feels like holding the whole bright and whirling world.

whatever heart you can make
for yourself

No one can say his name to me.

Whenever anyone stumbles into dangerous territory—the Delbos, for instance, or where I went and what I've been doing—I can see their eyes skid away from any mention of my foster brother. I can hear his name dropping like a pebble, vanishing into silence before they voice it. They maybe aren't conscious of the force at work in them, but I keep a close watch for moments like these. The world is dotted with emptiness, wherever Josh is erased from it—even though I'm fairly sure he's still right here in town. Back with the Delbos, back in school, with some hazy story obliterating the reasons for his absence. Maybe people think he followed me to Buffalo.

We were gone for nine and a half months, it turns out. I had no idea. If I'd had to guess, I might have said two at most.

In general, though, everyone prefers to avoid any subject that might lead to Josh, which in effect means anything connected with my past here. It's as if I live severed from my own history, and everyone focuses compulsively on what's next for me. So I have a counter job in a bakery downtown, and a tiny room above it to crash in, and Lexi's parents pulling every string they can get to find me programs and scholarships and *possibilities*. And if the cynical part of me says that they're just trying desperately to make me into someone halfway good enough to be Lexi's girlfriend, below the cynicism there's gratitude so fierce that it staggers me. Because who else ever bothered?

They've accepted me way more than I ever would have dared to hope, the Holdens. I won't let them down.

Lexi has called him, I know. Maybe even talked to him in person. I see the strain in her face when she tries to tell me, and the shake of her head when she gives up.

I'm not entirely sure she'd approve of what I'm about to do—but, thanks to the magic throttling us, there's no way I can ask her. She must guess it will happen sooner or later. And she knows I'm still crying myself to sleep every night, not because I want to tell her anything that could possibly hurt her, but because she insists on knowing the truth of what I'm going through.

I've just closed up the bakery in the lingering late-May twilight. Locked the metal gate and tucked two loaves of end-of-the-day bread into my backpack—one for me, one for the Holdens—along with a small box of Marissa's favorite daisy cookies. And then I start walking. Away from downtown, toward Whistler Drive.

Which seems on the face of it like an uncomplicated thing to do, just an evening stroll. But my body knows better. It's as if a shivering in the ground rushes up my legs at every step. It's as if the May evening transmitted a kind of cold that traveled from a place far beyond temperature.

For all I know, it's deep winter in that not-world where Josh and I were trapped, and a wisp of its breath still follows me.

There's so much I don't know—what happened to Kay and all the other imp-creatures, for one thing. Did they just fold themselves back into us when we returned here, and forget all about having independent lives? I don't know what became of my changeling, but I sometimes dream about her. She's always trailing behind me, always asking me to find her lost heart. I tell her to go back and look in my grave, and then I realize that grave isn't there anymore. It's gone as if it had never been, along with little Olivia Fisher's. Just like Lexi thought, all the kids are back with their families, though they do have kind of a haunted look when you see them. Do they remember?

Prince, Unselle, their whole uncanny tribe—I don't know if they were killed by the tide of implings when we escaped. But probably they're fine, enduring on and on in their sluggish half-life, bored out of their minds and ravenous to feed on human prisoners. On our emotions, the pungency of our despair, the kick of our rebellion. If I'm right about them, then Josh and I were hardly the first, or the last, of their victims.

From what Lexi's told me, there's no guarantee they won't come after us again too. There was something about that mink tasting our blood that means Unselle can track us, wherever we go. We're free for now, and that has to be enough.

As for what's going to happen once I'm in front of number 32—I have a rough idea. It doesn't matter. I still need the snap of empirical proof, or I'm always going to wonder.

So the drowsy streets roll back, and kids scamper through sprinklers, and adults lug groceries. No matter how long I live in this complacent normalcy, I'm always going to carry the buzz of the impossible. Because I've been there, I've seen it for myself, and that kind of madness gets in your flesh. It's like one of those viruses that scorches its way into your DNA, stays part of you years after the fever has broken.

Fine.

The Delbos' house slides up on me. The irony is that I almost miss it and walk right past, because I've half forgotten that it's only a single story high. A bland, butter-yellow split-level ranch. A home where I was always a stranger, except when Josh was smiling at me.

I stand and look at it, searching the windows for any stir that might be him, even though I know that will never happen. No matter if I go right up to the glass, or how I stalk in circles around the house, the magic will always arrange for Josh to wander into some room where I can't see him. He's in there, I could almost swear it, but at the same time he's unreachable.

I had unsettled plans to storm up and ring the bell, but now that feels preposterous. What will happen if I try it? I take the first step onto the Delbos' front walk and feel weakness bursting in my knees, ready to topple me. A warning shot. Whatever. I'm here and I'll take the worst it can throw at me.

A window in the living room jerks up. Against all reason, my heart leaps and my hand flies out, as if Josh's hand will be close enough that I can grasp it.

But of course it's not him. Emma Delbo is there, looking a bit less decrepit than she did last time I saw her. Still, even now that Josh is back and everything that happened has been wiped from her mind, I can tell her forgotten experiences aren't really gone. She's weighed down by something blue-gray and terribly heavy, until it's visibly distending her skin. Maybe her mind doesn't remember, but I can see what happened in the sag of her lips.

"Go away. You're not welcome here," she calls to me. I notice, of course, that she doesn't say my name. That's another thing since we've been back—no one calls me Kezzer now, like it's a facet of everything they can't say. I don't think Emma's a fan of *Ksenia*.

But maybe that's not the only reason. Maybe there's someone who can overhear the faintest edge of Emma's voice, and so saying my name is impossible for her.

"I never thought I was welcome," I snap back. But the truth is, a flush like fire races through my skin. It made more sense, her hating me, when she thought I'd murdered Josh. But now? I try to tell myself it's just the enchantment shoving her emotions around, but that's not as convincing as I'd like it to be. She probably thinks I duped him into running away with me.

"Why did you even come back to this town? You should have stayed in Buffalo!" She slams the window, but I stay where I am. Did I hear—or maybe I'm only imagining—a few rapid footsteps coming behind her, with a cadence that I know like my own pulse?

No one else comes to the window. No one else will.

The air is so blue, so vibrant, that it cradles me and stops me from falling. Windows wink golden, and I can see everyone else—*anyone* else, actually, in all the world—going through their everyday motions. And I know I have to stop staring into the void of the one person I can't see, even if that void pretends to be a magnolia tree and an expanse of vinyl siding. I turn to go.

Half a block later, I halt. Light footsteps are echoing just behind me, each one deliberately timed to coincide with mine. And this time—how?—I already know, I accept in my gut, that those steps aren't his.

I swing around and meet her grubby gray eyes. Awkward as hell that she's here, of course—does she think she can take my place? Lexi and I are both horribly certain that the *Xand* who still lives in town is as fake as tinsel. But at least she's had the sense to button up that hideous dress, though the crude red rag of her autopsy incision still pokes above the neckline. She gawps at me, maybe embarrassed, with her jagged blond hair twitching and her mouth hanging open.

"Sennie," she whispers. Ugh. Then, with a shade more confidence: "Did you find it? Give it back to me, and I'll go away!"

Of course. She's still after one thing. "Our missing heart?" I say. "Neither of us can get it back. You're going to have to forget it."

"Ours?" Her eyes narrow. "It was mine, it was all mine! Prince made it and put it inside me, and then they stole it right out of me! It's *mine*."

"It belonged to both of us," I tell her. "And no matter how much it hurt sometimes, I know we both would have given almost anything to keep it. But we couldn't. It's lost forever." I nod toward the Delbos' house. "You know where it is as well as I do."

Her head twists to look, with a suddenness like a convulsion. When she stares at me again she's gone bone white, her lips are trembling, and I pity her as much as I can. Which turns out to be a lot, actually.

In a dried-up riverbed, at the bottom of a gorge, I buried a heart full of water.

Now it lives in a yellow house. But that house is deeper than any gorge in the world. There's no getting to the bottom of it.

"I'm sorry," I tell her. "But I have to go home. And so do you. Or—look. You can go to another town, if you want. Invent a new name for yourself. I won't rat you out. Why don't you try that? Just be as alive as you can, with everything you have left."

She stares at me a while longer, both of us suffused in blue. I have a lingering sense—of what? responsibility?—that keeps me from turning my back on her and leaving. For a fake person, a poppet, a mannequin cobbled out of magic and mind scraps and maybe a rotten log, she's done pretty well, in fact. When she pointed me toward the way out of nowhere, she showed a kind of spirit and independence that has to be worth *something*.

"You think I can do that," she says at last. It's not a question. "With no heart."

"Yeah," I say. "I mean, I think you stand a decent chance."

She nods, twitchily, like there's nothing else that either of us could possibly add to that. No smile—it occurs to me that she might not have learned how to smile yet. She just pivots sharply on one heel and marches off, leaving me with the sick dread that I was spewing lies at her. It would be cruel to feed her false hope.

But maybe she'll pull it off and forge a life somewhere. She's what you'd call socially awkward, but so are a lot of people. And anyway, does it have to be with no heart?

With whatever heart you can make for yourself. Make it out of the surging trees. Out of this twilight that doesn't try to erase you anymore—that lets you burn on, Ksenia Adderley, at the core of its simultaneous peace and wildness. Out of a dark girl working on her term papers, but with a touch of her awareness still tuned to you. She'll expect you to stop by, even if it's just for a few minutes, because you always do.

acknowledgments

It's often impossible to pinpoint where inspiration starts, but in the case of *Never-Contented Things* I know precisely the night that set the book in motion. My beloved husband, Todd Polenberg, and our brilliant friend Ben Bartelle were sitting up late by a fireplace in Maine, talking crazy talk with me, when Todd volunteered that he would take a cocktail from a bartender with snake-head hands. "You will do no such thing!" I cried, distraught. "You do not accept food or drink from nonhuman visitants. That's rule number one!" The conversation unraveled through wild digressions, and by morning I knew what I would write next. (Thanks to this book, Todd is now convinced. No serpentine cocktails!)

The epigraphs that begin each section of this book point to its older roots in faerie literature, but they also trace personal influences to which I owe a lasting debt. My mother, Betsy Hart Porter, read me *Goblin Market* when I was a small child; it scared the bejesus out of me in that indelible way that can return, decades later, in the form of a new book. My wonderful editor, Susan Chang, casually introduced me to the medieval poem *Sir Orfeo,* which had a deeper impact on me than she could have anticipated. (An Orpheus and Eurydice retelling where Eurydice is stolen by faeries!? How cool is that?) The wise and charming Morgan Fahey suggested the Poe poem that gave this book its title and pointed out the eerie beauty of the titular line. Another friend, Laura Henze, sent me a volume of Yeats's faerie lore after that same Maine trip, which not only led me to "The Stolen Child" but informed subtler atmospherics as well.

I also want to thank my incredible agent, Kent D. Wolf, who believed in me when no one else did and hasn't stopped yet;

everyone at Tor Teen, but especially Susan Chang and Kathleen Doherty, for believing in me now, and Zohra Ashpari, for being so consistently awesome. Todd always, Kevin Messman for his insightful readings of basically everything I write, and Tera Freedman, also always.

And to a particular dream I had about a bowler hat: thanks for being there when I needed you. You were creepy as hell.

about the author

SARAH PORTER is a writer, artist, and freelance teacher who lives in Brooklyn with her husband, daughter, and two cats. She is the author of several books for young adults, including *Vassa in the Night* and *When I Cast Your Shadow*. She has an MFA in creative writing from City College. Look for her online at www.sarahporterbooks .com, www.facebook.com/sarahporterauthor, and on Twitter as @sarahporterbook.

More books from
SARAH PORTER

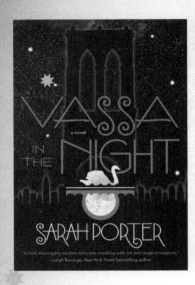

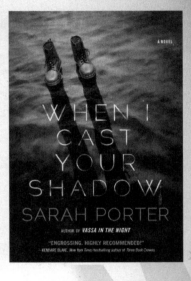

Step into the enchanted kingdom of Brooklyn, where magic—and danger—lurk around every corner.

A teenage girl calls her beloved older brother back from the grave, with disastrous consequences....